HEARTLESS HERO

MARY CATHERINE GEBHARD

Line editing by James Gallagher of Evident Ink
Content Editing by Edits in Blue
Proof Reading by My Brother's Editor and Amy Halter
Cover by Hang Le

Heartless Hero
ISBN-13: 978-1-7338510-2-2
An Unglued Books Publication
www.MaryGebhard.com

For the girls who like mean boys.

ONE

ABIGAIL

My head pounded as I dragged my feet through the gate. Carrying my strappy Jimmy Choos, I walked alone past towering wrought iron, along cobblestone and perfectly trimmed emerald-green hedges, past crystal-blue fountains and dower-faced guards. They didn't look at me, but I felt their stares all the same.

I'd lost my bodyguard. Again.

I'd been caught by the press. Again.

"You're in so much shit."

My older sister, Gemma, leaned against pretty white embellished walls, a cup of tea in her hands. When she saw me, she came forward, like she'd been waiting. I wouldn't doubt it.

"I think I heard Mom say the words 'complete disappointment.'" A smile curved her red lips just as a laugh echoed through the great halls.

Grayson, my brother.

"No, it was 'utterly hopeless,'" he added. "The word 'nunnery' was also tossed around." Gemma joined in his laughter, and I fought the urge to throw my strappy heels at their heads.

Both my siblings were tall and shared my mother and father's iconic blond hair. It looked like spun rose gold. I, on the other hand, was barely five foot five, and had my great-grandmother's hair, so brown it was almost black—just so it was obvious I was the black sheep.

"Where is she?"

"Take a wild guess," Gemma said.

I swallowed my grimace, walking in the direction as my siblings followed after me, eager to watch what was about to unfold.

My mother, Tansy, loved her tea and cupcakes almost as much as she loved doling out my punishments. Most days she could be found in the sunroom, overlooking three miles of gardens, blue skies, and Atlantic Ocean.

Outside the sunroom, I knocked lightly with a sigh. "Mom—"

I stopped short, locked on the figure at the end of our pearly hallway. It had been years since I'd seen him, but I'd recognize his piercing green eyes anywhere.

Theo Hound.

"Abigail?" my mother's lilting voice called.

I blinked, and he was gone. I must have seen wrong. That person was on the opposite side of the country, in California guarding my grandfather.

"Hello, Mother," I said, coming into the room. I took my usual place before her feet, the midafternoon sun warm against my back. My siblings went to stand by my mother, both resting their hands on the curling back of her sateen chaise, as if really wanting to rub in how apart from them I was.

Mother placed the book she'd been reading on a table adorned with tea and cookies to her left, starting in on her usual censure. She wasn't surprised, but she was disappointed. She both expected this and expected better.

"What is it?" I asked, holding back a sigh. "Am I under house arrest? Are you taking away my allowance? Or maybe denying me dinner?" Those were her usual go-tos. None of them explained the growing smiles on my siblings' faces.

"We've assigned you a new guard. This is not like the others you've ditched. This man is not there to protect you, this man is to watch your every movement and keep our *reputation* safe."

My gut dropped. The Crowne Guard was *filled* with sycophants who had their noses far up my siblings' and mom's assholes. I didn't have one friend on it. I *did* have one enemy, but surely they wouldn't choose him. My mother had always hated Theo, and she'd practically rejoiced when he left. She would *never* choose him to guard me twenty-four seven.

"So what?" I asked. "He's going to follow me around?"

Mother nodded. "Twenty-four seven."

"A male guard?" I nearly gasped. "But surely not at night."

"Twenty-four seven," she repeated. "We've redone your en suite into a room."

"That's not proper," I stammered. "Rumors will spread. People will think things." People already thought them. I'd been branded a slut since Rosey, our boarding school, years ago.

Screw the fact I was still *almost* a virgin, right?

Mom tossed magazine after magazine at my feet. The

one where they'd caught me getting out of a limo with my legs—and no panties. The one where I was topless on the yacht, making out with an Oscar winner. The one where I was lip-locked with Hollywood's *it* girl and guy.

I said *almost*.

"Rumors?" She arched a brow, then continued unperturbed. "This will be the *least* scandalous thing you've done. Believe me when I say he was not my first choice," my mother said, almost bitterly. "Despite my objections, your grandfather is resolute."

Now I was even *more* confused. Who had been chosen to watch me? What man could have my mother so bitter, yet be in such good graces with my grandfather?

"*Grayson* is on the cover of more tabloids than me," I tried desperately. I don't know why I even bothered. The bar was always placed on the floor for Gray.

My gaze kept drifting back to the door, beyond my sibling peanut gallery. *Had* I seen him? I didn't know anyone else who somehow both stood out of, and blended into, the shadows.

"Abigail!" my mother snapped, and I quickly looked at her. Only I could make my mother snap. I took perverse satisfaction in that; it was the only attention she afforded me, after all. "Did you hear a word I said?"

"Doubt it," Grayson said. "She's still standing."

I glared at my brother in the doorway. My siblings and I were so close in age. Gray was just a year older than me at twenty-two, and Gemma the eldest at almost twenty-three, yet we couldn't be further apart. Both he and my sister watched me, twisted smiles on their faces. Watching our mom torture me was one of their favorite forms of amusement.

"*Grayson* isn't going to marry the son of a man whose

company your grandfather has been courting for over three years."

Everything came to a crashing halt.

I wish I'd heard her wrong, but I *knew* I hadn't. I'd known this day was coming for as long as I could remember. You don't get to be me and not have *this day*. My sister's day had come in boarding school. My brother's would come soon as well. I darted my eyes between my siblings and back to my mother, a sinking feeling growing.

"You're marrying me off?" I took a step back. "When? To who? Have I even met him?"

My mom waved her hand as if what I'd said was trivial. "Before the end of the summer."

"*This* summer?" At my distressed face, behind our mother's back, Gemma pushed out her bottom lip, pretending to pout for me.

"Fuck off, Gemma," I said.

Gemma clutched her heart. "Mother, do you see how she speaks to me?" Behind our mother's back she mouthed *fuck you* and gave me the bird.

"Enough," my mother said without heat. "This shouldn't be news to you, Abigail. Your grandfather has been working on this trade for years."

"Yes, but—" I started, only to be cut off.

"We can't afford your little...dalliances...ruining it."

Gemma laughed. "That's a nice way to look at them."

"But—"

"We're done talking about this, Abigail," Mom said. "Why don't you try following your sister's example for once? She handles her engagement with grace."

"And if I say no?" I tested.

My mother sipped her tea, my question not worth a response. Since Father's death years ago, Crowne Industries had been untenable. Never mind what happened to our *family*—our father had been the glue holding an already dysfunctional unit together—the company was always the most important.

On the surface, we were billionaires who had it all. Beneath that veneer, we were barely sustained by my ruthless grandfather Beryl Crowne and my narcissistic mother, Tansy. We stayed afloat, because we did what they said.

Whatever they said—anything so we didn't lose the crown, or *Crowne,* I should say.

I knew what would happen if I disobeyed. I'd end up like my uncle, the cautionary tale in our family for what happened when you disobeyed: penniless and excommunicated.

Over mother's back, Gray blew me a kiss.

I ground my teeth. "I won't disappoint you, Mother."

Mom didn't even bother hiding her incredulous laugh. Without another word, she went back to her book. Our conversation was over.

Maybe if I was someone else, I would've told Mom to screw off. It didn't go over my head that she hadn't even bothered to tell me whom I was marrying.

I wish I didn't want my mother's approval, but it was the one thing I wanted most in the world, and there were days I would do *anything* to get it. On those days, I tended to disappoint her most.

I watched her a moment longer, playing the conversation I wished would happen in my head.

I'm sorry, Mom.

That's okay, because I love you, Abigail. No matter what you do, I will always love you.

After I'd stood there too long, Mother waved a hand for me to go.

I stopped just before the huge portrait of my father, Charles Crowne. He'd had a hard, square jaw and arresting reddish-brown eyes, and in certain lights, they looked purple. His eyes were the only thing I received from him, the only hint I might be a Crowne. He'd been gone for so long this was how I remembered him, in paintings and pictures.

"God, that was so much more satisfying than I imagined," Gemma said to my back. "I think I came."

"Oh, eat a dick, Gemma."

"I would, Abby, but you've already gotten to them all. You're the Pac-Man of dicks."

It doesn't count if it happens in Crowne Hall.

I spun around and raised my hand to throw one of my heels at Gemma's head, but my hand froze midair, captive in someone's grasp. When I looked over my shoulder, my knees buckled, and I nearly fell.

Theo.

Theo held me up by my wrist, unperturbed by the sudden weakness in my legs. I had questions...a lot of questions. Almost five years had passed since I'd last seen him in person. I'd seen pictures of him, but only in tabloids, and always in the back behind my grandfather, out of focused or cropped. Grandpa rarely visited our town of Crowne Point —and even more rarely so our home, Crowne Hall—which meant I never saw Theo.

Never saw the boy I'd saved.

The boy I'd loved.

"What are you doing?" I tried to yank my hand out.

He wouldn't look at me.

It was a rule all servants and bodyguards followed, but it had never been one Theo had obeyed. Not with me.

He'd grown into his features, his jaw now square and hardened. His cheekbones so sharp they were almost hollowed. Thick, silky, lustrous brown hair fell over hazel-green eyes so clear they were like gemstones.

He was in a suit too.

I don't know if I've ever seen Theo in a suit. It was tailored perfectly to his tall, lean muscular build.

"Your poor bodyguard is already having to save your ass," Gemma said.

"My—my what?" I stammered.

He still hadn't released me, the blood draining beneath his touch.

Heat rose to my cheeks. I tried not to think about how it was *Theo* touching me and instead attempted to pull my arm from him. He held tight, fingers bruising.

I was above him. I shouldn't be thinking about the delicious, spicy way he smelled, or his calloused touch. Did his voice still catch on a growl?

"You're my bodyguard?" It came out on a whisper. "Why?"

But then Gemma laughed, Theo's gaze snapped to her like a magnet, and I knew.

"Have fun with your new personal *babysitter.*" Gemma waved airy fingers over her shoulder, her laugh disappearing down the polished halls.

All at once he dropped me.

The heels I still carried clacked to the floor.

It was just me and Theo, alone.

I peeled my eyes from my manicured fingers.

Theo was watching me. I sucked in a breath. If I said something, I could get him fired. I was drawn to him, though. He looked at me with nothing in his crystal-clear green eyes save callousness. I picked at my blush nail polish, staring right back.

"Are you really my new guard?"

Aren't there easier ways for him to get closer to Gemma? I wanted to ask.

Less... *painful* ways? For me.

The grandfather clock ticked away a full minute as I waited for him to respond. In the end, I caved.

"Are you back for me?" My words slid out as a confession.

Are you finally back?

He arched a dark, impassive brow. "What do you think?"

It wasn't necessarily a no, but the way it was spoken made it clear it wasn't a yes.

I'd waited years for Theo.

Five years I'd waited for a word from him, five years I'd yearned and tried to hate him, and only ended up hating myself.

In the end, this was how he came back, with more betrayal.

Down the hall paparazzi were being shuffled in by staff, getting ready for Gemma's birthday party, one of the bigger parties this summer. It wasn't uncommon for them to be in Crowne Hall, and I chewed my bottom lip.

Theo's eyes narrowed on my lip right before I lunged at him, pressing my lips to his. Theo was stone beneath me, just like he'd been the night I'd kissed him, the night before he left.

He shoved me off, and I stumbled back.

Hurt ricocheted inside my ribs.

"I love when you tell me how hard you're going to fuck me," I yelled, eyeing the paparazzi.

Our eyes locked, the flashing of cameras reflecting in his glare, and then Theo gripped my wrist, yanking me out of their view into the ornate hall. I let him tug me down the hallway, our footsteps echoing.

The exterior of Crowne Hall was famous for its inky black shingles and castle-like spires; inside it was pearly white with gold trim. It was a darkly romantic aesthetic, black railings and white, matte walls with intricately cut molding, the occasional gilded accoutrement, and the inescapable smell of salt air.

"Grandpa will fire you when he sees the photos," I said with a smile, masking my hurt in triumph.

I couldn't let him know how much power he still had.

Theo drew his thumb across his lush bottom lip, dragging it out in a distracting way, before ending on an exhale.

"Spoiled little princess... you know better. House paparazzi don't publish anything without written approval."

Hurt welled in my chest.

Where was *my* Theo? Did he ever exist? This heavy-lidded, gaunt, square-jawed imposter was just like everyone else now, seeing only my scars.

His pale eyes narrowed. "You have a party to get ready for, *Ms. Crowne.*"

He said my name with such venom it slid inside my blood and burned; then he grabbed my arm, tugging me toward my wing.

Gemma's birthday party had been planned months before, but I couldn't help but wonder, *Would I meet my fiancé tonight?*

"I can—" I yanked myself free. "I can *walk.*"

My chest rose and fell with heavy breaths, and his eyes

dropped to the movement before sliding back up my neck. There was no heat in his gaze, just ice, and it burned in a different, more painful way. He raised a brow, slightly tilting his head toward the wing. I summoned all of my imperial, God-given *Crowne* right to raise my chin, and I walked past him.

Even though everything in me wanted to crumble.

Especially as I felt him behind me, like a hot, heavy shadow.

Theo Hound wasn't like the other bodyguards in my grandfather's employ. Once upon a time, he was mine. We were just teenagers then, but I found Theo. I kept Theo. I almost gave him my heart, but like everyone else, he chose my sister.

TWO

ABIGAIL

It was awkward and shadowy back in my wing. Theo hadn't said a word, and I didn't want to be the first one to break the silence. When I imagined our reunion, it was never like this, with another barbed wire kiss to shred us.

The last time we'd been together I'd kissed him. I was sixteen years old and head over heels in love with him. It didn't matter he was eighteen and my grandfather's protégé. Or that I could never be with someone like Theo, not without losing everything that made me a Crowne.

I'd kissed him.

Hours later I'd found him professing his love to my sister.

"You're not supposed to look me in the eyes," I muttered. The silence was killing me. I was Abigail Crowne, fire starter, scandal maker, the Wicked Bitch of the East Coast. I'd ruined reputations and destroyed lives, but a few minutes of silence with Theo and I was muttering like the schoolgirls had with Grayson.

Theo arched a brow. Slowly, deliberately, he trailed his gaze upward, landing on the petite crystal chandelier. Almost as if he was rolling his eyes at me.

I rolled my lips together, searching for pieces of myself Theo couldn't take. I straightened my spine, folded my arms, and took a breath.

"I don't need a babysitter," I said. "The sooner you accept that, the easier this will be."

His eyes flashed to mine, and heat seared my stomach.

I knew things about Theo.

Wicked things. Dirty, naughty words he'd whispered in my ear came drifting back, ghosting along my throat like his fingers.

"I—" A stutter threatened to erase the image. I swallowed, lifting my chin. "Stay out of my way, or you'll end up back on the fucking streets, Theo. I brought you here; I can put you back."

The words hurt me more than they did him, I think, because an almost-smile twisted his square jaw. He seemed to take up all the space in the room.

Outside, the crash of waves and trill of seagull caws amplified our silence. The sun was setting, and I knew I should be getting ready for Gemma's party.

Theo walked across my room to the mini fridge hidden beneath discarded silk blouses and unmatched heels—Mother always said I was a mess even the maids couldn't wrangle. He pulled out a water, and I was reminded again that Theo *knew me*, knew every hidden spot in my room and heart.

Theo had been in my room before, but I'd always snuck him in. Now my favorite pearly-pink couch had been replaced with a foldout—a *foldout*. I must have really fucked up to have my mother put such a thing in my wing.

He twisted the lid off the water, handing it to me. "I think we got off on the wrong foot."

I took it warily. I didn't want to be enemies with Theo. Sometimes I did things without thinking—*most of the time*. My heart was sore and bruised from him, but if I could go back in time, I wouldn't have kissed him.

Both times.

I took a sip of water. "Why are you here, Theo? Really?"

He tilted his head. "Truth or promise?"

My breath hitched.

Laughter echoed in my ear, salt air and summer nights, Theo and I curled together on the sand.

Play a game with me, Theo. Truth or promise?

Theo stepped closer, pulling me from the memory. Instinct had me shoving him away before he could get too close. He slammed large palms on either side of my head, grin stretching like a lion about to eat its prey.

"I'm here for you, Abigail."

Why didn't that put my stomach at ease?

Then all at once, he shrugged, stepping back. "The sooner you get your shit together, the sooner I'm back with your grandfather. I'm here to protect your and Crowne Industries' image until your wedding day. Nothing else." He folded his arms. "Even stunts like earlier aren't going to deter me, Abigail."

Until my wedding day. I swallowed a rock at his words.

I knew it was coming. I've been to all the other weddings. First it was my unmarried aunts, then it was my uncles, then they went for the cousins, and even the second-cousins, so on and so forth. Slowly we rebuilt our family on the unsuspecting backs of those who dared to rise above us, until we were back where we belonged: above *them*.

To date, the only one not forced into a marriage was, ironically, my mother.

Rationally, I know it's not the end of the world. Gemma says when she gets married, she won't move out. She's already planning on forcing Horace to move in. Crowne Hall is big enough that they need only see each other for events. They'll continue to sleep with whoever they want, as they already have been.

But I don't *want* that life.

I'm stupid enough to want love.

I lifted my chin. "I want to be the best Crowne I can be."

He gave me a look, and for a moment I thought he was going to call me out. There was a time when I'd told Theo all my deep dark secrets.

Like what I really wanted to do with my life, or how I hated myself for wanting to be better than my sister. How I wanted to be something, *do* something, more than be just a Crowne.

How I wanted my mom to love me more than anything.

He smiled, but it wasn't the smile I knew. It was cruel, his pale eyes gleaming with something wicked beneath the shadow of his dark brow, and his plush lips curled.

It sent shivers down my spine.

"Like I said, Abs. I'm here to help."

He'd used his old nickname for me, but there was no caressing lilt. If anything, he may have called me a bitch for all the warmth there was.

I narrowed my eyes. "Truth?" I asked, trying to use our old game, the one he'd just called upon moments before.

He shook his head. "Promise."

I watched him a moment longer, as if he would suddenly break and reveal all his motives.

He didn't.

So I left him in my newly finished en suite—his *room*.

I turned to shut my double doors, and right before they closed Theo's black leather shoe slid between them. I stared at it, dumbfounded, and in that second Theo slammed open the left door.

"It stays open," he said.

"I'm—I'm changing." The absurdity of having to say it aloud had me stammering over my words. I hated that.

His eyes traveled a slow, cutting path down my body before coming back to me, bored. "And I'm not interested."

I couldn't so much as scoff before he turned, giving me his back. My fingers itched with the urge to pelt him with the nearest hard object at his head—a lilac-scented candle.

I didn't have it raised for a second before Theo said, "Sure you want to do that?"

How did he know? He hadn't so much as shifted. His shoulders were broad, his legs spread, his hands behind his back in the perfect bodyguard position.

I dropped it with a thud to my feathery white carpet.

Theo wasn't my best friend anymore, that was for sure. He was a bodyguard through and through, and I was beginning to worry he wasn't like the others I'd scared away.

He looked at his wrist and, like he knew I was still staring, said, "You have forty-five minutes."

I straightened, going to my walk-in.

When I'd first found Theo, he'd had to sleep with the rest of the servants in the servant wing. No amount of pleading had changed Mom or Grandfather's mind. It wasn't proper. It wasn't right. Now Theo definitely wasn't the sixteen-year-old I found, and neither was he the eighteen-year-old boy who'd left me. He was a twenty-three-year-old man. Hard. Chiseled.

Dangerous.

And he was just outside my bedroom.

I swallowed, trying to focus on getting dressed.

My dress was truly fit for a princess. A sheer white boned bodice, dipping low with a sweetheart neckline and mother-of-pearls dotting the boned corset and falling like raindrops down the tiered tulle.

They called us royalty in our town, and we couldn't afford to ruin the image.

I added my finishing touch: a teardrop pearl necklace hanging just above the lace sweetheart. I touched the soft pearl resting just above my cleavage, wondering if Theo still remembered this secret. This piece of myself I'd only ever told him.

I couldn't completely finish dressing myself. The silky rose laces corseting the back of my dress were impossible to tie. Normally I had someone dress me, a girl who was just a year older than me. She was new to me and her name was Story.

So where the hell was she?

I called down to the servants' wing.

"Busy?" I all but gasped. "What do you mean she's *busy?"* I wasn't like Gemma or Gray, who had entire legions attending to them.

All I had was this girl.

When it was horrifyingly clear no one was going to help me, I hung up the Crowne Hall house line. A part of me wondered if this was another punishment, and if making a scene would make Mom even more upset with me.

So I determined to handle it myself.

I struggled, flexing in ways no person should flex, and I

knew Theo could hear me. My breath was too loud, coming out in short gasps. Theo remained stoic at the door, not so much as flinching. When I fell off my chair and knocked over my coral porcelain lamp after another attempt, his cool, even voice finally drifted inside the room.

"Need help?" His head was still forward, his shoulders loose.

"No," I snapped.

Yes.

"Five minutes," he replied.

I chewed my bottom lip, staring at his back. Theo was a sentry. He didn't so much as straighten his spine at my presence.

I watched my clock tick down. *Four minutes. Three...* I was going to be late for Gemma's party, and Tansy Crowne would have me drawn and quartered.

"I need your help," I blurted.

A barely-there perk of his slightly crooked ear was the only response I got before he came to me.

Theo was behind me for a long time, his fingers just beneath the lace of my dress. It only took Story only five minutes tops, yet he leisurely worked the laces. My heart rose and rose with each skim of his finger, the pad of his pointer sliding along my spine, teasing to the base. It took everything in me not to grasp the doorframe for support.

"What's taking so long?" I demanded.

Silence.

Then, "Done."

But his touch stayed, as if memorizing each traitorous heartbeat beneath my flesh.

"Thanks," I said. *Thanks?* I didn't *thank* people, especially not bodyguards. Not getting them fired was *thanks* enough.

Theo froze, and his grip tightened on the laces, forcing the dress so taut against my skin I couldn't breathe. I opened my mouth to suck in air, but nothing came. I think I squeaked out a word, but if he heard, he didn't act like it.

Suddenly he let me go, and I stumbled forward.

"It's part of the job, princess."

We were late, rushing through nearly empty halls to the ballroom where the party was being held. We were almost there when I heard, "Oh shit, the mutt's back!"

Geoff, one of my brother's friends, laughed with his friend Drake. I didn't see any drinks in their hands, but it smelled like weed.

"Does that mean we can't make the princess cry anymore?" Drake mused, watching me with sparkling interest.

"Not if you don't want to get bit," Geoff sneered.

I snuck a clandestine glance at Theo, wondering if their words affected him as much as they did me. There'd been a time when he'd been the only one at my back, and of course our world had afforded him cruel nicknames for his kindness.

Dog. Mutt.

He was stone.

Fine, I would be too.

We kept walking, leaving them to their laughter.

We rushed straight down and sat at the table high above the party without doing the regular meet and greet, and I could tell Mother was already upset.

I quickly scurried to the table and found my seat, but froze when I saw the item in my chair: a long-stemmed gold rose. I brushed the rose to the floor and took my seat. Roses were perfectly normal, especially at such an opulent party.

It wasn't possible he could be here. It wasn't. Crowne Hall was more fortified than the white house.

Still, my heart hammered.

Theo was a hot shadow at my back, his presence a boiling pressure. I was seated above everyone else, and I folded and unfolded my linen in my lap.

Crowne Hall was known for its extravagant parties, and tonight was no different. All the elite of Crowne Point were here to celebrate my sister's twenty-third birthday.

I was seated at the very edge of the long, elegantly decorated table, and Gemma was at the center, wearing the Crowne family tiara. Mom didn't even let me look at the thing. I folded my arms, trying not to feel envy, but it boiled venomous beneath my skin.

Grandpa wasn't here.

I missed him.

The only one who showed me any sort of affection.

I shifted again in my dress. Something felt wrong.

I looked over my shoulder at Theo, standing sentry against the only wall that wasn't a floor-to-ceiling window.

"Are you sure it's on correctly?" I asked. I knew if I had another wardrobe mishap I'd be in deep, deep shit.

Theo gave me a deadpan stare.

I looked back out at the hall, at the rows of perfectly dressed partygoers seated beneath the domed ceiling and massive imported Italian crystal chandelier. No fiancé tonight, it seemed—just us Crownes above everyone else. Which meant I'd been spared.

Barely.

Before long the trill of crystal sounded, and eyes turned to me. It was my turn to do a speech for Gemma. I swallowed my urge to vomit and stood. My old high school classmates were in the crowd, having returned from their lives for the summer. From college or internships, things my family frowned upon, but I dreamed about.

I'm only twenty-one, and as the summer looms to its end, I fear it will be another year I won't be afforded the same privilege.

Technically I have three younger half-siblings, the triplets my father had with his official mistress before he died. They're still in boarding school in Switzerland. Some days I envied them. We'd been plucked from boarding school and told to amass influence at public school. Gray and Gemma *ruled* Crowne Point High. Back then, I thought it was the worst time of my life.

It was nothing to now.

I tapped my crystal glass with a smile.

I gave some bullshit speech about love and family, even looking to Gemma with a smile—she crinkled her nose at me. When I finished, I set down my drink. I was afforded the duty claps owed me. However, when I turned around, giving my back to the room, everyone went silent.

My gut dropped.

A billion thoughts went through my head.

Did I have panties stuck to my dress? Was it see-through? Did Theo forget to lace the back properly?

We hadn't been seen by anyone on our way down. What an awful way to learn my new dress was see-through. I was frozen, waiting for the pin to drop.

"Oh my God," someone whispered.

"What is wrong with you, Abby?" Gemma hissed, suddenly at my side, her perfect nearly nude manicure digging into my elbow.

"Currently? I have a bitch-barnacle stuck to my arm." I yanked Gemma off me.

Gemma scoffed. "This is low, even for you."

Fear crawled up my throat, but I couldn't let Gemma win. Still acting like everything was fine, I caught my reflection in one of the many gilded floor-to-ceiling windows surrounding the room. They opened out to the Atlantic Ocean, sapphire in the night, like looking into a black mirror.

My dress had been vandalized. Smeared along the pretty sheer skirt in red lipstick were the words: *Gemma is a SLUT*.

I gasped, grappling with the material to try and get a better look.

What. The. Fuck.

"You're a fucking psycho," Gemma hissed, still smiling.

"Pot meet overly priced plastic kettle," I spat, dropping my dress.

"You're envious, you're hateful. You've *always* been that way," Gemma said. "There's a reason you don't have friends, Abby. A reason we vacation without you. A reason Mom constantly wonders if you were switched at the hospital."

I looked over the crowd, seeing my old classmates. Suit-clad arms were folded. Beautiful, professionally made-up eyes glittered under the low light, watching me. A hushed murmur began to rise like a slow wave.

I knew what they were thinking, and it gutted me like a harpoon. It was the same thought keeping me from being invited to parties, spurring me to show up uninvited and armoring me to act like I enjoyed ruining their fun.

God, Abby, take a fucking hint.

I just hoped someone would say they were happy to see me.

Once.

"Take a fucking hint."

I launched at Gemma. I tangled my fingers in her silky blown-out curls, and I knew it wasn't going to end well. People think I'm malicious and vindictive and did things because I like causing drama. But have you ever been so hurt and torn open you'd do anything to make the throbbing pain stop?

You can't think about the after, only the now?

Why do I have to get married before Gemma? And why so rushed?

Why does everything in my life have to revolve around Crowne Industries?

I yanked at my sister's hair, and she gripped my wrists, pulling me the other way.

"You're such a disgrace to our name," Gemma said, our foreheads touching.

"You're a kiss-ass."

"Yeah, well you're a kiss-ass wannabe." Gemma was *strong*. She held me there, forcing me to listen. "And that's fucking pathetic."

Another spear to my heart.

I redirected my grip from Gemma's hair to her nice dress, tearing at the lace, and she was trying to do the same when I was pulled off, back into the arms of Theo. Gemma tore my dress as I went, and I only managed to slightly wrinkle hers.

Theo's heat wrapped around me, arms like corded iron. Gemma's perfect blonde curls were mussed and tangled, and the Crowne tiara was now askew. That filled me with bitter-sweet joy.

"Stop." His low, commanding voice vibrated against my ear. I relaxed, my hurt melting into his chest.

For a stupid, blinding minute I felt safe. Theo had been the only one I'd ever felt safe with.

Then he dropped me. I watched as if viewing a car crash as he went and helped my sister off the floor, even going so far as to fix her tiara. Pain tore my heart down the middle.

"Well, happy birthday to Gemma," I said. "The real whore of Crowne Industries."

"Cover yourself," my mother hissed. I looked down, finding my breasts exposed where Gemma had ripped. I quickly slammed my arms over my chest, but it was useless —everyone had seen.

My eyes snapped from her to the crowd watching with delight, then back to her. I ground my jaw so tears wouldn't spring. I know what they're thinking. I'm pulling an Abby, making a mess of things, acting like a fool. I can't wait to see what the hashtag would be tonight.

"It is such a relief your father isn't here to see this." There were few times I'd heard my mother's voice shake, an anger reserved only for me—her greatest disappointment.

"Get her out of here," my mother said to Theo.

Theo nodded, coming back to me, beginning to usher me away.

"But Mom—"

"Abigail," my mother hissed, cutting me off. Her smile remained, glancing at the people who watched us. "Are you so fatally jealous you have to ruin everything?"

"Mom, I didn't *do* it," I said weakly.

Her eyes narrowed. "The words just crawled up your dress?"

I opened my mouth and closed it. I didn't know how they'd gotten there.

"It wasn't my fault," I said weakly.

She shook her head. "It's never your fault, Abigail." My mother walked away, joining the crowd to presumably do damage control.

"At least playboy Gray understands his role. You..." Gemma sighed, righting her tiara. "You are so deeply, deeply unworthy of this family."

I mashed my lips together, trying to control the heat crawling up my cheeks. I could feel them all watching me, the whispers, the laughter, the rumors that would spread.

So I laughed.

Because I didn't want to cry. "I *wish* I wasn't part of this family."

I ripped myself out of Theo's hold, running out of the great hall and into the gardens, falling on the lush green lawns overlooking the ocean. I pulled at the ends of my curls, looking at the dark waters.

We weren't ever like other families, but then Dad died, and everything became about preserving his name, *our* name.

My mom has always been Tansy *Crowne*, but there was a time when my sister and brother weren't only Gemma and Gray *Crowne*. And me... who was I before I became the girl pitted against them?

The girl destined to lose.

The real truth about me? The lives I destroyed were casualties. I wasn't wicked.

I was unworthy. Unlovable. Rejected.

I heard a crunch and jumped, but when I saw who it was, I relaxed.

"Theo." His name came out on a breath. The glow of

Crowne Hall created a halo around his lean figure, making him look dark and ominous. He'd been there for me, held me, even if it was just part of the job, and I couldn't shake the reminders of the past. Hope bloomed in my chest that, despite earlier today and five years of distance, we could go back to before.

He slid out of his jacket, draping it over my body.

"Thank you," I said. Sincerely. Once again, Theo had been the only one there for me.

Something flickered in his eyes.

Disgust?

I tugged at my chestnut curl, trying to get my heart rate under control.

Wary, I pulled the lapels tight around me, watching him through my lashes as he walked around me until he was blocking the ocean. He bent down, suit stretching across his knees, his face still half-engulfed in shadows. His sharp cheekbones even hollower, more gaunt in the darkness.

"Poor Abigail," he said. "Always second best." He wiped the tear off my face with his knuckle and a smile that made me shiver.

"Theo, what are you—"

He cut me off, my words disappearing into my throat as he spoke. "Never good enough. Not loved by her mommy. Hated by her siblings. Reviled by her peers." His hand didn't leave me, knuckles resting on my jaw, lighter than air. "Poor little Abigail only wants to be loved, but no one could ever love her."

"Stop." I tried to tear my face from him, but his light grasp turned furious. He held my chin, hard and bruising, forcing me to look into his eyes. The warm Crowne Hall lights reflected in them, dancing like devil's flames.

"So easy. So predictable. Still lashing out without thought, starting fires that consume her."

My heart pounded louder than the ocean as a realization curled in my gut. There was only one person who had access to my dress. I just didn't understand *why* he would do it.

"You did this?"

"I fucked up your dress. The rest was all you."

"Why?" I whispered.

He released my chin, and this time I was frozen in place, his presence holding me captive. He trailed his knuckles against my jaw, up and down in a tender fashion that utterly belied the wolfish, vicious way he watched me.

A ghostly breeze blew salt air between us.

He wasn't going to answer.

"Why are you here?" I tried instead.

His knuckle grazed my chin as a smile curled his lips. "Truth or promise?"

I had a thought as he perverted the sweet game we used to play as teenagers.

The thing between us was darkening, twisting, and I should run. Run before I darken and twist with it. I was the Wicked Bitch of the East Coast, but I wasn't the words they called me. Not really. I liked to pretend I was as callous as my brother Grayson, as cunning as my sister Gemma.

In reality, I was soft. As they said, there was a reason I'd never fit in. I was a marshmallow. Easy to step on. Easier to squish.

So I answered. "Truth."

Theo smiled, easy and slow. "I'm going to break your heart, and you're going to thank me for it."

THREE

THEO

She blinked, blue eyes wide, then laughed. "You're out of your mind."

"Maybe," I answered, dropping her chin, standing up. The grass was made unsteady by the sand beneath, and the ocean roared angry behind us.

I liked her at my feet. Liked having Abigail Crowne where she belonged.

Thanks.

Abigail *thanked* me. Abigail Crowne didn't show soft sides, and if she did, it was only because she was about to put the dagger in your back. Thank-yous. Promises. Confessions. They should all be treated like enemy fire.

In all the truth or promises Abigail Crowne and I had played, she'd only ever made me one promise, and she broke it before the sun could rise.

Now, Abigail watched me, keeping a taut smile on her

face, the moonlight liquid pearl on her skin. It was as if she thought I wouldn't see through it, like I wouldn't remember what a real Abigail Crowne smile looked like.

I speared my pocket, finding the friendship bracelet I couldn't throw away. "You have a nickname, you know, around Crowne Hall."

Her smile dropped.

"Oh." I smiled, licking my top two teeth. "You already know it."

"Fuck off." She stood and took off the jacket I'd given her, throwing it at my face, trying to push past me, but I easily grasped her by the elbow.

It wasn't like before. She had no fight.

I'd thought about this moment for five years, what I would do when I finally saw her again, how I would make her suffer like she'd made me.

I'd expected her to fight back.

"The girl who opens her legs for anyone," I said quietly, working the blocky beads so hard they bit into my skin. "The girl who begs for insults, because they come easier than adoration. The girl who'd ask to get slapped if it meant someone would touch her."

"Please..." Abigail bit her lower lip and looked at the grass. "Stop."

"The Reject Princess." I licked the words with a humorless smirk.

Her eyes flashed back to mine, haughty and filled with fire. For a minute she looked just like she had the night she'd started this.

I was sixteen when they'd found me.

When *she'd* found me.

I don't know much about my life before the Crownes.

I'd lived on the streets of our small town, when one night a shiny, black car stopped. Abigail Crowne got out of the car. I remember it had been an unusually cold July, and the streets popped with fireworks every night.

She was the most beautiful person I'd ever seen in my life. Her black hair had curled in the wind like silk ribbons and she had an entitled, callous sheen to her violet veiled brown eyes I'd only ever seen on the rich.

She'd bent down until we were eye to eye and said, "I've been looking for a pet. Grandpa's allergic to dogs and Mom hates cats..." She'd trailed off, biting her bottom lip, looking at me. Her front teeth were a little crooked, but it had only added to her allure.

You're going to be mine forever, and you're going to thank me for it.

"The Reject Princess... yeah." I laughed, grabbing her elbow, pulling her closer. "I'm going to break your heart, and you'll thank me for it. You'll beg me to do it again."

Fear flickered in her eyes, and she searched my own.

Whatever she was searching for, she wouldn't find it.

She lifted her chin high, and whatever vulnerability she'd shown me before vanished.

"If I'm the Reject Princess, what does that make you? The pathetic dog asleep at her feet?"

A humorless smirk chilled my lips; then I bit the air between us, stopping a feather's distance away from her lips. She jumped back, heels losing purchase in the sandy grass, falling on her ass.

My laugh barely reached my lips, let alone my eyes.

Her eyes widened. "What happened to you?" Abigail scrambled back, getting tangled in her tulle. She spun around and tried to stand, tried to leave. I stepped on the hem, and she fell forward on a gasp.

I yanked her up by the laces of her dress just before she hit the grass.

"I dunno." I gripped her satin laces, pulling her to me. "What happened to me?"

I didn't give her a chance to recover. With one hand on her laces, I trailed my other lightly along her collarbone.

As far as I was concerned, she'd had five fucking years to be comfortable.

Her heartbeat pounded against my touch, and hard, heavy breaths escaped her spoiled, pouty lips, but she held her face in a firm grimace. Still, her skin rose to meet me.

"You're not the boy I remember," she said, a wrinkle marring her perfect porcelain brow. "You're not the boy I saved."

"You're not the girl I remember either, princess."

There was a time I thought Abigail was like me, but she'd always been a spoiled brat. Today proved that, shattered any lingering doubts.

"I'm *exactly* the person you left me to be," she said.

"I'm going to take everything from you," I said, voice soft. "Until you regret ever making me believe you were different."

Until you regret making me believe I could have something more.

"I won't play your games," she said, a slight stammer to her words.

I bit back my laugh. Abigail Crowne was a master at games, but this time I'd be the one to ruin her, break her to pieces, build a safety net with rotting promises.

I'll take everything from her. Her family. Her dreams.

Her heart.

Until there's nothing left.

"Princess..." I ghosted my touch at her collarbone up to

her throat, forcing her neck back, flush against me, ears to my lips.

"You're not a player. You're a pawn."

FOUR

ABIGAIL

"Up and at 'em, Reject." Theo threw open the windows. Yellow-gold morning light assaulted the shadowy corners of my room.

He eyed the porcelain lamp by my bedside, now muted in the morning glow. "Still afraid of what's under the bed?"

He shot me a twisted, red-lipped grin, and heat crept up my cheeks, embarrassment drenched my blood. Only he knew *why* I slept with the light on. He knew and was using the memory as a shard to stab me.

I quickly slammed the light off and deflected. "You're not supposed to come into my room. I could have you fired."

"I wonder who they'd believe? The misbehaving heiress or the nothing-but-exemplary bodyguard tasked with watching her reject ass."

I glared at Theo, willing it to turn him into ashes, pushing past how his street clothes fit on his muscular yet lean frame. His hoodie, gray jeans, and tennis shoes were designed to blend in, but he stood out like a model on the runway.

Theo Hound was undeniably gorgeous, and he was also dead set on ruining me.

He was supposed to be *my* person, and instead he left me like everyone else. I wasn't ever a very good Crowne. I never filled my room with extravagant purchases like Gemma, or played games with the desperate like Gray, but when I saw Theo, I took him.

Last night I'd trusted him, and once again he'd betrayed me. I'll never make that mistake again. From this point on, Theo Hound is enemy number one. I don't care he's been charged to guard my life. If I let *my* guard down, he'll ruin me.

I know it.

If my glare affected him, it didn't show. In fact, his blush lips curved. "Sleep well?"

"I hate you."

"I don't know how I'll go on," he said without any emotion, turning his attention to my ornately carved wood desk. There was only one thing atop it, my laptop—Mother liked to keep things neat. When he began opening drawers, I darted out of my bed so fast I forgot I was in only a small slip of a nightgown.

I slammed the drawer shut.

Our hands touched over the cool metal handle, Theo's stare on mine, as my heart rose into my throat. I couldn't fight him off. If he wanted to open that drawer, he could.

Inside it I had a secret: college applications. A belief I could do something, *be* someone, better than arm candy, better than the last name *Crowne* and the girl I'd been raised to be. It was a fairy tale, a fantasy, but I liked to look at the applications and dream. The same way people who drove by our manor on tour buses did, I bet.

"What do you think you're doing? You can't just tear apart my room."

"Actually, I can." Theo took a step closer, pressing me against my desk, until my back bit into the wood. "I'm not like your other guards, Reject. You can't scare me away. Your secrets are mine. Your mind is mine. Your body is mine. How else could I *protect* you?"

All too aware of his body pressed into mine, I tried to control my face, not let on how unnerved I was. Protect me? More like destroy me.

I gave myself away with a hard swallow, and Theo stepped back, a cruel smirk on his lips. His eyes landed on my open laptop, on the pictures wallpapering the back, and slowly Theo withdrew his hands, a grin spreading. He snatched the laptop, holding it high so I couldn't get it. Maybe I should've worried more about what was on my laptop, but as long as he didn't see my college applications, I didn't care.

The pictures were of the one day Gemma and I hadn't been at each other's throats. She'd just turned twenty-one, I was nineteen. She'd allowed me into her bedroom for once, and we'd gotten drunk and taken naughty photos.

She had the matching set, the ones of me.

That was how Crowne sisters bonded—blackmail.

He arched a brow. "Naughty."

"Nothing you haven't seen before," I said under my breath.

His stare dug into me like he wanted to press. Press what? The reason you obliterated my heart?

Then he slammed the laptop shut and shoved it under his arm. "Get dressed."

"So you can make Mom hate me even more? No, thanks. I'll stay here." Today was one of my most favorite days, but if Theo wanted me dressed, instinct said I should do the opposite.

A cruel smile. "Scared?"

"No. I'm just not in the habit of listening to my bodyguards."

"Get dressed, or I'll dress you."

A ripple of excitement raced up my spine, one I quickly disregarded as shock. "You wouldn't dare."

"Want to test me, Reject?"

Before I could respond, he grabbed my elbow, dragging me to my walk-in. He tore open the frosted French doors, throwing me inside like I was a rag doll.

"Get. Dressed."

"Get. Out," I responded in the same tone.

His eyes raked over me, and I folded my arms, as if I could shield myself from the piercing stare.

He laughed. "Nothing *half the world* hasn't seen already."

He spoke to me like I had to him just moments before, but a stab of hurt sliced through me.

Everyone *had* seen me, because I'd been betrayed the same way Theo had betrayed me. Getting out of a car to paparazzi who'd been tipped off, after being persuaded to go commando by people I thought were friends. Kissing an actor on a yacht who thought it would be hilarious to kiss the famous train wreck and let the world see.

As if he knew I was hurting, he said, "I'm disappointed. I thought it would take more than one night to break you."

The only thing not completely stone on his hard features was the slight mocking lilt to his soft-as-sin lips.

Without another thought, I tore off my satin nightie and

threw it at his head. The *fuck you* was apparent.

For a split second, shock registered over his features. Then heat blazed, peppering goose bumps along my skin like tight-fitting lace.

I was utterly naked in front of Theo for the first time in my life, and all he did was stare. We'd shared dirty promises, but we'd never fulfilled them. A cool ocean breeze whispered across my nipples, and I fought the urge to cover myself.

I wouldn't lose.

All at once he slammed the French doors shut so hard they rattled.

I stayed there in the center of my walk-in closet, the plush carpet cushioning my feet as I fisted my hands.

I couldn't decide if I'd won or lost.

I'd had *years* to train for this. Every guard assigned to me either quit or relocated. Theo Hound wouldn't know what hit him. He wanted to play?

Game. On.

The town of Crowne Point is known for three things: my beautiful sister, my playboy brother, and the time I pulled the First Daughter's extensions out at our annual Fourth of July barbecue. In my defense, she "mistook" me for the help.

The help doesn't wear bespoke Zac Posen.

Bitch.

We're a small eastern beach town nestled at the southernmost tip of New York, home to some of the wealthiest people in America. My grandfather, of course, and the people he'd made rich. Years ago, when my great-great-grand daddy made his money in railroads, we'd been one of the first and most important commercial lines, and Crowne Point used to be an industrial hub. Now that stop is a tourist attraction, and my family is involved in everything from fertilizer to Big Pharma. Chances are there's something in every home that's made us money.

We make the Hamptons look like a trailer park. It's almost hard to believe we came close to losing everything. My home, Crowne Hall, was as much a landmark as the swans inhabiting our beaches. It's visible from anyplace in Crowne Point, and from Main Street, you can see the jutting black towers past the olde-style shops.

Most importantly, my family owns this town. People outside of Crowne can't really understand what it's like to live here. A journalist did a piece on Crowne Point once and called us an "entrenched monarchy hidden inside America's East Coast," like it was a bad thing.

There's a hierarchy.

A way to things.

You're either royal, or you're not.

We have a native swan population people travel from all over the world to see. In the summer their populations surge for a few months. In a few hours, this place would be crawling with tourists and townies alike, flocking to see the hundreds of swans that consume our beaches the week before the Fourth.

"Today is seriously still important to you?" Theo asked, eyeing me.

"No," I responded too quickly, giving myself away. Historically, the Swan Swell had always been one of the only times my grandpa came home, and he'd come hold the swans with me.

It was a tradition I'd had with my father, and when he

died Grandpa stepped in. It meant the world to me.

Theo laughed, obviously picking up on my lie.

I glared.

"Those are so pretty!"

I blinked out of my glare, finding a pretty young woman eyeing my earrings.

"Did you buy them here?"

She gestured down Main Street where various pop-up shops and artisan craft stalls had appeared overnight. During the Swell, Main Street closed down to make way for them.

I touched my found-glass earrings with a smile.

"No, afraid not."

"Do you mind telling me where? I would love to have a pair."

Love to have a pair.

I glowed at her words. I have a secret, one I'm certain Theo has forgotten about, and one I don't want him to remember. He'd nearly discovered it this morning in my desk. I make jewelry, and someday dream to study the art in college. I only ever use found items, because there's magic in revealing the beauty of what people discarded.

I smiled at the woman. "I'm sorry. I can't remember."

She frowned but accepted my lie.

I watched her walk away, disappearing into the crowd forming in Main Street. There was a warmth in my stomach that wouldn't easily dissipate. When she complimented me, it was so much more poignant than the millions I'd been showered with simply for being a Crowne. Those compliments were like everything in our world, done for vapid, unyielding custom.

But that woman complimented *me*.

When I finally looked back, Theo was watching me

with too much interest.

"You have a nickname too, you know," I said casually, fingering seashells on a pop-up shop's stand. It was my secret dream to have my own shop and one day have my jewelry for sale for women like her.

My secret, unobtainable dream.

Theo spared me a look. "Trying to get in my head?"

String lights drooped overhead that would glow in the evening, and we would soon be shoulder to shoulder.

You can always tell the difference between a tourist and a townie. Townies know us. They glance at us. Tourists stare.

"Just wondering if you remembered, if you knew you were Crowne Point's very own lost dog. What's it like not knowing who your parents are?"

"What's it like knowing yours, and knowing they don't love you?" he responded easily, sounding bored.

I glared. "My dad loved me."

"Mmm... past tense."

I ground my teeth.

Focus.

"I need to use the bathroom."

Theo narrowed his eyes but said nothing.

When we got to the bathroom, Theo tried to push his way inside first. I jumped in front of him, blocking the doorway. His hair was wilder in the salty humidity, sticking up yet still soft looking, falling over his piercing eyes.

"You have to be kidding."

"If only," he deadpanned. "I go everywhere you go, Reject."

"I'll tell everyone you're a pervert," I threatened. A leonine smile spread his plush lips, and he leaned forward, forcing me to arch and strain my back to get away.

"Then I'll have to make sure what you threaten comes true."

My lips parted, momentarily stunned by his response. So many of my guards had been concerned with reputation. All it took was one artfully placed threat and they kowtowed.

"Stay outside and I won't lock the door," I said it with a glare, but I knew I was negotiating with him, and I itched to slam the door.

A spark glittered in his pale eyes, and I swore he knew what I was planning, but then he shrugged and gave me his back.

I slammed the door and focused on the window at the back.

There's an underground in Crowne Point. A place where elite and townies collide in mutual drug-fueled non-judgment. It takes place about a mile east, in the old amusement park on the now-abandoned pier, once called Crowne Park, now known colloquially as Horsemen's Wharf. It was named after the four boys who oversee it, who run the meanest gang in town. I never really interacted with them, and that was a good thing.

The Horsemen take pride in their drugs, to the point even people like Grayson begrudgingly acknowledge they have good, clean shit. The Wharf is also one of the quickest places to score.

I kicked over the trashcan, hoisting myself up, shimmying my legs through the window, trying not to think about Theo. There'd been a time when he'd lifted me up through windows, and we'd jumped down together.

I released my grip, hopping to the ground.

"Where are you going?"

"Shit!" I jumped at Theo's voice, falling back against

the brick wall, heart racing. Did he really remember our move?

As if he could read my mind, he said, "You haven't changed."

His clear green eyes roamed my body. My satin black tank scorched beneath them, and I jumped back to this morning, when I'd been in nothing but my silky pajamas. I hardened my glare, refusing to fold my arms.

With a wicked grin, eyes lingering on my chest, he added, "Strike that, you've changed some."

I fought the urge to kick sand at him.

"Wanna tell me where you were going, or should we do it the fun way?"

I stayed silent.

He rubbed his bottom lip with his thumb, watching me. "There isn't much around here." He focused on me. Studying me. Digging into me. Once again it was like he was reading my mind.

As if he was commanding me to do it, my eyes traveled left, where, in the distance, barely visible against the darkening sky, was the decrepit Ferris wheel that marked Horsemen's Wharf.

"The Wharf? Really?" He sounded disappointed in me.

He pushed me against the brick wall. "What was your plan, Reject? Go to the wharf, get some drugs, put them on me, and call Grandpa Crowne?"

Yes.

Dammit.

It had worked with so many of my other guards.

Theo kept pushing into me, knee grinding up against me in ways I liked too much.

"Get off me." I tried to push him off and he gripped my wrists.

A cruel smile spread those devilish, heart-shaped lips. "Are you *still* a virgin?"

I felt like a doe about to be caught in the jaws of a mountain lion. For a brief moment, I showed him my neck. Ice-cold water drenched my spine, and I locked eyes with him. No one in the world would accuse Abigail Crowne of being a virgin.

But Theo had never been just anyone.

I quickly shook out of it, re-dropping my walls, but I took too long to respond. "No."

He laughed.

Hiking his knee up just a little bit, pressing on that deep, aching spot inside me.

"You *are*."

There was wonder in his voice, but it was drowned by the cruelty. It reminded me of a photo I'd seen of tourists on a beach taking selfies with a dead baby dolphin.

Vicious delight.

I'd done everything *but*—so technically I wasn't. Right?

"This changes things." He pressed his knee *hard,* and a traitorous gasp fell from my lips. I hated myself for grabbing onto him, wrinkling his shirt.

His touch threaded into my hair, pulling my head, exposing my neck. "How much would you give me to make your first time *magical*, Reject?"

"I'm not having sex with you." Why did my voice shake?

Another laugh.

Trying to see his eyes, to calculate his next move, caused a painful strain in my neck. It was so much easier to give in. Give in to his fingers digging into my hair, massaging one minute, and bruising the next.

I tried to focus on my breathing, but the more I did, the

more my lungs shrunk. All I knew were his soft lips on my ear. His breath too hot, burning up my neck. His knee causing a curling ache inside me I'd never known.

An ache threatening to consume me.

His lips were so close to my flesh. Something deep and traitorous inside me screamed *kiss me. Bite me. Mark me.*

"I won't do it," I said, voice breathy and treacherous.

"Keep telling yourself that," he said. "You'll give me so much."

My eyes flew open at his dangerous words.

His lips fell on my neck.

"Theo?"

At the voice, Theo dropped me like fire and stepped back. My hand came to my neck, where his lips had left a venomous tattoo, threading into my blood, turning my view hazy as a sunset. I couldn't string together a thought.

I needed to get my shit together, because a few feet from us was a man in a dark-gray, three-piece suit despite the summer weather. He was almost as famous for the look as he was for his ruthless business practices.

Mr. Beryl Crowne, aka the third richest man in the world, aka my *grandpa.* Theo's boss, the only person to ever show me affection outside of Theo, and Theo's meal ticket.

Beryl Crowne had been accused of many things—and indicted for none. He was a man who cared as much about his reputation as he did the price of his company's stock. Anyone to ever publicly accuse him of something nefarious either rescinded it within the next few hours or ended up... curiously missing.

"Oh, did I forget to mention Grandpa's home?" I said to Theo, manufacturing a frown. "I saw his motorcade right before I went to the bathroom. Must have slipped my mind."

Grandpa loved Theo like the hardworking son he lost too early, and like the diligent grandson he never had in Gray. He'd been grooming Theo for a position in Crowne Industries since I picked him up off the street. The distinction was clear, though. Theo wasn't blood. He wasn't a Crowne. Don't date my granddaughters, don't even look at them, and don't get any ideas about biting the hand that feeds you.

Theo stood there, dumbfounded.

I adjusted my top, acting like whatever happened between Theo and me was nothing.

It *was* nothing.

I ran to my grandpa.

"Papa!" I jumped into his arms.

"Princess..." He caught me in a hug, tone skeptical. "What did I just see?" He looked over my shoulders at Theo.

"You'll have to ask Theo, Papa. You know I would never do anything to disappoint you."

Papa had been called a megalomaniac, a narcissist, a sociopath, but he was the only one who ever gave me the benefit of the doubt.

Pantiless photo? Topless on a yacht? Three-way lip-lock? All the result of unscrupulous reporters.

If only my grandfather had been around more. The only time I saw him was for a few days in the summer, and occasionally—if lucky—on holidays.

Grandfather and I separated, and after agreeing to meet up for our swan-feeding tradition, I walked back toward Theo, who still wore a shocked look.

"*That* was my plan," I whispered, walking by Theo.

Me: 1

Theo: 0

FIVE

ABIGAIL

I watched my grandpa and Theo talk, trying to read their lips as I held a baby swan. My grandfather was frowning; Theo was frowning harder.

Abigail! Abigail! Give us a smile.

A few feet to the left of me, reporters snapped pictures, their bright flashes stinging my eyes. I ignored them. It was all I could ever do. I squinted harder, past the flashing, trying harder to see my grandpa and—

Rules.

Ha! I jumped, unable to control my happiness. I'd caught *that* word. Grandfather had mentioned the rules. No looking me in the eyes and definitely no *touching*. Theo was getting his ass handed to him. Maybe he'd even get sent back to LA.

"What are you smiling about, Abigail?" a reporter yelled. I glanced in their direction.

"It's a beautiful evening," I murmured.

It was the time of night when the sky looked like a painting as day faded. The stars were diamonds caught in a swirling purple-orange-pink watercolor above us. Tourists were flocking to the beach to watch the swans. Adult swans were way too mean to hold or even go near, but there was a little embankment where you could feed the baby ones.

If you were a Crowne, you could even hold them.

My eyes traveled down the soft, white-sand beach dotted with swans, a diaphanous memory of sixteen-year-old Theo, glittering beneath the pier.

I've never told Theo why I stopped for him. Not the truth. I made it seem like it was a rich girl's whimsy, and I think that was the only lie he ever bought.

He'd been sitting on the sand, smoking underneath the pier. I drove by him three times before I made the driver stop. I'd just been called back from my boarding school, Institute Le Rosey in Switzerland, mentally steeling myself for the years ahead. I didn't have many friends at Rosey, but I had zero in Crowne Point. I hadn't liked the plan to return home, but I wouldn't do anything to disappoint my grandpa.

You're not supposed to be alone. Forget what the world tells us about soul mates and family. It's something you feel, the very essence of loneliness.

Theo had it.

He radiated it.

He was the only person I'd ever seen like me.

All at once, Grandfather walked away from Theo, and I was torn from the memory. I took a step, lips caught on a word. Grandpa was supposed to come hold the swans with me, but if Theo was glowering, whatever happened with my grandfather wasn't good.

Grandpa probably had to walk it off. His precious

protégé had disappointed him. Still, I watched my grandfather disappear into Main Street, gut clenching.

I plastered on a smile as Theo came to a stop next to me. "Rough chat?"

He said nothing, though he shifted and held his arms behind his back. I ignored how it made his biceps pop beneath his hoodie.

"I'll understand if our little relationship is coming to an end. Nice try, though."

I stroked the feathery head of my swan. Theo stared straight ahead. His brown hair fell unruly over his gemstone eyes. His nose looked like it had seen some fistfights. There'd been a time when this wounded, broody boy smiled for me...

I shook that intrusive thought away.

"Did you know swans mate for life, Abigail?"

The hairs on my neck rose. He was calling me Abigail, not Reject, but it wasn't sweet. The calm way he spoke reminded me of the moment in a horror movie before the monster jumped out of the dark.

"Yes..."

"When they lose their mate, they grieve like us. They mourn. They're never the same." He wasn't looking at me, but down the beach like a good bodyguard, scanning for threats.

He was the biggest threat.

"Some swans change so much, they never find a flock again. They wander lost and alone. Forever."

I didn't realize I was holding onto my swan too tightly until it bit me. I let go with a gasp, and it jumped away with fluttery wings, running down the beach. Blood wept down my wrist, but I was stuck on Theo.

His eyes locked with mine, and another one of his bone-curling grins broke his cheeks. It was chilling juxtaposed against his pink lips and almost angelic features.

He was oleander, as beautiful as he was betraying.

Still with that smile, he asked, "When I'm finished with you, will you be lost forever, Abigail?"

It wasn't a rhetorical question, and it froze me.

Suddenly his hand shot out so fast I flinched and closed my eyes, expecting to be hit. When nothing happened, I opened one eye and saw what he'd grabbed: a camera. A reporter was on the ground, about to take an upskirt picture of me. Theo had grabbed the camera before the reporter could take a picture, his entire hand encapsulating the lens. The reporter tried to pull it back, but Theo yanked it away and threw it to the ground.

It shattered on impact, glass shards flying. Theo shoved me behind him before the shards could sting.

The reporter yelled something about suing him, and all Theo said was, "Bill me."

I couldn't keep the awe out of my eyes. No one ever did things like that for me. One of the reasons I'm in the tabloids so much was because I don't have any protection from paparazzi. My siblings have entire armies dedicated to getting them from point A to point B. I only have me.

After Theo left, I haven't had one guard stay longer than a month. I have a reputation for scaring them away. It started as an accident, then it spiraled.

I just wanted *one* to stay.

Like Theo, it was all so easy for them to leave. They were supposed to guard me, life or death, and one threat and they went running. Some even went to Gemma after me, but I suspect those guards would've used any excuse to get off my detail for hers.

Theo narrowed his eyes, and I quickly cleared my

throat, rolling my eyes. "Now everyone is going to say I break cameras."

Theo grabbed my hand.

On instinct, I tried to pull it out of his grip. He was too strong. Veins throbbed along the back of his hand, disappearing into his wrist, beneath his hoodie, and no doubt up his forearm. I pulled on his hand with my other one, trying to break free as he dragged me from the beach toward Main Street.

No use. If he registered my struggling, he didn't show it.

"What are you doing?" I asked, giving up—for the moment.

In response, he threw his head over his shoulder. A horde of shark reporters had gathered around the fallen one like chum, the flash of their cameras bright and pointed at us. I quickly turned away. I definitely didn't press myself against Theo's back.

I didn't notice his muscles, or how it felt to be protected for once.

His hand wasn't warm, strong. I didn't feel safe. I wasn't thankful.

Theo was *bad*.

Yet as he dragged me farther from the beach, I looked once more over my shoulder at the broken camera, the reporter who would have made a story of me, made me a fool, the Crowne Slut... again.

If not for Theo.

I shoved an ice cream cone at Theo. He eyed it like I'd given him a ticking bomb.

"Hurry, before it melts," I said, wiggling it beneath his

nose. "It's your favorite, licorice." I wrinkled my nose. *Gross.* "I should've known you were a psycho back then. Consider it a thanks for, you know, before..."

My words faded into the air, disappearing into the twinkling lights above us. Thanking Theo Hound was not easy for me to do. Another excruciating second passed, Theo's bright eyes shadowed beneath his thick brows.

Then he took it.

A weight lifted off my chest when he did so.

"Sharks are clear," he said, eyes lifting over my shoulder, back to the beach. "Don't want you to miss your tradition."

I looked over my shoulder, finding my grandfather facing the beach, surrounded by a legion of guards and swans.

I narrowed my eyes back on Theo. "I thought you wanted to take everything from me?" Wouldn't he want to keep me from my most valued tradition?

"Maybe it's a *thank-you*." He lifted the ice cream with a soft smile.

I chewed my lip, unsure what to do with a Theo who took ice cream and seemed to care.

"Probably shouldn't bring this to the sand, though, unless we want to re-create the swan riot."

The memory blasted through me. One year we'd been forced to run down the beach, chased down by a horde of angry swans gunning for our ice cream. Theo had held my hand, dragging me down the sand as the tide nipped at our feet.

I rubbed my thumb and forefinger together, trying to banish the feel of his hand.

"That was your fault," I said on instinct.

Neither of us wanted to take the blame.

"Your ice cream," he said.

"*Your* idea."

I laughed as we walked to the beach but quickly swallowed it. Not hours ago, Theo had made it clear how much he hated me.

To my shock, he laughed too. Theo's laugh was an unassuming soft sound, so quiet you could miss it easily, but once you heard it, it never left you.

Like him.

I'd missed it so much.

I eyed him warily, but he only licked the purple ice cream.

Still, a small part of me hoped.

"Papa," I called when we got to the sand. "I'm ready!"

His wall of guards parted, and Papa turned around. My gut dropped. Grandpa had the frown reserved for mergers that fell through, the dark, stormy eyes used when he learned someone had dared say something bad about Beryl Crowne. Now that frown was directed at me.

I tugged on my gauzy pink summer dress. "Papa?"

"When I really get your thanks, you won't be smiling, Reject." Theo's lips grazed my ear, his whisper harsh and bitter.

I tore my gaze from Grandpa, just in time to see Theo turn the peace-treaty ice cream cone on its head. The purple-black globe of ice cream landed with a splat on the boardwalk. He then dropped the cone to the ground and smashed the waffle beneath his shoe into a hundred crispy pieces.

My mouth fell open, but I barely had a second to be stunned or angry before my grandfather's harsh shout brought me back.

"Abigail!" he yelled.

A few of the swans around him fluttered their feathery, white-and-tawny wings nervously.

"Papa, you're scaring the swans—"

He raised a hand. When Beryl Crowne raised his hand, you shut up.

"Theo had a very hard time telling me this." Theo and Grandpa shared some kind of look I couldn't decipher. The rock in my gut sank deeper. "I practically had to dig it out of him. When I did, I almost didn't believe him." Grandpa rubbed the wrinkle between his dark, red-brown eyes.

Enough time passed for me to brave a response.

"Dig what out of him?" I glanced at Theo. He had his bodyguard mask on now. A stoic, hard jaw. Eyes forward on potential threats. Legs spread and ready to move, arms behind his back but ready to attack.

Then all at once, his eyes found mine, and he winked.

I sucked in a breath.

Have you ever had a sinking feeling something horrible is about to happen? Something that will change your life?

My smile flickered, a dying light bulb. "Papa, if we start now we can still hold the swans..."

Though most of them had scattered because of his yell, a few still lingered. I knew I should stop; something worse was happening than my tradition being ruined.

"I heard the rumors, Abigail," Papa said. "I heard them and I didn't listen. I should've listened. Are you so attention starved you would sell out our family name? Your own sister?" My grandpa's eyes were back on me, his ire hot, unexpected, and before now, unfelt.

I didn't know what to do with it.

I'd heard rumors of my grandfather's anger, but I'd never experienced it firsthand. I wanted to sink into the crowd and disappear.

"Weeks before your wedding and the most important merger in our company's history?" he continued.

"I don't understand." My gaze flickered between my grandfather's and Theo's.

"Cut the shit, Abigail."

I swallowed air.

My grandfather never spoke to me like that. He called me *princess*, *sweetheart*, and *darling*.

I still couldn't speak.

Grandfather held out his hand; a moment later one of his men placed a stack of papers in them. He held them to my face. Front and center, paper clipped as if it had been printed separately: the blackmail bonding photos I'd taken with Gemma, and beneath them, emails printed from *my* address to make it look like I was planning on sending them to the press.

I'd never written those emails, and I never *would*.

My stomach dropped, my eyes shifted to Theo, a small, wicked smile quirked his right cheek.

"That's your email."

"Yes, but—"

"And that's your room."

"Yes, but—"

"And that's *your sister*."

"Yes! *But*—"

"I already have one famous slut for a daughter." He paused, shook his head. "Did you think you could get out of your marriage this way? As if I wouldn't realize the trick you were playing?" Grandpa raised his voice, and I startled as someone looked over. He smoothed down the sides of his salt-and-pepper hair, regaining composure.

"I want to marry him," I said, scrambling. "I want to get married. I'm excited to marry..." I trailed off, heart paralyzed as my grandfather's eyes narrowed, and I realized I still didn't know the name of the man I was marrying.

I withered and died under his gaze.

"Edward Harlington," he said.

"Yes, Edward Harlington," I said quickly.

His red lips thinned. "I've been too lenient, too understanding. You are worse than a disappointment; you are a liability. I should have listened to your mother."

There were no swans anymore, the sky dark and stars too bright. My main course punishment had already been doled out by Mother; Papa was handing out dessert, taking away his love. Leaving me alone, empty and bereft, like the sand.

He lifted one finger, signaling for his guard to follow him, heading toward Main Street.

I couldn't breathe. My heart was crumbling inside my chest.

I know there's a reason there's a no-tolerance policy on marriage in our family. It's not some archaic tradition, it's our lifeboat. After my dad died and a string of bad luck and bad business decisions nearly left us ruined, marriages saved us. When Uncle Albert canceled his wedding and we almost collapsed, it became law.

As my grandpa likes to say, "You can't be a Crowne without many sharp points. You're either part of this family, or you're against it."

Grandpa was my *one* constant after Dad, the only love I'd felt in a home of strings and conditional affection. I was watching it burn down, frozen as debris floated past me, breathing in the ashes.

Without another word, he turned away. Panic strangled my lungs. My world was giving way beneath me. I couldn't breathe.

Paparazzi had gathered around the perimeter, sensing something was happening in the Crowne family. I knew I had to let him leave. We could combust in private, but *never* in public.

"Grandpa!" I ran after him and tried to grab his arm. "Papa, please. I want to get married. I'll get married tomorrow."

Just don't leave.

Papa eyed the sharks.

"Goddamn it, Abigail!" He shook me off with distaste that ricocheted through my entire body.

I stood, watching him walk farther and farther away.

"When will I see you again?" I yelled.

He stopped. People walked on either side of him in pretty sundresses and polo shirts, the twinkling lights making the night that much blacker blurred.

Then he kept walking, and the crowd ate him.

I locked eyes with Theo as a slow smile spread across his face. When he saw me hurriedly swipe my cheeks, his smile grew.

He mouthed one word.

Point.

I will not cry for him.

I will not let him *see* me cry.

I knew without a doubt he was behind this. Theo had been in my room. He'd seen the pictures. He'd had my laptop. The point I *thought* I'd gained had actually led to my demise. He'd made me the Crowne Slut with the one person who always saw me otherwise. He'd taken the one thing I had in this family. The one person who loved me.

THEO: 1

ME: 0

Tears were threatening to fall, and I was using all my

energy to keep that from happening, so I didn't see the change in Theo. I definitely didn't see what was happening a few feet away. Theo grabbed my wrist. In the same instant, I tried to yank myself free.

Theo was unaffected.

Someone must have been talking in his ear, because he pressed his thumb to it, nodding, saying something I couldn't catch.

All at once his attention was on me. "It's time to go."

Incredulous, halting laughs broke free. As if I would go *anywhere* with him ever again.

I gave him the finger, still trying to break free. "Let me go."

"No dice, Reject. If I let you die, I'll get a real shitty Christmas bonus."

"I don't want you to fucking save me." I kicked the back of his knee. Success! He stumbled forward, only a little, which was more than I'd ever managed with him.

"If you don't stop struggling, I'm going to throw you over my shoulder." He turned around, tongue edging the seam of his top lip. Anytime his tongue pushed his upper lip it meant Theo was frustrated.

So what did I do?

"Fuck you." This time I really did spit in his face.

The moment was heated. Pressurized. A second teetering like a penny on its side as I waited for him to react, our stares locked and unblinking. Theo slid his tongue between his teeth.

Why was there a small part of me that *wanted* him mad?

Mean.

Punishing.

With one, heated exhale, he wiped my spit from his

cheek, and I was in the air, his strong arms locking my ass in place. I slammed my fists into his back, even though it was useless.

A few feet away from where we'd just been a fight had broken out, but that's not what had my heart hammering, the blood in my veins turning to ice.

No... *no, no, no.* It had been *weeks* since he'd bothered me. *Weeks.* I was starting to believe he was leaving me alone. He was gone.

Anyone might believe it was a coincidence, but not me. I learned to take coincidences as deliberate. Resting inside the melted black ice cream Theo had dropped to the ground was a single gold rose.

A message from my stalker.

SIX

THEO

Abigail slammed her fists against my back, but they may as well have been raindrops. Once we got to the safe house, I dropped her to the sea-warped wood, and she immediately jumped back. With both hands she wiped hair out of her face, finishing with a searing glare.

Fuck, she was cute. Her pale cheeks red with anger, nostrils flared. I liked her mad.

Too much.

The perfect size for me as well. Small, but never someone to overlook, despite what she might think. The thought pierced me like a bullet, fast and without any way to defend against it.

"Theo!" she yelled, waving a hand over my face, and I realized she'd been talking. "What are you doing?"

"The fuck does it look like, Abs?" I shoved her aside, checking the lock on the door behind her, giving the place another once-over.

Abigail's only memories of me were as a teenager. She had no knowledge of the man I'd become. I'd been trained. I knew what I was doing. This was one of the many safe houses scouted and assigned in the city of Crowne Point. It wasn't designed to be lived in, merely a place to stay until a threat passed. Right on the beach, small and inconspicuous.

Abigail might even think I was a bodyguard in title only, that I was here only to mess with her.

I should be.

I should be here just to fuck with her. Shouldn't give a shit that there weren't enough exits in this supposed safe house. Shouldn't care that a glass window was bullshit. They should be tempered.

After checking the window, I went back to Abby.

"A Crowne Industries protest turned violent. We're staying put until further notice."

Her brows furrowed. "And that's definitely all it was?"

I folded my arms, arching a brow. "Did you have something else in mind?"

She cleared her throat, raising her chin. "I don't want to be within three feet of you, and you want me to stay in this cramped closet? Fuck off."

She tried to unlock the door so I grabbed her by the elbow, planting her against the many colored wood planks holding up this ramshackle cottage.

I pinned her with one arm.

"Be a good girl and stay fucking still."

"A *good* girl?" Abigail started in on me, but a shadow near the window caught my attention, and I tuned her out. The ocean was just outside, as were swans. The occasional hiss or snort or whistling as they feathered their large wings, drifted in.

The life of a Crowne had its perks, but the higher you

rise, the deeper you fall. Beryl Crowne received at least thirty death threats a day, and of those at least ten were substantiated. Abigail was a bit too naïve to the darker side of being a Crowne.

"I'm trying to think of another way to say *fuck you*," Abigail said. "Because it's clearly not getting through. Go do some unaccompanied fornication."

After a moment, once I was sure the only things outside were swans, I turned my attention back to Abigail.

"Someone has to make sure you're safe."

It was meant to be cutting, not a confession. Of all her siblings and family members, Abigail received the least attention. At least, that's the girl I remembered. Sad. Lonely. Like me.

But the girl I remembered was never real. She was always spoiled and privileged; she just did a better job of hiding it.

Her glare sharpened. "And that's you?"

I ground my jaw, pressed my arm tighter, trying to ignore the way her breasts rose and fell beneath it.

It used to *only* be me, but like everyone else, she abandoned me. She stomped on my fucking heart. Left me bleeding, lonely—and just like with my mom, for years I wondered what I did to make her leave.

Anger made my voice raw. "Unfortunately. I'm *your* bodyguard."

She laughed, blew out a breath that made the dark strands of her hair whisper against my jaw. "You're the asshole *ruining* my life. And you know what, I don't even know *why*! Why are you doing this? I don't understand what happened to make you this way. You didn't used to be like this. You used to want to help people. I remember the boy whose biggest dream was to save kids like him."

Her words nearly made me drop my arm.

Yeah, I didn't dream of being a bodyguard. My life's goal wasn't making sure assholes like Beryl Crowne could safely keep *being* assholes.

"Don't you remember?" She peered at me. "You wanted to make sure no one was left behind, no one was abandoned. What the hell happened to you?"

Abigail didn't just play games, she played *dirty*. She really was so fucked up that what happened between us meant nothing.

I pushed her deeper into the wall, her nails clawing the wood behind her, and my free hand wrapped around her neck. Her lips parted, too pretty and fucking distracting.

"What the hell happened to me, Abigail?" I didn't recognize my voice. It was low and without feeling, venom the only thing left. "*You* fucking happened to me."

"Let me go," she breathed.

I leaned forward until my lips were against her ear, my words singeing her skin. I dug my thumb into the hollow beneath her jaw and ear, torn between the part of me that wanted to mark her and destroy her.

"You're stuck with me," I growled.

"What about Gemma?" The bite to her words had me pulling back. There was anger in her eyes to rival mine.

The fuck about Gemma? She had an entire legion of security forces.

A moment later, the head of security came through my earpiece.

False alarm. All clear.

I let them know I'd heard the message, still studying Abigail, locked on her anger. She rubbed the spot where my thumb had been. I ground my jaw. I wanted to pull her back, rub the spot out with my thumb. *Fuck.*

Possessive.

Too fucking possessive when I came here to ruin her.

I should take her back.

Put much-needed space between us. Get my head clear. I needed to focus on why I took this job. I had a win today. I'd separated the daddy's girl from her only living father figure.

"Well, we have some time to kill. What should we do?"

"I have an idea," Abigail said. "You shut up and I'll stare at the ocean and imagine I'm anywhere but here."

She walked to the other side of the one-room cottage, sitting on a stack of crates covered in thick, ropy fishing net, folding her arms. I leaned against the wall, one foot propped. True to her word, she stared out the window.

"You really fucked up this time, Reject. No daddy alive to love you. No grandpa to pretend to love you."

Abs shifted at my words but said nothing.

"Is that why you're so angry, Reject? I'll be your daddy, if you ask nicely."

Eyes still out the window, she said, "Fuck. You."

I shook my head, halting my smile with my tongue. "That's not very nice."

The whistle of swan wings sounded. I walked to her, taking a spot next to her against the window, blocking her view. She shifted her eyes to the door, muttering, "Asshole."

"You think that's all I am?" I pulled one of the crates from the stack beside her. It caused the one she was on to rattle, and she fell to the floor.

I stepped on either side of her, pinning her with my legs

so she couldn't get up. "If I was only an asshole, you wouldn't have anything to fear."

She stared up, eyes wide and betraying her hesitation, before she shook it off with a glare. I bent down, leaning forward until I could taste her breath, placing a knuckle to her chin. She jerked but didn't move.

"When I make you cry and scream, it's because you'll like what I'm doing so much..." I placed my other hand on her bare thigh, just beneath the hem of her dress, and she swallowed, throat bobbing. "You'll beg me not to stop, Reject."

I trailed my knuckle along her jaw, stroked behind her ear, and grasped her silky hair, tugging her ear to my lips.

"And now you have no one left to love you. No one. Not your daddy. All you have is me." I licked her ear, tongue caressing along the shell, top to bottom, before biting the lobe. She breathed in a way that sounded suspiciously like a sigh. I tightened my grip on her hair. On her thigh. "Only me."

At the same time she shivered, she said, "Stop."

There was no force in her voice, but I did. I stood back up, and she tried to scramble away, but I stopped her with my shoe, digging into her thigh.

"Let me go, dog," she spat.

Her dress had ridden up, her panties now visible.

"God, you're so fucking wet." I laughed, then kicked up the rest of her dress with my other foot. "Is that for me, or are you really a whore?"

I wanted to rub my thumb across the lace between her thighs. Press the fabric against her. *Feel* how wet she was.

I dug my heel into her thigh.

"You look like you need to be fucked, Reject."

"Fuck you."

"Nah..." I shook my head on a smile. "I don't fuck rejects, but admit all you have is me, and maybe I'll touch you."

I dug my shoe into her thigh until she gasped. Her eyes found mine, lips parting. Wet. My eyes fell to them, to the way her spoiled, pouty pink lips parted, her tongue begging to lick them.

Was she enjoying this?

I shifted, and when I spoke, my voice was hoarser. "You want me to let you go? Just say the words. Admit the truth and I will."

She didn't speak, but her breath was like the wings of the swans outside, and she was wearing the most painfully see-through white lace panties.

Fucking *white*.

Fuck. I was hooked on that.

"Say it," I pressed.

My heel would leave bruises on her thigh.

"Just say it," I growled.

Fuck.

I was losing myself. I used to torture myself over what Abigail Crowne sounded like as she came. Turns out, it was nothing like my imagination. My imagination was a scratchy recording compared to this. She was a live symphony.

And she wasn't even coming; this was just the fucking prelude.

She gripped the ropy netting behind her for dear life.

"Do you still want me to let you go?"

A heartbeat passed like an eternity, and then she whispered, "No."

I took my heel off her thigh, kicked apart both of them

until she was obscenely spread and I could bend down between them. Moonlight made her eyes bolder, rawer.

"Maybe I shouldn't." I caressed my knuckle along her jaw. "Maybe I should rip off those panties and finally find the truth of you, see how wet and wanting you fucking are."

In that moment, I almost did.

I almost kept going. Nearly slid my hand inside her thigh, up to those torturously tempting white panties, inside to what I'd been dreaming of since the day she'd picked me up on that fucking beach. Would she be hot, as wet as I'd imagined? Would she moan when I slid inside her? No... Abigail Crowne would be a meteor shower.

Quiet, magical, over too fast.

I untangled myself from her, standing up slowly. I didn't bother adjusting myself. Abigail's stare focused on my jeans, before she tilted her chin.

Her wide, violet-brown eyes were still hazy. I was always thankful for being sent to California; at least I didn't have to see Abigail every time I looked out the window. The night sky there didn't glow the same dark-red indigo. Back here... I can't say the same.

I dragged my thumb across her still-parted bottom lip. "Told you it would feel good."

Shock and recognition hit her at once, and she tore her face from mine.

"Can we go?" Her voice shook.

"Sure. Threat's been gone for a while now."

I couldn't see her face; she'd hidden it in shadows. When she didn't respond, I bent down until we were eye to eye.

"Are those tears?" I reached out to thumb them.

She slapped me away. "Leave me alone."

"Is that really what you want, Reject?" I thumbed her

chin. Abs tried to jerk away, so I gripped her hard, yanking her back. I don't know what came over me. Maybe it was her red eyes. The fact she still hadn't fixed her dress. Or it could be the pounding in my chest that wouldn't stop. I don't know. It happened in a split second. One minute she was glaring, the next I was kissing her.

Hard. Brutal.

Addicting.

Until sanity returned, and I let her shove me off.

When I was done her cheeks were wet, her glare was fierce, her bottom lip bruised from my teeth—and her taste was fucking imprinted inside me. I wiped her off with the back of my hand, as if it would do something. Then I threw her a smile.

"Remember, I'm the only one you have left."

SEVEN

ABIGAIL

Theo and I climbed the stairs to my wing in silence, and he took his place just outside the doorway to my bedroom. Part of me itched to slam the door, but I knew I'd lose that battle.

I couldn't lose another.

I'd said nothing to him on the way back, but I wasn't a fool. That didn't give me any bit of power. He'd stolen it the moment I'd urged him to go further.

Outside the Swan Swell after-party was in effect in the gardens, the trill of laughter and music floated in through one of my windows.

My dress had been made months before and once again required aid to put on, but Story *still* wasn't anywhere to be found. I refused to let Theo help me get dressed again. I'd learned my lesson. So, I tugged on a black, plunging-neck dress with a lace bodice that hugged me much too well for this kind of party. It had a sheer black-lace stomach and a flowing black velvet skirt, with two high slits up my legs.

The Swan Swell dress code was a *strict* white.

What-the-fuck-ever. I guess I was going to officially embrace my role as the black swan.

I had my leg propped on my chaise, clasping the strap on my ankle, when I saw it. My dress had fallen away, the slit showing the oval bruise on my thigh. Light, but it would darken.

Just say it.

I couldn't breathe, heat crawled up my neck, consuming my oxygen. I should hate him. I should. I shouldn't wonder what it would feel like to have his marks elsewhere visible, for everyone to see.

He'd treated me like dirt.

Stepped on me with his fucking shoe.

And I... *liked* it?

I wish I could say there's nothing left in our relationship, but that would be a lie. Theo and I are inverse, a dark, twisted version of love. We're still connected, but not through sweet words, through torment and ache. Theo is still inside me. He's still in my heart.

Now he's just determined to break it.

I touched the bruise just as Theo's bored voice drifted in: "Hurry up, Reject."

Theo was looking at his phone when I came to the door, but he looked up at the sound. He all but froze.

"What?" His silence made me uneasy, almost as much as the foreign look in his eyes. I fought the urge to fist the velvet skirt of my dress.

Apathy returned, and he shoved his phone in the inner pocket of his suit.

Theo was *divine* in a tux. I'd never had a problem with our guards matching our clothing to blend in, but then I'd never had Theo as a guard. I thought casual Theo was gorgeous, but it was nothing to him in a tux.

I still wasn't used to seeing Theo so dressed up. He'd come to parties with me in the past, but like everything else with us, I'd had to sneak him in.

It was perfectly tailored to his tall, lean build, and his bedhead brown hair made him look casually elegant.

"Trying to catch flies?" he asked wryly.

I blinked and closed my mouth. I hadn't realized I'd been staring, but Theo watched me with a smirk. I rolled my eyes, shoving past him and making sure to elbow him hard, not speaking the entire way to the garden.

When we reached the garden, he stood beside me, just a little behind, like the good bodyguard he pretended he was.

In the garden, women were dressed in flowing white dresses with feathery white fans, and swans floated in the fountains—PETA *loved* this party. There was an empty seat at the table where Grandpa would have been seated, I noted with an ache.

The ocean was dark. Twinkling lights floated like fireflies. Swans glowed in the backlit fountain and feathered their wings, drops of water flying as diamonds before disappearing into the night.

By the maze, hidden somewhat but the tall hedges, I spotted servants setting up fireworks. If there's one thing a Crowne loves, it's fireworks. We do them all summer long, culminating in a *huge* show at our Fourth party.

"I thought you would've pulled an Abby by now," Theo said quietly. No one would've known he was talking to me. "You know, started a scene, thrown a few priceless vases."

I looked at him out of the side of my eyes, then back at the party.

He took a drink, then paused, looking at his water. "Did you put salt in my drink?"

A small smile curved my lips.

I had.

"Your revenge is very *Home Alone*."

It wasn't my revenge, of course, but I couldn't resist the urge when he'd left his glass unattended. There'd been a time when he'd done the same to me. I'd told him I'd get him back.

That was a month before Gemma... I never got the chance.

Anguish strangled my heart.

"That's not even clever..." He pulled out an ice cube, shaking off stray water. "I did it first, Abby."

My eyes popped, but before I could even think about the fact he remembered our pranks, ice was pressed against my lower back, dripping a cold trail. I tilted my head to see. His hand had disappeared inside the open back of my dress, and his hand must be holding the ice cube.

I shifted, the spot where he pressed burning cold.

Theo arched a brow. "Something wrong?"

I refused to capitulate, instead focusing on the empty chair where my grandfather would have sat.

Grandpa was the one person who paid attention to my Christmas list, the only one who checked in on me after another tabloid fiasco. I thought he was my constant. In the end, though, Theo only proved what I already knew, love is conditional. Some people were obvious about their strings, but everyone has them. If you love someone, it's only a matter of time until they take it away.

As if she *knew* I was thinking about parental neglect, my mom appeared. Dressed to the nines as always in a bespoke, flowing white dress that may as well have been haute couture.

She eyed my outfit. "What are you wearing?"

I swallowed, the ice dripping down my ass, sliding deeper. "A dress."

Her frown deepened. "Sarcasm isn't clever or cute, Abigail."

"But it..." Melted ice inched closer and closer. "Is..." Farther down between my lips. "*Efficient.*"

Theo laughed, so low only I heard him. He glided the melting cube down my dress, hand slipping inside my panties, along my ass, until he had the ice pressed cold to my lips.

"And where is your fan?" my mom asked.

"Uh..." I couldn't focus, looking around, wondering if people could see what was happening. Theo stared forward, at my back like the good bodyguard he was pretending to be, meanwhile he was spreading me wide with a freezing-cold ice cube.

I focused on not making a scene.

If I moved, Theo would win. If I moved, Mom would know.

"My what?" I breathed as the cube spread me wider, frigid cold. His fingers hadn't touched me, but I was too aware we were separated only by slowly melting water. Theo Hound, who'd once made dirty promises and now promised to ruin me, was millimeters away from my most private of places.

"Your *fan*." My mother's perfectly plucked brows caved in disappointment.

Theo started to press the cube inside me.

I jumped forward, breaking contact. I could breathe

again. I waved my black-feathered fan in Mom's face, forcing her to step back, needing a distraction myself.

Theo Hound's fingers had almost been inside me.

"Honestly!" she said, fixing unseen flyaways in her updo. "Have you spoken with your grandfather?"

"My... my grandfather?"

It was a perfectly innocent question. Everyone knew Dad and I had the swan tradition, and with him gone, Grandpa had continued it. But I couldn't answer the question.

After everything with Theo, I'd forgotten about earlier. My grandpa. *The rose.* For over a year I'd been relentlessly harassed. First it was social media. After blocking him, it was emails. I could only block so many of those. Then it was letters. Then it was strange coincidences. A single gilded rose waiting on the hood of my car. Another rose waiting for me at my favorite boutique.

People like me can't go to the police because "a Crowne doesn't call 911, they call their lawyer." The first time I heard that was on my fifth birthday—or, rather, *remember* hearing it.

This was the closest I'd been to the person who left the rose; usually it'd been there for hours. An icky feeling lurked in my gut. What had he planned? What if Theo hadn't been there?

My gaze collided with Theo just as he dropped the nearly melted ice cube in his mouth.

His tongue swirled around the ice, and heat seized my stomach. Theo was tasting *me.* I didn't give him permission to learn that secret part of me, but like every other torment, he'd taken it anyway.

Now he forced me to wonder what his lips would feel like, his tongue doing to me what they did to the cube. He fucking knew it, too, as a wicked grin curved his beautiful lips.

"Abigail." My mother's cold, irritated voice drew me back. "Did you hear a word I said?"

"No," I admitted. "Sorry."

She clicked her tongue, eyes narrowing.

"Your fiancé's mother has joined us tonight." She gestured to a plump woman wearing a flowing, feathery white dress, her light-brown hair piled high with more feathers.

"Be on your *best* behavior, and do make an effort to introduce yourself. Eleanora will want to know who exactly she's getting as a daughter."

For a moment I'd allowed myself to forget I was engaged to a man I didn't know.

I swallowed. "Of course."

With a deep exhale through her nostrils, my mother walked away.

Mom wasn't gone a minute before Theo's hot breath was on my ear. "I always wondered what you tasted like."

He slowly moved back into position, staring straight ahead, a cocksure tease to his lips.

"My imagination was better," he said like it was an afterthought.

My heart bottomed out, still locked on his lips.

Theo had kissed me. It could hardly be called a kiss, bruising and punishing, but that's what it was. Five years since I'd felt his lips, and now they were used to torture me.

I was a lot of things—hated, reviled—but I was never pathetic.

Theo made me pathetic.

I couldn't get the thoughts of his calloused hands on my thighs out of my head. I could still feel the way they dug into my skin, so torturously close to where I really wanted them. His wet lips on my ear, biting me *just right*. I was agonizing over it. I wanted to hate his touch. I wanted to revile him.

He was still torturing me. Still teasing me. *Still* using his lips to break me.

I *wouldn't* let him take my heart, no matter what my traitorous body felt. I would put an iron lock on it and throw away the key. Even if it meant I couldn't love anyone else.

Love is ephemeral, anyway.

Across the room, I spotted my sister and her fiancé, Horace.

Time for a taste of his own medicine.

Time for him to learn a girl who lost everything is dangerous.

She has nothing left to lose.

"So you're planning something," Theo said.

"Am not."

I hadn't been thinking of my plan five minutes when Theo spoke. Was I really so obvious? The thing about Gemma's beaus is they've always been so very... distractible. I planned to do what I always did when my heart hurt, when I was burned by Gemma's spotlight—show how much damage you can do in the dark.

This time it had the added benefit of maybe hurting Theo.

I grabbed the nearest champagne off a server, looking from Horace and my sister to the beach. They were setting up the fireworks.

"You have your bad idea face," Theo said simply.

"I don't have a bad idea face. I don't have *bad ideas.*"

Theo didn't say a word, but his expression said everything. He rolled his lips, eyebrows raised, nodding like *okay, sure.* I folded my arms, glaring.

"You're doing that thing with your lip," he said. "You did it the day you brought me home. You did it the night we broke into the school and freed the frogs from the science lab. You did it yesterday before you lunged at me like a sex-starved lunatic." He leaned closer, breath heating my neck. "You're doing it now."

I unlatched my teeth from my bottom lip, not realizing I was biting it.

"You know me so well, Theo Hound," I said with bitter sarcasm.

"Unfortunately."

"Oh yeah? Then what's my favorite color?"

He scoffed. "Trick question, Abs. You love them all."

I turned from him, the air between us suddenly stifling.

I hated these parties.

When we were kids, Theo and I used to steal a bottle of liquor off the bartender and go up to the balcony overlooking the ballroom, making up backstories that would *shock* all the pretentious people who showed.

She definitely wears off-the-rack.

He secretly votes Democrat.

We'd laugh, sharing one bottle, getting so drunk Theo would have to carry me to my room on his back. A sharp ache slammed into my gut at the memory, and I took another drink of champagne, trying to drown the hurt.

"Am I going to have to carry you to your room?" He eyed me, then leaned close until his lips grazed my ear again. "She looks like she secretly enjoys *la délicatesse* Big Mac."

I followed his eye to a particularly extravagant woman.

I took a big gulp of champagne, but my hand shivered and I dropped my glass. The golden liquid spilled into the grass and sand. Theo's eyes narrowed, reading into what happened. I tried to cut it off at the quick. "What? I'm clumsy."

I turned away, waving down a server to come and clean up the mess.

He laughed. "You danced for twelve years, but okay."

I spun on him. "Stop that!"

He arched a brow, waiting for me to elaborate.

"Stop acting like you remember things about me."

Stop acting like you *care*, like we meant something more.

Theo watched me, his eyes narrowed, taking a torturously slow sip of water.

"I remember everything about you, Abigail. I've tried to forget you. It's impossible. You are..." He looked away, bitter fury and contempt swirling in his eyes. "You are *stuck*." He clipped the last word, like he wanted to spit it out of his mouth the same way he wanted to spit *me* out.

I don't know if I'll ever get back my breath.

Before I could respond, we were interrupted.

"Hey, freeloader." Grayson walked up to us, eyes on Theo. In a black suit, the sleeves folded to the forearm, tie undone and wrinkled as only Gray could get away with. "Gemma needs you."

"What?" I asked. "Why?"

"Something about a fan stuck in a tree. You're the tallest one here."

I waited for Theo to tell him he was needed *here*, with *me*, but he shrugged like it wasn't a big deal, heading toward my sister by the fountain.

I shouldn't have expected anything else.

"You still in love with that loser?" Gray asked. To our left and right, girls watched him from beneath fans. Some demure, others obvious.

I glared at my brother. "I was never *in love* with him—and he's not a loser." I don't know why I added the last bit, and I hoped Gray didn't notice it.

But Gray, despite his devil-may-care demeanor, rarely missed a thing.

We had a twisted relationship, the same way I had with everyone in my family, but it was nothing compared to mine and Gemma's. Mom pitted us all against one another, but Gemma and I were in direct competition. There could only be one winner, which meant there was always one loser.

"He's a freeloading gold digger."

"He's the only one in this family who actually *works*."

Gray looked at me like I was an idiot. *"Exactly."*

"You never liked him—" I broke off.

Someone stood out among the fanning groupies. She was someone you would normally overlook, but I'd been looking for her. Because of *her*, Theo had been able to sabotage my dress, and because of *her* I'd been scolded by Mother—*again*. Story.

My jaw dropped, eyes narrowing. Why the hell was she out here?

Gray stepped in my line of sight, blocking her and distracting me. "He's not good enough." For a moment, I thought Gray was giving me a rare compliment, then he added, "You're barely good enough to stain a shirt—"

"Gee, thanks."

"But you're a Crowne, so we have to pretend."

Gray downed the rest of his amber drink, slammed it on

a server's tray so hard she stumbled, and left. I looked for Story in his absence, but she'd disappeared again.

I focused back on Gemma. The fountain glowed on her skin; she was luminous. Her white dress caught the breeze. My mother laughed at something she said. Everyone watched her, transfixed. Horace, Horace's bodyguard, men lingering on the side, the women.

Theo.

It didn't look like he was trying too hard to get anything out of a fucking tree.

She was pure, perfect. She'd had a fiancé since we were teenagers, but it wasn't like my engagement to a man I've never met. It wasn't rushed, forced, and ugly. They were everything you thought when you imagined elite marriages. Aristocratic. Beautiful. Destined.

At least... that's what it looked like from the outside and isn't that all that mattered?

Maybe I was what they called me. Imperfect. Dirty. Vile.

Maybe I could get some of it on them.

I watched, waiting until Horace left the group. I intercepted him before he reached the buffet.

"Abigail?"

I touched his shoulder. "Has anyone shown you the maze?"

EIGHT

ABIGAIL

I didn't like the way he kissed.

I didn't like his hands on my hips.

I didn't like any of it.

I thought it would make me feel whole, better, special. Instead I was emptier than before we'd started. He didn't bother asking if he could put his hands between my thighs. I didn't bother telling him to stop.

I don't know how long we were like that, him kissing and me waiting for *something* to change. All I know is when I saw him, when Theo found me, a part of me came alive.

I started moaning. Real porn star stuff. I grabbed Horace's hair, pulling him to my neck. It was greasy with too much product. I jerked his head to the side so I could lock eyes with Theo.

Theo was a shadow in the night, looming, taking up almost all the light. I wanted him to come and grab Horace off me. Fling him by the collar to the ground. He just watched. A muscle in his jaw twerked. Clenched. Making his cheekbones that much hollower.

Horace's lips roamed my neck. I couldn't pretend anymore. I couldn't even move. I was sucked into Theo. When I totally froze, Theo's lip twitched. Not quite a smile, but the arrogance in his eyes flamed.

I wanted to kiss harder at the arrogance, but I couldn't.

"Horace?" Gemma's husky voice called out, her white chiffon dress following after, a fairy among the dark leaves. She stopped next to Theo, spotting us.

Horace jumped off me like I was on fire, running to my sister's side as if he hadn't just been climbing up my thigh and moaning my name. I was alone on the sand, surrounded by the looming hedges of the maze, shimmering black-green in the night.

"Oh, hey Gemma." I stood up, brushing off invisible grains of sand. Inside, my chest was on fire. They were both by her side, *again*. In the dark, someone might call out my name, but in the light, everyone always chose her.

Gemma folded long, lean arms, tilting her head so rose gold hair fell down one side.

"You didn't used to be *this* awful," she said. "Remember the late nights? The pictures we used to take together?" At the mention of the pictures, my grip involuntarily tightened. Pictures that had once been the only evidence of any affection in my relationship with my sister were now concrete proof I was unlovable.

"We've always been competitive," Gemma continued. "But you weren't so *vile*."

"You stole him!" I screamed. "You stole the only thing that was ever mine."

The words fell out of me, having been caged inside with a broken lock. I was never any good at keeping my cool like

Gemma. I knew I gave up too much, and I prayed Theo didn't put two and two together.

I couldn't look at him, but Theo's silent presence sucked me in like a black hole.

"What the fuck are you talking about? You act like you're the victim, but you've tried to steal every boyfriend I've ever had. If our life was a novel, I'd be the princess and you'd be the shitty, jealous villain begging a mirror to say she was pretty. I'd be furious if it wasn't so fucking pathetic. They let you blow them or finger you, then come back to me because anyone with a brain can see you're not worth it." She paused to let me breathe from the brutal tongue-lashing before she delivered the final blow. "You're one step up from a Fleshlight."

"Your fiancé didn't think so." I could feel my insides squishing beneath my sister's silver heel. Even I didn't believe my words, and as her perfect pink smile grew wider, my uncertainty cemented.

"Did you think he did that without my permission?" She laughed. "My only condition was I got to see the look on your face when you found out once again you weren't a second, or even third choice. You were barely a choice at all."

I couldn't breathe. I wanted to make them like me— imperfect, stained. Instead, I'd been used as a rag to make them cleaner.

My gaze connected with Theo's brutal and unyielding green eyes, and that was when my tears fell. It wasn't quite arrogance in them, it was almost... disappointment.

My tears burned like acid.

I couldn't let them see.

My choices were humiliation by running away, or staying for a public, brutal shaming. So I ran. I pushed past them. I heard her laughter, but I kept running. I couldn't listen to this; her truths cut like knives. A Crowne always learned truth hurt more, was cleaner, more effective. More than that, when you're as powerful as us, you don't need to lie. However vicious and razing a lie, you can always be assured you'll rise above the rubble.

A Crowne didn't lie... to others.

To ourselves, well, we were masters.

I ran and stumbled in the grass, my heel getting caught in the uneven, sandy terrain. I kept running until I tripped. I stumbled into a servant, and we both went down.

At first, I thought the most damage I'd done was to my ego, and maybe bruised the servant I'd knocked down a little, but I learned quickly enough how wrong I was when the *pop* and *squeal* sounded, followed by screams.

Fireworks.

I'd knocked into the servant setting up the fucking firework show, just as he was lighting the first one. I looked around frantically as one by one fireworks exploded without direction. It was a domino effect, the first lighting the second, and so on.

I stood up in time to see them explode in the garden.

"I didn't do this," the servant said, desperation leaking from every syllable. "You know I didn't do this Ms. Crowne."

I glanced at him. Maybe if it had been Gray who'd caused this, he'd be blamed. But it was me.

He had nothing to worry about.

One after another my mother's artfully trimmed hedges were set ablaze, the dark night illumined in orange and yellow. Tonight's firework show ruined.

Servers rushed to put out the fire in the garden. Party-goers screamed, running away from it. Startled swans jumped out of the water. It was a total fucking catastrophe.

I swiped tears out of my eyes.

Why couldn't I ever do anything right?

Theo had asked if I was going to pull an Abby. In the end, I guess I had.

"Abigail Genevieve Crowne." My mother clenched my arm so tight I swore it might bruise. "I know you're behind this somehow, but smile and act like everything is fine." Behind her Mrs. Harlington watched us, light-brown brows furrowed.

Out of the bushes, I saw Gemma walking toward me from the maze, laughing with Theo and Horace.

Everything was spiraling out of control, faster than the shrieking fireworks. Fire rose in my chest, and I clawed for a distraction. Something to make this not *hurt*.

"Am I ever going to meet my fiancé?" I yelled, tearing my arm out. "Or are we just going to exchange cattle on my wedding and call it a day?"

Mrs. Harlington's mouth dropped.

My mother's lips thinned.

And a little bit of the fire in my chest dissipated.

I kicked off my shoes and ran past my distraught mother and my soon-to-be mother-in-law, into the house and up the stairs, down the hall, to my wing. I didn't stop to catch my breath until I was safely in my wing, back in my room. Then I fell, grasping the sateen chaise at the foot of my bed. I counted my breath with the ocean waves outside.

Minutes passed with their crashing.

1...2...3... heart almost steady.

"*Bad* plan."

I lifted my head sharply at Theo's voice, still holding the arm for support. Just like that, my heart was tachycardiac.

Theo leaned with his back against the doorframe, head canted, watching me with a darkly amused expression.

I looked back at the white carpet.

"Where's Gemma?" I sounded petulant.

I hated that.

I saw his shadow first, then his soft black leather shoes. He bent down, lifting my chin from the carpet.

"You act like you're this broken little victim, but I see you." He rubbed my flesh gently through his vicious words. "You're an attention whore. You get off on it. Good or bad, Mommy didn't give you enough growing up so you seek it out."

His thumb strayed from my chin, gliding along my bottom lip.

"Am I not giving you enough attention, Reject?"

Anger rose hot, almost masking the hurt. I snapped at his thumb; he drew it back just in time with a laugh.

"Go away," I tried to growl, and it came out a mumble.

"Did you think that would bother me, Reject?" His voice was too calm, too quiet.

"It wasn't about you," I lied.

"Hopefully. Because watching you treat yourself like an old couch doesn't do much for me."

My heart cracked.

Then his fingers came back to my chin, vicious, dragging me up off the floor with a force that felt like it would snap my neck if I didn't comply.

"It's my fault. I wasn't clear."

The hand at my chin pushed the hair from my face violently, locking into place at the back of my neck—locking *me* into place. His other shot between my legs. Cupping me —no, *imprisoning* me.

I sucked in a breath.

"You're mine. I own this. The next time you feel like getting sloppy with my property..." His grip tightened, and the little air in my lungs vanished. "I won't be so forgiving."

Shivers raced up my spine.

I glared. "Oh, I'm so scared."

A small smile hooked his right lip, like he knew my lie. "Were you just as wet for him?"

The closest Horace got to me was above-the-panties action, and I nearly vomited at that. Either way I answered would damn me, but Theo didn't seem to want one anyway.

Theo traced my lace panties, barely lifting the edge with his thumb, just grazing the crease of my thigh. I sucked in air, trying to keep my head clear. It was a torturous rhythm. Expose, cover, expose, cover, until I felt I was going to die if he didn't move his thumb closer to where I throbbed.

"If I moved these aside, would I find my answer?"

God, yes, please do it.

The apathetic curiosity in his voice *killed* me, like he didn't give a shit he was touching me. I could be a rock for all the affection in his tone.

Meanwhile, I was burning up under his touch.

I moved, trying to force him under my panties, just a little closer. Somewhere along the line, consequences had given way to aching, throbbing need.

Then it happened. His thumb slid just enough, hovering featherlight above my pussy.

My breath rushed out of me.

Our eyes locked. In that second something crashed. I saw him again. I saw Theo Hound, my best friend. Sweetness, tenderness—it was faint, but it was *there*, a softness in his eyes like dawn breaking.

He pressed a little, barely spreading me, but not nearly

enough.

I whimpered, and the sweet look vanished.

"I already came," I said, desperately grasping at straws, anything to keep control. "You saw. Whatever happens, it doesn't matter."

His eyes narrowed; then a mean smile spread his heart-shaped lips. "Is *that* what that was supposed to be? You don't think I know what you look like when you lie, Abigail? It's classic you. Turning up the volume so loud no one will see the scared little girl beneath. I see you."

He leaned forward, breath ghosting my neck, until his words shivered down my spine. "I'll *always* see you."

He pushed deeper, spreading me wet and aching, too slow and too tender for the vicious way he spoke.

"When you come for me, you won't have to put on a show." He trailed his lips up and down my neck, below my ear, my jaw—not a kiss, not a tease—a ruthless torment.

The steam and heat from his breath, the constant ache built from his thumb, had my eyes rolling back.

"And that's okay. I won't need it."

Finally his thumb just barely grazed that tender, aching spot. I caved, grasping his shoulders, feeling his muscles bunch, pulling him closer.

Then he dropped me.

Shoved me to the chaise. I wasn't sure I could stand if I tried.

Theo licked the back of his thumb, one long, agonizing swipe, our eyes still locked. "Sleep well, Reject."

THEO

. . .

I woke to Abigail's sob. Instantly I was up, through her open gilded double doors and inside her room. Next came a whimper, then another sob. It was two in the morning, but the large room glowed hazy marigold. Abigail didn't do dark. She didn't do nightlights. She couldn't sleep unless all shadows were gone.

My training had me scanning the room. I jiggled the windows—still locked. Closet, bathroom—clear. No threat save the ones in her dream. I was double-checking the windows when she whimpered again, tossing in her quilted satin sheets.

I kicked the post of her king-sized bed. "Wake up, Reject."

Her bed rattled, but she didn't wake.

Abigail has no other guards but me, because the spoiled fucking brat scared them off. So I only sleep for, maybe, three hours tops because there's no one to relieve me. In those three fucking hours, she wakes me up for a fucking nightmare.

She slept with one lean, pale leg bare. All the way up to her hip. I chewed my bottom lip.

I can still fucking taste her.

Fuck.

Goddamn it.

Another sob, this one muffled by her pillow.

I ground my jaw and went to her bedside.

Abigail hadn't had a hearts-and-flowers childhood. We'd bonded over that, once. She was a princess, I was a street kid, but we'd both been scarred by rejection and abandonment. Back then, she fooled me into thinking I got off easy compared to her.

My mom only left me once.

Hers never stopped leaving.

I lifted her up by the shoulders, shaking her. "Wake the fuck up." Her eyes fluttered open, hazy. Brown-black strands of hair stuck to her forehead and flushed cheeks. Lips parted.

The urge to let her drop back to the mattress and leave was strong. It was no longer my job to chase away her nightmares, and I was dangerously close to crossing a line I'd drawn in cement.

My grip tightened on her shoulders.

"I can't find anyone." Sleep-coated distress colored her words. "They promised they wouldn't leave this time, but I can't find anyone."

I should get up. It was only a matter of seconds until she came back to reality.

I peeled strands of hair from her face. "It's just another nightmare, Abs."

Her brows caved. "I don't want to spend Christmas alone."

"You're not alone, sweet girl."

The term of endearment slipped out, but she'd be too tired to notice. Hopefully she'd be too tired to remember any of this.

Her cloudy gaze cleared, focusing on the room, the bed, then me. Recognition slowly washed over her features. "Oh."

My hand lingered longer than necessary on her cheek. Abby was a siren in her floaty black slip and I was the sailor ready to jump into the rocks for her.

I pushed the rest of her hair out of her face. This was Abigail at her most dangerous. Because when Abigail dropped her walls, mine fell with them. I forgot. I forgot to hate her, forgot why I had to learn to hate her.

"You good?" My voice was soft.

"Yeah. Thank you."

Thank you.

I flinched. Whatever tenderness snuck insidiously inside me vanished. Disgust slid as sewer water through my veins. First at myself, for being so goddamn stupid, then at her.

It had been a night like this when she'd told me she loved me. She'd looked at me like this too.

My voice was too soft, deadly.

"Thank you?" I tightened my grip on her hair to a yank. "Thank you, promise, please... Abigail Crowne's four favorite words."

"What are you doing?" Her voice shook.

I laughed, biting my tongue. "You're so fucking predictable."

A small, bluish-green dot caught my eye, visible on her small wrist. I let go of her hair, gripping her wrist, pulling her small body to me and holding her in the air and off the bed in an awkward position so she was at my mercy.

Fuck.

She still looked so beautiful.

"Did you think you could get into my head? *I'm* your worst nightmare, Reject."

I pushed her back into the mattress. "I know everything about you. I know the deep dark secrets you don't even tell yourself. I know the truths to all your lies."

I pressed down on the freckle until it disappeared into the bloodless white of her skin.

"I will *always* be inside you."

A fear whispered back: She *would always be inside me.*

I let go, got off the bed, and left her behind, slamming the double doors shut as she yelled at my back, "All I said was *thank you!*"

NINE

ABIGAIL

I rubbed the small blue-gray freckle to the left of my vein, the tattoo Theo had given me, made from the tip of a graphite pencil. He'd said everyone would think it was just a small, irregularly colored freckle, but I would know. Forever.

I was tired, having stayed awake after Theo came to me last night. At least he'd shut my doors, given me that sliver of privacy.

For a brief second, I thought I'd seen the old Theo. Sweet and kind Theo, the one who woke me up from nightmares. Of course I was wrong. There was nothing about the old Theo left.

Theo used to wear a friendship bracelet every day. It was made of bulky, pastel beads and had the letters BFF sandwiched between hearts. Seeing someone like Theo, a guy who only wore shades of black, with a penchant for smoking, smirks, and brooding, with a pastel bracelet on his wrist was unbearably sexy. He'd worn it like he wore everything else, with effortless confidence born from not giving a shit what anyone else thought.

Like everything else Theo, it drove me insane.

Who gave it to him? Why didn't he ever take it off?

Anytime I'd asked him, he'd always said I already knew the answers.

I used to hate seeing it on his wrist... now it drives me insane to see his wrist bare. Another reminder the old Theo is gone.

A knock at my door had me sitting up and righting shoulders achy from hunching for hours after Theo left, wiping sleep-tired eyes. I expected it to be Theo, so I steeled myself. Today was another stupid party. Another expensive invite. Another day for Abigail Crowne to ruin. Some famous cellist was playing, one of the women people would cream their panties just to sit hundreds of chairs away from. Naturally, everyone at Crowne Hall wouldn't give a shit.

When I was a kid, we used to sabotage such parties.

Before my siblings and I totally hated one another, we ruined them together.

When my mom pushed open the door, I realized I didn't need steel. I should've poured liquid cement inside my veins.

I quickly scrambled off my bed. "Uh, hi, Mom."

She had a small unreadable smile on her face as she came to the side of my bed. I could count on one hand the number of times Mom had been to my wing.

Mom pushed my hair behind my ear. "It's a shame your father had to miss last night." Her smooth, nearly wrinkle-free hand lingered on my ear. I couldn't breathe. "To see your beautiful, masterful magic trick."

I frowned, biting the inside of my cheek to suppress a

swallow. Mom's sweetness barely veiled the sharp edge of her words. Anytime Mom brought up our late father, something awful was about to happen.

"A quarter of my garden and two point five million dollars disappeared in thirty seconds."

Still she played with my hair, the same smile on her face. If I were any other person, I would've thought *that* was what got me in trouble, but money didn't matter to us.

I waited for the shoe to drop.

"The acquisition and your engagement nearly went with it."

Her voice was deathly quiet, but her grip on the lock of my hair tightened. If I moved the slightest bit, it would be painful.

"I'm sorry, Mom," I said, straining my neck to stay still. "It was an accident."

Her eyes narrowed. I looked the most like Mom out of all of us. I had her small stature and her almond-shaped eyes, button nose, and bee-stung lips. I think she resents me for it.

All at once she let me go.

I loosed a long exhale.

She stood, walking over to my desk. I watched silently as she opened the drawer with my college pamphlets, the found jewelry I'd been building as a portfolio, my treasures and my dreams. One by one, she picked up my jewelry, walking over to my open window.

I didn't bother wondering how she knew. Tansy Crowne knew everything, saw everything, heard everything.

"Should I show you my trick?" She dangled my necklaces, earrings, and bracelets in the empty air.

She dropped all but one, holding the glimmering item in her grasp.

Fear crawled up my throat. "Mom—"

"You know how this works, Abigail. You take, I take."

She dropped the last one.

My mouth parted, staring at the open window as she walked by me, whispering in my ear not to be late for the party later. Staring even after she left. Years of artwork lost in a second. The only pieces left were in my secret box, stowed away in my closet.

The worst part... I wasn't mad at her. I was mad at myself for believing I could be anything more.

I don't know if my family was ever happy, but we weren't so... *unhappy*.

There was a time when I wasn't so *vile*.

With Dad gone, all I ever really knew was Mom, and for as long as I can remember, she'd favored my siblings, specifically Gemma. Nothing I ever did was good enough for her. She set Gemma and me against each other, but Gemma always came out on top.

I keep hoping one day she'll let me win, or at least, let me know why I'm losing.

When I finally turned around, Theo was in the doorway, watching.

How long had he been there?

Vulnerability scraped at my throat. I couldn't handle whatever he had planned, not after my mother. Something flickered warm in his light eyes, but it was gone before I could decipher it.

He kicked off the frame. "Let's go, Reject."

I *felt* Theo's judgment at my back. It's what everyone would think. How could Abigail Crowne even dream of college? Dream of anything other than the life she was given? Abigail Crowne was less than. Abigail Crowne was second best.

Abigail Crowne was worthless.

"Not gonna fight back?" Theo asked.

Dark, silky cello music grew louder the farther we descended downstairs. Today I could dress in jeans, Chanel pumps, and a bulky, oversized crewneck sweatshirt, which meant Theo was dressed casually in dark-gray fitted jeans and a cable-knit sweater that outlined his biceps and fore-arms too well. We had a world-class cellist, and we liked to show our privilege by dressing down.

The party *should* be in the garden... but it had to be moved, for obvious reasons, and was now in the terrace over-looking the ocean and unburned parts of the garden— though it had been mostly fixed, the only evidence of Abigail Crowne and her near-constant fuck-uppery the smell of burnt leaves.

Bloody Marys, mint juleps, and assholes await me. I can't wait.

Theo grabbed me by the collar, yanking me backward right before I would enter. He pressed me against the wall.

"You in there?" He ruffled my hair and curls fell over my eyes, blurring his face. I saw only important parts of him, the parts that defined Theo Hound. His sharp jaw. The cut of his gaunt cheeks. His piercing green eyes.

Theo's soft voice and playful actions cut worse than any of his harsh words. After Mom's reminder this morning, I knew how dangerous it was to believe in something good.

I turned my head.

He pushed one strand behind my ear. "Abig—"

Laughter cut him off, and he dropped his hand, taking a step back.

"Morning, Reject."

Geoff, this time with Alaric. Another asshole I was unfortunate enough to be "friends" with by the forced proximity begot from wealth and power.

"Uh-oh, don't make the reject cry. Look, her dog is already growling."

I glanced at Theo, who oddly enough *did* look upset.

They kept talking, but I was focused on Theo. I don't *get* him. He probably thought I'd been too asleep the night before to notice him say nice things to me—but I wasn't.

One minute he's hot, the next cold. When I show him any hint of sweetness he throws it in my face, as if he prefers me when I'm a bitch.

Geoff and Alaric walked outside, joining the others in their casual attire outside on the terrace.

Theo stared after them, a look on his face that made me shiver.

"People call me that all the time," I said quietly. "*You* call me that."

It was a moment before he acknowledged I'd spoken. So long I thought he wouldn't. Then he looked down at me with a look so intense, so ripping, it cured my soul.

"Exactly. Only *I* get to call you that."

Then it vanished from his face, and I was summoned by one of my mom's friends, forced to play Abigail Crowne.

THEO

I stood behind Abigail as she talked to some older woman with so much work done she had a constant Joker smile. We were on the upper part of the terrace. Above us, a tiered chandelier cast soft light, and Grecian columns slatted our view of the iron-blue ocean.

I rolled the bracelet in my pocket between my fingers, weathered from all the times I'd rubbed it during the years Abigail and I'd been apart.

You belong to me now, forever.

I worked the bracelet in my pocket harder, focusing on the blocky beads, not the arch of Abigail's neck, exposed when she moved her hair over one shoulder. I could still feel Abigail's skin beneath my fingers. She was a tempting lie, a promise I wanted to believe wouldn't break.

The woman wandered down one of the two forking stairs to the lower deck of the terrace—probably to wreak havoc on Gotham—and Abigail was alone again.

"Hey," I said. "Reject."

Nothing. *Still.*

This was what I *wanted.* Abigail broken.

I was so busy working the bracelet I didn't notice the music grow distorted, cacophonous, and shrieking.

"Someone switched her bow," Abigail said absently. I glanced at where Abigail was looking. The cellist was red-faced.

A smile came—that used to be our move—but it vanished just as quickly. Abigail was watching her mother, brows drawn.

"Do you know what would really piss her off?" I asked, voice low so only she could hear. She tilted her head to listen. "Fucking your bodyguard."

Her breath caught and she tried to cover it up by clearing her throat.

"You're just trying to trip me up, get me caught and in trouble."

I grinned. "Definitely." She looked at me, catching my darkening eyes. "Doesn't mean I'm not right."

"I'm not falling for this."

My grin widened. "The Abigail I knew wasn't such a coward."

"The Theo I knew wasn't such a dick."

I pressed a tongue to my teeth, halting a laugh. "That's just not true."

"I don't even want to see you. I definitely don't want to fuck you." She turned back so fast her hair whipped my face.

"My little liar," I said. "When will you learn just saying words won't make them come true?" I leaned forward, breath skating along her neck, goose bumps betraying her almost as much as her pulse. "You wanna fuck me...but I'm gonna wait till you beg."

She canted her head, eyes meeting mine over her shoulder. Something sparked in the clay depths. Desire?

She tore her body away from mine before I could decipher and said, "I have to pee."

I followed her inside silently, leaning against the wall opposite the door, waiting. Many windows and arched doors opened onto the terrace, but most partygoers were farther down. This was not a cramped patio. Like everything Crowne it was luxurious, opulent, and extravagant.

I kept rolling the beads between my thumb and forefinger.

Abigail thought she saw me first, that the first time we met was when she got out of that car on the beach. She thought *she* found *me*.

I let her believe it too. Shit, I let myself believe it.

The truth was, I found her.

Before everything, before the day on the beach, before I

broke her heart and she broke mine. She always wondered why I got in her car. I've told her half-truth after half-truth. I had nowhere to go. You were the best option. It was either sleep on the beach or get in your car.

What I didn't tell her was we'd already met, and the bracelet in my pocket was the reminder of the week Abigail Crowne had cemented herself in my heart.

When we were apart, it was a lot easier to paint her as a villain. Now *she* painted insidious strokes across that picture.

Loud laughter carried on the ocean wind, and my eyes landed on the chucklefucks walking toward me, Alaric and Geoff. They passed without noticing me, walking down the terrace steps to the private beach.

There were so many assholes and bitches in her world— too many to keep track of—but I remembered Alaric and Geoff. We'd fought once before, but then it had been five against one.

Abigail was broken. Broken from her bitch of a mom, from assholes like these who'd made her life hell since birth. *Broken*. Only I wanted to break her. She hadn't smiled *once* today.

I kicked off the wall.

"Oh fuck, it's the dog," Alaric coughed on a laugh when he spotted me walking down the steps. The overcast sky made the pale sand shadowed and cool.

"Did we bring a spray bottle?" Geoff asked.

They laughed again, then turned back to the ocean, lifting a small, sterling silver spoon to their noses. Could be cocaine, could be fucking Oxy for all I cared.

I crooked my neck. "You owe Abigail an apology."

A pause, then another laugh.

I debated giving them one more chance.

Fuck it.

I grabbed them both by the collars, throwing them to the sand. I didn't want them too bloody, couldn't have what I'd done be obvious. As they attempted to stand, I grabbed them by their necks, pushed their faces deeper into the grainy sand. They coughed and choked on it.

Above us, the party continued. The melodious laughter, crystal champagne glasses tinkling, and the deep shiver of the cello flowed despite us.

"Don't make the reject cry. Next time you'll bleed."

This was nothing, I told myself. It meant *nothing*. It was part of the job.

I shoved them harder into the sand; then I let off and wiped my hands clean, grains of sand sprinkled into their hair.

"You think we're going to take this shit lying down, dog?"

"You're fucking dead!" they called after me. "Dead!"

ABIGAIL

When I came out, I couldn't find Theo. A few days ago, I would've been thrilled. I'd expected to find him opposite the wall, pale eyes piercing, and for some reason an odd ache settled in my gut.

I quickly brushed it off.

Back in the ballroom, the cellist had fixed her bow and the music was low, sweet, and haunting. I caught sight of Alaric and Geoff. Their eyes were blackening, noses red and running. Another trip to their on-retainer plastic surgeon. Something in my gut spurred me to stop walking and turn to them.

"What happened to you?" I asked.

Geoff gave me the finger. "Fuck off, Reject."

Alaric shoved my shoulder so hard I stumbled back.

"What the fuck? Eat a dick, *Rick*." I called him by the nickname he hated. He was *Alaric,* not some "blue-collar working man."

Alaric was, quite honestly, the worst.

Alaric spun around, holding his nose, black and bruising eyes slits. "Keep your dog on a goddamn leash, cunt."

The words stole any comeback I had prepared, and I stared long after they'd disappeared into Crowne Hall. Could Theo have had something to do with their faces?

No...that was impossible.

I should follow them back out to the patio. I *should* be watching the famous cellist, mingling with whatever politicians and wealthy elite had come. No doubt my sister Gemma was doing that, and my mom would notice my absence.

Instead I walked up to the balcony overlooking the empty ballroom, sitting down and scooting to the edge so my legs swung over open air. To my left one of the tall, gilded, latticed windows was opened onto the overcast sea. I pulled out a joint from my clutch, tracing my fingers along the inscription etched in the marble floor.

AC + TH

I'd etched this the night I fell in love with Theo.

My relationship with Theo was always different. From the very beginning, we were connected. Something *else,* something *other*. But this was where it became love.

"Thought you would have grown out of your bad teenage habit."

I coughed out smoke at the voice, looking up to find Theo staring down at me.

Some habits are impossible to break.

I lightly punched my chest, trying to stifle the coughs. When I spoke, my throat was sore. "I only smoke—"

"When you have a problem you can't solve," he finished.

"I was going to say *sometimes*."

"Oh, you were going to lie." He did his Theo laugh. Not quite a laugh. Not quite a scoff. Like he wasn't laughing with me or even at me, but because he knew something I didn't.

He pulled a cigarette out of his pocket and said, "Give me a light."

That was Theo. Never asking, only assuming.

I leaned forward, cupping my hand against the low, salty wind blowing in from the open window. He bent forward, a strand of his hair falling over one eye. As I was lighting his cigarette, I focused on that. The closeness of him, his face a devilish temptation behind the flame.

The flame caught.

He grinned and fell back, blowing out smoke. "Good girl."

The words seized my gut, but Theo wasn't even watching me. As if the words came out of his mouth without thought, as easily as the shivers racing up my spine following them.

He leaned with his back against the railing, staring out the open window, cigarette between his pointer and middle finger. The sky was overcast, a soft gray muting the sand. He took another drag, then turned.

And caught me staring.

I quickly looked at the ballroom far beneath my feet.

"How did you find me?" I asked after a minute, voice quiet.

"I'll always find you, Abigail."

My eyes snapped to his, finding him watching me already. Those devilish lips were wrapped around the cigarette, pale stare narrowed on me with something too close to possession, made even more searing through the smoke. Maybe it was supposed to be meant as a threat, but his words punched me in the chest as I imagined an alternate world, where Theo still cared.

"So...cigarettes now?"

As far as I knew, Theo didn't smoke cigarettes. We had a bad habit of smoking together, but it was weed, not cigarettes. I guess that was another thing that changed.

He eyed me down from his nose. "Can't be high. Not while watching you."

My gut somersaulted, and I coughed out more smoke.

"So you still come up here?" he asked, blowing out smoke, eyes still locked.

I was hoping he'd forgotten this place. The alcove where we'd laughed and I'd spilled secrets and desires to him. Where he'd held me when I cried.

Theo broke my heart, and I'd tried to forget everything about him, but trying to forget only made me remember him more.

I shrugged. "It didn't mean that much to me."

He narrowed his eyes, and I thought he'd call me out, but then he tapped the ash of his cigarette out on the banister. Ash fell like muted glitter to the ballroom.

Then he sat beside me, dangling his feet with mine like we had so many times before. Our thighs and shoulders almost touched, his legs stretched so much farther than mine. There was only enough space for the *AC + TH* now sandwiched between us to pop out, bold and taunting.

His thighs were thicker now too, but still lean. Were his hands bigger? That seemed improbable.

I knew one major difference for certain. I couldn't look at him. I could barely breathe.

He traced the very same inscription I had moments before.

"Cute," was all he said.

"I was young and stupid." Had I responded too quickly? I took a shaky drag from my joint.

Suddenly he was at my wrist, pulling my joint from my mouth, thumb at my freckle and rubbing it with too much purpose.

"Young and stupid," he repeated. The wistful edge said there was so much more beneath his words and my heart *pounded*. His pressure deepened, and my breath caught.

"Truth or promise?" I asked, needing to distract from whatever was happening.

"Truth..." He narrowed his eyes, seeing through me.

"Did you beat up Alaric and Geoff?" I noticed his knuckles were abraded, not quite bloody, but something had definitely happened.

He nodded slowly, curving his lips to blow a puff of smoke to the side and out of my face.

"Why?" I asked.

He smiled slowly, shaking his head. "My turn. Truth or promise?"

I bit my lip, my turn to look away. Away from his deep eyes.

But then his thumb was at my lip, pulling it from my teeth, and I was drawn back to him. I could taste the coppery remains on his thumb.

My gut somersaulted.

Pancaked.

Bottomed out.

He was *Theo Hound* and he was my *enemy*. So why did I want him to push his thumb deep into my mouth? Why was I stuck on the way he was watching me? Why were his lips the only thing I could focus on?

Sucking the smoky taste off them.

We were getting too close.

I was going to get hurt, again.

I jumped up. "I have to go."

He took a slow drag, staring up at me, eyes sharp. "That's not how this works."

"I don't care."

He looked almost disappointed, then stamped the cigarette out, smashing it into the *AC + TH* before standing up.

"You owe me."

On our way back to the party, we passed by Alaric and Geoff. They'd since cleaned up, but their eyes were black. When they saw us, they flipped us the bird with a laugh. I kept walking, because fuck those guys, but Theo stopped. Full stop.

"Did they apologize to you?" he all but growled.

"What?"

"Did they say they were sorry?"

"Uh... no?" Was he kidding? Alaric and Geoff say *sorry*?

I kept walking and was nearly at the patio when I noticed Theo had changed direction—toward Alaric and Geoff. He expertly grabbed them and had them incapacitated before I reached him.

"Theo, what are you doing?"

We were just inside the many open French doors that

led to the patio, barely shielded by Mother's favorite potted black orchids. The cello's haunting shiver ghosted on the wings of feathery ocean air, servants would be coming in and out, and, if anyone looked in our direction, they would see us.

He grabbed them both by the collars, thrusting them in front of me. "Apologize."

They winced. "Fuck off, dog."

Theo used to get in fights when we were kids. It was a weekly occurrence. He was the wild dog I'd let into our china shop, and it wasn't uncommon for him to be outmatched. He'd give a good fight, but he always got his ass kicked.

I'd always had to clean him up. He'd never understood why it hurt me so much, but then, I'd never understood why he had to fight. I'd always had people talk shit about me.

He forced them to their knees with a yelp of pain. "Apologize."

"Theo, it's okay—" I attempted, hoping to stave off the moment it changed and Theo was thrown to the ground.

"Apologize," his command caught on a growl.

They met my eyes, their own burning with hate. "Sorry," they gritted out at the same time.

I barely had a moment to register shock before Theo had thrown them both down. They laid their hands out just in time to stop from smacking their heads against the marble.

"Let's go," Theo said.

He gripped my wrist, stepping over them like they were dog shit and dragging me with him.

I looked over my shoulder at Alaric and Geoff, still prone, then back at Theo, at his grip, firm yet unbruising on my wrist.

When had Theo become someone who could not only hold his own but take on Alaric and Geoff? And what the hell did it mean that he'd asked them to apologize to me?

Nothing.

It had to mean nothing.

The alternative was too damning.

TEN

ABIGAIL

I barely slept, tossing and turning all night. Yellow-gold morning light lit up my room and warmed my bed. Tomorrow is our annual Fourth of July party, and maybe my last chance to gain my mother's approval.

Even still, my mind isn't on Mom.

It's on Theo.

I can't stop thinking about him. I'm supposed to be above him. He's my bodyguard, but my strings are attached to *him*. In public, he stands behind me. In private...

In private my heart beats for him.

With a groan, I banged my head against my pillow. I *can't* give him that power. This is just lust. I'm over-the-top horny, and once I have a clear head, he won't have any power.

I rolled over, fixed on my gilded-ivory crown molding, sliding my hand beneath my silky white sheets and pushing down my panties, sliding my hand between my thighs.

Theo means nothing. Once I take care of myself, I'll stop thinking about him.

I closed my eyes and spread myself, sliding two fingers up and down, slowly finding the right rhythm.

If I moved these aside, would I find my answer?

Theo popped into my head. I couldn't help it. With my eyes closed, his piercing green eyes and cocksure voice consumed me. If I opened my eyes, I could probably banish him, but just imagining his thick, sure fingers between my legs had my body heating, my breath short, and the ache between my legs growing. Theo was a flurry of agonizingly sweet juxtapositions. Rough but silky, gentle and firm.

He'd left me hanging, but maybe I could force his mirage to finish.

Do you know what would really get her attention? Fucking your bodyguard.

His voice was in my ear now. Low and quiet, but never unsure. Almost infuriatingly confident. Like how he'd commanded Alaric and Geoff. That rough, grating growl I only heard when he was consumed with emotion—so *Theo*. No one ever stood up for me like that—no one.

Apologize.

His name was on my tongue, slipping past my lips before I could pull it back.

"You're having a good morning."

My eyes flew open, finding Theo in the doorway, a slight smirk hooking his lips.

My heart pounded with the possibilities of what he'd seen... or heard. I lifted my hand from between my legs, prepared to stop and die a slow death somewhere, humiliation coursing hot through my veins, when he growled, "Don't fucking stop."

It was only a split second hesitation.

I kept going, slower at first. He leaned with one shoulder against the doorframe, glued to me. At first, there was that damn apathy in his gaze. It was infuriating, but somehow *so* hot.

There was something about the impassive way he studied me that made my heart pound. It was as if what was happening was no more interesting than finding a penny on the ground. My heart pounded harder to the rhythm of his disinterest. I ached and the knot in my stomach throbbed.

Everything about this was a *shouldn't*, but it *did*.

I tried to be stone, too, to show him he meant nothing, that this was nothing, but I couldn't.

A whimper escaped my lips, and then his eyes blazed like the joints we'd smoked clandestinely when we were teenagers. I could practically hear the snick of the matches.

What am I doing?

I don't like this.

I do.

I like him watching me. I like his hungry, ravenous eyes.

I like how he pushes his shoulder harder into the frame with my breathing. I like his jaw tightening with the deepening of his brow, the darkening of his gaze.

I like being on display for him.

It's wrong.

But it makes me feel so good.

He ran his thumb over his lip, nail digging into the flesh like he wanted to dig into *me*, and said low and casual: "Faster."

I listened, sliding along myself with fervor. My breathing rose in cadence—I couldn't stop it. I slid inside myself. One finger, two. *Wet.*

I've never been so wet and I know he can hear it.

It's traitorous.

It's not enough.

I know why, it's because of him. I'm empty with the memory of Theo's fingers only feet away, even if they were barely touching me.

If I were with anyone else, I'd put on a show.

With him, I'm quiet.

And God, that's so much more betraying. Only the sound of my thighs rubbing against the sheets, magnified like thunder, my breathing gusts of wind. He said he wouldn't need a show, and I can feel the truth of those words. He reads every hand movement, every rise and fall of my chest. I can't hide from him. I can't pretend.

He sees me.

Theo slid his thumb from his lip, biting the tip. Jaw flexed and eyes hard, like he was memorizing every small movement. I can't help but imagine his teeth on me, biting into my flesh. Marking me.

Before *I* even realized I was about to come, his lip curved. Then I felt it, the pulse, the ache, the throb growing and spreading deeper.

I can't take my eyes off him. He's spurring me further and further. I want to beg him. For what, I don't know. I'm captive, held taut on this throbbing thread by his half smile, his bitten thumb.

Then he lowered his head, just a half nod, a quirked brow.

Go ahead.

His name was on my lips again as I come completely undone.

Theo hadn't said a word as we came downstairs for breakfast, and I was grateful he had to walk behind me. I couldn't look him in the eye.

What was I thinking?

Breakfast was painfully overdone, as always. Even more so, because Mrs. Harlington was now staying with us in anticipation of my impending marriage to her son.

Her presence was like seeing the executioner at the gallows.

We had every type of breakfast food available. Fluffy eggs, colorful fruit, sweet and syrupy scones and crepes all laid out on a table stretching the thousand square foot dining room. Morning light streamed in through windows like diamonds.

All the personal guards were seated at the table today, probably because Mom had noticed the Harlingtons sat with theirs, which meant Theo would sit next to me too. We'd barely taken our seats when my mother's sickly sweet voice stopped me in my tracks.

"Did you think I wouldn't notice?" she asked. "That I wouldn't know?"

"I—" I stumbled over my words. "I didn't... we didn't..." How could she know? How could she possibly know?

"What does this look like?" Mom continued.

"Um... a cherry?" a servant's weak voice answered.

Conversations went quiet, all eyes traveling to where she spoke with a servant who'd gone sheet white. I practically sank into my chair. *Of course* she didn't know.

I'd nearly given myself away.

I refused to look at Theo. I could feel his stare trying to force me, so I smoothed a napkin over my camel-colored leather skirt.

My mother laughed. "Yes dear, a braindead woman could see that. What does it *look* like?"

The girl trembled.

Opposite my mother, Gray leaned back, arms overhead, a smile growing.

"Does it look *round* to you?" My mom trailed manicured nails down her neck, waiting for the maid's response.

"Um... no?"

"Are you asking me?"

"No?"

"Are you asking me that too?"

My mom's face was pinched in the way she got when dealing with help. *It's not like I'm asking them to solve world hunger,* she'd say.

"Do you want to start your day off with an ugly piece of fruit?"

The girl shook her head furiously. "No."

"Take this," she sighed, handing the servant a bowl of bright-red cherries that looked perfectly round. She scurried off, mumbling apologies.

Like clockwork, my mother sighed. "It's not like I'm asking them to solve world hunger." The room laughed, and conversation continued.

"Still seated at the end with the rejects and forgotten," Theo said, reaching for a glass of water in a crystal goblet.

I clenched my teeth.

His cruel words shouldn't be a surprise but after this morning... they hurt worse.

"I don't care about her. I don't care what they think. They can ship me off to Antarctica for all I care." I couldn't help myself. I spared a look down the table where Mom, Gray, and Gemma were seated together, laughing. Was I seated down here alone on purpose?

Of course I was.

He laughed, low. "You are so fucking transparent, Reject."

I glared at him. If I thought earlier today meant something, that quickly taught me wrong.

"Well you're pathetic," I said. "A pathetic, lonely dog begging for scraps from our table."

I folded my napkin neatly in my lap, pressing the silky linen, ignoring him and trying to ignore my family.

Then I felt it, his hand under the table, sliding up my thigh.

I jumped.

"Abigail," my mother called. "Edward was just here."

I lifted my head, trying to see past the row of people between us. "Who?"

"Your *fiancé*," she answered, irritated.

Excuse me for not knowing the name of someone no one has introduced me to.

"Had you not spent the morning sleeping, you could've said hello."

Well, *thank fuck* for that.

"We just learned you were in the same class at Rosey," she continued. "Come share some of your stories with Mrs. Harlington."

We'd gone to Rosey together? I tried to remember anyone with the last name Harlington. I'd had no friends, and, like most of my classmates, sobriety wasn't really optional.

"He may join us later this week, for the Fourth," Mrs. Harlington said.

I was getting used to the idea of having just a name for a fiancé. The idea I'd actually have to meet this Edward and actually *marry him*, made my throat close.

"Oh, that would be wonderful..." My mother trailed off.

I prepared to stand and make up some bullshit when Theo curled his hand inside my thigh, a halting grip. All I could focus on was how close he was. Too close, not close enough. I should've worn pants.

Thank *God* I didn't wear pants.

"Stop," I whimpered.

"What were you thinking about?" he whispered. "What had you saying my name like a fucking plea for mercy this morning?"

"Abigail," my mother called out again, voice clipped, losing patience.

"*Fuck.*" Theo cursed low when he realized I hadn't put on any panties.

I focused on my ugly cherry, on keeping my fork from shaking. Not his fingers *almost* grazing me, igniting goose bumps that invaded my core and made my stomach ache and throb. Not how I wanted him to touch me. How I wanted him deeper, satiating what I couldn't earlier.

Why wouldn't he just go inside me?

"Abigail!"

Mother rarely took that tone in public. I was about to stand—conditioned like a fucking dog.

Theo's hand on my thigh tightened. "Don't move."

"My mom is calling me," I said weakly.

His finger plunged inside me. The fork I was holding dropped to my porcelain plate with a clang.

"So answer."

With him deep inside me?

"Abigail? Are you *trying* to make me lose my voice?" Mom had a bored, unaffected tone, one I knew meant she was close to losing her patience.

"I..."

Theo pulled out, then pushed back in, deeper, curving

his finger at just the right angle. I tried to focus on my breathing and failed.

What was I going to say? The room blurred. He was hitting that perfect, *perfect* spot I'd dreamed about this morning. His finger was big and thick and—

Fuck.

"Abigail?"

"I spilled champagne on my dress," I managed weakly.

Theo's low chuckle raced up my spine and made my teeth tingle.

Mother took a deep breath. I could picture her nostrils flaring.

My thighs fell open for him, begging for *more*. His ruthless rhythm all I knew. More fingers, more pressure, more pace.

More Theo.

Theo who had one tantalizing, taunting finger inside me —and was focused only on his food. Eating eggs and talking to the person beside him like he wasn't driving me to the brink.

I was going to come. I was going to come on the hand of my bodyguard, surrounded by my family and my soon-to-be mother-in-law.

My breath shook. The room faded away to nothing.

Salt. Seawater. Sunscreen.

Him.

Him.

I gripped his thigh beneath the table, trying to anchor myself.

The only way I knew he even *realized* what he'd done to me was the way his voice slightly roughened when my grip tightened on his thigh as I came.

I quickly excused myself to the terrace for air.

Everything was in technicolor. The salt air brittle in my nose and on my tongue. The wind biting. The sun too bright, its heat on my neck fierce.

I could still feel him inside me, a throbbing memory.

I wanted more.

I couldn't want more. He didn't do that to me because he liked me. He did that to me because he knew it would wreck me, humiliate me.

I gripped the railing to steady myself, when I saw it.

A single gold rose sitting on the railing, and this time it came with a note.

See you soon.

Just like that, fear eclipsed everything. I didn't want to believe it. I couldn't believe it. He couldn't reach me *here*. I lifted it and pricked myself on the stem.

"Abigail?"

I jumped at Theo's voice, dropping both the rose and note to the sand out of sight. I spun to face him, heart pounding. Blood dripped from my finger into the velvety, soft-white dunes. His eyes sharpened on it.

"What happened?" he asked, taking a step to me. Any closer he would see the rose, the note.

"I cut myself on the railing. I don't know." My shaking voice betrayed me. Before he could take another step forward, I walked past him. "Come on, dog. Let's go or Mother will throw a fit."

I felt Theo's suspicion coming off him in waves behind me.

I couldn't focus on it, because all I could think was... my stalker had gotten *inside Crowne Hall*?

ELEVEN

THEO

I stayed outside Abigail's room well into the night, not putting a toe past the bodyguard line, but I watched her. She'd been weird all day, ever since brunch. Jumpy and skittish. I played it off as what had happened between us.

But something in my gut said otherwise.

She was atop her silky white sheets now, with some kind of mask on her face, in an oversize shirt that read ADULT-ISH and black satin sleep shorts, her long sable-brown waves tied in a messy bun atop her head.

Beautiful.

"This is the Abigail I know," I said, leaning against the door. "All her pretty makeup and lies washed away to show the troll beneath."

She looked up, surprise flickering in her clay eyes before disappearing into a glare. "Shouldn't you be barking at a car or something?"

She flipped a page in her book, ignoring me.

Abigail masturbating.

That's an image I won't get out of my head... fucking ever.

Before, I was never allowed in her wing. Didn't mean she didn't sneak me in. Let me lie on her bed with her in the glow of her lamp as I waited for her to fall asleep. We'd talked into the night, about anything and everything. What food we liked (she liked Crowne Drive-In Diner burgers, I liked licorice ice cream), our favorite movies (hers was *Silent Hill*, oddly enough), or just how much she wished her mother would love her. She never said it aloud, but it was obvious by how often she spoke of her.

Back then the farthest we went was holding hands.

Hers were always too small in mine.

I made her promises, though. Whenever we played our game, she never promised, but I made so many.

I promise someday I'm going to kiss you, Abigail.

I promise someday I'm going to fuck you, Abigail.

I'd whisper dirty promises along her neck as she gripped my hands. She always responded in the same way: *Please.*

Abigail looked up. "What?"

I cleared my throat. "You owe me."

I walked into her room and threw myself on her bed. Her book went flying. Abigail bounced. She looked at her fallen book, then at me, as if deciding which problem to deal with first. She decided on me.

"Uh, get the fuck off."

I threw my arms behind my head, situating myself against her quilted satin headboard.

She ground her jaw. "You could at least take your shoes off."

I put one leg over the other, really rubbing my shoes

into the comforter as I went. "As I was saying, you owe me. Truth or Promise?"

She scrunched her nose, and I could tell she wanted to fight it.

But she said, "Truth."

"Why did you look so freaked out earlier today?"

Her eyes grew. "I..." She bent over the bed, busying herself with the fallen book. "I don't think I looked freaked out."

"Not what I asked."

"Well, I don't think I look freaked out so I obviously can't answer that question." She sat upright, placing the book in her lap, fixing the mask on her face.

I zeroed in on her nervous hands, the way she chewed her bottom lip and wouldn't look me in the eyes.

"What book you reading?" I asked, deciding to push it off.

Abigail Crowne was stubborn and trying to force something out of her was generally fruitless.

"It's a romance novel. You probably haven't read it, because your brain is small, unlike mine."

I bit back a smile. "Right, that's it." I shifted, throwing one of her ridiculously sized pillows off the bed. "What's it about?"

There was so much tension in her eyes, a needling mistrust. She eyed me like I was a lion being nice to a mouse.

I was beginning to wonder myself why I wasn't eating the mouse.

But that was a problem for another night.

"A guy," she finally said.

I couldn't halt my laugh. It came out of me, real and

genuine. I was brought back to the old nights, when we would laugh until the black night faded into sun.

"No fucking shit, Abigail," I said. "What's the story about?"

Another one of her side-eyed uncertain glances, but she started telling me all about it. How she'd just started it yesterday but was almost finished. How the hero was so *hot* (her words) and the heroine kind of annoying, but the hero made up for it.

Romance isn't my genre. When I read, I tend to gravitate toward nonfiction, horror, or classics. But Abigail Crowne was a romantic, and she got lost in her stories. As she told me the story, I got lost with her.

I used to read every story she loved, because I loved talking to Abigail, so it didn't matter the subject. When we were teenagers, she got into *Twilight*, which meant I read four books about a sparkly vampire and had to deal with Abigail being Team Jacob.

Team fucking Jacob.

I eyed the forest green book in her hands.

She sat up straight, looking at me funny. "Why do you care?"

"Maybe I'm in the mood to read some, what was it? Stepbrother alpha..."

"Stepbrother alpha*hole*," she enunciated.

"Right." Another grin I couldn't stop. "That."

Fuck, she was cute. It got under your skin.

Her shorts were too fucking short, showing too much of her silky thighs. The memory of her coming on my finger blasted into me. She was tight, so fucking tight. Just the thought of what she'd feel like wrapped around my dick had me shifting.

Our eyes connected.

"Theo, this morning—" she started.

A timer went off, and she peeled off the cottony mask, dropping it into her porcelain trash can. Now her skin glowed; she was too damn pretty.

I'd wonder forever what she was about to say.

"How did you do that thing to Geoff and Alaric?" she asked suddenly. "With the arm."

I shrugged. "Training."

She moved her mouth around, not happy with the answer. Her lips looked poutier tonight, I don't know if she'd added gloss or what. I couldn't take my eyes off them. Moving them around didn't help.

I wanted to bite them.

First the top one, then the bottom.

"Do you ever wonder about your mom?" she asked, dousing my fantasy in ice water. The fuck? Could she stay on one topic?

"Is that my truth or promise?"

"No," she said. "Just a question." She picked at the forest green spine of her book. "I know you were in foster care for a while, and then you were on your own... before me. But your mom's alive somewhere. What if she wants to know you?"

"She doesn't."

I could tell she wanted to say more. She kept picking at the green edge of her spine, watching me like a turtle was in her mouth trying to burst out.

I exhaled. "Speak."

"I'm just saying." She dropped the book entirely. "Your mom was so young when she gave you up. She's an adult now. *You're* an adult now. What if she's tried to contact you?"

I was dropped at a fire station with my mother's diary

and only a name—Theo. There is no record of my mother. My last name came from the firefighter who found me. His favorite Sherlock Holmes' novel was *The Hound of Baskervilles*.

Abigail fucking knows this.

"Maybe she gave you her diary for a reason... I've never seen anything like it. The beautiful red-leather and tree burned into the face is so beautiful. I'm positive it's custom."

This was classic fucking Abigail. She lives in a fairy tale, and has had a fairy tale image of my reunion with my mother ever since she learned I wasn't an orphan, but was abandoned at birth because my mother was too young to raise me.

Some days I regret showing her my mother's diary. For me, it was something to remember her by. But romantic-fucking-Abigail had stars in her eyes from that point on.

Abigail continued. "We could hire a private investigator to find where it was made."

I narrowed my eyes. "We?"

There is no fucking *we* anymore. I moved to get off the bed. I don't know what I was thinking, coming in here in the first place. Acting like it was five years ago.

She grabbed my arm, stopping me, eyes wide. "Do you still have it?"

"Have what?"

She rolled her eyes. "The diary."

Of course I still had it. If Abigail had her box of secrets, her jewelry and dreams she *thought* I didn't remember, then I had my diary.

Everybody has a dream; mine is finding my mother. But more important than having a dream, is hiding your dream, putting it in a box or in my case, a black backpack under the couch I slept on, so you don't fall to pieces when it inevitably doesn't come true.

It was my most valued possession, and Abigail was the only person I'd ever let know it existed.

"Why do you care?" I asked.

She dropped my arm, turning away. This was the moment I should have gotten up and left, remembered why I'd come back in the first place.

"Maybe I just want to know if there's any of the old Theo left..." She started out strong, then trailed off.

An odd ache clutched my chest at her words and the soft way she spoke them.

A dangerous part of me wondered if there was any of the old Abigail left too. The same part that couldn't get the way she felt coming on my fingers out of my head, and couldn't stop wondering what she would feel like around my dick.

But I couldn't wonder that.

I couldn't let her get close.

Not again.

Because you can't be left if you never let them stay.

Our eyes were locked, and she mashed her lips together, as if deliberating something. The air felt too still, too hot.

"Theo, I'm sor—" she started, but before she could push it further, I grabbed her by the arm, spinning her and pinning her to the mattress. She was beneath me before she could blink.

"What are you doing?" Her voice was breathy, a whisper against my lips.

I liked that. Way too much.

"Showing you how I did that *thing* to Geoff and Alaric."

"You've learned a lot."

Those bitable lips were only a breath away from me.

I had it in my head to tell her about the years I spent doing nothing but training. About my awards and how I knew all kinds of fighting styles, from Krav Maga to jiu jitsu to line to Muay Thai. I wasn't the boy she'd sent away.

But I was focused on her lips. The way her tongue darted out to wet them and her chest pressed against mine. My knee separated her thighs. Her sleep shorts had ridden up, and I was insanely distracted with what her bare skin would feel like if I wasn't wearing jeans.

So all I got out was, "Yeah."

"You're like this badass bodyguard dude," she breathed. A smile flickered against my lips at her wording. "I remember when you used to get in fights for no reason."

My brow furrowed. "No reason, Abigail?"

She shrugged. "I guess not. They're dicks. They deserve it."

Every single fight had been for *her*. There was a reason they called me her dog.

"Just when I think you can't get any stupider, you say shit like that."

Abigail glared. "Fuck you, Theo." She got redder, trying to squirm her way out. I pinned her harder, drinking in each slight movement. Her furious breaths, the way her hair fell out of her bun and across her eyes, her shirt riding up, her hot slice of skin pressed against my abs.

"One minute I think you're going to be nice to me," she huffed. "But that's like impossible for you now. You're such a—"

I cut off whatever she was about to say with my lips.

ABIGAIL

. . .

I don't move. I don't even breathe, eyes wide and stunned. Theo is kissing me—*again*. This kiss is different. Still bruising and brutal, but not nearly as mean. It almost feels... worshipful.

My anger quickly gave way to white hot *heat* as Theo deepened his kiss, slanting his mouth, tongue searching.

I parted my lips, surrendering too easily.

He grasped the back of my neck, lifting me, and suddenly we were spinning. I was no longer beneath him but on top as he lay against the headboard. His hands were all over me—on my back, my neck, my thighs, along my arms. Goose bumps echoed their path.

I should push him away. He's the boy who calls me *Reject* and made it clear he wants nothing but my tears. But his kisses feel like devotion, and his touch is close to reverence. I'd dreamed of kissing Theo on this bed. When I was a teenager, it was *all* I dreamed about. He'd hold my hand, and I'd wish for courage to make a move, fulfill his dirty promises.

Theo wasn't a teenager anymore.

He was a man.

He bit my top lip, the hand not anchoring my neck sliding under my shirt, up my stomach, stopping just beneath my breast. I arched like I could force him to touch me. Theo can't be forced. He just thumbed the curve beneath my breast in a tortuously slow and gentle rhythm.

Next his hungry mouth came for my bottom lip, this time more furious, dragging it out.

Ravenous.

His desire was hard against my thigh. I rubbed. I moved.

I was rewarded with a slight groan, the tightening of his grip against my neck, biting my lip harder.

I wonder if I'll bruise. I hope I do.

His hand on my neck pinned me in place for his carnal assault. I couldn't move, only grind harder as his tongue dove deeper and he fucks my mouth.

Then I heard it.

Abigail.

My name from his lips against mine. It was so quiet, barely a night breeze. Maybe it was just a hope sprung from too many jagged memories, but his barbs on my heart tighten anyway.

"Please," I begged.

It was like icy water was dropped on his head.

He threw me off him, and I bounced on my mattress with the force of it. Theo was off the bed before I could even brush the hair out of my eyes.

I was still so hot and bothered. I must look a mess. My shirt rode up and so did my shorts. My hair was tangled, my bun fell out. He was putting so much distance between us, and this should be the moment I come back to my senses.

When I realize Theo is not the boy who used to hold my hand on this bed, but the man who calls me *Reject.*

Instead, I held my arm out to him. "Theo?"

Theo paused. He was still hard, distractingly so, the outline rigid and mouthwatering in his jeans. His bedhead hair was even more messed from our make-out, falling across pale hazel-green eyes churning with a storm of emotions.

Then he shook his head, looking a little spooked.

He turned, walking out of my room, making sure to slam the door in his wake.

TWELVE

THE NEXT DAY, Crowne Hall was bustling with energy for our Fourth of July party. Our Fourth party is world famous. Everyone who is anyone is in attendance. I'd had my hair and makeup done, and across my vanity gilded and silver makeup cases were scattered and catching sparkles of morning light.

Tonight I would meet my fiancé, Edward.

I touched the orange sea-glass pendant on my neck, another one of my originals, as a shadow formed behind me in the mirror.

Theo.

I hate that the first thing I think of is kissing him. It's like a brutal flashback, a car crash I can't escape. His lips on mine.

It's fucking distracting.

I looked away.

I knew I'd have to marry someday. For a Crowne, it was just like everything else in life, perfunctory. It never made me feel any sort of way. Yet for some reason the idea of meeting my future fiancé has my heart aching.

"Time to go, Reject," was all Theo said.

I saw Mrs. Harlington and my mother talking, but there was no man with them. I slouched, hiding behind a hundred-layer croquembouche with sparklers jutting from the hilt, hoping they didn't see me.

I wasn't going to go out of my way to find my future husband. I have my entire life for that.

"Poor lonely Reject," Theo said. "Don't you know you're hiding from a family who couldn't give a shit where you are?"

I stood up straighter, glaring. "At least I *have* a family to hide from."

As if I need a reminder the kiss meant *nothing*, Theo is making sure to be a complete and utter asshole. He was in a suit again too. A deep, charcoal gray that somehow brought out the vivid green of his eyes and seemed to magnify the sharpness of his cheekbones.

Why couldn't he be hideous when he was being such a dick?

Theo was so confusing. He'd been *worshipful*. Reverent. Kissed me like he was dying of thirst and I was water. I was learning to dread his moments of affection, because they quickly led to this. Complete indifference.

Who actually has the power here? I thought it was me, but all I can think about is Theo. What he says. Thinks.

He's inside me.

He's my guard, but I feel like his slave.

I touched my lips, still remembering him.

As if he knew, he laughed. "Someone on your mind, Reject?"

I looked away, pulling out my phone and pretending to be busy on it. The sun was a citrine line on the horizon, casting the revelers in its hazy glow. Theo was at my back the entire time.

Unlike my siblings who keep their finstas—our secret Instagram accounts—updated, I don't really *have* anyone to talk to. The hashtag *fourthofcrowne* is being used and easy to track if you're in the know. Somewhere my sister was skinny-dipping with a prince off the back of his boat. My brother had his arms around this year's Victoria's Secret runway models. There was a whole, separate world happening right around me, a party filled with fun and depravity. I was supposed to be part of it, instead I'm more separate than someone who wouldn't know it didn't exist.

This is the party of the year, and I don't want to be here.

I stuttered on one of the photos. A—a rose?

It was, under the hashtag, and I was in the background out of focus. I snapped my head up, looking left and right, trying to find who took the photo.

I didn't realize Theo was over my shoulder until his breath is against my ear. "Looking for picture evidence of how little people care about you?"

I chewed my lip, putting my phone on sleep.

It was nothing. Just a weird coincidence. Still, my gut won't stop roiling.

"Sad, lonely Reject. No one to love her, only people to loathe her."

I spun on Theo. "Even if I was pathetic, my pathetic life is still a thousand times more wonderful than yours could ever be."

He grinned. "If only you believed that."

I took a step, until I could smell his fresh, minty breath. So close to kissing once more. "You'll never be anything more than a dog. An abandoned puppy crying out for its mother."

Suddenly his grin dropped, he pressed a finger to his ear, and his eyes narrowed on me. "Get behind me."

"What? Fuck off." I tried to brush by him, but he grabbed my elbow, his finger to his ear again.

"Get. Behind. Me." He thrust me behind his body.

Then I saw a commotion near the gates. Someone had tried to break into the party. It wasn't uncommon for that to happen. Usually there were a few attempted party crashers every year.

What was uncommon? Someone giving a shit about my safety.

Once there was a bomb threat on Crowne Hall, and all guards went to make sure my mom, Gray, and Gemma were taken care of. They forgot I was even there. Even my own guard at the time rushed to save *Gemma*.

Fear assaulted me. Could it be *him*? The guy who left the rose? I don't know what he looks like.

It was an odd mix of emotions I felt. No one ever saved me. Ever.

I couldn't help myself. I placed my hand on his arm, feeling the muscles cord beneath my touch. His back flexed beneath his tuxedo. I felt safe. I felt cared for. These weren't feelings I was used to.

Dangerous.

Especially with the man who'd said he was going to destroy me.

So I shoved him off.

Theo ripped his hand away from his ear, all attention on me. "Why can't you just fucking listen?"

"I don't want you saving me. Stop saving me! Stop acting like you fucking care. You're not a hero. You're cruel and heartless."

He ran a thumb along my jaw. "You're right. I'm no hero."

"So why do you keep saving me?" It came out a plea, a whisper, when I meant it to be fierce and angry.

He grabbed my jaw, dragging me close by his fierce grip. "Only I can hurt you, sweet girl. You're mine to torment. Your tears are mine to free. Your heart is mine to break."

Whatever commotion was happening at the gates faded away. My eyes dropped to his soft lips, and his grip on my chin softened.

I was certain he was going to kiss me.

I wanted it too. I could still remember his bruising kiss, the way he'd worshipped me just last night. I even angled my chin closer, my body a traitor.

Then early test fireworks popped, and we each came to our senses, separating.

THEO

There's something Abigail isn't telling me. I'd been picking up on it, but now I was certain. She's jumpier, looking over her shoulder more. At first I thought it was because of *me*, but now I know.

Abigail Crowne is afraid.

There's a lot Abigail doesn't tell the world, truths she keeps hidden, but she isn't someone to be afraid.

A few party crashers won't scare Abigail, especially when they'd been rounded up and sent to jail.

I gently shoved her shoulder blade. "Hey, Reject."

Fuck, Abigail in her white dress looked like something

out of a damn fairy tale. The sand interlaced with the confetti and glitter, and as she walked barefoot through it, I wondered if she actually was.

A Crowne July Fourth is not your average backyard BBQ. Politicians, CEOs, and celebrities were among the attendees, and they all used it as a chance to network. You don't just show up; you don't buy a ticket to this thing; you get invited. Invites are some of the most sought after in the world.

I don't give a shit. I focused on Abigail.

I shoved her again, harder. She ignored me, acting like she was so damn interested in her fucking phone. I reached over her shoulder and snatched it out of her hands, holding it high above her head as she tried to grab it back.

A gold rose?

It had the stupid hashtag they'd used for this party. I handed the phone back to her, suspicion creeping up my spine. It was the same jumpiness Abigail had yesterday. Was she hiding a boyfriend?

"What's this?"

"Nothing. I don't know—"

"A guest has made the request I send this to you, Ms. Crowne." A server appeared, interrupting her. He held up a fucking gold rose on a silver platter.

"Got some boyfriend I don't know about?" I asked.

Abigail froze, then slammed the thing out of his hand. The platter and the rose fell to the sand.

I didn't have a chance to ask her what the fuck she was doing, because a moment later she fell to the ground with it.

A few heads turned to look.

I bent down. "Not getting enough attention?"

Abigail turned into me, grasping my tuxedo lapels.

Shock stunned me. She shook, fucking *shook*. Abigail didn't shake.

Her skin is sheet white, breath raspy, but it's her eyes I was locked on. Wide yet far off. I'd seen this reaction before, in the eyes of every employee at Crowne Industries when the building was under lockdown for an active shooter.

The beach faded out. The people watching us disappeared.

Whatever black blood existed between us vanished.

"Abigail," I whispered. "I've got you."

I covered her hand with mine, slowly lifting her up with me as she held my lapels for dear life. I placed my shoulder over hers, shepherding her from the beach into Crowne Hall. The smell of sparklers and pastries and salt air was at our back as we climbed the stairs up to the alcove, where she would be safe from prying eyes and cruel hashtags.

I was too aware this was where we'd come as teenagers. Where I'd comforted her before, when she'd cried about her mother and first dropped her walls.

"Abigail, look at me," I said evenly.

She was shivering uncontrollably, whatever terrorized her about to consume her entirely.

I gripped her chin, lifting her violet red-clay eyes to mine. The fear in them filled my gut with acid, just as much as the utter helplessness I felt. I was supposed to protect her.

"Focus on me," I commanded.

She searched my eyes, fear fading as she locked on me like a magnet.

"Take a deep breath," I said.

She did.

A barely-there smile broke. "Good girl."

Fear lingered in the air, muggy and choked. As long as

Abigail focused on me, stayed anchored to my gaze, I knew she wouldn't dissolve into fear.

The words I was planning on saying were, *Who did this? Who are you afraid of?*

"I'm not going to let anyone hurt you, Abigail." My grasp on her chin tightened. "Do you believe me?"

A pause passed like an eternity.

She swallowed. "Yes."

ABIGAIL

Theo ripped apart my room.

"What's going on?" He tore silk and satin pillows off my bed. Outside fireworks had begun to pop, lighting my window in shadowy glows of red, white, and blue.

Theo flipped over my mattress, reached down, and lifted up his suit leg, pulling out a knife. A harsh rip sounded as he dragged it down the middle. Then he laid waste to my satin and quilted pillows.

He'd thrown off his jacket, and it lay as a casualty in the middle of my floor.

Sufficiently satisfied I was hiding nothing in my bed, he turned to me. Feathers floated as snowflakes and fairy dust around him, and he looked like a conqueror amidst them.

"What's going on?" he repeated.

His hair was wild and messy and I wanted to push it out of his eyes. His glare was somehow even more wild. Theo folded his arms, and I ignored the way his biceps popped, how with his shirt rolled to his elbow his veins bulged.

"Nothing," I said.

"Then who gave you that, Abigail? Why did it freak you out?"

"No one. I mean, I don't know." Technically that wasn't a lie.

The muscle in his jaw popped with anger in a much too delicious way. For a minute, I thought he was giving up. Instead, as if suddenly remembering, he took a sharp left. I realized he was heading for *the spot*. The one spot I kept all my secrets, desires, and fears.

Only one person besides me knew about it.

Of fucking course it was him.

I should've changed it.

Panic gripped my stomach, so I did the smart thing...I jumped on his back. He was too wide. I was too small. My legs spread out behind his back, and I clung to his neck. We must have looked ridiculous, me in my bespoke white party dress, him in his suit, utterly ignoring my existence.

He laughed darkly. "Nothing to hide?"

It was useless trying to stop him. I was literally on his *back,* and he carried me like I was a backpack, digging through my room without pause. He bent down, and I climbed higher, looking for leverage. Absently, I noted how tight the muscles on his back had become.

He paused. "What is this?"

I knew what he'd found by the tightening of his muscles even though I couldn't see.

Oh, just my *collection*. So many photos of me. Some of them harmless, and many of them public, but somehow so sinister.

Like the tabloid upskirt photo, but zoomed in at an obscene angle.

The picture of me topless, again zoomed in and with the man in the photo's eyes crossed out in red.

My stalker went into great detail about exactly what he would do to me when we were finally together, but they were all signed off *beloved*, as if he didn't know he was being creepy.

As if... we were a couple.

It was nausea inducing. It was a strange motivation that moves you to keep things like that. Fear that if you don't, no one will believe you when it happens.

When.

"It's nothing," I said quickly, even though I couldn't see what he'd grabbed.

He shucked me off him without effort. I fell to my ass with a minor thud. My heart hammered as Theo thumbed through each one with a torturous meticulousness, pausing occasionally to reread a letter or examine a photo. He gave nothing away in his look.

Slowly, his eyes found mine.

Theo bent down until we were eye to eye, suit stretching across his knees, a kindness in his pale green eyes that made my gut tighten.

"What is this?" he asked again, holding up the stack of papers and photos. His voice was like earlier, as if I were a frightened doe he had to soothe off the road.

I was more terrified of that than any of his cruelty.

I stood up, dusting nonexistent items off my dress. "I'm a Crowne, Theo. Death threats and stalkers kind of come with the package."

I stared into Theo's eyes, acting as if fear wasn't strangling my chest. He got an odd look across his face before folding something and shoving it in his pocket.

I looked at his pocket. "Theo, you can't tell anyone. *Especially* my mom."

His brow furrowed in pity. "She could help, Abigail."

"We're both thinking of the same person, right? Tansy Crowne, the woman who told me my incessant need for attention was exhausting, you know, that one time I had the gall to start my period during the annual Christmas party?"

His nostrils flared, but he nodded. For a moment I thought that was the end of it.

"How long?"

I shrugged. "I don't know." Over a year. No one checked my mail the way they did my grandfather, mom, and siblings'. They didn't think anyone cared about me. And at first I didn't think it was a big deal either. By the time I realized it was too late. I'd tried desperately to keep my last guard, but in the end, he ran when I needed him most.

I had no one to blame but myself.

Theo leaned forward, clear eyes shadowed under his hard brow. "How. Long."

Like I'm going to tell you— "A year."

Theo's eyes softened, and I lived for that moment.

I could forget myself, forget Theo was just as much a threat as the man planting dangerous, lascivious promises atop the hood of my car and in my mailbox.

"You've been dealing with this for a year?" Theo asked softly.

I shrugged and played it off like I always did. "Yeah. Sorry, Theo. Someone beat you to the punch. It's not a big deal."

Just like that, he was rough again. "Not a big deal? Are you fucking kidding me, Abigail?"

"Careful, Theo, it sounds like you might care about me. Are you actually taking your bodyguard duties seriously?"

His glare returned. "You've been keeping this from me?"

"Fuck off, Theo."

The fireworks were reaching their crescendo. *Pop, pop, pop* one after another, until brightness eclipsed the sky, illumining my entire bedroom.

He grabbed my elbow, eyes searching. "What else are you keeping from me?"

Theo didn't mean it *that* way, but my heart pounded, a liar about to be caught. I struggled in his hold. This was too real, too close.

"Let me in, Abigail. Let me protect you."

Time froze, the deafening *pops* faded, and all I saw was Theo. His earnest eyes, blazing by the colorful fireworks' light.

He didn't know how much I wanted that. That was *all* I wanted, but he'd already taken so much from me. I couldn't give him more.

I yanked my arm free with one final, painful tug, stumbling back into my double doors.

Outside my window, drunk girls stumbled on the pier, holding each other for leverage, bottles of champagne gleaming gold beneath the fireworks. Boys with their backs to the massive white yacht also held champagne, but theirs had sparklers shooting white and gold from the bottle.

"The after party is starting," I said instead.

Theo narrowed his eyes. "You hate after parties."

I shrugged. "A lot has changed, Theo."

With my arms behind me, I opened my double doors.

Theo moved to follow me, so I put a hand out. "I don't need a bodyguard to go on my yacht. I don't need *anything* from you."

Because you can't give me what I need, your heart.

Theo's jaw clenched, grinding his teeth, watching me until I disappeared out of my wing.

THIRTEEN

ABIGAIL

One word to describe a Crowne after party? Opulent. Wealth and excess were flaunted like the Louis Vuittons we used once then never again. We were kids raised without any worries or rules, and we stanched our boredom with debauchery.

To my left, three girls hooked arms and jumped off the boat, still in their glittering party dresses. Probably more than some people's entire house payments... but that was the fun of it. In boarding school, I'd once seen a classmate use the back of a MacBook to write his notes, because he'd run out of paper. Now, one girl held a bottle of Cristal in her hand, and their laughter disappeared with the splash.

I kicked off my heels, wishing I'd had time to change. You didn't wear your party clothes unless you planned on ruining them.

"Who let Reject on the boat?"

I paused at my "name," turning to see the First

Daughter doing a line of cocaine as one boy I recognized from some new teen drama did a line off her naked back. She stood up, pressing her nose, and shot me a glare.

Never mind it was *my* family's boat; she never did get over the whole ripping out her extensions thing.

"I really like what you've done with your hair." I did a circle with my hand, gesturing to her hair. Her glare dropped, uncertain. "It's so brave to use rat hair for extensions."

Her hair was a long, luxurious auburn. The best extensions money could buy.

She flipped me off, then leaned in as the teen heartthrob held his phone up to take a selfie, boobs out and all. She stuck her tongue out, holding up a bottle of Cristal. It wouldn't go anywhere save our finstas. There was always an unspoken rule at these parties: never share publicly.

Because as long as we didn't end up on the news, our parents let us do anything.

If we did... well, I served as the cautionary tale.

I moved through the party, noticed and unnoticed at the same time. The Crowne shadow. The *thump thump thump* of electronic music pulsed an upbeat, luxurious music. Designer shoes hung from a chandelier. And a fear twisted in my gut that maybe I should've let Theo stay. What if my stalker was here, somewhere?

No. It was impossible.

He couldn't be *here*. I eyed the guards at our docked yacht's entrance. The after party to the Crowne Fourth of July was the most exclusive party in the world, even more so than the party that preceded it. Even if he'd somehow gotten into the Fourth of July party, he wouldn't get here. Still unsettled, I headed toward the balcony to hopefully watch a drunk idiot make a fool of themselves.

"Abigail..."

I nearly jumped at the voice, then I settled.

"Khalid," I said.

"Call me *Prince*," he said with a gross smile.

I barely stifled my laugh. "No, thanks."

Real-life prince and princesses from places like Dubai and Denmark often attended our parties. Maybe somewhere else that would've been impressive, but in Crowne Point they were just another douche.

"Your hands are empty," he said, noting my lack of drink.

I stared off the balcony toward the horizon. Below us, someone was lighting off what looked like anti-tank weapons, by the rattling *boom* and accompanying tangerine flash in the sky. A sign everyone was getting drunker, and the night was getting darker.

"I see you're putting that Yale degree to good use."

He laughed, but it was empty. The kind people like him use to try and butter me up, as if I wasn't raised around his kind, as if I can't see right through him.

I side-eyed him. "What do you want?"

He laughed again, then slid one arm along the railing, getting closer. "Straight to the point, Abby. I like that."

Then his hand was on the back of my neck, his alcohol-laced breath on my cheek.

I pushed him away.

Ew.

"C'mon, Crowne. You've never said no before. Why start now?"

Sometime in boarding school, someone started the rumor I was easy. I never denied it, because denying it was akin to ratifying the thing. Sort of like with this asshole—the more you say no, the more they hear *yes*.

He came at me again, with more fervor.

So I pushed him with both hands. His drink fell from his grasp, landing on the bottom deck with a shatter. Someone yelled *party foul.*

"So you open your legs for every other guy but not me?" He came back at me, pushed me flat against the railing. "What's the deal, Abby?"

No sooner had Khalid pressed his hand between my legs and fear wrapped its ugly hands around my throat, than he was yanked back. Violently.

Theo.

His name was a sigh of cool relief in my veins.

He held Khalid by the collar, practically lifting him on his tiptoes.

"Don't touch her," he growled.

Khalid rolled his eyes. "Someone fetch a bone; the dog is growling again."

Theo grabbed his other arm, putting it behind his back the way he'd done with Alaric and Geoff, forcing a yelp from Khalid. Anytime Theo acted like this, my heart fluttered. I could get used to it, I thought. I *was* getting used to it, and that was the problem.

Theo shoved Khalid against the railing with so much force the railing shook. "Apologize."

I couldn't imagine a prince, third in line to the throne, saying sorry to anyone, much less a *girl.*

And I was right.

"Fuck off," Khalid gritted.

Theo paused. For a second I thought he'd let Khalid go. Then, in almost slow motion, he bent Khalid's finger back. *Crack.*

Khalid screamed.

Sounding all at once bored and furious, Theo said, "Keep your hands to yourself."

My eyes locked with Theo's, still holding Khalid. The pale green depths were filled with an inscrutable emotion— if I didn't know better, I'd say *need*. There was a fire in them matching the burning sky. Blood rushed fast and furious through my ears. Unintentionally, I wet my lips. His eyes dropped to them.

Theo stepped back. Khalid hung over the railing, using it for support. Theo grasped my elbow somewhat gently, considering what those very hands had just done seconds before. He steered me away from Khalid's moans and the menacing words he yelled at our backs.

He careened me all the way to the front of the boat.

People made out and more on white leather, but I was stuck on Theo.

"You broke his finger." Awe laced my words.

He scoffed. "He got off lucky."

I blinked in surprise. Lucky? What else could Theo do, if provoked?

I pulled my elbow out. "Why are you here?"

He quirked his head to the side. "Hmm... that doesn't *sound* like thank you." He stepped closer, and I took a step back. My back bit into the railing. "Did you really think I would let you out of my sight? After tonight?"

Yes.

No.

I don't know.

"Why do you care? You've made it clear you don't care what happens to me."

"Don't care, Abigail? There's a reason they call me your dog."

"Stop," I said weakly, turning my head away from him.

"Those fights I got in when we were kids?" He gripped my biceps, thrusting me to him. "For you."

I slowly looked back, eyes locked.

"Every single broken bone. Every bloody knuckle. It was all. For. You."

"Stop!" I yelled.

Funny Theo. Sweet Theo. Aggressively *protective* Theo.

It was too much.

"You want to talk about not caring? Look in the fucking mirror. All I've ever done is care about you."

My heart pounded like the *pop pop pop* of fireworks as his grip tightened, pulling me closer until our lips were only separated by the breath of ocean air.

I darted my tongue out to wet my lips, and his eyes dropped to them, hooded.

"Ooooh! Theo and Abigail are about to *fuck*."

I was pulled from Theo's searing gaze to the boat's leather couches where we'd drawn an audience. My classmates and peers made kissing noises at us, and a few made the jerking-off motion.

"Isn't bestiality illegal?" one of them asked.

"You would know," another countered, and the guy who'd asked threw a vape at his head.

"Get the fuck out," Theo practically growled, his grip tightening on my arms painfully. I didn't think they would listen, but they all quickly scrambled off the couches, mumbling something about a rabid dog.

The time it took for them to leave was enough for me to come to my senses.

I pulled out of Theo's grip, but his eyes were back on me, and that was almost worse. They dug through my walls.

"Let me fucking protect you, Abigail."

"You *can't*. You're the one person who can't."

I was always Abigail *Crowne*, and my last name always eradicated anything else about me. Abigail *Crowne* needs her mother's approval. Abigail *Crowne* has no friends because Abigail *Crowne* is a fire starter, an attention seeker, a whore. Abigail *Crowne* hurts before she can hurt.

With Theo, I was always just Abigail.

And that was the problem.

"Abigail—"

"You broke my heart!" I think I yelled, but the sound of fireworks, music, and illegally obtained weapons was so loud I couldn't be sure. "You talk about how you're going to break my heart, but you already did, Theo. You shattered it into a billion pieces."

His grip loosened, eyes wide, lips parted.

I took the opportunity to run. I ran back into the party, into the black and glitter and flashing lights, deep into the pounding music. Away from Theo, from someone who saw *me*, disappearing into a world where no one saw me.

Because that was *truly* safer.

I took another shot of vodka, then slammed the glass down.

I can't believe I told Theo that. *Fuck.*

Slam.

I can only imagine the ways he's going to use it against me.

Slam.

Deciding to forgo the shots and grab a bottle, I carried it with me into the master bathroom. Astonishingly, no one was in the bed, but laughter and giggles trickled out of the bathroom. I saw their shoes before I saw them. Spiky, silver, sparkly heels sticking out of the bubbles. They drank from a champagne bottle, curls sticking to their perfectly done makeup. Only their jewels and shoes were left on their naked bodies.

"Get out," I said, taking a drink, not bothering to hide my glare.

"Um, fuck off, Reject."

They giggled harder.

I vaguely recognized them, the way I vaguely recognized everyone. I think one of them was friends with my sister, or maybe had sat on the face of my brother.

With an exhale, I threw the bottle against the wall. It shattered by their feet. It wouldn't cut them, but it was enough to get them scrambling out of the tub.

"Are you a psycho?" they screamed, bubbles stuck to their artificially tanned skin.

"Um, maybe?" I said in the same annoying tone, bobbing my head like they had.

The door slammed shut behind them and I headed to the balcony.

Fireworks still reflected on the ocean. Laughter was almost as loud as the music. We'd reached the point in the night where clothes had become optional. I hung my arms over the balcony. The water looked blurry, and I felt... off. I attributed it to the alcohol and heartache.

"Abigail."

I turned around at the voice.

I hadn't heard the door open.

A man stood in the bedroom with the same vaguely familiar face everyone here had.

"What do you want?"

A smile speared his lips. "Finally making an introduction... though it's unnecessary. We've met before."

"I've never met you."

He frowned. "You don't remember me?"

I rubbed my head, blinking through the fog. I'd barely had anything to drink—the hell was wrong with me?

"You kissed me. You loved me."

"I think you have me confused—"

That was when I noticed the rose in his hand, like all the other roses terrorizing me this last year. My eyes flashed between that and him. It *couldn't* be him, right? Instinct had me stepping back, clinging to the railing.

"Who are you?"

I knew in my gut, but I still didn't want to believe it. Stalkers are supposed to be ugly warts of a person. He was not. He was beautiful. He reminded me of the boys I'd gone to school with. Perfectly groomed, with soft skin and softer lips, and bright, clear eyes. His light-brown hair had a slight wave to it only professionally done hair could achieve.

In any other situation, I might have found him cute.

"You know me, Abby." He took a step closer. "I was with you at Rosey, Abby. Roses for our time at Rosey." He smiled like what he had said and done was sweet, not absolutely terrifying.

His words hit me like a struck gong, and I gripped the railing harder. I thought back to my time in Switzerland. I'd attended boarding school until age fourteen, my brother fifteen, my sister sixteen, when Dad was barely in the ground and Grandpa thought we should attend public school for "appearances." I'm sure it had nothing to do with his briefly considering politics.

Rosey was a blur of drugs, partying, and going to school hungover. Boys and girls were divided into two campuses, but that hardly kept us apart.

All this time I'd assumed he was some weird, obsessed fan.

He was *one of us?*

"You promised you would stay in touch," he continued. "You wouldn't even accept my friend request. You never followed me back. You *blocked* me."

The music warbled and bent inside itself.

"You give someone like the dog attention and not me? I could give you the world." He traced his knuckles along my jaw. When did he get so close? "You're Abigail Crowne. You deserve so much more."

I tried to focus on the man in front of me. My tongue felt thick. I moved it around my mouth, as if that would help. My head was suddenly fuzzy. I rubbed it but it didn't help.

Suddenly, it came to me.

"Newt?"

A flash of violent anger cracked across his face like lightning, and I sucked in a breath. *"That's* what you remember?"

I knew it was a nickname, but my head was spinning so hard I couldn't remember his real name. His last name was something with an H? Hollingsworth? Hathaway? That didn't sound right...

Newt had gone through a growth spurt. He'd also lost the baby fat. But I saw it now. He was Newt, the boy I'd played spin the bottle with.

Once.

"I've had to watch you all over the news. With other guys. Naked and showing off." The last part he nearly bit off.

"Newt, that was years ago..." Dizzy. I was dizzy. My grip was slipping on the railing. "We were kids."

I *barely* remember you, I almost added.

"Stop fucking calling me that," he snapped and snatched my wrist in a violent grasp. "My name is Ned."

For some reason I couldn't move, couldn't fight him.

All my life I'd wanted to be the center of attention, to be noticed and appreciated. Outside of the shadows.

Newt, or Ned, smiled, his knuckles still on my cheek. "I'll give you the attention a Crowne deserves."

Then everything blurred.

FOURTEEN

THEO

I followed Abigail into the party, but she disappeared. So I grabbed a water and stewed as the disgustingly wealthy became more disgusting.

I broke *her* heart?

I scoffed into my water.

What kind of mental gymnastics was she pulling to think that up?

She'd kissed *me*, promised she'd never leave me, and then the next day I was sent to California. She knew what it meant to promise to never leave me.

She knew.

Didn't she?

I sat up straighter, spotting Abigail coming out of a room, her arm around some guy's neck. Classic Abigail. Pushing me away. Pushing everyone away. Show her a bit of affection, and she runs to a stranger.

"Hey, dog!"

Alaric, Geoff, Khalid, and two other fuckers I vaguely recognized, surrounded me, blocking my view of Abigail.

I raised a brow, lifting my chin at Khalid's swollen finger. "Looking to break some more fingers?"

"I told you, you're dead," Alaric growled.

I looked over their shoulders, finding Abigail again, studying the guy all but carrying her. He looked like everyone else here. Entitled. Soft. Like if we were back in the Middle Ages he'd have an executioner, and that guy would be me.

"Five on one." I eyed all of them. "Feeling brave now?" They glared. Abigail stumbled again.

"Listen..." I said, eyes still on Abigail. "If you're looking to get your ass kicked, let's do it quickly."

They laughed; then, without further pretense, Alaric swung at me.

I dodged it easily.

Next Geoff came at me, then the two fuckers whose names I couldn't remember, then Khalid. I dodged, letting them get tired.

All the while I kept my eyes on Abigail. She couldn't keep her head up, and he was holding a little too tightly to her wrist. How drunk was she?

A sucker punch to the gut from Geoff temporarily distracted me. I grunted, focusing on them, ending it quickly.

Khalid got a broken wrist, Geoff and Alaric broken noses, the nameless idiots a few broken ribs. When I'd finished with them, we'd gathered an audience, and they lay on the ground, moaning.

They all got off easy.

"Last warning," I said. "Find me again, you're dead."

I wiped my bloody nose, looking for Abigail. I might

have a black eye, and my ribs would hurt, but they were still rich boys relying on privilege to win their fights. They didn't know what to do with someone like me, someone who not only fought back but knew how to fight.

I looked for Abigail and just barely found her before she left the boat. She stumbled, her head lolling to the side.

That was when I intervened.

The guy gave me one look before trying to brush me aside. "Get out of here, dog."

I ignored him. "Abigail?"

She barely lifted her head, eyes glassy. "Theo." She smiled brightly when she said my name.

That more than anything made me suspicious. Had she been drugged?

"Abigail, how much have you had to drink?" I narrowed my eyes, trying to see how dilated her pupils were.

"I like it when you glare at me." She said it like it was a secret, giggling.

Definitely drugged.

My attention turned to the fucker holding her. "What the fuck did you give her?"

"He's giving me roses, Theo. I think he likes me. I wish you liked me."

A heartbeat hung in the air. I didn't have a minute to contemplate her confession, because I was too busy realizing this guy was *the* guy. I thought he was another date-raping privileged fucker who didn't understand the meaning of the word *no*, like the assholes I'd just reacquainted with my fists.

He was the fucker terrorizing her?

His eyes widened, then he dropped her. He fucking dropped her. I grabbed her by the waist before she hit the floor, holding her up. He sprinted out the door, pushing drunken and high revelers out of his way, heading for the dock.

Everything in me wanted to run after him. But if I let Abigail go, she would fall. Or worse, go to the hands of someone like Khalid. So I watched him run, memorizing everything about him. Chestnut hair. Blue eyes. About five foot eleven. Cleft chin.

Abigail leaned into me, murmuring something I couldn't hear. I attempted to get her walking, but she was fading fast.

I lifted her into my arms. Her head fell to my shoulder, arms around my neck, burying her head in the crook of my neck. I couldn't help but think about how nice she smelled, how good she fit in my arms, and how fucked the reason for holding her was.

Her asshole peers made whooping noises as I carried her out. Bright flashes went off, taking pictures.

When we got to her room, Abigail fell to the bed easily, already asleep. I made sure her head was situated properly on her pillow. She hadn't worn shoes, and the bottoms of her feet were dirty. I wondered if they'd hurt at all tonight.

An ache in my chest formed that I quickly ignored.

She was like a princess amid all the downy silk sheets. Her dark brown hair curled around her face.

I pushed away a stray strand, pausing.

Eyelashes fell on soft cheeks, and her pouty lips parted for hushed breaths. She didn't look wicked when she slept. Could she really have been hurting all this time?

I tried to shake off the thought, but it lingered.

Still caressing her cheek, I looked at her secret spot that housed a box filled with piles upon piles of pictures of Abigail. Alone, the pictures were mundane, but by the hundreds, they were downright sinister.

I stepped back, fiddled with the notes in my pocket, thinking of the disgusting promises that asshole had made.

That he'd nearly been able to make good on.

This was my fault.

I let her run. I let the shit between us come before her safety.

Never again. *Nothing* would come before Abigail, not even my heart.

A few hours later, when dawn was just breaking gray in the sky, there was a knock on the door to Abigail's wing. I stood off the wingback, stiff from watching Abigail for hours.

I left one of the double doors open so I could still see her.

Tansy Crowne stood in the doorway, as if she didn't even want to step one foot in the wing. One perfectly plucked brow arched. "I assume this is important."

"Abigail needs more security," I said, getting straight to the point.

She laughed, closemouthed. "Abigail needs a lot of things. More attention isn't one of them."

I eyed the box I'd set on a gold-and-glass coffee table, preparing for Tansy's arrival. I'd had a bereft hope when I called for Tansy that maybe I could convince her with a simple plea. Abigail kept her secrets in a box for a reason. She acted like she doesn't want her mother's approval, but it's the one thing she wants above all else. If I told Tansy, I was betraying her.

I lifted the box for Tansy, filling her in on everything as Tansy flipped through it with bored disinterest. It was a betrayal, and I hoped it was worth it. The thought of what would have happened to Abigail had I not been there…

Tansy was quiet after she reached the bottom, her eyes ever calculating; then she spoke. "Did you tell anyone else?"

"No."

Tansy nodded. "We can hardly afford any more bad press."

It was moments like these I was reminded with a dousing of ice cold water to my spine how different I was. You could almost think you were like them, and then they said shit like this. I told her her daughter had been drugged, almost carted off to God knows where, and her mind was on shit like the *press*.

"Abigail needs more security," I said again, trying to keep the venom out of my voice.

She flipped back through the photos. "Mmm…"

"You can afford a small army for your other children, but I'm here telling you someone wants to harm your youngest, and you don't care?"

"Where were you when all of this supposed drama was happening?" She lifted her head, pinning me with her gray eyes, taking in the dried blood on my shirt, the bruise forming around my eye.

Tansy had never liked me.

She glared when I didn't immediately avert my eyes. I exhaled, looking away. *You're not supposed to look a Crowne in the eye.* It was the rule all servants followed on threat of punishment, being fired—or worse. Me? I've always been in the gray.

I wasn't a servant when Abigail picked me up. Now… now I'm something in between.

Even Beryl Crowne didn't always have me follow the rule.

Tansy smiled and went back to photos she'd already seen.

I should've ended it there.

"Are you going to be so calm when your daughter is raped and left for dead?"

She cut herself on the corner of a photo with a barely audible hiss.

Slowly her eyes landed on mine.

"Abigail is not the sweet girl you make her out to be, Theo Hound. I thought you knew that most of all." She didn't bother stopping the blood. It dripped onto the photos. "When she was eleven, she skinned her own knee to get my affection. When she was twelve, she bled through her party dress and started a scene. When she was fifteen, well..." Her eyes pinned me, Abigail's fifteen-year-old attention grab. "What makes you so certain Abigail isn't behind this?"

Tansy left me with that question; however, she took a few of the photos and notes. I stared at the closed doors, hoping she would at least look into it.

Whoever he was, he had money and power. This went beyond some crazed fan's imagination. He had the means to make fantasy a reality.

The most chilling part about it was that every letter is signed off *your beloved*. The photos are written alongside letters as if he was there with her, two couples going shopping together, or going for ice cream on a date.

It's clearly a love letter, so what will happen if he can't make the fantasy a reality? If it all comes crashing down?

Abigail was already starting to sit up when I got back. I went to her side, pressing her chest and telling her to lie down.

She pressed a hand to her head. "What happened?"

"That's what I'm trying to figure out. You were

drugged—"

Abigail cut me off with a gasp. I thought it was about her being fucking drugged, but then her eyes widened on me, soft fingers coming to my split lip.

"Theo..." Her words were plush, almost as much as her touch trailing my cheek, down to the blood staining my collar. She tried to get up again, so I pressed harder on her chest.

She rubbed three fingers at my lip like she wanted to wash away the blood and pain. I shouldn't like it. I definitely shouldn't remember all the times she *had* washed away the blood.

"I don't like you getting in fights," she said, fingertips dancing lightly around the circumference of the bruise.

"Only for you, sweet girl."

She lowered her hands, eyes down, working her now bloodstained fingers.

"Who was he, Abigail?" I asked softly.

She rolled her lips, eyes finding a gold-encrusted clock. "I need to get ready for France."

"Paris? That's what you're worried about?"

"And Spain. Switzerland. I'm worried my siblings are packed and ready to go, and my mother is once again going to point out *I'm* not."

I let her stand.

She walked around her room in a wrinkled party dress, clearly still disoriented. It tugged on my chest, and I wanted to help her.

I tangled my hands in my hair. "Who the fuck was that?"

"I don't know. I was drugged, remember? Have you seen my suitcase?" She exhaled. "This isn't my job... where *the fuck* is Story?"

"I know you're lying."

No one batted an eye when he had Abigail on his arm. There weren't a lot of rules at those parties, but one was written in stone: only the invited were allowed. Some average loser fan wasn't going to weasel his way in.

Everyone knew everyone, so Abigail knew him.

"Why won't you just fucking let me in?"

She froze, looking over her shoulder at me with a wrinkle in her brow.

There was no reason for her to let me in, no reason for me to want it. Not anymore. Yet my chest still pounded with almost losing her, and I couldn't get what she'd said to me on the boat out of my head. It was rough and raw in my voice.

She looked away and continued packing.

I fiddled with the bracelet in my pocket. Abigail said I broke her heart, but she left me. She ditched me after taking me in and making me think I belonged somewhere, finally. For no fucking reason. One minute she was kissing me, the next I was gone.

I'd remember the day forever. When I learned I was being sent away, I figured a few thousand miles was nothing.

I'm going to California, Abigail.

Good. Don't ever fucking talk to me again.

Then she slammed the door.

She'd made me feel safe, she'd made me feel like I could let down my walls, and then she'd gutted me.

Anger rose hot and acidic up my throat.

"I don't know what the hell you think happened, Abigail." I tossed the bracelet on the stand. It landed with a clack. "But *you* abandoned *me*."

FIFTEEN

THEO

The Crowne family jet was just one of many they owned. It was over $500 million, paid for by Crowne Industries, and used mostly for shit like this—holidays. Every summer after the Fourth of July they went on vacation, ending with a few days with their grandfather in Switzerland. It used to be Abigail's favorite time of the year; now she looked at the massive plane with melancholy.

A pang of guilt hit me.

"You're late," Tansy said, arms folded, standing at the foot of the grand staircase leading to the open doors of the plane. The ocean was a steely-blue line beyond the emerald manicured lawn and tarmac that was the Crowne Hall landing strip.

Abigail sighed, not bothering to explain herself, following her mother up the steps.

Inside, Gray had already kicked up his feet, remote in hand, video game on one of the many razor thin televisions inside the plane. Next to him, a girl sat, hands in her lap, eyes down.

Abigail zeroed in on her, jaw dropping like she was going to do a classic Abigail outburst, but then Tansy stepped in the way.

"I'm sure I don't need to worry about you this time," Tansy said, eyes thinning to a glare. Abigail closed her mouth, nodding, and Tansy headed to the master bedroom in the back, where she would take a cocktail of pills and wake up when we landed.

I briefly wondered what had happened when I was away to make Tansy say that.

Abigail sat down, eyes on the girl next to Gray. Though she was vaguely familiar, she didn't look like Gray's usual conquests, with their professionally blown-out hair and even more blown-out lips. Nearly every inch of her cocoa skin was covered in fabric, from her wrists to her neck, like she'd stepped out of the Victorian era. Her curly hair was done up in a bun, but stray spirals fell in a halo across her face.

For some reason, Abigail fumed.

"Did she break your heart too?" I asked.

Abigail flinched, then turned her attention to a huge round window. There were many like it on the plane, letting in bright-white light. I drummed my fingers along my knee. Sunlight was an ethereal line along her profile.

I knew I should let it go. She was just trying to get under my skin the way I'd been getting under hers.

"How exactly did I break your heart?" I prodded.

Abigail stood abruptly, not bothering to look at me. I quickly followed. She walked past Gray playing his video game. Gray yelled when she blocked his view. She walked through the dining room, past Gemma on her phone and

Horace picking something out of his nail, until she reached the bathroom.

She held the door open, glare sharp. Behind her vanity lights were hot white and a marble countertop held every assorted accoutrement the rich could possibly need.

I placed my hand on the doorframe. "What the hell do you think happened? What story have you been telling yourself?"

"I have to pee." She slammed the door in my face, forcing me to jump back.

Abigail was in the bathroom for an hour, until Gemma knocked to be let in. I leaned against the opposite wall the entire fucking time, grinding my teeth.

"What did you eat?" Gemma yelled, slamming her fist.

The door flew open as Gemma was about to slam her fist again. Gemma fell forward, stumbling and almost falling on white marble just as Abigail walked out.

"There are other bathrooms," Abigail snapped.

"This is *my* part of the plane," Gemma huffed, fixing her blonde waves.

Abigail walked by me like I was nothing more than a painting or the on-plane fireplace they lit during the winter.

"Abigail—"

"It's in the past. It's over. Stop bringing it up."

"God fucking dammit, just stay still." I slammed my hands, bracketing her. Next to us, a vase of freshly cut flowers shook. Too hard. Too loud. Gray shot us a barely curious look, and the girl he was with did too, but she quickly averted her eyes.

I lifted my hands.

"I saw you with her," she said. "After I kissed you, you told Gemma you loved her, just like everyone else."

She *saw* that?

But I didn't have time to dwell, because Abigail was on the move again, determined to walk all six thousand square feet of this fucking plane.

I caught up to her, whispering low as we passed Gray, "It's not what you think."

"I heard you say *I love you!*" she yelled, spinning on me. "You can't trick me on this, Theo."

So fuck being private?

Gray threw his remote to the side, crossing his arms overhead. "Okay, this is way more interesting than demolishing eleven-year-olds."

Abigail shot Gray a look, then kept walking, picking up the pace.

"Stop, no, come back," Gray said without any vehemence, grabbing the controller out of the girl's lap.

"I wasn't saying that to *her*. I was saying that about *you*."

Abigail stopped in her tracks and I nearly ran into her shoulder. I thought I was about to get through to her, but then she steeled herself again, shooting me a glare.

"How dumb do you think I am?"

"Abigail—"

"Tea?" A stewardess appeared with a plate of small, steaming cups and rolled white cotton. "Or towel?"

Are you fucking kidding me? I nearly dragged my hands down my face.

Abigail affected a smile. "Thank you."

She took a cup of tea and headed back over to the couch Gray was sitting on. Gray eyed Abigail before going back to his video game. There was an unwritten rule on the Crowne jet: all of the Crownes kept to their own section of the plane.

I stood between the fully stocked bar and a couch, watching Abigail just a few feet away. I was at an impasse.

All this time, all this trauma and trouble, was because she'd *overheard* that night I went to Gemma?

There was a part of me, a very ugly, jagged, and calcified part, that said to ignore it, to continue on as I had. It didn't erase the years of heartbreak. It didn't erase what she'd done—she'd sent me away without bothering to ask my side of the story.

But I also couldn't ignore what it *did* do.

It gave me a reason. All this time I thought she'd abandoned me for nothing.

Abigail used Gray as a shield. It was already hard enough ripping my heart out of the concrete vines it grew. If there was one person in this world I didn't want to watch, it was Gray fucking Crowne. The guy thought I was worse than gum beneath his shoe.

I dragged my hand through my waves. "I knew we couldn't be together."

At my voice, Abigail looked up from her tea, surprise written across her features.

"A guy like me, with someone like you, Abigail? I was your dog. I was only good enough to sleep at the foot of your bed."

"Yup," Gray said, without taking his eyes off his video game.

"Theo—"

I waved a hand, silencing her. I had to get this out.

"You weren't just my best friend, Abs. You were the best thing that ever happened to me. I couldn't lose you... but if I loved you, I would. Every day with you I got closer to telling you the truth and ruining everything. When you kissed me?"

For a minute I'd let myself believe I was worthy of love. Let myself believe she might not abandon me.

I exhaled, shaking my head at the memory. When I looked up, our eyes locked across the small space.

"I just wanted to go back to being your friend—*needed* us to go back. I knew if I told Gemma what I felt, she'd give me the truth. She might stand a chance of fixing what I felt before it was too late."

"What did she say?" Her fingers clasped the porcelain cup, joints white.

"That I wasn't worthy of thinking those thoughts about you, let alone saying them aloud. She was right. She reminded me how lucky I was to just stand next to you."

Abigail opened her mouth, but it was my turn to leave. At least five miles in the air, I could be certain the man who wanted to harm her wasn't aboard. In a plane bigger than most houses, I could keep my distance.

Even still, I made sure she was always in my sights.

Abigail was oddly quiet. Maybe thirty minutes passed, and she didn't so much as grumble, even when Gray elbowed her as he played his game.

When Gemma came in from the back of the plane, Abigail tracked her. I could see the tension rising in her neck. Gemma went to the cockpit, probably to ask on flight time. She had a bottle of wine in one hand and glass in the other, laughing at something the captain had said.

"Why is Story with you?" Abigail sniped, eyes still on Gemma.

"Who?" Gray asked.

"My *servant*."

That's when I realized why she was so familiar. When I lived at Crowne Hall, I'd seen her around, though five years had shaved some of the youth from her features, and she hadn't been Abigail's girl then.

Gray glanced at the girl to his left like he'd just noticed her for the first time. At the attention, the girl's eyes widened like a bug under a magnifying glass.

"You took her from me. She doesn't belong to you."

Gray shrugged, eyes back on his video game. "Tell me her favorite food, and you can have her back."

Abigail sputtered. "Are you kidding? Can you name any of your servants' favorite *food*?"

Gray shook his head, an amused smile on his face. The girl rolled her lips, watching Gray.

"This is so. Fucking. Ridiculous," Abigail practically screamed. She stood up, eyes still on Gemma, closing the distance between them.

I knew before she'd reached her, Abigail was going to explode, so I was already standing up.

"Bitch." Abigail shoved Gemma. Gemma stumbled into the cockpit, hitting the back of the captain's chair. The plane wobbled, the wine in Gemma's hand miraculously unspilled.

"Take this out of here or we'll have to land," the captain said.

"What the fuck?" Gemma looked at Abigail.

"You ruin *everything*."

The pilot said something again about taking it out of the cockpit, but Abigail was blind. She shoved Gemma again just as I reached her, grasping her by the elbow.

"What did I do to make you hate me so much?" Abigail demanded, tears in her eyes.

"Hi, stealing the words out of my mouth!" Gemma said.

Abigail lunged with so much force she slipped out of my grasp. They were at each other, tearing at their hair. I put myself between them, but they still managed to get at each other.

Only Abigail would start a catfight five miles in the sky.

Abigail slapped Gemma, knocking the bottle of wine from her hand. It flew in a spiral arc toward the front of the cockpit. In retaliation, Gemma threw her glass at Abigail. I blocked the brunt of it, so it got in my hair, stained my shirt and jeans. The captain yelled as the bottle finished its trajectory against the front of the cockpit, shattering against the window and spilling onto the controls, some even splashing back onto us.

"Abigail Genevieve!" Tansy yelled, and it all came to a stop.

Tansy stood in the doorway to the cockpit. It was one of the rare times you saw Tansy Crowne not entirely made up. She had an emerald silk mask around her neck, matching silk pajamas, and her hair tied in a scarf.

She closed her eyes, taking a deep breath. "Last year you threw a fit because a *few* of your things were forgotten..."

"It was my entire wardrobe. I had nothing to wear. I had to go shop and replace everything—"

She opened her eyes, pinning Abigail. "*Hush.* Are you incapable of going even *one hour* without making a scene?"

Ever calm and collected Tansy Crowne looked on the verge of explosion. Her cream hands in tight, white fists, her jaw clenched.

"We'll need to make a landing, Mrs. Crowne," the pilot said. "There's wine on the dash. We'll take you back to Crowne Point."

"Landing?" Tansy asked, a frown making what little lines she had on her face pop.

"But we've barely been in the air," Gemma said, then turned to Abigail. "I hope you're fucking happy."

"I won't be happy until you're dead," Abigail yelled.

The fighting nearly started up again, so I pulled Abigail away from her family, away from everything, all the way into a secluded bedroom.

The pounding of my heart was louder than the engines and wheels of the plane as the pilot began the descent.

"It's her fault," Abigail said, staring at the door.

"What's her fault, Abigail?" My words were quiet. It felt like a secret, one we'd been holding in for far too long.

She kept staring at the door, so I cupped her neck and cheek, turning her to me. Her eyes settled on mine.

"All of it," she finally said, but like there was more she'd wanted to say. "What do you mean I abandoned you?"

My grasp on her neck and cheek tightened, my thumb fanning to encase her entire jaw.

"You sent me away to California, Abigail," I replied, the memory still stinging. I stroked her jaw with my thumb, kept my grip on her neck possessive. "You left me. You took me in and then abandoned me just like my fucking mother. At the time, I didn't know why, but now I do. You saw me with Gemma—"

"I didn't send you away," she cut me off, eyes wide. "You were my best friend. You were all I had. I loved you... even if you didn't love me."

A weighted pause followed her words, our eyes locked. I didn't know if I could believe her, if I *wanted* to believe her.

If Abigail didn't send me away, then who did?

Before I could think too long on *who* had actually sent me away, turbulence jostled the plane. Both Abigail and I lost our footing. I fell backward into a black leather chair, catching Abigail in my lap. The plane steadied, but neither of us moved.

She pulled the bracelet she'd given me out of her pocket.

I thought she would've thrown it away.

"I always assumed you left me," she said, fiddling with the beads. "Because you wanted my sister and were tired of pretending to like me."

Her quiet confession cut through me. All this time she'd been hurting just like I had.

I stroked my thumb across her cheek. "Sweet girl, I would never leave you, not willingly, not unless I had to."

Her eyes found mine, lips parted. Warmth radiated from her clay eyes, affection a luminous glow. My eyes landed on her lips, when all at once she jumped off me. She took two quick steps back until she was almost at the door.

"I-I don't believe you, Theo."

There wasn't determination in her voice; if anything, she sounded afraid. She tugged on the bracelet, pulling the beads apart, the white twine shiny.

I tilted my head. "Yes, you do."

She mashed her lips together, eyes darting around the room. I stood up, walking to her leisurely, grasping her wrist and anchoring her attention on me.

"This could all be another elaborate trick," she said, allowing me to drag her into my embrace.

I don't know if I was ready to completely forget five years of resentment and pain. When your view of someone is stained in heartbreak, it's hard to completely wash that away, even if that view is wrong.

But love or hate, I couldn't go another minute without Abigail.

"Could be," I admitted.

I rubbed my nose along her cheek slowly, her sharp inhales spiking my heart rate.

"You say you... *care*... about me, and you don't actually like my sister, and you even tattoo me, yet you wear someone else's bracelet—"

I crushed my lips against hers, quick and harsh, shutting her up. Enough to bruise and leave her breathless.

When I pulled back, her eyes were hooded, locked on mine.

I thumbed her bitten-red lower lip. "*You* gave me that bracelet."

SIXTEEN

ABIGAIL

Theo was in my room.

A nervous laugh bubbled out of me. I quickly smothered it with the back of my hand, trying to pretend it was a
cough.

Theo shot me a curious look, the one that said he saw
right through me, then turned from me, busying himself
with something I couldn't see on my nightstand. Grateful
for the momentary respite from him, I breathed.

Mother was furious we had to reschedule the flight. It
appeared no serious damage was done, yet a full top-to-
bottom inspection had to be done before we could fly out,
which meant a night back at Crowne Hall. A night alone
with Theo...

I fiddled with the bracelet on my wrist. All these years
I'd wondered *who* gave him the bracelet. Making up ridiculous stories like he had a girlfriend he pined for, or a long-
lost soul mate, and all this time it was *me*?

My heart cracked open.

For all his bluster, Theo hurt the most.

Another laugh threatened to burst.

I was acting ridiculous, like he hadn't been here a thousand times before.

He'd replaced the light bulb on the light not inches from him.

Theo Hound had been in my room more than anyone. As a best friend. As an enemy. And each time, he was the only person guarding my door. Now... as a lover? The thought seized my throat.

What would he think? I wouldn't be good enough. I never was. Not for Mom or Grandpa, not for the world, definitely not for *him*. I didn't have practice in this. I should've practiced. *Why didn't I practice?* Maybe he would be fine with just oral.

I could *do* oral.

I was so busy weighing the pros and cons of presenting my just-oral-for-life idea that I didn't notice he'd left my nightstand and come before me.

"Hey." Theo pushed my hair behind my ear, and I nearly jumped at the contact. He laughed, but it was soft and low. "You're so transparent."

I looked away, mumbling, "Only to you."

"Good," he practically growled. The way he spoke, as much as the meaning behind the words, curled my gut.

He grasped my chin, lifting my eyes to his. I leaned on my tiptoes, angling for his lips, wetting my own. His burning, pale eyes dropped to them and his breath warmed my mouth. I could practically taste him.

"Show me your art," he said against my lips.

I tried to ignore the flutter of him calling my found jewelry *art*. Garbage, junk, those were words I'd expect...

but art? Only in my dreams. I didn't bother questioning *how* he knew I still made jewelry. That was Theo; he always saw into me. What I did wonder was *why the fucking fuck now?* I was still on my tiptoes angling to kiss him, and I could feel him against my hip—*hard*.

I blinked, bringing the hazy room back into view.

"Now?" I asked.

A slow grin curved his right lip, melting my insides like butter, and then he nodded. He released my chin, and I walked in a trance to grab the box where I kept my secrets and jewelry.

"I think that's the first time you've listened to me," he said to my back.

"Don't get used to it."

After grabbing my jewelry box, I turned around. Theo was in the process of tearing off his wine-stained hoodie. I nearly dropped the porcelain box to the floor. As if in slow motion, he revealed his body to me.

Theo had always been muscular.

But oh *my* God.

I tilted my head, pushing my tongue into the muscle of my cheek. He slowly revealed the ridges of his cut eight pack, his tapered waist leading my eyes to his sculpted Adonis belt, which disappeared beneath jeans slung low on his hips. I licked my lips, too easily imagining where those toned vee muscles led.

"A guy could get addicted to the way you look at him."

I quickly busied myself with my box.

Theo laughed. "Is Abigail Crowne *shy*?"

My cheeks heated, and I lifted the box to cover it. "I'm not *shy*."

I'm petrified.

But Theo doesn't get to know that.

I kept fiddling, pretending like it took more than one second to open a fucking box. Art, that's what I was focused on. Not Theo's abs.

Rigid. Cut. *Hot.*

Suddenly his lips were at my ear, and I couldn't breathe.

"I promise..." He spoke the words of our game, trailing off as his teeth grazed my ear, barely a bite, the pain a shiver of its own promise for more. "I'll take all night fucking you."

He ended on a growl that vibrated through me. My hands shook. His breath was hot on my skin, his body hard against my back.

"I promise by the time I'm done with you, you'll be ruined for everyone but me."

Breathe. Remember to breathe.

When his tongue caressed the tip of my ear, I dropped the box entirely. He grabbed it, reflexes so fast, but didn't cease licking me, kissing me, sucking on me, until the room faded, and all I knew was him.

When he was done devouring my ear, and I was sufficiently putty, he handed the porcelain box back to me.

"But we'll go at your pace, nice and slow."

He grinned, then made his way to my bed. Feathers from my massacred pillows lingered on the floor, and my mattress was askew on the frame, but he lay on it without so much as a blink, and something about that made him even *hotter*, sitting among his carnage like nothing.

There was something in my hands. I looked at my jewelry with foreign interest. Why did I have this? What was my name again?

Oh. Right.

I took a seat on the edge of my destroyed bed, afraid my

legs would stop working. *Jewelry*, I said to myself, *show Theo my jewelry*. I repeated it like a mantra.

"Do you know why I want to go slow?" I didn't respond, but he didn't care. "Seeing you like this is fucking hot, Abigail. It's the greatest foreplay. Wide-eyed and without walls. No more lies. But that lip." He zeroed in on it. "Bite it again and I might change my mind."

My eyes met his as he adjusted himself. There went my thoughts again. Even through his jeans, I could see the outline of him.

I wetted my lips. "Aren't your jeans wet?"

"Are you trying to get me naked, Abigail?"

"No," I said too quickly. He was still drenched in wine and it had to be uncomfortable—*maybe* a naked Theo crossed my mind.

His grin spread. All white teeth. Somehow both sweet and vicious, carnal and loving. All *Theo*. I nearly sighed. I missed his smiles.

Theo slid his zipper down—an act that was far too sensual—then slipped out of his jeans and tossed them to the floor. I briefly thought about all the stains. Dark wine on my perfect white satin sheets, now on my plush feathery rug. I loved it. A dark, twisty part of me wanted the memory of him forever.

Theo grabbed a joint from his discarded jeans, and with the *snick* of the match, something inside me lit ablaze as well.

A *joint*.

I swallowed, trying not to read too much into it.

He was in nothing but satin-looking gray briefs, and once again I was distracted. They clung to roped thighs, and if I thought he was hard in his jeans, it was nothing to now.

My throat dried.

His laugh filled the room like the butterflies in my stomach.

I forgot showing him my jewelry. I forgot everything. Theo had one arm folded behind his head, bicep popping and carved, muscles I didn't even know catching the fading sunlight. Wine drenched strands of hair, dripping down onto his full lip, as he smoked with his free hand.

He blew out a puff, watching me with an intensity that stunned me, drew me in, until it was nothing but us.

Theo Hound *was* art.

Hedonist. Hellish. Art.

I dropped my jewelry, and it fell with a clatter of beads and sea glass and silver to the floor. I crawled atop him. He kept smoking, blowing in and out, but if it was possible, the look in his eyes sharpened further. Musky smoke enveloped us in a warm haze, softening us, but through it all, his eyes were clear.

I stopped just before his jaw, his sharp, smooth jaw. Nerves strangled my stomach. I could feel him hard and digging into my stomach. This was *Theo*. This wasn't some random asshole. I cared desperately what Theo thought of me.

Heat blazed in his eyes.

I wanted to kiss him so badly.

So of course I distracted myself.

"I don't remember," I said. It was barely a whisper. Theo arched a brow at my non sequitur. "Giving you this bracelet," I explained.

He blew out smoke. "You were small."

His hand settled casually yet possessively on the back of my thigh, just beneath my ass. I swallowed air. I wanted him so badly I felt like I was going to combust. All the while Theo just watched me.

As if the memory came back to him, a small smile tugged his lips. "Little Abigail Crowne, in black jeans, a fur vest, and leather boots... an outfit that cost so much it could probably get me off the streets. You know what I remember most?"

His thumb grazed the underside of my ass. Slowly. Easily.

"What?" I couldn't breathe.

"You had the same fucking look in your eyes. Lonely..." His eyes softened. "But so damn tenacious. I thought you were going to hand me money, but you gave me a fucking bracelet. I was hungry, so I was pretty pissed."

As he told the story, it came back to me. We'd spent the day at Crowne Point Day Camp, a nonprofit camp set up by Mom and Dad. It was only for appearances, and the last time I ever went somewhere like that, but I got to make a friendship bracelet. I didn't have a best friend to give the bracelet to, but I loved the thing. It was the first thing that was *mine*, not Abigail Crowne's, but *mine*. Still, when I saw him, I wanted to give it to him. I don't know why. Maybe my heart knew what my mind didn't.

I guess I'd latched on to that feeling, even if I didn't remember its inception. From that point on I made jewelry until I reached an age where I had to start hiding it from my mother.

A Crowne isn't a petty craftsman.

I did it in secret, and it saved me. I was so young—so young I forgot Theo—all I remembered was that feeling. I forgot the boy who played an integral part of the dream that saved me from disappearing into Abigail Crowne.

I stared at him with newfound amazement.

His thumb traveled higher, into my linen floral shorts

and sliding over my panties, and I could barely get out my next words. "You kept it."

"I kept it."

His thumb disappeared too soon, now using the arm to wrap around my waist, sliding me higher, pushing me against his dick.

Hard.

Rock hard. And he felt like heaven between my legs, hitting that aching spot, making me ache even more but in a delicious way.

I couldn't stop the moan that dripped from my lips. At the sound, he pressed his head against my headboard and groaned. I think I could get addicted to that sound. Rough, a little strangled and pained. My eyes dropped to his lips, waiting to hear it again.

"Condom?" he asked, voice rough. His head was still against my quilted headboard, only dropping his gaze to meet mine.

"I don't have any condoms," I said. "I mean... I just... I never..."

I mean, I did, but I bought them when I was sixteen.

Theo lifted his head, brow furrowing. "You're really a virgin?"

I looked away. "If we're going by heteronormative norms, but I've done everything else so—"

His lips were on mine.

He tasted like wine and smoke and sex, like some heathen god. His kiss was soft but unyielding, and it was over too soon. He broke off, my eyes still closed.

"You just said heteronormative." He caressed my cheek with the knuckle of the hand that held his joint. "Careful, Abigail, someone might figure out there's more to you."

I didn't get a chance to respond, because then his hand

disappeared from my waist, and he was sliding up my thigh, into my shorts, fingers pushing aside my panties, spreading me. Breath left me in gusts, my fists curling into his chest.

God, the way he watched me... it was intoxicating. He drank me in like the wine clinging to his skin, registering my smallest movements, the quietest sigh. All with one finger, all while he smoked, the air growing thicker and hazier.

Every bit of his focus was on me, and that made me feel worthy.

"Please." I wasn't sure what I was asking for, but I knew I needed *something*.

His green eyes narrowed slightly, a barely-there smile hooking his right cheek.

"Abigail Crowne." He stamped out the joint on my nightstand, eyes still locked. "There's no going back from this."

SEVENTEEN

THEO

We collided like atoms.

Tongue, teeth, and bruising lips. Abigail ripped at my clothes, tearing and stretching my shirt, fingers flying from my hair to my shoulders, nails biting into my flesh.

It's so fucking hot.

It's not right.

"Slow, sweet girl," I said softly against her lips, pressing her down on my cock, spreading her thighs around my hips.

I was aching to be inside her, but this is her first time —*our* first time. The night can't end quick and dirty. So even if we explode into a billion pieces tomorrow, when she puts them back together, I'll be inside her forever.

"I'm not going anywhere," I said. "Let me make you feel good."

I kissed Abigail like I should've years ago, memorizing her with my tongue, marking her with my bite, not even breaking as we shoved her shorts past her hips. I couldn't help my smile when she finally got out of them, tossing them to the feathered floor. For the world, Abigail was black and red lace. For me... she's cotton polka-dot panties.

Next went her silky shirt, thrown over her head. My touch feathered the clasp of her bra, still tonguing and consuming her even as the lace slipped off her shoulders, falling to the bed.

I froze.

Fuck.

Shit.

I'd imagined Abigail since the day she picked me up—got a view of it briefly when she threw her pajamas at me—but it was never like this. Without anger, willingly, about to give me everything.

She's everything.

Soft, so soft, with a smattering of barely-there freckles along breasts perfect to palm and massage and suck and *bruise*. I ground my jaw, fighting the urge to flip her beneath me, slam my dick into her, and taste every inch right then.

Tonight we'd go slow, tonight she sets the pace.

"I know it's nothing you haven't seen already..." She trailed off. "You and everyone else..." Abigail looked away, swallowing.

I traced the bob of insecurity she could never hide from me, gliding my finger from her throat, down between her breasts, until I could edge the cotton seam of her panties. Her breathing picked up with my movements, and goose bumps pebbled her breasts.

Gorgeous. Distracting. I'd map them with my tongue, then lick them away, one by one.

But she still wouldn't look at me.

I lifted her chin, dragging her to me, our foreheads

pressed, until I could taste her truth like sweet candy on my tongue.

All I've ever wanted was to make Abigail feel safe, special. To give her a taste of what she gave me.

I captured her lips, and say against them, voice hoarse, "No one has seen this."

Don't hide from me, I nearly say. *With me, you're perfect. With me, you're always enough.*

But something stops me. Feathers floated around us, the discarded reminder that not everything is perfect.

Our eyes connected and I gripped her ass with both hands, hiking her up my body, slamming her lips against mine. It was faster, more furious. Even though she was still in panties, she was so wet, getting all over my fucking cock, drenching my gray underwear black. I slid my hands up her thighs, stretching her panties, spreading the cotton between her pussy lips and rubbing it against her clit until she broke from our kiss on a groan that went straight to my dick.

"Fuck, Abs," I said, dragging her bottom lip out with my teeth. "Get out of these goddamn panties."

I sucked on her neck, watching as she shimmied out of them. Each movement rubbed against my dick. I wonder if I've been dropped into a dream as Abigail slowly revealed her round, peachy ass. When her pussy spread on my thigh as she kicked off the last of her polka dot panties, I'm sure of it.

Abigail fucking Crowne, spread, naked, and all *mine.* I didn't give her a second to breathe, crushing her back against me. I slid my finger into her pussy from behind, priming her for my dick.

She gasped at the fullness, before biting down on my neck. *Hard.*

I groaned.

Fuck.

I want her marks all over me.

I teased another finger near her entrance, smearing her wetness all over my finger, all over *her*. She pushed back on me with a whimper that made my dick punch at the seams of my gray boxer-briefs.

"You want that, sweet girl?" I punctuated my question by barely thrusting inside her heat. "You want more of me?"

She nodded, nails digging into my shoulder.

In my wildest dreams, I never imagined it would be like this. Abigail was so tight and wet, dripping down my hand. She made sweet, stuttering gasps and quiet moans.

Never imagined how goddamn hard I'd get.

"I've almost memorized everything about you," I said casually, sliding a second finger inside her. The quiet moan that dripped from her lips was pure goddamn heroin. I slid out, only to push a third finger in. When her mouth opened around a wide O and she struggled to form any sound, I knew right then I'd spend the rest of the night chasing that high.

"Soon I'll know it all. I'll know every goddamn way to get you to make these sounds. Only me."

"Only you," she breathed, sounding disoriented.

I paused at her words only for a second. Then I slid out, gripping Abigail's chin with fingers still wet from her, eyes locked.

"Take my underwear off," I rasped.

Abigail didn't need to be told twice, pushing my underwear off with shaky hands. When my cock sprang out hard on my stomach, she gaped. She eyed my hard cock, lips parted, tongue slightly out.

Abigail sat back on her heels, thighs spread around my

hips, and I could see everything—every glistening fold, every bead of sweat lining her golden abdomen.

"One more out, Abs," I said. "Once I get you back down here... no promises."

Still, I was no saint. I palmed my cock, encouraging that dark look in her eyes. Abigail took her lower lip between her teeth.

Fuck.

I'll never be able to look at that lower lip the same way again. I'll start encouraging all her bad decisions.

In answer, her fingers slid along my cock, whisper light. I threw my head back on a groan and she threw me a mischievous smile.

"Playing around, Reject?" I grabbed her wrist, dragging her back to my chest, spreading her pussy against my cock. Our groans wove into one wicked melody.

Her fingers dove into my hair, tangling the strands. "Theo..."

Her clay eyes met mine, bright with need.

I reached off the bed, fishing for a condom from the pocket of my discarded jeans. If it was possible, the dark, hungry look in her eyes as I slid it over my cock made me even harder.

Something about fucking Abigail on a mattress I'd ripped open to spill her secrets seemed... inevitable. Our twisted, brutal destiny.

I placed my hands on her soft, honey thighs, notching my thumbs in her hipbones, lifting her up so she could reposition herself on my cock.

"Ready, sweet girl?" I asked.

"Yes," she whispered, biting that lip so hard I could see the white.

I pushed the hair out of her eyes. "It's just you and me,

Abs. Go *slow*." I slid one hand away from her hip, thumbing her clit. "This is my pussy now and I plan on using it whenever the fuck I want. Go too fast and hurt yourself, and I'll be pretty damn disappointed."

I released her clit and she fell forward on a breath, catching herself on my abs, fingers splayed. She blinked up at me, swiping her tongue across her bottom lip, then nodded.

I pushed a sweep of hair still veiling her from me back behind her ear. "Good girl."

Beneath long, feathery lashes her eyes found mine, and she gave me the prettiest, sweetest, close-lipped smile.

Goddamn, that smile.

She wiggled, spreading and taking me in just a little. Her lips parted on a sharp, surprised gasp. At the same time, something too deep to be a groan rumbled out of my chest.

Hot, wet—perfect.

Now *this* was an image I'd never forget. Abigail Crowne struggling to lower herself on my dick, her pretty pussy spreading to accommodate me. She dug her nails into my flesh as wisps of her silky hair floated across my chest.

The look on her face will forever be etched into my memory, most of all. Lips parted, caught on a breath, eyes locked on mine.

"Breathe," I soothed, voice rocky.

Abigail took a shaky, musical breath, moving another torturous inch, then froze, eyes growing, nails pricking my lower abs.

"Abigail?" I asked, trying to keep the strain in my voice hidden.

It was fucking cruel torture to stop. I can't decide if pausing on the image of me being swallowed by her is some kind of heaven or of some kind of hell.

At the same time, I'm worried it's too much. I'm too big, and it hurts.

"I don't want to do it wrong," she blurted. Her eyes popped as if she'd let something slip, and she looked away, blushing *hard*.

Fuck, Abigail without walls was addicting.

Dangerous.

I laughed. "You can't do it wrong." I reached out, threading my palm in her hair, grasping her head, dragging her to me. "You could break my goddamn dick, Abigail. It still wouldn't be wrong. Not with you."

I placed a slow, hot kiss on her cheek, until the tension in her shoulders faded, and she melted back into me.

"But..." I said, lips still against her cheek, her jaw. "Maybe don't aim for that."

She laughed—that fucking *laugh*. Abigail *laughing*? I hadn't heard that sound in years. When Abigail really and truly laughed, it was spectacular. Not the fake, rehearsed pretty laugh she gave the world. The real one. The one with the little snort. The one that made her cover her mouth in adorable embarrassment.

That more than anything had my heart pounding, my dick throbbing.

"Your pace," I reminded her, voice a lot rockier than I'd expected.

She nodded. I was about to drag her to me for one last kiss, when she impaled herself, taking me to the hilt. A wicked gasp left her lips, nails biting into my chest. Every image I'd dreamed of her was blurry. This was technicolor.

"Oh, *fuck*," I groaned.

"What?" Her eyes grew. "What's wrong?"

"You feel fucking amazing," I managed.

She smiled, biting that lip again.

"The fuck happened to slow, Abs?" I asked.

"You said *my* pace..." Abigail trailed off, rolling her hips, testing me inside her, and I pressed the back of my head into the pillow.

Holy shit.

Head still back, I found her eyes. "You good?" She sucked in a breath, focused on my chest, pretty pouted lips sucking in breaths. I squeezed her thigh. "Talk to me, Abs."

"I'm... perfect." Her eyes lifted, finding mine on a smile. She twirled her hips again, grinding back and forth. Oh *shit*. I can't remember the last time I felt like I was going to come this fast, but if she kept doing that fucking thing with her hips...

I dug my fingers into her flesh, keeping her still. "Wait," I said, voice hoarse.

Her brow furrowed. "Is something wrong?"

I bit the corner of my lip on a smile. "Nah, sweet girl. You're perfect."

Too fucking perfect.

Abigail was a dream in the hazy, smoky light, hair a veil across her breasts. Maybe it would shatter in the morning. Maybe I'd wake up and it would all be gone, but right now I pushed her hair behind her ear, anchoring my hand, the other on her hip.

Her eyes found mine and the room disappeared, an irrevocable connection rooting itself deep inside. She looked at me with awe, with affection too close to something else, something deeper.

"Ride me, sweet girl," I said.

"But..." I could see the worries, the fears spreading in the furrow of her brow like cracks in glass. "I'm not sure I know—" I pushed up inside her until all that came out of her lips was a perfect, beautiful sound. Not quite a gasp, not quite a moan.

"Do what feels good." I thrust up again just to hear that sound again, until her nails dug deeper and she fell on me a little more.

Slowly, her insecurity faded as she lost herself in pleasure.

I learned her rhythm. She liked it deep and gasped every time I pushed deeper, closer to the limit. Each inhale had me wanting to slam harder.

Later.

I slid my hands up her thighs, up her rib cage and her breasts, before spanning my palm along her neck and sliding my thumb into her open, gasping mouth.

"I should give it to you hard," I growled. "I should fuck this pussy until you can't walk. Until you learn to listen."

She clenched with each rough word and that, almost as much as her bottom teeth biting into my thumb, her hot breath fanning the skin, fueled me—knowing how much she loved it.

"You'd like that too much, wouldn't you?"

Her head fell back on a sigh, clenching so fucking tight around my dick. I knew she was on the edge, and I nearly fell right off.

"Look at me, Abigail." I gave a gentle squeeze to her neck. She sucked in a breath at the pressure, eyes dropping to mine. "Yeah, sweet girl, like that."

I gave another deep thrust, free hand finding her clit. She sucked in a sharp gasp and reached out blindly, gripping my jaw, thumb disappearing into my mouth.

"I think I'm..." As she hit her peak, her eyes glazed over.

I pulled her to me in a violent tangle of lips and limbs, consuming her gasps and sighs as she fell apart around me.

She cried my name into my mouth and it dripped like whiskey into my gut, warm and empowering. The taste of Abigail Crowne's utter and complete vulnerability, a secret flavor no one had ever known, ignited a possessive need.

A protective urge.

I held her tighter, even as her nails dug into my shoulder, even as she bit my lip bloody. I would carry the marks proudly, the scars of a secret only I know.

Only I would *ever* know.

My sweet girl *was* a meteor shower when she came, a blinding, life-changing, divine experience.

When Abigail came back down to earth, she smiled. Fucking smiled. Her nose crinkled with it and I saw a little bit of her pink gums.

I rubbed her smile with my thumb. "Look at that smile."

She buried her face in my chest, and I laughed, stroking her hair. "Fuck, I like this side of you. If I'd known all this time I could've been fucking the sweet into you..."

I memorized her with my touch. From the slope of her shoulder, down her spine, to the bone at her ass, over the curves of her ass and back up again to her hair. I hadn't stopped touching her, learning her. She has a small birthmark on her ass, and her goose bumps were small, like her.

Part of me knew it was because I didn't know the moment this would end.

Abigail lifted her head, and I kept my fingers in her hair. Her own found mine, running through the strands.

A wrinkle formed on her brow. I rubbed it with my thumb. "That's not the face you should have right now."

"I'm worried you're going to go away," she admitted,

voice too dark, too serious. "I'm worried all of this is going to disappear."

I dropped my thumb from her brow, trailing my knuckles along her cheek, and joked, "Worried you're going to lose your dog?"

The wrinkle deepened. "Yes."

I paused.

I realized just how fucking much I'd been vulnerable. Instinct had me itching to get up and leave, but her eyes were open and watching me with so much affection it anchored me. I wanted to know everything in her head that made her look at me like that. I never wanted her to stop running her fingers through my fucking hair.

"What are you thinking?" she whispered.

I traced her lips, from corner to center. "All the dirty words your pretty lips are going to say."

A shaky smile speared her lips, and she lay on my chest. "I like this side of you too," she whispered.

I don't know how long we were like that, her on my chest, me stroking her hair. It was an intimacy I'd never known.

"Spoiled rotten Abigail Crowne has a sweet pussy," I mused, her silky brown strands of hair falling through my fingers.

By the way she stiffened, I could tell she wasn't sure if she'd heard me correctly. I should've probably let her rest, but shit, she did have the sweetest pussy, and I never came. I was still hard.

I lowered my lips to her ear, dropping my voice. "You have the *sweetest* pussy, Abigail. Makes putting up with all your bullshit almost worth it."

Her swallow was audible, and to me, that was a fucking

invitation. I fisted her hair, pulling her head to the side, exposing her neck.

"Admit it." I licked a trail along the muscle of her creamy throat, back up to her ear. "Tell me all about your sweet pussy, Abigail Crowne."

"I-I..." Abigail stuttered in a way I was growing addicted to.

With my free hand, I thrust two fingers up inside her, before removing them in the same breath and shoving them into her mouth.

Gagging her.

She swallowed my fingers eagerly. Her nails dug into my shoulder, her other hand anchored on my hip. Having Abigail splayed and twisted across my chest as she earnestly deep throated my fingers ignited the possessiveness that had sparked earlier. It emboldened it, engraved it, fucking wrote it in blood.

She was mine.

"Fuck, I'm so hard watching you taste your pussy. You get me so hard, Abs." I took her hand from my hip, dragging it, making her palm my still hard cock. "You come on *this* cock. Your hot, wet, *sweet* pussy only comes on this."

She nodded through my fingers gagging her throat, somehow also *blushing*.

That was a sight.

I slowly withdrew from her mouth and saliva dripped from her full bottom lip. I brushed it away with my thumb, her lips still parted. She watched me, transfixed.

"I have a sweet pussy," she whispered with a smile. That smile got me almost as much as the dirty words coming from it.

"Yeah." I crushed my lips against hers, bruising and hard. "You do."

I pulled her across me until her small frame was back atop mine. There was no better feeling in this world than Abigail's soft body pressing into my hard one.

Nah, strike that, her pussy clenching around my dick topped it.

Suddenly she pulled away and sat up, thighs spread on either side of my hips.

Fuck. Would I ever get used to a naked Abigail Crowne? I don't even think she realized the effect she had on me.

"Did you... you know..." She chewed her bottom lip. "I did...but did you?"

Yeah.

I *really* like this side.

"Did I what?" I flipped her over and hoisted one thigh over my hip so I could grind my still hard dick against her pussy. "Did I *come*?"

Abigail inhaled a melodic gasp that went straight to my cock, arching her back. I was learning the differences, what sharp inhales meant versus the ones she'd just made. How much to push, how much to let her take the lead, or when she needed direction.

I nipped at her collarbone. "We have all night, sweet girl."

Abigail arched her back, pussy hitting my cock. Fuck. She was still so wet. I could slide into her, take her from above, behind, the side. Every fucking way until she couldn't move.

Except...

I lifted my head, finding her eyes.

"Unless you're done," I said. "Then your ass goes to sleep."

It was her first time.

She could be sore.

In response, Abigail clasped my cheeks between her palms and kissed my cheek. Then my jaw. Then my lips. She feathered soft, tender kisses all across my face until I melted into her lips with a groan, parting her mouth with my tongue.

Abigail Crowne had the sharpest thorns and the softest petals. Maybe that's why I was so addicted to bleeding by her, it made her soft touches, looks, and kisses all the more intoxicating.

We took a breath, foreheads still pressed, as I reached for another condom from my discarded jeans.

"You..." She swallowed. "You kept your promise." Maybe she saw the confusion on my face, because she grasped my face in her palms, pulling me to hers.

There wasn't a single filter in her clay eyes. Emotion poured out of them like a broken faucet, drowning me. This was the dangerous part. Not the fucking. This.

I'd do anything to keep that glow in her eyes.

"There's no going back. You said when you were done with me—"

I slammed my mouth over hers. Kissing her deep, harsh, brutal.

You'll be ruined for everyone but me.

"Sweet girl," I said, eyes still closed, lips still pressed. "I'm not even close to being done with you."

EIGHTEEN

ABIGAIL

I woke sore, rested, and *happy* for the first time in, I think, ever? Light filtered hazy through my curtains. The joint was dead and had burned the nightstand. I got a vicious glee thinking of how much it would piss off my mom if she ever cared enough to come in my wing.

I stretched my arms with a small groan, turned my head —and shot up.

Theo wasn't in my bed; he wasn't even in my room or at the doorway. I clasped my satin sheets to my chest, working the material beneath my fingers. Theo's clothes were gone. Only the burned joint and the wine stain evidence anything had happened at all.

Beneath my fingers the stain had set; in the morning light, it was bolder, a deep burgundy.

Horrible, ugly, intrusive thoughts ran a mile a minute.

It meant nothing.

It was all just a game.

This was his plan all along—the door opened, cutting off my thoughts.

Theo.

He leaned against the frame, face unreadable. Wild, chocolate hair fell over one eye. His cheekbones were sharper in the shadow of the doorway, the muscle beneath dark and hollow. He folded his arms, back to his regular bodyguard uniform of a shirt and jeans, designed to blend in. Once again, that was a fool's errand. He looked like a clandestine picture of a celebrity.

His shirt read: YOU'RE TOO CLOSE.

"Get up," Theo said. "We have a plane to catch."

He turned around, leaving the door open and empty in his wake. I could hardly breathe.

Did it really mean nothing to him?

I suddenly felt naked. So very naked.

We were in the air for an hour before Theo spoke to me. He was too close to me. His jeans rubbed against my bare thigh, and it was all I could think about. I was doing my best to act like I wasn't bothered, and that meant I stared out the window.

For an *hour.*

I should've known he could see through me.

"Something wrong, Abigail?" His breath was against my ear, voice low and sultry like an intoxicating drug. I folded my arms.

Clouds. Focus on clouds.

"No." The grumpiness in my tone must have been much too obvious, because he smirked.

He placed a hand on my bare thigh, and I nearly startled at the contact. *When will I learn to wear pants?* I looked around to see if anyone was watching—of course not, no one ever paid attention to me.

A sudden thought came to me. "Did you tell my mom anything?"

He was acting weird again, and paranoia was taking hold.

At my question, he turned, rotating me with him, and slid a jean-clad knee between my bare thighs. His eyes locked with mine.

"Maybe."

Mischief floated in his pale eyes, and fear collected like beetles in my gut. At my face, he grinned, sliding his knee deeper between my thighs.

"I told your mom you needed more security. She told me a lot of stories, like how you skinned your knee to get her attention."

My gut dropped, and I tried to focus on anything *but* his jeaned thigh sliding between my bare ones, getting closer. Everything blurred—his eyes, his thigh—the plane's engine the only thing clear.

"She really painted a picture of Abigail Crowne," he said lowly. "A desperate, attention-seeking liar."

Hurt and pain at being once again betrayed, and in the most brutal and primeval of ways, somehow *heightened* Theo. He slid deeper, getting closer to the apex between my thighs, and I was stuck on his eyes. His hand on my thigh. The coarse sensation of his jeans against my bare skin.

Move, Abigail.

Run.

I swallowed. "Oh." It was all I could manage.

The plane hit some turbulence, and I broke out of his spell, using the opportunity to run away before Theo could do any more damage to an already brutally bruised heart, sprinting to the bathroom. Before I could even close the door, Theo slammed it open with one hand. The mirror shivered.

I should have known I wasn't safe.

He shut the door behind us with a *snick*.

Inside, my mind was screaming: *Please don't do this, please don't obliterate me once and for all.*

I couldn't let him see my vulnerability, so I looked left, right, eyes landing on a vase, and chucked it at him. He dodged it easily with a laugh and it shattered to pieces behind him.

He took a step closer and I turned around, focused on the black marble sink. The bathroom was the size of some of our guest bathrooms at Crowne Hall, but it felt too small. Much too small.

He wrapped his body around me, and I felt every inch of him—the roped muscles of his forearms, the warmth and security of his biceps.

His sharp hips.

His hard cock.

I tried not to like it, tried not to melt into his embrace. I turned into my shoulder so he couldn't see my cheeks heating.

He pushed into me, and a small, treacherous groan fell from my lips. I ground back against him, losing myself.

"That was the moment I knew, Abigail."

My stomach dropped. He was going to gut me, but I was a junkie searching for her next fix. Even though I knew he would hurt me, I couldn't *not* ask for the pain.

"Knew what?"

"There was no going back. Not with you. I'd rather be kicked to the curb by you than brought home by anyone else. You could leave me over and over again like the fucking dog I was, it didn't matter. All I could think as she spoke was..." His lips found the side of my neck. "I'm yours forever, Abigail."

Our eyes met in the mirror. "Don't you know that yet?"

He bit the skin he'd previously been sucking and his name fell from my lips, relief flooding my veins like an opioid.

Theo tortured me. All morning he'd kept me on the brink of misery. And the sick part? I *liked* it.

Because Theo knew me. In the same way he'd physically kept me on the edge last night, twisting the high inside me until I rode the razor-thin line between pleasure and pain; he did it emotionally. Fuck me physically, emotionally; I needed what only he could give me.

"Where were you this morning?" I practically breathed.

I felt his grin on my skin before I saw it light up the mirror. "Miss me?"

Yes.

I glared back. "No."

"Liar." He buried his face into my neck, then reached one arm over my shoulder, dangling something shiny.

I couldn't tell what it was at first, but then it focused. A small, rose gold key chain of a little dog, with crystals for eyes.

"You were worried about losing your dog," he said into my neck, lips warm. "Now you'll always have one."

A gasp fell from my lips. "Theo, thank—"

"It's nothing." His gruff voice cut me off before I could get my thank you out.

It wasn't *nothing*.

While I thought my nerves and fears were falling on

deaf ears, he was listening. But of course he was... that was Theo.

"Now shut up and let me fuck you."

Theo dropped the key chain, and I stumbled to catch it; at the same time he slid a hand under my shirt, grasping my breast. His other free hand dove beneath my skirt, not pushing aside my panties, but *ripping* them.

The key chain fell out of my hand, skittering across the sink. I grasped the marble edge, needing stability.

"I went easy on you last night."

That was easy?

"I'm not stopping until you're breathless and broken."

I heard the tear of a condom wrapper, then he was at my entrance.

He was waiting—what is he waiting for?

"You want my cock, Reject?" he asked.

Reject. Hearing him say it like this wrapped up thorny torment in desire, sharp but soothing like my inhale. I shouldn't like it.

I pressed against him, trying to force it.

His hand was at my neck, pushing away my hair, sliding down my spine, cool and hot at the same time. "Say it."

"I-I want it," I gasped. "I want your cock."

He laughed, biting my shoulder blade. "Good girl."

He was so big last night, and it was no different now. I couldn't speak. I couldn't breathe.

"Breathe." His voice was soothing and brutal all at once.

How does he know? How does he *always* know?

I exhaled and he slid into me.

I see stars. I see the sun. I see the entire fucking universe.

It didn't escape me that my mother, everyone, was just outside. If Mom caught us, she'll send Theo away, I know she will. Bodyguards weren't even supposed to look us in the eyes, and mine is making me go cross-eyed with pleasure.

Part of me *likes* it. It feels reckless and wrong.

With one hand on my hip, simultaneously holding me in place and *up*, my legs weak, Theo built a slow, torturous rhythm. Theo fucked like he torments. The same calculating mind that ripped apart my walls and drove me to misery, is now used to bring me absolute pleasure. He knows things about me I never dreamed would work.

A kiss on my spine. A biting tug on my earlobe. A hot, quick pinch of my nipple. His touches were quick and calculated. Slow and luxurious. I couldn't see. I could hardly breathe. Just like before, the only thing keeping me tethered was Theo.

And when his strong hand tightened possessively around my neck, I swear, he unravels me.

"I like you like this." His lips are at the base of my neck, whispering against my spine. "Too strung out on my dick to put up walls."

In. Out. In. Out.

I could barely focus on anything else.

"I can see all of you, Abigail. Your wants. Desires. *Needs.*" His grasp on my neck pulls me back, bending me until his lips touched my ear. "I'm not stopping till you've had them all."

I could feel him in my *toes*, all starting from that one, *perfect* place.

I grasped his forearm, digging into the flexing muscle. He didn't even react. His grip fanned to cover almost all my collarbone, and his breath skated along my neck.

"Look at me."

He said that last night too.

I lifted my head, catching his eyes in the mirror.

"Hi, sweet girl."

His smile *melts* me. Devious and sweet and devouring all at once.

I can't say if that's what does it. Or if it was the gentle term of endearment leaving his cruel lips, his soft touch on my neck, anchoring me and grounding me, or his eyes, never once leaving mine, watching me with an almost brutal intensity. Maybe it was his cock hitting just the right spot.

All I know is it all comes together in the right time and right moment.

And I come undone.

Goose bumps shiver along my soul.

Theo is *everywhere*.

I must be loud, because Theo glided his hand up from my neck, to my mouth. I bite on his fingers, too hard, I think, but if he was fazed he doesn't show it. Through it all, he kept that torturous pace, and he watched me, eyes burning.

Theo.

It wasn't a name; it's a feeling, dripping inside me. His green, green eyes. His lips. His smile. When he broke our stare, head falling to my shoulder with a rough groan as he comes, it causes an entirely new flurry of goose bumps to erupt along my body. I know the feeling won't ever leave me.

We were still for an absolutely perfect minute. Theo whispered along my skin. *Stunning. Perfect. Mine.*

I don't quite catch them all, but I feel them.

He pulled out too soon.

I wobbled, but he caught me. He fixed my hair, adjusted my shirt, then skirt, ghosting his fingers briefly along my naked lips, causing me to shiver. He stuffed my torn panties into his pocket, and my breath caught.

A moment passed, his eyes locked on mine; then he trailed his knuckles along my still-flushed cheeks.

"Fuck," he cursed. "I like this look on you."

"What look?"

He grinned, looking more wolfish than man. "Me."

NINETEEN

THEO

The Crownes were not the type of people to stay in a hotel, unless they owned that hotel. In France they preferred to stay on their private island. Warm sun beat down on hot sand, and Gemma groaned.

"This is *torture*." She threw her phone down. It landed quietly in a small tuft of sand.

"Two more islands, sis, two more," Gray said, his arm across his eyes, blocking out the sun.

Gemma sighed, lying down on the sand. "Wake me up when we reach Switzerland."

Only a Crowne would be bored on a private island.

They were bored because to them, France, Spain, Switzerland—it was an obligation, not a once-in-a-lifetime vacation. Which meant they usually came up with more and more crazy and dangerous activities.

It made my abdomen clench in anticipation.

I wanted to take Abigail and lock her in a room.

She'd taken a liking to the key chain I'd gotten her and carried it everywhere. She called it T2, for Theo Two. She didn't know it was also a tracking device.

I wasn't sure how to feel about the guilt.

Normally the odds of the asshole stalking her following us out of the country was low, but that asshole was like them. Wealthy and without limitation.

"What are you thinking?" Abigail asked, shifting my focus from the turquoise sea to below me, where she sat on the sun-warmed sand.

I glanced behind me, checking that her family was too preoccupied to hear, and said, "Wondering what those pretty lips will feel like wrapped around my cock."

Her lips parted, eyes widening, and she looked away. My cheek twitched. I liked shocking Abigail. She was someone who acted impossible to shock.

I stood behind her like a good bodyguard, arms behind my back, legs spread, but below me... Abigail was nothing but temptation in a cornflower swimsuit that brought out her honey skin, the rich tones in her dark hair, and the bright color of her clay eyes. It hugged her pert breasts above the glowing lines of her abdomen. My eyes traveled to a barely covered pussy. Was she wet? She got so fucking wet.

As if hearing my thoughts, she shifted, uncrossing her smooth legs. I clenched my jaw.

A Crowne vacation was one of the only times *family time* was enforced, meaning all four Crowne family members sat in somewhat close proximity. Meaning I couldn't haul her ass over my shoulder and fuck her. She looked up at me again, and by the way she stared, wetting her lips, I could tell she was thinking the same.

"Hey, dog," Gray yelled from down the beach. I tore my

eyes off Abigail, finding him peering at me from under the shadow of his forearm. "Go get me a piece of gum."

I arched a brow. He was already chewing a piece.

"Don't call him that," Abigail snapped.

Gray shifted his gaze to her. "Because only *you* can?" He rolled his eyes. "Dogs are good at fetching things, and it stimulates their brain, sis."

"Why don't you have *Story* do it?" Abigail countered. Story was still perched beside Gray, knees to her chin, and still covered head to toe.

"Shut *up*," Gemma groaned, a wide-brimmed hat on her face now. "I'm trying to fall asleep."

"Children," Tansy murmured, not lifting her eyes from her magazine. She sat beneath a cabana in a sunhat and glasses, a pitcher of some fruity liquor beside her and two women in soft linen ready to attend.

Abigail flipped Gray off, and he blew her a kiss.

We went back to the sound of the waves and Tansy's ice clinking as her attendants poured her a drink.

I bent down, face blank, acting like I had some very important bodyguard business to tell Abigail.

"Truth or promise, Abigail?" I stared forward at the waves.

"Now?" she stage-whispered, looking over her shoulder at her family. "Truth..."

"If I were to slide my hand between your thighs, how fucking wet would you be?"

Her breath seized.

Gray opened an eye, but it looked like I was completely detached, eyes on the horizon. Gray closed his eyes, lowering his arm once more. I looked back at Abigail.

"Show me. Lift up your swimsuit."

"My family..." But Abigail was already trailing her

fingers down to the ribbed pale blue hem of her swimsuit bottoms. She lifted the hem just so, and I stifled my groan.

"You can't help it, can you?" I said, low and quiet. "You're so fucking wet."

Her fingers shivered, her breath halting—*nervous*. I loved getting Abigail nervous as much as I loved shocking her. She got high off the nerves; the fear was adrenaline. In Abigail's world, there wasn't much to be nervous or afraid of. They had everything, were above the law—it bred comfort and boredom.

I leaned in, my breath licking her ear. "If I asked you to finger yourself right now, would you?"

"Don't," she pleaded.

Making sure to keep my posture casual and give nothing away from behind, I leaned forward and bit her earlobe. Her finger dropped, spreading herself as if unconsciously. That image is going to be burned in my goddamn retinas, Abigail giving in, fingering herself in front of her family.

Then a second later, she shot up.

I followed suit, standing casually to my feet, crossing my arms in front so my hands hung over my dick.

Abigail ruffled her hair, cheeks red. "I'll get you your gum, Gray."

"What gum?" Gray mumbled, but Abigail was practically running to the main house. I caught up with her just inside the foyer.

Her glare was on me. That fucking Abigail Crowne glare. It shouldn't turn me on so much.

I pushed her against the door on a laugh, bending down until I was eye to eye with her swimsuit bottoms. I peeled aside the blue material. She was perfect. Naked. Bare. *Wet.*

I found her eyes. "Fuck, Abigail, when was the last time someone ate you out?"

Her eyelids fluttered. "S-Stop tormenting me."

"Tormenting?" I laughed. "This is torment?"

Eyes still locked, I took one slow lick from the bottom of her slit to the top. Her mouth parted, eyes stuck on me.

I sucked her lips slowly until she shuddered, tasting the image that had tormented *me*. A taste I hadn't been able to get out of my fucking head since the Swan Swell. Now it was a font I could drown in.

Abigail was ambrosia. She was sunscreen and cocoa butter and *her*. A taste I wouldn't ever get off my tongue.

I tongue fucked her, ate her, consumed her, watching her disappear to ecstasy. She bit her lip raw, her eyes grew hazy, and goose bumps peppered her flesh. I could hear her family just outside the door. I didn't give a shit, spurred on by her taste. She didn't seem to mind either.

"My little attention whore," I said, sucking her clit harsh enough to draw a gasp. "Do you want to be caught?"

Her hands found my shoulders, nails digging. "Don't stop."

At her words, though it killed me, I tore myself from her. I stood up and took a step back. Her swimsuit was torn to the side, messed up in the most distracting of ways, showing too much of her pussy and not enough at once. She looked at me with hazy, confused eyes.

I threw her a grin. "But you asked so nicely before."

I wrapped my arm around her waist, thrusting her to me, crashing her lips against mine wet with *her*. My free hand dove between her thighs, finding her swimsuit still pushed aside. As our tongues met, I fingered her deep, hard, and fast, but only for a second, before I stopped.

More confusion muddled her pretty clay eyes.

"I don't want to torment you, Abigail," I said, licking her off my fingers.

Realization gave way to anger, and she clenched and unclenched her fist. I thought she might throw something at me, but she only exhaled and raised her chin.

Her eyes glittered, and she adjusted her swimsuit. "I'll get you back, Theo."

I grinned. "Looking forward to it."

ABIGAIL

I would get revenge on Theo. I couldn't think about anything save him all damn day, and he knew it. He had the smuggest half smile on his face. Not even "accidentally" kicking sand in his face took it away. He'd just brushed the grains out of his eyes like he *knew* why I'd done it.

By the time the sun was setting in a violent sapphire-violet, I almost had an idea of what I would do. He needed a taste of his own medicine, and I couldn't do that on this fucking island. Gemma and Gray *always* snuck off the island, and I never asked to go out with them. They never wanted me, and I didn't feel like taking that hit to my ego.

Revenge might be worth it.

At dinner, we sat outside beneath the rising stars with the breath of salt air. When I sat next to Gemma, she looked like I'd spat in her food. We always made sure to keep at least one seat between one another or, if you were Gray, you claimed an entire side.

"Wait for me tonight," I whispered. Gray looked up from his phone at my words, the same look Gemma had written across his face.

"Um, what?" Gemma asked at last.

"You're not invited," Gray said slowly, like he was teaching algebra to a toddler.

"Just save a spot for me on the boat," I hissed. I could tell Gemma was about to not so kindly repeat what Gray had said, so I added, "Or I could tell Mom..." I glanced down the table to where she was eyeing her bouillabaisse like someone was about to get fired.

Gemma's eyes narrowed to slits. "Fine."

"Abigail..." my mother trilled. "The Harlingtons will join us in Switzerland this year for an unofficial engagement party."

I was still smiling from my win with Gemma when she spoke. How could I have gone so long without thinking about my *marriage* and my fiancé? I was supposed to meet him, and when I didn't, when everything happened... I got swept away.

I glanced at Theo. He gave nothing away. If he cared I was getting married, he didn't show it. Beneath the table I rolled T2 between my fingers. I looked at my stew, picking at the fish and onions and tomatoes with my other hand.

"My *fiancé* didn't even bother showing up to the Fourth," I muttered.

Mom glanced at me. "Lying is very beneath a Crowne, Abigail."

"He didn't!" I dropped my spoon with a clang. "Am I really supposed to marry someone who doesn't fucking show up when they say they will? How will I recognize him on my wedding day? What if I accidentally fuck the usher?"

"Let's be honest," Gray said. "It won't be an accident."

Mom had gone quiet, the time it took for her to speak counted by the waves.

"I think you're done eating," she said at last.

I didn't argue. I pushed away from the table with so

much force my bowl toppled over, spilling red stew onto the soft satin linen. Theo followed me quietly back inside.

Theo and I didn't speak at all after dinner, and I almost didn't go through with what I'd planned. But what choice did I have, really? If I didn't, we would be stuck together with the third wheel that was my unmet fiancé.

The reality that was being a Crowne.

After getting dressed, I found Theo in the adjoining room, bent over behind the couch. He turned his head at my footfalls. His profile was breathtaking—then I saw the item in his hand.

"You *do* still have her diary."

He shoved it back in a black bag. I tried not to be hurt he was still hiding it from me. I chewed my lip as an awkward silence stretched.

"You really don't want to look for her?" I asked.

Theo stood to his full height, folding his arms, taking in my pale blue cropped tank top with a plunging vee, my tight skirt that barely hit my thighs. "Where are you going?"

"You didn't answer my..." I trailed off with a sigh and shrugged. "Off the island."

He arched a brow. "You don't get invited to that."

Ouch.

"Well, tonight I was." I mashed my lips so he couldn't see the pain, but it was futile. His eyes softened, seeing through me. I raised my middle finger, showing my dangling T2, trying to change the subject.

"I'm bringing my dog. Nothing to worry about."

He didn't argue when I opened my window. I could've taken the door... but I liked having him catch me; it was like before everything went to shit. Theo went first and held both his arms out for me, hoisting me down from the window. My chest slid against his, and he held me in place long after I was safely down.

"Sure you want to go out?" he asked, low. My eyes were locked on his soft lips, dusky pink in the dark. The Mediterranean night air was warm, and his lips were so, so close.

There was still so much debris between us. The longer we went without addressing it, the harder it would be to dig ourselves out, but the emotion surging behind his luminous eyes brought me back to the simpler nights. The nights when he caught me from my window, when we both fell to the night dark grass and tried to keep our laughter hidden from roaming Crowne Hall guards. There were times when I thought he would kiss me. When he stared at my lips the way he did now.

I lifted my eyes, meeting his burning ones.

In the distance, a bird squawked and I used the distraction to separate.

I won't lie, I was terrified as we approached the dock. I wouldn't have put it past my brother and sister to leave without me. They were there, though, boat churning water, Gray at the wheel and Story seated behind him.

I took a seat in the stern, watching her. Story looked absolutely miserable. I wasn't ever one to wonder why Gray did the things he did, but now I couldn't help it. What was he doing with her? Or... to her.

Gray pulled us away from the pier, and in no time we were rushing toward our destination, sweet, salty air kissing my cheeks. The Riviera skyline was like a colorful chest of treasure opened and shining against the black sky. Gray turned off the engine when we arrived, steering us into a hidden cliff. The stars above us vanished and for a moment it was utterly pitch.

The thumping beat hit us first.

Then the dark opened up into a dazzling cliffside grotto that looked out over an ocean, enclosed by rock on three of its sides. A DJ spun on a dais in the middle of the water, colorful jewel-toned spotlights flashed from him into the crowd. Girls in bikinis and skimpy dresses danced on stages built into the rock, hair flying with their movements. Some jumped off rocks into the water below.

Gray docked our boat amid many others.

This was the most exclusive club in the French Riviera. Only a few knew its location and how to get here. I already recognized Khalid and the teenage heartthrob from our after party. The thing is, exclusive just meant *small*. We all frequent the same clubs and places. If you don't like some-one, tough shit, you learn to tolerate them.

Someone was there to help each of us out of our boat.

Theo, Gemma, and I were the last to leave.

"Let's try to avoid each other," Gemma said to me, her hand still encased in the man helping her get out. She stepped onto the polished floor, her hair all but whipping me in the face. She spotted her friends—the Gemma troop-ers, I called them, because they all looked like mini fucking Gemmas—and ran to them with a squeal.

"Yeah, they really wanted you here," Theo said at my back, a laugh all but on his tongue.

I ground my jaw, letting the man help me out of the boat as I eyed the girls dancing on the stages, my plan set.

"You have your bad idea face again," Theo said when he was out of the boat.

"I don't have—" I exhaled, blowing a strand of hair.

"Will you do me a favor, Theo?" I asked, batting my eyelashes, tone saccharine.

He pushed his cheek out with his tongue, looking me up and down with sharp eyes. A small barely-there smile hooked his cheek, and it nearly buckled me. It was like he was reading all of my thoughts, and it amused him. I was a mouse the lion had decided not to kill for a few minutes.

"Oh yeah, Reject? What favor?"

I ignored him calling me *Reject*. "Um... could you get me a drink?"

Another one of those sharp looks, then his grin spread. Slow, feral, devious. "Sure thing. I'll get you a drink."

I watched him walk away, his broad back disappearing into the crowd. That *grin*. It lingered in the jelly in my thighs. It made me nervous even though he was playing into my plans.

I shook it off—physically shook it off—then ran to a stage.

The club had multiple stages on all floors leading to the top. Every one was open so you could jump into the ocean with the DJ. From the bottom looking up, you could see them all.

Every stage was taken, but I didn't care. I made my way to the top, eyes on the best. There were few above a Crowne, and this girl was not one of them.

"Get off."

She was about to argue, but when she saw who I was, she quickly scampered off the stage.

I spent years dancing, and I got a delicious thrill thinking this is how my training was used. Dear mistress Alexy, all those fucking hours spent *en pointe* are now being used to shake my ass for semi-random strangers.

Dear Mom, all those hours you forced me to stretch are now being used to bend over—

I was grasped by the wrist, and I stumbled into Theo's piercing, pale green eyes. "What are you doing?"

His voice was rough, like sandpaper, and it rubbed me in the best way.

"Tormenting goes *both ways*, Theo." I leaned in like I was going to kiss his cheek, then pulled back with a wicked smile. His eyes darkened, sending thrills down my spine. I tugged my wrist and he narrowed his eyes a fraction but loosened his hold.

Like he wanted me to *know* he'd let go.

He didn't stay at the base of the stage like a lot of the men. He went to the edge of the floor until his back was to air and the water below.

Song after song, Theo let me dance, but I could *feel* him. All other persons faded away. Through the crowd, Theo's dark and twisted wire throbbed.

I lifted up my shirt and the crowd went wild.

I had a half second to register the rush before I was grabbed at the ankle. I was yanked *hard*, flying up and into the air, catching Theo's upside-down glare. At the same moment I was certain I was going to slam into the shiny stage, Theo's arms wrapped around my waist. He threw me over his shoulder, ignoring my shouts.

He yanked my skirt down, then his arm wrapped tight around it so it couldn't ride up. I could barely register the gentlemanly action, when his thumb was at my panties, sliding through the material, and he was *on me*. Pressing into my slit, grazing me back and forth, driving me hotter and higher, as he carried me through the club like I was a feather.

Torturer.

Theo Hound was a cruel torturer.

He carried me into a room carved into the rock, but by the hanging chandelier and plush carpet you wouldn't know it. It overlooked the sparkling night and dark ocean. I could only hear the thump of the beat, the occasional happy scream and splash. We were totally hidden.

He tossed me down with something like savage tenderness. I landed on my feet hard, but his hands came to my cheeks, pushing the hair out of the way.

Then he kissed me, hard and brutal and over too fast.

"Fuck, I love that color on your cheeks, Abigail. Only make it for me." I think I must have flushed harder, because the grin on his face spread. "Yeah, sweet girl, like that." He trailed his knuckles along my cheeks, down to my jaw.

Goose bumps rose along my spine.

"I thought you were going to..." I swallowed at the memory of him touching me. "In the club," I finished on a whisper. I couldn't say it. Theo sucked out my bravado and made me a puddle.

In dark gray jeans and a black leather jacket, he was somehow both dressed up and casual, quintessentially Theo, and it was driving me nuts.

His knuckles continued down my neck. "Would you like that?"

It wouldn't even be a shocking sight to the kind of people out there. Which is why the fact he brought me back here, to someplace private, had my gut twisting. It was more taboo to do things in private, more scandalous to keep a secret than tell it.

"With you, Theo, there's a lot I shouldn't want... but I do."

He held my shoulder now, thumb at my collarbone. "Like?"

A voice in my head whispered at me to say dirty things. I wanted them, of course. I wanted to do all the dirty things with Theo, but that's not what I was thinking when I spoke, and if I said that, I would only be pushing him away. The look in his eyes, the gentle way he stroked my collarbone, told me not to push him away.

"I want you to sleep in my bed, Theo," I said honestly. "I want to wake up in your arms."

Emotion flitted across his face, too quick to discern. "Sure thing, sweet girl."

And then he kissed me.

TWENTY

ABIGAIL

I woke up in Theo's arms, warm and safe for the third night in a row. We were in Spain now, having made the two hour flight last night. Now we slept in a custom bed bigger than a king, with soft sheets to complement the softer air. The room opened up to a wraparound porch with baluster railings overlooking the warm ocean.

I folded my arms on his chest, resting my chin on my hands, and looked up at him. "Why do you call me *sweet girl?*"

A flicker of a smile. "Because that's what you are."

"I've been called a lot of things…"

"You're *my* sweet girl, Abigail. Just for me." He pushed the hair out of my face, trailing his caress down to my lips. "You slept with the light off again."

"I guess I did," I said. With Theo in my bed, I didn't feel the need to keep it on. The meaning was clear and I felt too raw, but thankfully Theo didn't press further.

I angled to kiss him, stretching my arms out from sleep. As I did so, I swiped my arms across the nightstand to our left, accidentally knocking off his backpack. It fell to the floor, and his mom's diary fell out. With it, the nice moment shattered.

Theo slowly untangled from me, leaving me cold in bed, to put it away.

My gut clenched at the sight. We hadn't really let each other back in, not really. We'd stepped outside of our walls, into neutral territory. Neither of us had really torn them down.

How long could that last?

"It wasn't random," I said, watching him shove it back in. "That night on the beach, I mean. I know I acted like it could have been anyone, but it could only be you."

The muscles in Theo's naked back were tight and coiled.

I worked the soft sheets between my fingers.

"It was *you* I wanted," I continued. "Theo, it's always been for a reason, from the very beginning."

He stood, diary in hand. His jaw was clenched so hard the muscle feathered. He came back to the bed, sitting on the edge. I sat up, resting my chin on his shoulder.

"There's nothing worth reading in here..." He held the diary out toward me, not quite giving it away. I waited on a heartbeat's thread, hoping for something I was too afraid to even think.

He feathered a caress along the edge of my cheek. His touch was too nice. Too sweet. Too addicting. You could almost forget the crash that followed such a high.

My phone buzzed on the nightstand. I reached an arm out and grabbed it. An unknown number flared on my screen, followed by a picture of a single gold rose, and a promise: *Can't wait to see you.*

I dropped the phone, too shocked to pretend it was nothing. It fell loud and ugly to the floor.

"Is that him?" Gone was Theo's tender voice, in its place rough words that abraded my spine. My eyes flashed to his.

I'd almost forgotten my stalker in our sweet bubble.

"I just realized I don't have your number—your new number," I said, trying to deflect. I reached for his phone, putting my number in and then texting myself. "There. Everything is as it should be. Guess it's easy to overlook when we're always together." I gave a shaky laugh.

My deflection didn't go unnoticed. "You don't need to hide, Abs. I'm here to protect you. I've always been here to protect you."

"Not always," I whispered.

The bed was too hot, the sheets stuffy. I sat up, throwing the Egyptian cotton off and stretching. Warm Spanish air drifted in through the window, sliding along my shoulder blades.

"He's not like your other problems, Abigail. You can't stuff him into a box and act like he doesn't exist."

I dragged a nail along my thigh, hating his words, hating how he could always rip away my armor.

"I know he's one of you," he said more softly.

I looked over my shoulder, barely catching Theo's eyes.

The door to my wing opened and our tenuous connection snapped. I quickly dressed, throwing a threadbare pink sweater over a vintage Chanel skirt. If Theo and I were caught together, he'd be taken off my assignment. Nothing would happen to me, because as a Crowne it only mattered if I tried to love him, if I tried to marry him and be with him.

And that wasn't happening...

Theo didn't care. He slid languidly into his gray jeans, cavalierly putting on the same shirt he'd worn the night before.

Gray was in the sitting room, leaning against the door.

His blue eyes sparked with suspicion when he saw us, but all he said was, "We're doing a DiCaprio tonight, you in?"

My eyes lit up. "Really?"

A DiCaprio was named after Leonardo DiCaprio from his scene in *Titanic* where Rose sneaks down into the basement. We would go out and party with the peasants—Gray's words. Usually I wasn't invited, because they *never* invited me to anything unless they had no choice.

An uncontrolled bubble of excitement filled my chest.

I heard Theo scoff beside me. He never approved of doing a DiCaprio, mainly because we usually left the "peasants" in some kind of trouble, whether it was emotionally or legally. Gray raised an eyebrow in his direction before landing back on me.

"Unless you want to stay on this Spanish Alcatraz."

"No, no. I'll meet you."

Gray nodded. "See you tonight by the pier."

I chewed my bottom lip so Gray didn't see my smile. I could hardly contain my excitement. All I'd ever wanted was to be included.

Theo blocked the door almost instantly after Gray left, arms folded.

"You're not going."

"Why do you get to tell me what to do?"

He shifted, biceps, triceps, and deltoids flexing in a truly unfair way. "Because I'm your—"

"Your *what*, Theo?" I interrupted.

We still hadn't labeled it, whatever *this* was. My body-guard? My best friend? My bully? My boyfriend? Or simply nothing at all? Another long, pressure-filled minute passed.

In the end, he never answered.

I eyed the diary still in his hand. "Why are you hiding your mom's diary from me?"

"Why are you hiding your texts?" he countered.

I narrowed my eyes. "It was a friend—the person who texted me."

He laughed, a harsh, barking noise. "Fuck off it was a friend. I'm not letting you out of this room, Abigail."

"That's how it's going to be?"

Another agonizingly tempting flex of his arms, and this time he shifted, spreading his legs as if to say, *Just fucking try getting by me.*

"Your safety is my first priority."

"I'm getting married. Does that bother you, Theo?" I asked. "I'll belong to some stranger for the rest of my life."

I was poking at something perilous, but I couldn't stop. I felt untethered and crazed. Theo's jaw was so tight the muscle popped and flexed.

"You'll still need a bodyguard," he gritted. "Day or night, I'll be there."

I ground my teeth. *Why* did his response bother me? It's how it should be.

"You'll listen to me fuck him?" I goaded. "Listen to me come?"

Theo laughed. "You won't come." He grabbed my wrist, yanking me so I spiraled into the hard planes of his chest. "Only I can get this spoiled pussy off."

Before I can speak he shoves aside my panties, thrusting roughly inside me.

One, then two fingers.

I should pull away. This is the moment I should prove he doesn't have the power he thinks he has. But dammit, I lean into him. I let myself melt into his chest and the worshipful yet brutal way he watches me.

"I hate you," I managed, even though inside I lived for his smoldering green-eyed gaze and the ruthless rhythm he worked inside me.

He did something absolutely wicked with his fingers and I gasped, clinging to him as my knees literally weaken.

He grinned. "Yeah, I can tell."

Theo curled inside me, pumping, pressing his thumb hard on my clit. He shows me the truth of his words with his touch. My pussy is marked by him, attuned, forever his; only he can make my soul glow. I'm on the edge, about to drop, when suddenly he stops.

Steps away.

I'm left aching and barely able to stand, and Theo is completely aware of what he's done to me.

I know, because his next words are, "Day or night, Abigail."

Theo's grin is gone, and he's put his arms behind his back, returning to his good bodyguard stance. His face is a complete fucking mask.

I adjusted my skirt, swallowing my anger.

"I'm going out tonight," I said, hating how rough my voice was. "You're my *bodyguard*, so you listen to me."

Theo seemed to think on that a moment, then turned from me, walking out of the room. He paused in the doorway, only to turn back and chuck his mother's diary into the center of the room. "When you're ready to stop telling lies, come find me."

He slammed the door shut.

I felt awful. The one thing he kept locked tighter than his heart now lay split open on the floor. I picked it up, heart pounding, holding it with more care than a bird's egg as I went to the door.

"Theo, I'm sorry—" I broke off when the knob wouldn't budge.

I tugged on it.

Locked

He fucking locked me in.

My fist was poised to slam, when I paused. The open window blew silky air on my skin. This wasn't the first time I'd been locked in my tower.

Abigail Crowne had perfected climbing out windows.

"Hey, are you Abigail Crowne?" Some kid sidled up next to me, trying to get a look at me under my baseball hat. "You are. I've seen your vag!"

"Congratulations," I said with faux cheer. "You're almost as special as a used tampon."

He muttered something about me being a bitch and walked away.

This night *sucked*.

I tugged on the bill of my baseball cap, hiding my face. The key with doing a DiCaprio was not to stand out. Whoever looked the least wealthy got the most props. Gray tended to take it to the extreme. Someone actually *gave* him money tonight.

I pulled T2 from my bra—the only spot I could put anything—spinning it around on my finger, rose gold catching the light.

I missed Theo.

Stupid, broody Theo and his cocky smile. His slightly slumped shoulders, like he didn't give two shits if people noticed him—but that's *all* I could do.

I'd read each page of his mother's diary before I left. She'd lived in Crowne Point and the one guy she'd slept with skipped town. She never saw him again, though she didn't love him, and by sleeping with him she'd been forcing herself to be someone else.

A lot of the pages were rambling thoughts of a teenager, but each she addressed to him, sometimes to Theo or just "baby boy."

When I'd finished, I hadn't realized how much time had passed until the sky was dark and it was time to meet Gray.

My siblings hadn't included me in anything past the boat ride, and I wasn't sure where they were. So I drank in a dark bar, elbows on the sticky counter, occasionally rebuffing assholes. Everyone looked in their early twenties, and a few maybe younger, in their teens.

With nothing else to do, I opened the browser on my phone, searching for private investigators, toying with the idea of hiring one for Theo's mom, but guilt kept me from sending them an email. It felt wrong to do this behind his back.

Gray and Gemma appeared, sprinting out of the basement, laughing. A few seconds later, a mob followed them, yelling words in Spanish I couldn't catch.

I set my drink down.

"Ladrón!"

Thief.

I sat up straighter.

I came outside in time to hear Gray say, "I didn't steal shit. I just let that fat ass dog out for a much needed walk."

"Vete a la mierda, maldito ladrón!"

Gray doubled over, holding his gut and onto Gemma for support.

My Spanish wasn't as good as my French or Swedish, but I caught enough to know the guy was pissed.

Sirens sounded in the distance and Gray and Gemma pointed at me. "We gave it to her."

Everyone focused on me at once.

"*¿Dónde diablos está mi perro?*"

Something about a dog, and once again, not happy with me.

"Uh..."

When I looked back, Gray and Gemma had vanished.

FUCK.

I slowly raised my hands. A mob of about ten angry Spanish hipsters were waiting for me to give them information about a dog I'd never seen.

"Have..." I took a step back. "You..." Another step. "Checked..." I turned on my heel and sprinted away. "*Idon'tfuckingknow.*"

I reached the pier, finding Gemma and Gray already in the boat. The air was extra brackish, and the wind had picked up, whipping my oversized hoodie.

"What did you do with the dog, asshole?"

Gray rolled his eyes. "The dog is fine. It's in the bathroom." He turned on the engine, and that was when I noticed they were unanchored and pulling away from the dock. I ran to the edge, but there was already too much space between us. The sea was a dark void.

I could've asked them to stop, to come back, but it would've been pointless. I was such a fucking idiot. It hit me in the gut hard as they laughed, pulling the boat away.

I was the fall guy.

There was always one in every group.

I don't know why I'd thought tonight would be any different. Of course the only reason they would invite me was because I was the fall guy.

But it *hurt*.

It hurt to be abandoned. Flashbacks to boarding school assaulted me. When Gray paid a boy to ask me to the dance, only so he could abandon me the night of. Or the time I thought I'd fallen in love with another boy, and he'd sent my dirty pictures to everyone.

And then Gemma had bribed someone on the yearbook to include them.

I'm no saint, either. My hands are bloody, my soul is stained. We're all stuck in this vicious cycle of hurting and being hurt.

I glanced to my right, where paparazzi and officers had gathered. My options were slim. If I wasn't home by morning, Mom would kill me. If I got spotted tonight, Mom would kill me. It was looking like Mom was going to kill me.

Gray waved, and the engine revved, dark water churning white as they got smaller and smaller, fading into the glittery night. "Enjoy the nunnery, Newt."

Oh my God.

Newt.

Newt! After Isaac Newton, the nickname given to any fall guy at our boarding school. I'd totally forgotten he had a real name, because Newt—err Ned—was *everyone's* fall guy back in Rosey, and no one called him anything save Newt all the years we were there.

I was on the precipice of remembering something important, *so close* to remembering his full name, his *real* name—

An arm yanked on my shoulder, pulling me back.

Theo.

"Did you think you could run from me, Reject?"

Theo dragged me to another boat in silence. This boat was nowhere near as nice as the one we had. It was a small, wooden one that fit two, maybe three, people and the engine sputtered. I wondered if he'd got it off one of the servants.

I kept thinking back to Newt/Ned, trying to remember his last name, but I couldn't remember one person calling him by it in all the years we went to Rosey.

We tiptoed from the dock up whitewashed steps to the Spanish colonial, pausing to hide from Mother's servants beneath the shadow of a wooden trellis. Theo's chest was pressed to mine. His chin barely grazing my scalp. Below us, the sea slapped against the dock walls, a soothing melody.

"I read it," I whispered. "I read her diary."

Theo cleared his throat. "Told you, not much in there."

There was so much in there. All of it was filled to the brim with love and longing. Our walls were *finally* falling down. Even in the past, Theo had never let me look through his mother's diary.

I had to tell him about Newt.

"How did you find me?" I whispered.

That brought his attention to me, our eyes locking. "I'll always find you, Abigail. Remember that next time you spend the energy falling out a window. I used to be the one catching you."

Though his words made my heart leap, I pulled away. "That doesn't answer my question." The longer the silence pressed, the deeper my gut sank. I took a step back, night air and Spanish stars between us.

"How, Theo?" I pressed.

He worked his jaw. "Your key chain has a tracker in it."

My heart dropped. "I'm such a fool."

"No, Abigail—"

"I thought this gift meant something." I tore the key chain from my bra. "I thought you cared about me. You told me to trust you. To stop telling lies."

I'd been played the fool... *again*.

"Why can't it be both?" Anger usurped his breath and he gripped my shoulders, dragging me to him, eyes blazing. "It's because I care about you. Fuck, can't you see that? Am I supposed to just sit around and hope nothing happens to you?"

"You could have told me. Why did you *lie*?"

He dropped me, and whatever remorse I'd seen vanished. "Following your lead, Abs. I know there's something you aren't telling me."

Guilt swamped me. I knew I should tell him about Ned. Maybe I should've told him about him the day I realized we'd gone to school together, but there was still so much shit between us.

And now there was even *more*.

So I deflected. "You didn't use this to save me. You used it because you trapped me in a room and didn't like that I climbed out." I chucked the pretty key chain into the open sea.

It hurt.

It hurt so much.

Theo watched the glimmering gold disappear into the black waters before turning back to me. "What happens if I can't be there for you?"

"I guess we'll have to do it the old-fashioned way. With trust."

"Abigail."

My mom's voice was like a damn Taser. I sprang off Theo, feeling caught despite having done nothing.

I rubbed my dark hair. "Uh, Mom. You're up late."

An agonizing silence followed my brilliant observation. Then she turned away, walking toward her bedroom. For a second I had hope she'd leave it at that.

"Are you coming?" she asked, impatience thin, feathery, and sharp.

Into her room? At two in the morning? Anxiety crawled like ants under my skin, but I followed. I could feel Theo watching after me.

A single lamp lit up the sitting room inside her wing. She sat on the antique love seat beside it. I could tell she'd been awake for some time, because her makeup was on, her curls were done, and, though she was in pajamas, they were the kind meant to be seen in.

I took a shaky seat across from her when my eyes landed on the items on the table between us. Photos and notes of me—of me? I looked more clearly. They were the ones Newt had sent. The only place they could have come from was my box.

My box.

A trillion questions flitted through my mind. How long has she had them? *Why* did she have them? And what could it possibly mean that it now sat between us?

"We need to talk," my mother said.

I dragged my eyes away from the box, finding her dark-blue ones. Warm, Mediterranean night air whispered through gauzy curtains.

"In a few weeks' time your grandfather will close this deal, and then your fiancé will meet us in Switzerland."

The wrinkle in my brow deepened. This hardly seemed

so important to discuss at two in the morning. My eyes flittered to the box.

"Okay..." was all I managed.

She pulled the box into her lap. "I've seen your evidence. A few pictures are nothing to be concerned about."

She flitted through the photos and letters. I was missing a key bit of information. I still wasn't grasping it. It was there, close, a needle digging the tip of my tongue.

She lifted her head. "What are you hoping to accomplish, Abigail? All I see here are love letters from a future fiancé. Ned Harlington is a good..."

When she said his name, all the rest of her words faded to darkness. I stared at the box in my mom's hands. Harlington, the very same Harlington I'd heard spoken over and over since the acquisition began. The dots had been there, but I'd never quite connected them.

"Ned... is *Edward* Harlington?"

"The son of the man your grandfather has been trying to back into a deal for more than a year, your fiancé."

Everything clicked into place. The roses in Crowne Hall. The Fourth party where I supposedly met my fiancé.

I could barely breathe. "Why is everyone calling him Edward?"

My mother blinked slowly. "Why do people call you Abby, Abigail?" Silence followed as my heart raced and nausea consumed me.

I was going to marry someone who'd drugged me, stalked me, threatened me. What would happen when there was no distance between us, no walls to keep me safe?

"We can't afford a classic Abigail scene," my mom said. "Nothing seems to be working with you. The only reason I submitted to having that boy back was to keep you on a leash. I think it's time to send him away—"

"No, no. I'll be good." Send Theo away—again? "I'll be better."

Her sharp eyes narrowed, catching. Had I let on I cared too much? I knew if I backtracked, it would solidify what she suspected.

"I..." I swallowed. "I didn't know. I didn't realize who it was."

I should've known. I should've connected the dots. I hoped in vain we could end it here, and Mom would let me pretend this never happened.

But he would be in Switzerland?

My throat closed at the thought.

She exhaled through her nostrils. "Edward Harlington is from a good family, he could marry any girl he wants, and he chose *you*. He chose us. I can't even find it in me to be shocked you're trying to ruin this—"

"I..." I cut her off, voice scratchy. "I made a mistake."

I stared at the floor, willing a hole to open up and suck me in.

She eyed me with a sigh. "Come here." I stood up, finding a seat next to her on the antique couch. "You know I don't like being harsh with you." She hugged me. She caressed my hair, holding me like she had when I was a little girl.

"I know," I mumbled into her shoulder.

She sighed again, her disappointment seeping like water into my bones, deeper still, until I didn't know where it had gone and could only feel it. Weathering and cold. Her fingers stroked through my hair, separating it like water in the way only she could.

Mom rarely hugged me, and anytime she did, it was

usually after she'd emotionally obliterated me. How fucked up was it to live for these moments?

We sat in disharmonious silence. I didn't count the minutes, and I tried to enjoy the rare mother-daughter time. Tried not to think about what led to it.

"I almost eloped, you know," she said absently.

I don't think I could have spoken if someone put a gun to my head. I stared at my mother, wondering if I'd heard her correctly.

"I guess you could say he was my Theo. He worked for my father in the mailroom, because back then there was such a thing as a mailroom," she added, raising a brow at me. "He brought me cheap chocolates and we listened to music that would make my father's toes curl."

A small smile curved her lips, a *real* smile, soft and so un-Tansy-like. I tried to imagine my mom as anyone other than the woman who sent back perfectly fine cherries. Someone who ate cheap chocolate and listened to popular music.

"What happened to him?"

It was foolish of me to hope for a happy ending. She'd married my father; obviously she hadn't ended up with her Theo.

Still, my heart stood on tiptoes.

"He died."

Mom spoke as if we were discussing the weather, always composed, but I was struggling to breathe. Both her husband *and* her first—maybe only—love had died?

"Not at first," she continued. "But watching me marry your father killed him slowly until he wrapped his car around a tree."

She turned to me. "I made a mistake, Abigail. I made

him think we could be together, and I let him fall in love with me."

My eyes traveled to the door, as if I could see Theo on the other side. I'd always been selfish when it came to him. Selfish to take him, selfish to keep him, selfish to want him to stay.

"Did you ever think about giving it all up for him?" I asked quietly.

"You won't marry Theo, Abigail. You can't be a princess and marry a pauper."

I didn't know what to say. I just sat in the dimly lit room, picking at my jeans. The single lamp didn't seem like enough light for the dark words.

"I know you think I'm a villain."

"No, I—" I attempted, but she cut me off.

"I don't want you to be like me, Abigail. Don't make the same mistakes. Men like Edward are dangerous only if you let them be. He isn't like your grandfather; he isn't cunning." Something flickered in her eyes, something like fear, but it was gone before I could be sure.

I couldn't help my next words. "He threatened me. He stalked me. He drugged me."

"He's a coward. Cowards are easy to control."

She smiled at me.

This was the first sincere conversation I'd ever had with my mother. I couldn't help but wonder if anyone else knew this side of her. As uncomfortable as the subject matter was, I couldn't help wondering if we were finally getting closer.

Then she sighed. "Maybe we should send you home. It might be easier for... everyone."

All my hopes shattered.

Send me *home*? So that entire conversation meant nothing? We all hated this forced family time, but it was a Crowne tradition. They were cutting me out of the family picture, and I could feel the scissors scraping along my soul with each cut.

"I can handle it," I said. "I'll... I'll marry him."

A long, palpable silence followed my words. When my mother finally spoke, it was about a completely different subject.

"Have you been to see Dr. Brenner recently?" she asked lightly, referring to our on-call plastic surgeon.

"No. Why?"

Her eyes lingered on my bare midriff, then returned to mine with a tight smile. "Maybe make an appointment when we get back."

I rubbed my eyes as I left my mother's wing. I wouldn't cry, but they still stung. I could handle Ned. I'd *been* handling him. What I couldn't handle? Being yet another disappointment to my mother and losing Theo in the process.

TWENTY-ONE

ABIGAIL

Uneasy is the girl who wears the name Crowne.

My grandma told me that on my seventh birthday. Everyone said she was losing her mind and not to pay attention to her words.

I'm not so sure.

Since Spain, things with Theo have been off. On the surface, things are okay, but it feels wrong, a strong current beneath still waters. Our time in Italy flew by, and now we're heading to Switzerland.

I haven't told him the truth about my fiancé.

He hasn't apologized for the key chain. Not really.

I want to tell Theo everything, but we're hours away from Switzerland.

Switzerland.

Where I might see Ned and have no choice but to act like everything is fine, like he hasn't been tormenting me.

Theo would rip Ned apart, and if Theo did that, Mom would rip Theo apart.

I glanced at Theo, sitting stoically beside me on the plane.

It feels like fate in a way. I haven't seen my grandpa since the Swan Swell, since the day Theo ripped us apart. It prods something inside me, opens up the parts of me I've been pretending didn't exist. The odd distance between Theo and me, the lies I'm telling, the secrets I'm worried he might be keeping.

We're ignoring a chasm between us, and my grandfather might be the thing to shove us inside.

"Something's bothering you, Abigail," Theo said the moment we landed. Cool summer air whipped at our skin, the jet still powering down. "Something more than what I did."

"I'm nervous to see my grandpa," I lied. Guilt ripped apart his face, and he went quiet. Shame settled in my stomach.

A black town car pulled up, one of four, and I was seated alone with Theo in one as my mother and siblings took their own.

It wasn't a short drive to the house, but it's worth it. Switzerland was my favorite as a child. It's our very own fairy-tale castle, with steepled roofs, turrets, and crenellations. Built into the top of the mountain and rising high into the blue sky, we took a winding road into verdant snow-capped mountains. A shimmering clear lake was below us, and evergreen spruce surrounded us on all sides.

Inside the castle, I looked around, as if Ned was going to pop up any minute, but it was just us and the servant staff.

"He'll be here tomorrow. Remember what you promised." My mother smiled and walked away, up the winding staircase toward her room. Servants followed, carrying her luggage.

I was jumpy in my skin. Itchy. Emotions were eating me alive. I couldn't think about them.

So I did what I did best. I reacted.

Gemma was leaning against the wall, on her phone.

No more classic Abigail scenes.

My mom's words were fresh in my mind. I opened and closed my fist.

"Have you seen Dr. Brenner recently?" I asked lightly, approaching Gemma.

She looked up from her phone. "No, why?"

"No reason..." I lingered on her midriff, long enough for a wrinkle to appear between her brows, then kept walking. I saw her tug down her shirt out of my periphery.

Why was it when I should be on my best behavior, I was always on my worst?

I hadn't even crossed the foyer when I caught Theo's gaze. He watched me too closely, seeing right through me. I walked past him like it wasn't a big deal he was there, or that he'd seen what I'd done.

He fell in step behind me.

Our footfalls echoed in the vaulted castle ceilings, haunting. While the castle was centuries old, inside had been entirely updated. Switzerland was the light to Crowne Halle's dark. Just as opulent but with pale blue, silver, and white decor.

My wing was no different, all silver and blue, with regal furnishings as old as the castle. The minute we got back to my room, I busied myself. I grabbed my suitcase, throwing it on my bed, wrinkling the satin. I had to unpack, because Gray *still kept Story.* So I focused on that.

"Are you ready to tell me what's going on?" Theo's low, steady voice was at my back.

"You're not making much sense, Theo."

Theo always had a hard time with how my peers got away with everything. I knew deep down that when it came to me, he wouldn't let it go. Which meant Mom would never give me another chance, and somehow, *worse*, Theo would leave my side.

I was already out of my mind trying to figure out how to keep them away from one another.

Theo gripped my chin, drawing my eyes away from my haphazard unpacking. "Abs."

Warning flared bright in my brain. Theo could see into me. He could rip out pieces of me I didn't give him permission to take. He was clawing into my soul at that very moment.

I dropped to my knees, reaching for a distraction as much as I was reaching for his buttons. He grasped my wrists, holding me off.

"Fuck off, Abigail. Do you think I'm that simple?"

I bit my lip, looking away.

Still holding my wrists, he bent until we were eye to eye. "Who is he? Who has you this scared?"

"I don't know."

He dropped my wrists with so much force I turned in the other direction.

"Classic Abigail. At any sign of pain or hurt you build your walls. Can't let anyone see those deep, dark insides, after all."

I didn't speak, focusing on his black sneakers.

"You spend so much time picking out the most precious items. You turn lost and forgotten things into treasure.

Would you ever put them on some weak, breaking metal band?"

"Of course not," I said.

"So why are you doing that with your soul, your heart?" He touched his pastel bracelet on my wrist. "Your bracelet will break if you keep building it with brittle wire."

I knew he was talking about more than his bracelet, more than my jewelry. My heart ached.

"Why are you hurting, Abigail?" he asked softly.

"Don't make me lie to you!" My throat was clogged with tears. I never cried. Theo was the only one who did this to me.

He watched me in silence for so long my knees started to ache. The muscle in his jaw twerked with how tight he clenched. The hollows of his cheeks even deeper, gaunter. His eyes were a campfire, blazing and fierce, yet soft.

"I can't let this go," he finally said.

"So don't," I said. "Just for now, for tonight."

When I reached for him again, he didn't push me away.

"What are you staring at?" I asked, peering at Theo from over a book. We were alone in the library, and every few minutes I'd look up from my book to see him staring.

"You." He leaned forward, elbows on his knees. "You get lost in a book the same way you get lost in my cock, you know that? It's fucking distracting."

I looked down, cheeks flaming.

"Shit, Abigail," he said. "You know what that look does to me."

Still looking down, I set my book on the studded suede arm of my chair, then got to my knees, walking to him. His eyes transmuted, burning coals. As I got closer, he spread his legs enough to allow me between his knees.

"Sweet girl..." Theo threaded his fingers into my hair, caressing from my scalp to the middle of my back. His eyes creased, and I knew he was about to rip open the wound between us.

"Don't," I pleaded. "Just... not right now."

At least Theo and I seemed to have perfected this part. Communication, our emotions, our truths, were all tangled in the barbed wires of our past.

But this? This was easy for us.

I placed my head on his thigh, and he slowed his caress.

"Your grandfather wishes to see you." I jumped up at the voice, hitting Theo's chin with my head. He cursed and I rubbed my scalp, turning to find my grandfather's guard in the arched doorway.

How much had he seen?

"M-My grandfather?"

I hadn't met with my grandfather one-on-one since the night Theo had ruined my relationship with him.

I stood, leaving my book discarded on the soft velvet wingback, and followed the guard.

When we reached my grandfather's office, the guard placed a hand on Theo's chest, not allowing him to follow me through the doors.

"It's okay," I said. "Nothing bad is going to happen to me in my grandpa's office."

Theo's frown deepened, his jaw clenched. Even I didn't quite believe my words, but I followed my grandfather's guard through the doors.

Grandfather's guard deposited me like a package, then shut the door, leaving us alone.

"Edward Harlington is joining us soon," Grandpa said,

facing an expansive window. "I know you're aware of his... predilections."

Predilections, that was a nice way of phrasing it.

"You knew?"

Grandpa turned to his desk, unlocking a drawer. He pulled out photos, placing them on the desk. At first I was expecting them to be the ones from my box, assuming my mother had shared them, but they were of me and Theo, all from the last month.

Mostly in compromising positions, like kissing, there were even photos of us the night out on the Riviera.

My lips parted, but no words came out.

"There's nothing I don't know, Abigail."

"Are you following me?" I finally managed.

"I would have been foolish not to, after what happened at the Swan Swell." Grandpa folded his arms, watching me. "I know now you were not behind those photos, just like I know that it doesn't really matter because, in the end..." He sifted through some of them. "You were still a disappointment."

A stale silence lingered, his disappointment etched in the wrinkles around his mouth. At me. At Theo.

"What are you going to do to him?"

"Do you remember the night you begged me to keep Theo?"

"U-Uh..." It felt like a trap.

"Theo doesn't have any family, anything to keep him attached to something other than the job. He was the perfect protégé. At least, he was. What can you take from someone who has nothing, Abigail?"

I rolled my bottom lip between my teeth, recognizing that either way I answered, I'd lose.

"You take away what you've given them."

I ran over to his desk, slamming my hands on it. "You can't send him away. *Please.*"

I couldn't lose Theo, not again.

He leaned forward on steepled fingers, eyes narrowed. "I think that's up to you, princess."

Princess.

He was calling me *princess* again, but the warmth had been replaced with an ominous lilt.

"This marriage isn't a death sentence, Abigail. You can have your cake and eat it too. You just have to remember... you can't be a Crowne without many sharp points."

I focused on the meaning behind his words. Beryl Crowne would do anything to keep the Crowne name untarnished. Fear and foreboding strangled my gut.

I swallowed. "I understand. You're either for this family or against it."

THEO

I can feel Abigail slipping through my fingers, and I don't know why, or how to fix it. Tonight will be the first meal she'd have with her grandpa since I'd wrecked that relationship, the first time she'd be in the room with him.

I was in Switzerland, which meant everyone had to dress for dinner. I was in a tux and Abigail was in an absolutely fucking cruel strapless black-and-emerald dress with a slit in the jewel-toned satin skirt that went all the way to her hip.

As I walked behind her to the vaulted medieval dining room of their Swiss castle, the grains kept falling. If I told him the truth, he'd fire me and make sure I never saw Abigail. Not telling him wasn't an option either.

"Theo!" Her grandfather spotted me, waving me over to him at the end of the table. Abigail watched me warily as I went to him.

He clapped my shoulder. "I think a promotion is in order when this wedding is finished. You've been handling her well. Not a peep by the press."

Abigail eyed me as she took a seat at the table.

Fuck.

"I'm curious, what could you possibly have done to get her so cooperative?" Beryl Crowne asked, digging his fingers into my shoulder.

"Just the usual..." I trailed off.

Beryl's death grip on my shoulder wouldn't give. "And did you enjoy your time on the Riviera?"

Abigail dropped her fork, eyes shooting to her grandfather's. I focused on the meaning behind the words, uncertain why fear clouded Abigail's eyes, why he was digging his fingers into me like I'd pissed him off.

Don't date my granddaughters, don't even look at them, and don't get any ideas about biting the hand that feeds you.

Did he *know?*

"Oh, you made it!" Tansy said.

"How was your flight?" Beryl dropped my grip with his question, voice light.

Tansy's thick wood chair slid along the marble floor, a servant at her back. A smile still lingered on my face when I saw who'd captured their attention. The mood didn't vanish; it faded like smoke.

Standing in the arched doorway was the asshole terrorizing Abigail.

He ruffled his hair, lazy smile landing on Abigail. "The flight was too long, but I'm here now."

I had him pressed against the gold-trimmed doorway before I could think. It was instinct. My forearm was at his throat, digging into his Adam's apple, applying just enough pressure to keep him conscious.

Tansy Crowne's shrill voice rang out behind me, telling me to let him go.

"You're here early." Abigail's voice shook, and for that, I dug the forearm at his throat deeper.

Wait—*early?*

"Couldn't wait to see you, babe," he coughed the words, face purpling.

My glare deepened into an ache. Did she *know* he was coming?

Tansy had welcomed him. Beryl had welcomed him. He had gotten into one of the most fortified houses in the world. This guy wasn't just one of them, he was somehow close with the Crownes. I stared at him, and as if reading my thoughts, he fucking smiled.

"Have you lost your mind?" Tansy shouted once more. "Let go of Abigail's fiancé."

TWENTY-TWO

THEO

"Theo, let him go," Abigail said, suddenly at my side.

A good Crowne employee let him go, because whatever he'd done to Abigail, he was in their good graces.

I would fucking kill him.

"Let him go," Abigail beseeched. She pressed her splayed hands into my side, trying to push me off.

From the corner of my eye, I could see Crowne guards making their way toward me. Mr. Crowne was getting out of his chair. While he had a smile on his face as he reassured Mrs. Harlington, there was nothing but coldness in his eyes.

I weighed the pros and cons of snapping this guy's neck right then and there. As if sensing what I was doing, and knowing the outcome, his blue eyes glittered smug and assured.

My grip at his neck tightened, happy to see him grow red.

"Theo, *please*," Abigail begged. Fucking begged.

I stepped off, shaking out my arms so I wouldn't wring his neck.

His collar was wrinkled, and he rubbed his neck, but the fucking grin stayed on his face.

I let Abigail shove me out of the dining room, into the hall and all the way back to her wing, until we were in her room. Then I yanked my arm out of her hold. I dragged my hands through my hair, looking into her searching eyes. Everything in my body wanted to beat the shit out of him, end this fucking problem right now.

All my helplessness came rushing out in rage. "You fucking lied, Abigail. Again. You know him."

What other secrets had she been keeping? She was sand. Slipping and slipping through holes I couldn't see. She looked away, to an ornate silver mirror cutting our reflections in half.

"How long have you known?"

"Spain," she admitted. "Well, I knew I'd gone to boarding school with him at the afterparty..."

Helpless frustration rose hot and acerbic, cutting through my chest and up my throat. I couldn't be helpless, so I got angrier.

"How long have you known Grandfather was aware of us?"

Her lips parted, a deer caught in headlights.

"Fucking typical." I laughed, but there was no humor in it. "You couldn't tell the truth if there was a goddamn gun to your head."

"I was trying to avoid this!" Pain strangled her. There was no Abigail glow and spark in her cheeks, she was hollowed and bone dry. Even the chandelier above couldn't warm her. She looked miserable.

I started moving toward the dining room again, not certain of a plan but fueled by the need to fix this.

Fix that look on her face.

"You can't." She grabbed my wrist. I kept walking, dragging her with me. She dug her heels into the silver-blue patterned carpet in an attempt to anchor me.

"Give me one good reason why I shouldn't kill him right now."

Her grip loosened enough for me to shuck her off, but I only made it a few more feet before she ran in front of me, arms splayed, attempting to block my path.

"You'll *die*."

I shrugged. "Not good enough."

I pushed her out of the way as gently as I could.

Blood.

That was the only way I'd be satisfied.

"What about the fact that even if you manage to get past all the guards in there, I'd never see you again?" she yelled at my back. "What about me? What about what it will do to me?"

I spun on her. "And what about me, Abigail? What do you think marrying him will do to *me*?"

Her eyes found mine again, shining even in the low light. "Are you offering me something different?"

I turned away with a curse.

I had nothing, no life to offer her. She was Abigail Crowne, and if she didn't marry who they told her to, she'd end up alone, abandoned, and discarded like I'd been.

I couldn't fucking do that to her.

Helplessness and fear bubbled up, and I slammed my fist into the wall. Plaster fluttered to the floor, my breathing roaring thunder in my ears, and then I felt it... her hands. They were so light at first I thought it was air.

I found her eyes, and she was already looking up at me. So gentle and fucking heartbreaking. As her world collapsed, she was still thinking of me.

After a moment, she pulled back.

I shook out my hand. "This isn't okay."

"It doesn't matter! It doesn't matter, Theo. When has it ever?"

I clasped her face between my palms and spun her around, pressing her against the wall. "You matter, Abigail. *You matter.*"

I slammed her against the wall, pinning her in a kiss.

ABIGAIL

Theo's kisses were everywhere at once. My neck, my chin, my lips. Biting, bruising lips that disappeared to my neck and came back to my mouth, robbing me of breaths and sighs.

"Theo." I tried to get his attention, but I could barely breathe through his kisses. He lifted both my hands, trapping them beneath one of his own. Loose plaster bit my back from where he'd punched the wall. In all my years with Theo, I'd never seen him lose control. Never. It was terrifying.

I didn't fear for myself. I feared for him.

"Theo," I tried again as he slid his hand up my thighs, inside the slit of my gown.

Lips, teeth, skin.

The room blurred, and I arched my back.

"Theo!" I yelled, as much to stop him as myself.

Theo froze, then slowly lifted his head from my neck. My heart broke. His lips were red from kissing me, his hair wild from how much he'd tangled it in his hands. His eyes were raw. An exposed nerve.

I wiggled my wrists in his hold, wanting to caress his cheek and soothe him. He tightened his grip.

"You have to let me handle it," I said. "Whatever happens, you can't do anything to Ned. You can't go to my mom. You *can't*." My voice was soft, looking at him with round eyes. *Pleading*. "Promise me, Theo."

He ground his jaw. "I'm not playing this game—"

"It's not a fucking game. *Promise* me."

Theo exhaled through his nostrils. I waited. I wasn't going to give in. I wasn't going to let Theo throw his life away for me.

"I promise," he said, spitting out the words like bitter coffee.

Before I could say another word, he slammed his lips against mine. The kiss was different—Theo was different. Rushed. Pressured. Intense. *More*. Like he was trying to use me up. All of me. It was exhilarating and scary.

He ripped apart sateen buttons holding my gown together, shoving it down until I was in a puddle of green satin and black lace. I took off his jacket in the same breath he unbuttoned his shirt, then his pants.

His large hands tangled in my hair, controlling my head so soft lips were on my neck, biting, bruising. He walked me back to the bed, hot skin flush against mine. His thick, muscled arms wrapped around me, holding me close.

I don't know why this feels like an ending.

He fished a condom out of his pants pocket, and I put it on him this time. He was hot and hard beneath my hand, and he watched me do it, a hunger in his eyes that made my hands shake. When I finished, I trailed my fingers up the sculpted ridges of his eight pack, sliding up his pecs, around his neck.

Theo pressed my collarbone, pushing me back to the bed with gentle force. Against the satin bedspread, I crawled on my elbows as he climbed on top of me. His lips found me almost as soon as they left me. Theo was looming, predatory, and ravenous.

Then he was *there—so* agonizingly close to sliding inside me.

I want to feel Theo without the barrier. I've never considered it before, but now it's all I want.

"Theo," I breathed his name like a prayer.

He pulled back so our foreheads were pressed, lips are a feather's distance from mine. Tenderness warmed his eyes, but some other grim emotion distorted it, made it raw and aching.

"I love you, Abigail."

It was so quiet, I thought maybe I'd misheard.

I *hope* I did.

He can't love me. He *can't*.

"Through your lies and your emotional garbage, I love you—"

"You can't," I blurted.

All the warmth was sucked out of the room with my words, and suddenly I was ice cold beneath him.

Theo looked like I'd slapped him. "I *can't*?"

He was still in that same aching spot. I was riding a wicked, dangerous edge, my heartbeat too loud in my ears. The throbbing between my thighs, the one in my heart, and the one rising in my throat all distort to one twisted feeling.

"I mean—" I could feel him pulling away and I didn't

want him to do it physically so I grappled onto his shoulders. "I don't know why I said that."

Yes, I did.

Theo Hound couldn't love me. It would be so much harder to keep him separate. To keep him safe.

Keep me safe.

Theo pushed off me and my heart rushed and pounded as he got farther away. I was screwing this up. I was fucking up *everything*. He was yanking on his jeans, throwing on his shirt, and I couldn't think of the right words to fix it.

"Theo, wait—"

He stopped, his jeans unbuttoned, giving me one last chance.

I had nothing. Nothing could make what he'd said okay. If the one boy—the one *person*—I couldn't lose in this world started to love me, then I could lose him forever.

The door slammed behind him. I should run after him and tell him how much I love him. I never stopped loving him. He was as essential to my heart as the blood that made it beat.

Instead I fell to my back.

The feel of our almost still lingered between my thighs, a deep-rooted, unsatisfied ache that now matched the one spreading from my chest. I was drowning. Wet, like he'd made me. Wet, from my tears.

Tears fell down my cheeks, but I didn't sob. I couldn't. I was too shocked. Of all the fuckups I'd ever made, this was the worst. I didn't just make him think it was okay to love me... I made him think I was worth it.

TWENTY-THREE

ABIGAIL

I'd fucked up so much. Theo and I hadn't spoken since last night, and now he just stood guard outside my room, like nothing happened. I'd opened my mouth so many times to speak, and each time closed it. I didn't know what to say or do to fix it.

Edward was the perfect needle to pop our rose-tinted bubble.

I was the perfect needle.

"Ten minutes until breakfast."

I slammed my laptop shut at his voice.

He eyed the action, pain flickering in his eyes, but said nothing, stepping back to position. Guilt slammed into me.

I'd caved and emailed a PI, and they'd messaged me back, told me they thought they weren't sure they could find Theo's mother, not with the little information I'd given them, but they'd try. I didn't know how to tell him. Theo had made it clear he didn't want to look for her, and I was worried he'd be mad, especially after last night.

"Theo, wait!" I threw my laptop off my lap, jumping off the bed. "Let me explain."

He stared forward. "You don't owe me any explanations."

"But—"

"You're going to be late for breakfast, Ms. Crowne."

Ms. Crowne. It was like the past months never happened. Last night never happened.

I sighed and walked back into my bedroom to get dressed. In Switzerland, we always had to dress up, but at least for breakfast a tea-length periwinkle tulle dress would do, rather than a gown. Theo was in another mouthwatering slate-gray suit.

We were just outside the breakfast hall when I grasped Theo's sleeve, forcing him to acknowledge me. Even though Theo had been keeping his distance, he'd been even *more* protective, if it was possible. He refused to let me walk into any room first. He was constantly on guard.

"Ask me a truth or promise," I said, tugging on his sleeve, wrinkling the perfect press. He turned around, shoulders tensed.

I took a step anyway, reaching for him. "Ask me."

"Rethink that step." The hate in his growl could set a house on fire.

I paused.

Had I really messed everything up so badly?

A moment passed, and then I noticed he wasn't looking at me. I followed his stare over my shoulder. Ned was frozen mid step.

That was all Theo said. He hadn't moved from his spot behind me, arms folded as usual, head slightly down like he was bored at a concert. But it was all he needed to say. Menace dripped off him.

Ned took a step back. "Guess the rumors about your dog are true…"

He smiled somewhat nervously, looking over my shoulder.

"He bites," I said.

"I'm just here to remind you you'll be sitting next to *me* tomorrow at lunch," Ned said, though he didn't take his eyes off Theo.

"Great," I said, disdain oozing from my lips.

"You can't be there all the time, dog," Ned said, eyes on Theo.

A foreign look flickered across Theo's face. Fear?

That couldn't be right.

When he saw me watching him, it vanished.

Theo leaned forward until he was over my shoulder, just next to my face. He clamped his teeth harsh and fast, the sound echoing, the motion fluttering the hair at my neck.

It made goose bumps of excitement pepper my flesh, but Ned jumped and scampered inside the dining hall.

The moment filled like a balloon, popping with our simultaneous laughter. For a minute I thought the mess I'd made last night was over, but then I caught his gaze as I wiped a tear from my eye, and his smile dropped. Silence descended once more.

"Theo—"

"Breakfast, Ms. Crowne," Theo cut me off, throwing his arm out toward the dining hall.

I studied his face, waiting—hoping he'd look back at me with anything other than boredom and disdain.

Then I sighed and walked inside the dining hall.

THEO

Abigail fell asleep late into the night, and now I dug my elbows into my knee, my chin on steepled hands, watching her.

I couldn't sleep, couldn't stop thinking. Edward knew the truth long before it hit me brutal and hard. He was untouchable.

"These little dates of ours are growing too common."

I lifted my head.

Tansy stood in the shadows, aglow only from the soft light leaking from Abigail's bedroom. Quietly, so as not to wake Abigail, I crossed the room and met Tansy outside the bedroom door.

"You know who that man is. You know what he's done to your daughter."

Tansy barely registered emotion. "The boy you assaulted like a common street thug? Or do you mean our daughter's fiancé? Our valued friend's son?"

"He's lucky he's not dead," I gritted.

She sighed through her nostrils. "Let's get to the point. You need something from me, and I'm... in a mood to give it to you."

As far as I knew there was nothing I could offer this woman. Tansy Crowne had everything, but I'd spent enough time in this world to know the fact that she even came meant there was something she wanted from me. Something money couldn't buy.

That thought didn't reassure me.

"What do you want?"

She pursed her lips. "Break up with her."

ABIGAIL

I woke to the sound of my mother's voice, drifting into my bedroom like a dream.

Abigail...

Next came Theo's voice.

Guards... Harlington...

I blinked, rubbing my eyes, adjusting to the soft light of my bedroom. I waited, ears perked, but only heard the sound of a door shutting, and silence.

"Theo?" I called out after a moment.

He came, still dressed in the suit he'd worn earlier today, though it was wrinkled now. Had he ever gone to bed?

"Did I hear my mom?" I asked, sitting up. "What were you talking about?"

His face was cold. It had *been* cold. It was worse than before; at least then he'd given me anger and contempt. Now there was nothing.

I rubbed my arm, trying to brush away goose bumps.

"She was reaming me for attacking her precious guest."

He slammed the door.

TWENTY-FOUR

ABIGAIL

The air was weird and toxic. For lunch, we all sat outside beneath a canopied table amidst the green gardens and sprawling lawn. It was reminiscent of a medieval tournament, minus the knights. At least the arranged marriages had remained.

I was next to Edward, and Theo? He was all the way down... next to Gemma.

Oddly enough, I had four new guards at my back, but I would trade every one for Theo.

"You look beautiful," Edward said to my left.

"You look constipated," I said without looking at him.

I couldn't take my eyes off Theo. Gemma's guard had come down with the flu. At least, that was what they said.

It shouldn't bother me, but I couldn't stop bouncing my leg. It shook the table. After last night and this morning, my insides were filled with fire ants.

It was just like before. I'd pushed and pushed and pushed, and in the end, scared him away.

Scared him off to Gemma.

He was with her. I was with Edward. This was not how it was supposed to be. Why couldn't I just tell him the truth?

Edward grabbed my hand and clenched so hard my bones felt like they were breaking.

I gasped, forced to look at him. "Ow!"

"Are your eyes caught in a glue trap?"

A tight smile wrinkled his cheeks, but there was nothing warm about it.

I tried to wrangle my hand free. "Let go."

He tightened his grip and I swear my bones caved in. I think a normal individual would feel a life-preservation instinct looking into the face of their stalker. Would *at least* weigh the pros and cons of their next move.

I bit my lower lip.

Bad idea face...

I knocked over his wineglass and plate of braised turkey, spilling them onto his lap.

He released me at once, jumping up.

I'd accomplished what I wanted, so I definitely should act like it was an accident and return to my food.

I grabbed my wineglass and, with shoulders back, stood up and threw it in his face. Pink liquid splashed and blinded him. He sputtered and scoffed, wiping it with both hands before blinking at me like I'd just killed his dog.

"Now you look a *little* bit more handsome," I said, folding the arm with the empty glass over the other. "But not by much."

The table grew quiet. My mother and grandpa, his parents, and my siblings were no doubt watching this unfold. No one had seen what Edward had done, and, honestly, they wouldn't *care*. So what if he'd grabbed me a little harshly? It was much worse to make a scene.

All this would be blamed on Abigail Crowne, fire starter.

Edward raised a hand like he was going to slap me, and on instinct, I closed my eyes. When nothing happened, I opened them.

My heart sank.

One of my new guards had stepped between us. It was just like every other guard I'd had before Theo. It didn't matter if I was about to be hit, you can't make a scene.

A part of me thought Theo might have saved me... I looked over to where he stood behind Gemma. He hadn't even so much as spared me a glance.

I couldn't fucking take this. I couldn't watch him choose Gemma. Screw third course or dessert or the fact that this was supposed to be for my engagement.

"Where the fuck are you going?" Edward snapped at my back.

"Darling?" my mother's voice trilled over my shoulder.

One word, but her tone spoke so much more.

Don't make a scene.

Edward had a dirty secret. He stalked and terrorized me, but all the wealthy had dirty secrets, some dirtier than others. No one gave a shit so long as they didn't air it.

"Literally anywhere but here," I said coolly.

My foot hadn't even landed on the first step when I was yanked back by my hair. I grabbed my scalp so I wouldn't fall and have my hair ripped out.

Conversation stopped, the clinking of forks silenced.

"Edward..." his mother's voice warned with the tone of scolding a child who'd taken a toy that didn't belong to him.

"She's mine. She's fucking *mine*. I saw her first." Another hard yank and I hissed, unable to hold it in.

I couldn't see anyone. My vision blurred on Edward's shiny black shoes... and then he let go.

I shot up, hands going to my head, scalp burning where he'd grabbed me. Two of my guards were at his back, holding him by his shoulders with a gentle yet firm touch. The other two stepped between us. How my mother would be proud, I thought venomously. They really knew how to keep up appearances.

Edward pushed wet hair out of his face, locked on me. The more he did it, the more unhinged he looked.

"Well..." my mom finally said, tapping fingers along her chin. "No need for coffee. I feel *quite* awake."

Gray, Gemma, and Horace were all uncharacteristically silent, with looks that might even be misconstrued as concern. I didn't want to be *pitied*, especially by my fucking siblings. Theo was finally looking at me, but his face was a mask.

Tears bobbed up my throat.

Humiliated at being used as a rag doll.

Humiliated because Theo had done *nothing*.

So I ran, sprinted until I was buoyed by silence, hidden in one of the many hallways of the castle. I leaned against a stone wall warmed by an opposite window, catching my breath.

My guards followed me from the garden, taking staggered posts along the hallway. I hated them, hated their very existence. They had gotten Edward off me. They'd done their job, but their presence meant Theo *hadn't*.

Had I ruined everything? Did he hate me so much? Or did he... did he maybe love her after all?

My scalp burned, but my eyes were absolutely on fire. I swiped tears.

"Abigail."

I snapped my head up at the voice. Light from cathedral windows bathed Theo in diamonds of chiaroscuro. White-gold sunshine warmed his lips, and shadows sculpted his cheekbones.

Feet of hallway separated us. His brows were drawn, his jaw clenched, and there was a war in his eyes I wondered if I'd started. Did he think I didn't love him, that everything was a lie?

"Hi," I managed.

Without a word he came to me and grasped my neck, pulling me to his chest.

He exhaled a soft sigh of exasperation, stroking my hair.

His shirt was soft too, and he smelled *divine*. It was so faint, so Theo. You only get to know the scent if you were paying attention, if you were close; fresh and clean, but spicy, and something else, something inscrutable. Something dark, a scent that made me curl my toes. He was home; he was safety. A scent I wanted to bury my nose in forever.

His palm landed on my scalp, stroking the aching place Edward had ripped.

He pulled back after a minute, but it felt like only a second. I searched his eyes. Even though he was staring right back, he was so far away. My lips parted to say something... I don't know, anything.

I opened my mouth and came up with nothing.

He took my hand, the one Edward had bruised, in both of his, tracing lines along the redness, brows drawn. Our breathing warmed the air like a summertime breeze, but desperation strangled it like storm clouds. He gripped me like it was for the last time.

"Ask me." It came out on a croak, and I swallowed, searching for courage. "Ask me, truth or promise?"

His ministrations froze, face hardening, then he dropped me, turning and walking back the way he'd come.

"You're going back to her? You're *my* guard."

"You have four guards; she has none." He didn't stop to talk, walking farther and farther away.

"Ask me," I yelled after him.

Desperation burned up my throat, acidic, panic heartburn. My hands went to the top of my head as I took deep breaths, trying to wrangle my heartbeat.

I practiced in my head over and over again. I didn't want to go back. Not to any previous iteration of us. Not the deserter, the enemy, the tormentor, or even the best friend. I wanted us as we almost became last night.

Now, as he kept walking, all I could feel was my beating heart. I eyed the four stone-statues guarding me, my potential audience.

If I told Theo I love him, I could lose him.

But if I don't, I definitely will.

"I never had a friend before you," I yelled to his back, voice trembling.

Maybe this is how I spill my guts to Theo, to his back.

It kind of makes sense.

"You were my only friend, but you were so much more. You were my best friend. You were my..." I fiddled with his friendship bracelet. "You know the areas of my soul I was too afraid to walk inside. You read the parts of me I thought I erased. You see my darkness, and you fill it with light."

Theo kept walking, getting closer and closer to the shadows of the stone hallway.

"You're my soul mate, Theo!"

Theo paused, then picked up his pace. He was almost out of my sight.

This was it, the moment when I'd have to jump off the cliff.

"I promise I'll never leave you," I yelled. "I promise I loved you. Even when you left, when I thought you loved my sister, even when you were cruel."

He stopped walking.

"I-I promise I love you," I said. "I promise I can't stop and will never stop."

He turned around, peering down the hallway at me with an inscrutable look on his face.

"You promise you love me?" he finally asked.

"Yes," I said quickly, hope filling my chest. "Yes, I love you."

He tilted his head, sharp chin catching sunlight. "What if I betray you?"

"Um..." I trailed off, at first thinking I'd misunderstood him.

Theo took long strides, closing the distance he'd just made.

"What if I betray you, Abigail?"

I fiddled with the pastel beads on my wrist, terrified, nearly snapping it. I wasn't expecting that. I didn't know how to respond.

"You won't."

"What if I did?"

I swallowed, picking at the beads, when his hand shot out, stopping me.

Anchoring me.

"Stop talking like this."

"You'd take away your love, wouldn't you? Because love isn't a promise, Abigail. It can't be broken or kept. Real love just *is*. It exists without consent. It *consumes*. You're just like everyone else. Love is something to forget. Love is something to break."

He wasn't yelling, but that was scarier. His anger was a razor-sharp blade slicing my veins.

So. Fucking. Angry.

And something else, too. Something like sorrow.

I tried to move away, but his grip on my wrist was steel, and he pulled me closer. His pale green eyes were shadowed under his dark brow, churning with some dark emotion.

"You won't," I said again, uncertain if I was telling him or myself. I searched his eyes back and forth, trying to find what happened. Where this went wrong. He searched back.

We were lost to each other.

"You make promises now because everything smells like fucking roses, but when the fire starts, all you're going to smell is smoke. It will choke you. You won't remember your promise."

He let me go. This time, I let him leave.

Back in my wing, I lay in bed for maybe an hour before my phone buzzed with a new email. I didn't quite register the shock at first. I stared at the information in the message: a response from the private investigator I'd hired.

Theo's mother. He'd found Theo's *mother*.

Just like I thought, the diary was unique enough he was able to trace it to the shop where it was made and find the owner. He was still trying to find where she lived, but he had a picture.

She looked a little like him. She had the same pale green eyes, and the same silky chocolate hair. Her name was Elizabeth, and she looked kind of familiar... and I wondered if I'd seen her in town.

With the weird distance between me and Theo, I didn't know what to do with this information,

Hours passed, and it was soon dinner time. Flanked by my new four bodyguards, I spotted Theo about to enter the hall.

"Theo?" I called out.

He barely turned his head, how he acknowledged me now, and yet another reminder of the bulwark separating us.

But it was his mother... his *mother*.

He held his arm out for my sister to pass, and a knife speared my heart.

"Um... never mind."

TWENTY-FIVE

ABIGAIL

The flight home from Switzerland was stifling. There's a wedge between me and Theo now, and I can't remove it. He was back on my guard, but so were the four new ones. He never strayed past the line of bodyguard. I never pushed him to.

Now we were home, the engagement party is tonight, and the only silver lining was Ned and all the Harlingtons weren't staying with us. I lay in bed well past the hour I woke, face planted into my pillow, breathing in silky fibers.

I would tell the world I was marrying *Ned* tonight.

I'd found Theo's mother.

Theo still wasn't talking to me...

My bed shook and jostled beneath me, followed by, "Get up."

I lifted my head, but Theo was already nearly out of my room.

Two women came in after him, carrying various weapons of beauty. They tittered back and forth as they pulled and curled and pinned my hair. They applied layer upon layer of makeup, until the girl in the mirror was shielded under makeup and hairspray.

I watched Theo's back in the mirror, wishing he would look at me. I just wanted to fix it. I expected anger. I *hoped* for anger, but he acts like I don't exist.

I'd found his *mother*. How the fuck do I tell him I'd found his mother when he won't look at me for more than two seconds?

"You're going to be the most beautiful girl there," one of them said as they finished packing up their supplies.

I wondered if they'd met my sister—oh, they probably said that to everyone.

They commented on how *stunning* my dress was, then left. It was hanging up against a tall, arched window. The golden lattices on the window shone through the white fabric, making it look a little mystical.

I still didn't have Story back, which meant I was once again dressing myself. My dress was a thin, shimmering gauzy material matching the flowing fabric of skirt that fell off my shoulders. It flowed like air and fell like water. I finished off the look with my handmade translucent sea glass earrings with rose gold adornments. They were small and added enough pop without overpowering.

I touched my lobes, wondering if they would keep *me* intact.

All I needed to do was tie silky white laces at the back of my dress.

Laces.

I glanced out my open door, where half of Theo's body

was usually visible standing guard. All day his hands had been behind his back, the soft material of his shirt clinging to broad shoulders and defined muscles, but now he was curiously absent.

I found him by the fold-out, holding his mother's diary, but he was just staring at it. It wasn't even open. I felt like I'd just walked in on something too intimate and immediately stepped back—but ran into the wall.

He turned his head at the noise, quickly shoving the book away.

Silence stretched.

Finally, I said what I'd come out for in the first place.

"I need your help."

I could see the objection forming on his face, so I tried to stop it: "Please."

He came inside my room and waited for me to put on my dress. His wary eyes transmuted when they saw me. I felt naked. How could he do that with just a look? I rubbed my arm.

His stare traveled to the plunging neck, where the built-in corset was encased in white lace. My long hair had been pulled up, and he looked like he wanted to rip it out and tangle it and get it messy.

"Is that held up by magic?" he asked roughly.

"That... and sophisticated sewing." I swallowed and turned around, exposing my naked back with its undone laces. "Lace me up?"

He walked to me, fingers finding my laces. I tried not to jump at his touch, but I couldn't control the goose bumps.

It was too quiet. His touch was too gentle.

"Are you writing something naughty back there?" I teased, but my voice shook.

"Maybe." I swear I heard a smile in his voice. It gave me hope, like the first bloom after a cold, desolate winter.

He finished.

An awkward silence weeded around us, then he nodded his head like he was going to leave and go stand guard.

"Wait!"

He stopped.

We were already so close to shattering. There were cracks between us; water and debris were seeping through. I didn't want to ruin this.

"Do you remember the first romance we read?" I blurted.

A bird's song trickled in through the open window, counting the silence in its melody.

I don't know why he read them, he wasn't a fan, but anytime I read one, he would too. When I got into *Twilight*, he finished them before me. He was Team Edward and I was Team Jacob. He said, and I quote, "I knew you were dumb, Abigail, but maybe we should check you for a brain tumor."

I like books, but Theo *loves* them. He teased me about my love of romance, but he's the only person who ever read them with me.

Theo didn't respond, so I kept talking.

"You said that fairy tales and happily ever afters were for rich people... bet you feel fucking stupid now," I said on a laugh. I worked the fine, shimmery fabric of my dress between my fingers, hating it. It was beautiful and a fucking *lie*—like everything in my life.

"I know things are messed up between us." I lifted my eyes and found his hard glare had softened.

"Abigail..."

God, I could forget everything with that voice and the

eyes behind it. He took a step to me, and I knew if he touched me, I'd cave.

"Do you ever think about looking for her? Your mother..." I whispered.

"No." His voice was firm.

"What if somebody found her for you?" I offered. "I know I screwed up everything..." I rubbed my forehead, probably messing up the artfully manufactured glow placed there only moments before. "I don't know why you're still here..." *If you still want revenge* a scared, uncertain part of my brain whispered. "I know that... you can... you should find her."

It went so much better in my head. I was going to say how he could do so much better than follow me around, and he deserved better than being the Crowne dog. He could find his real family. I know how much that meant to him. It was all he ever wanted.

I was going to tell him how I hired an investigator, and there was hope.

Instead it came out a jumbled, weird mess of alphabet soup.

"I miss you," I confessed. "You're here, but it's worse than when you were gone. I feel like you're getting ready to leave me again."

"Sweet girl," he murmured, a guarded smile on his face. "I would never leave you, not willingly, not unless I had to."

The words were so much different than the first time he'd spoken them. They tightened around my heart like barbed wire, instead of soothing like silk.

"You would tell me if you were going to leave, right?" I asked. Theo nodded, but it felt off.

"Promise?" I teased, and his eyes clouded, landing on

the bracelet of his I still wore. I fiddled with the beads, inse-
cure, and moved to slide it off to give it back.

His hand landed on my wrist, stopping me.

"No. Wear it. I like you having something of mine. To
think of me." He thumbed the beads on my wrist, that
foreign emotion clouding his eyes again. Was it sorrow?
That couldn't be right.

"Theo?" I placed my free palm on his cheek, and
instantly his hand was over mine. His grip wasn't light like
mine, he pressed my hand deep into his sharp cheekbone,
until I was sure it hurt.

"You were the most distracting fairy tale, Abigail
Crowne, but you were worth every harsh reality."

"I'm not a fairy tale. I'm here—"

His lips crushed mine, hands diving into my hair. I
gasped at the suddenness of his bruising lips. He took
advantage of my open mouth, tongue seizing mine, swallowing my sighs.

His kisses were rough and grating and tender at the
same time. After so many days of callous Theo, I didn't care
how his love came. I'd wrap myself up in the thorns of his
affection.

We pulled back for a breath, his eyes burning and
pained, our foreheads pressed together. His hands
smoothed up and down my arms, from shoulder to wrist.

I had thought that maybe I could tell him about his
mom and heal us. *Show* him much I loved him, and what
could be.

A grand gesture.

We could go back to before.

"I found her," I whispered. "I found your mother."

Theo didn't immediately pull away. I think it would have been easier if he had. He slowly withdrew from me. It was agonizing, like ripping out fingernails one by one, but all the while his stare was on me.

Digging.

Finally *I* turned away. I couldn't take it anymore. I grabbed my leather clutch to get my phone, finding the email, handing it to him.

For a long while, he simply stared.

Then there came a moment when I thought I'd done the right thing. When Theo's eyes cracked with what I thought was heartbreak, but eventually shone with wonder. His eyes found mine, and I believed I'd fixed us.

Then everything crashed.

"Are you trying to get in my head?" he asked.

His stare was bitter cold, his words even more so. Goose bumps rose along my flesh, a warning.

"What? No—"

Theo threw my phone at the wall, cutting me off. It cracked, breaking into pieces. I tore my gaze from the remnants of my phone, back to Theo.

I was fucking this up so much.

"Then why? I fucking told you to stay out of it, Abigail." He took a step toward me, still speaking with the chillingly callous tone, as if he hadn't just left a dent in the pretty color my mother fired numerous decorators to achieve.

"I just..."

"Why did you do this, Abigail? Why did you do this *now*—" He broke off and rubbed his face, turning from me.

His back rose and fell with his breaths.

"This is why you wanted so desperately to read it. Classic fucking fire starter."

"No!" I scrambled. "It's—I—what if she wants to see you, Theo?"

He turned back, glare sharp. "She doesn't. She gave me up."

"She was *fifteen*."

"And? You kept me. You *kept me* when you were fifteen."

"It's not the same," I whispered.

It was the wrong thing to say, again. Every shadow on his face was magnified by ten. The hollows beneath his sharp cheekbones, the dark of his brow, the muscle along his jawline. He was furious, and I was making it worse.

Was it the same? His mom probably felt like she couldn't provide for him, probably thought giving him up was the best she could do. She had no idea what would happen to Theo. She was selfless.

I saw Theo, and all I thought was how lonely he looked, and how lonely I was. I thought this boy might understand me. I might finally feel something other than emptiness. I wasn't thinking about providing a better life for him; I was thinking about making a better one for myself.

I was selfish.

"Goddamn it, Abby. What's inside this?" He went back to his black bag, pulling out the red diary.

"She tells you she loves you," I said. On every page, on every single page she told him she loves him. "She gave you that diary, Theo, and without it, we never would have found her."

"It's her reason for leaving me. It's not a map; it's a goddamn goodbye."

"Theo..."

"Fucking drop it, Abigail." All his careful bodyguard composure fell, eyes blazing. "Stop pushing your issues on me. You can't make her love me anymore than you can love yourself."

Tears blurred the edges of my vision. I swiped them away, absently wondering if they'd bothered to use water-proof mascara.

Theo glanced at his watch. "We should go."

TWENTY-SIX

ABIGAIL

Ned was just outside the gilded white double doors. Soon I'd link my arm in his and walk down the steps. His dad would be happy our families got along, happy I was keeping my worlds separate. The acquisition would be solidified. I'd probably make my mom happy. The rich would get richer. Great.

I didn't even give a shit about that at the moment.

Everything was so fucked up between Theo and me. I'd declared my love for him, and he'd declared his for me. Instead of bringing us together, it propelled us apart. Frantic, nervous energy zinged in my veins.

"I don't want to go through this door. I don't want to put my arm in his hand." Word vomit spilled out of me. "I don't want to do it. I want..."

I want *you*, Theo Hound.

"I won't let anything happen to you," Theo said from behind me. "I'll do whatever it takes to keep you safe."

There was a deadly determination in his voice that should've comforted me. Instead chills ran up my spine.

I tried to lighten the mood. "I know. You're my guard dog. You're always behind me."

The doors were opening, light and laughter and music seeping in through the crack.

Holding my dress up, I spun away from the doors, into the pale green eyes of Theo.

"I love you," I said. I'm sure my eyes were too wide, my voice too desperate.

The music got louder. Golden light bathed Theo's face. The door was open and waiting for me. It must've been only seconds, but it felt like an eternity for him to respond.

"For now," Theo said at last.

My heart bottomed out with the force of an elevator crashing and shattering to the floor.

I didn't want to, but I had to turn away. The gossamer of my dress floated against the marble floor as I stepped through the door. Ned stood to the side, waiting for me.

I linked arms with Ned, my guard dog always at my back.

Always.

TWENTY-SEVEN

ABIGAIL

Theo disappeared.

The second I hit the steps with Ned, I turned to look over my shoulder at him and he'd just...disappeared. I tried not to panic. He wouldn't leave me alone with Ned, not on purpose, not unless something was wrong.

Ten minutes later and I hadn't stopped looking for him, and neither had Ned left my side. He was sticky tape from hell.

"Give me a chance, babe," Ned said. "I'm such a nice guy"—I almost did a double-take. "The reason my dad is even considering merging with your company is because of me, Abby."

This time I did do a double-take.

"What do you mean?"

"I had to have you. I'd do anything for you. Even making my dad see the benefit of being part of Crowne Industries."

I bit my lower lip until pain drowned out all the awful emotions clogging my throat. It wasn't enough to terrorize it, he had to *ruin* my life too?

"I've done everything for *you*. Why not give me a chance? I promise I'll make you so happy. I'll buy you everything you want. I'll give you the fucking world."

"What do you like about me, Ned?" I asked.

"Everything."

I arched a brow. "What's my favorite color?"

"Um..."

Trick question, Abs. You love them all.

"My favorite food? What books do I read? Am I Team Edward or Team Jacob?"

"You like sports?" He shrugged. "I can get into sports."

Wow.

"So, what *do* you like about me?"

"You're a Crowne, Abigail. What's not to love? From the moment I saw you in Latin III, I was floored."

"Would you still love me if I wasn't a Crowne?" I mused.

That stopped him in his tracks.

I wondered if I'd convinced him. If he finally saw he didn't love *me*, he loved my Crowne.

"You'll never stop being a Crowne." He said it as if assuring himself.

Uneasy is the girl who wears the name Crowne.

Uneasy, unloved, unnoticed, uncared for.

"Maybe..."

Then I spotted silken brown hair, tall and towering above the rest of the crowd. Near the back, by the glittering glass windows.

Theo?

I stood on my tiptoes, trying to see more clearly.

"Is it because of the fucking dog?"

"Don't call him that." I shot Ned a glare. Funny how I found my strength the *more* Ned showed his face.

He's a lumbering shadow behind letters and pictures and threats I can't fight. In person, he's the teenage boy who shivered when I kissed him playing spin the bottle.

I looked back over the crowd, trying to see. I swear it was Theo. Why was he by the windows?

"As if the only reason I don't want you is because I want someone else." That nearly had me laughing.

"I see you wondering where he went."

I looked away.

Ned snatched my wrist, forcing me to look at him.

"What are you going to do, slap me?" I asked. "Slap the woman you apparently love?"

His grip tightened, but he let me go. I resisted the urge to rub my wrist.

"He doesn't want you, Abby. Not like I do." *Thank God for that.* "He's not like us. He's a social climber."

"Theo Hound is not a social climber," I said. Theo was so far from that you'd have to measure it in parsecs, but someone like Ned wouldn't understand.

"Everyone knows it. The story is famous. The reject fell in love with the only thing to ever love her back, a dog who abandoned her for a chance at her sister."

I chewed my bottom lip until I tasted blood. Ned's words ripped pieces of me I'd been pretending didn't exist, wounds that tore and tore and never healed. I wish Ned had laughed at or taunted me; it would've felt less real. He looked at me with pity. How dare someone like *him* look at someone like *me* with pity.

Theo didn't fuck my sister.

He didn't.

He'd promised it was all a misunderstanding.

Promises were sacred between us...

"The precious dog got sent away, and the moment he came back she forgave him, only for the dog to do it all over again."

Freezing water filled my veins.

Shut up. Shut up. Shut up.

"Clever," I managed, my throat stuffed with cotton.

Ned looked at his phone, an ugly smile spreading his lips.

"Do you really want to know where he went?" he asked, too quietly. His arm landed on my shoulder. I couldn't move to take it off, a deer caught in the moment about to kill her. "Because I just saw him, actually..." Ned showed me his phone. "We all did."

No.

The picture was under the finsta hashtag *Abbyslostdog*. Everyone was commenting, laughing at me. It had to be a mistake, a mirage, a deadly figment sprung from my darkest nightmares.

Then Ned gripped my chin, twisting my head to make me look. Through the crowd of ball gowns, tiaras, and tuxes, the picture came to life: Theo and *Gemma* kissing.

Theo opened his eyes, as if sensing me through the sea of tulle and satin, connecting with mine.

I dropped my champagne flute, briefly registering the cold gold liquid on my open toes.

Theo's hand grasped the back of my sister's head, his tongue diving deep into her mouth; then he looked back at her, and the crowd collapsed.

I shucked Ned off, pushing through the crowd.

Cries of *Excuse me!* echoed around me as my elbows flung to push them out of the way. I heard glass crash, red wine spill. My eyes were glued on the spot I'd seen Theo. Laughter, the trill of the violin, faded away.

Why would he do that?

It makes no sense.

Unless every little thing we've done has been...

I couldn't fathom it.

I was so close to the spot I'd seen them. Just a few more feet and I could confirm what I'd seen. I pushed aside the remaining satin and black... and was grabbed so tightly above my elbow I snapped back like a rubber band.

"*What* are you doing?" my mom demanded.

"I..." He was just beyond this wall of people.

I pushed my mom away, breaking through the last of them.

Empty. Just a dark window and glittering sconces. I looked left and right. Had I imagined it? As relief was about to cool my anxiety, I noticed my mother's *must*-sparkle-like-a-diamond window was smudged. I stepped closer and pressed my finger to the glass, imagining Theo and Gemma.

Their mouths heating the glass.

I fell against the glass. It had to be a mistake.

"What is it this time?" Mother pulled me from the window. "Not enough of a spotlight on Abigail Crowne during her own engagement party?"

"How did you find my box?" I asked, a horrible thought slicing through me. "Did you guess? Did you see me put it there?"

"I have better things to do than go rummaging through the FEMA relief zone that is your room. It was given to me."

I all but slid down the window.

There was only one person who could give it to her.

Tansy Crowne didn't lie. Truth hurt better than lies. Truth was a better, sharper weapon to wield. Lies were blunt, vulgar weapons used by weaker people, those who didn't have the power to ascertain truths.

And yet.

"He wouldn't do that. You're lying."

She didn't honor such an accusation with a response, lifting up her wineglass and waving to someone across the room.

That, combined with what I'd seen, chipped away what little hope I had left.

I'm going to break your heart, and you're going to thank me.

This had all been one, elaborate ruse. A game to trick me. To make me fall in love with him. The air was too thin. I took sharp, gasping breaths, but it just made it worse. My vision was going black, my knees giving way.

My mom was on me in an instant, eyes elsewhere, smiling like I wasn't having a meltdown. "Stand up before you make a scene," she said through clenched teeth.

"I. Can't. *Breathe.*"

"Then grow another set of lungs."

She hauled me off the floor, linking arms with me like we were going on a mother-daughter walk, when in reality she was tugging me out of the ballroom.

"Let me go!" I tore out of my mother's grip. "Can't you see something is wrong? Don't you care?"

The muscle in her jaw twitched. "I think you've had enough fun tonight."

"I think *so*," I agreed.

My mother's disappointment was apparent, but for

once in my fucking life, I cared more about something else than her approval. She breathed fire through her nostrils, then turned on her heel, disappearing back into the party.

I climbed the stairs to go to the alcove, my haven. How messed up was it that my one safe place was still intertwined with him? I let this happen. It was my fault. I opened myself up. He'd told me explicitly what he was going to do.

I pulled out my phone and texted him. I wanted one last chance for him to explain. To tell me everything was a misunderstanding.

You told my mom about my box?

I waited.

Three dots appeared and disappeared.

Why would you do that? Why would you go behind my back and spill all of my secrets?

Another three dots, and they vanished just as quickly.

Did you really kiss her?

Betrayal coursed through my veins, acrid and searing, and I asked the question I really wanted to know.

Did you plan this from the beginning? All of it?

Another three dots appeared. I was certain they would vanish, but I received a response: a photo. Whatever hope I had vanished with it, shattered into a million pieces.

No. No, no, no.

It was a selfie. He was grinning and appeared to be naked, but the selfie cut off *just* at the hard, muscular vee pointing down to his cock. It was lewd and sexy and suggestive.

The way he held the phone, I could clearly see behind him. He was in a bedroom, and I recognized it.

I spun around, looking behind me, then back at my phone.

It was the guest bedroom just a few feet down the hall.

On the bed, the dress Gemma'd had worn tonight was wrinkled. What removed all of my doubt—the silver-gray lingerie only Gemma wore was scattered on the hardwood. I nearly dropped my phone.

I told myself I wouldn't fall for Theo.

Love is ephemeral, conditional. Love can be withdrawn. Love is a fucking *lie*. It happened anyway. And here was the proof. The minute I believed I could have something real, where we used to drink and make fun of everyone, where we spilled our hearts, Theo fucked my sister just feet away.

He sent me only these words along with the picture: "Come find me, sweet girl."

Theo was waiting for me with one arm propped on the doorway.

Totally, unfairly naked.

"What did you do?"

I looked into his eyes, but there was none of the warmth I'd seen radiating these past few weeks. Cold, cruel Theo was back. The one who ripped away my grandfather, who'd promised to make me regret my love.

His grin was crooked, and he pulled off the condom still on his semihard dick, tossing it to the ground. "I don't know. What did I do, Reject?"

My eyes landed on the condom.

No.

"Did you really sleep with her?" I hated how my voice shook.

The past was coming back in a wave of nausea.

I wouldn't believe it. Not this time. I couldn't.

"Did you?" There was hope in my eyes. I knew it, because it wavered in my question.

Theo looked at me like I was a curiosity. "What if I did?"

Below us, the ball continued without pause, lilting music and laughter taunting me. They were having a wonderful time, unaware that above them a girl was shattering.

"I don't believe it," I whispered. "It's like before. You're lying. It's a misunderstanding."

He took a breath and leaned against the wall, one shoulder propped. "I wondered how the Crowne sisters compared. Gemma tastes better, but you're definitely more eager to please."

My lips trembled.

I didn't need to listen to this.

I turned to leave, but he gripped my bicep, spinning me flush against his naked body. When I struggled, he tangled one hand in my hair, the other at my lower back, anchoring me.

"You said you loved me, Abigail." His words were taunting, not sweet. "Even if I betrayed you. How does that lie taste on your tongue?"

"Fuck you—"

He tugged my hair until our eyes locked. He looked demonic. Crazed. His eyes searched mine like a police dog going in for a kill.

"You said you would love me, Abigail."

"Fuck *you*."

"If you *insist*." Then his lips were on mine.

TWENTY-EIGHT

ABIGAIL

His lips were punishing and consoling, taking my pain and sorrow and twisting it into something sweet. I couldn't escape our addicting ouroboros, and a moan threatened to escape me. The moment it left my lips, Theo broke our connection and shoved me to the bed.

The bed where my sister's ball gown now *lay beneath me.*

I couldn't see him; our ball gowns took up my vision. Fuck tulle. Seriously, fuck whoever invented it. He was a predator and I was his prey, trapped in the bushes of glittery and gauzy fabric, trying to find him.

"I'm not doing this *here.*"

I could've stood up, run out of the room and from this. Instead I made a weak proclamation even I wasn't sure I believed. I heard a creak on the hardwood to my left.

"Where I fucked your sister, you mean?" Theo's voice

came at me from the *right*, low and amused. "She's probably still on the sheets."

"Stop."

"Can you feel her?" His low voice took up all the space in the room until it was inside me, seeping cold amusement. "I fucked her bare before I put on the condom."

"Stop."

I was yanked by my right ankle, pulled roughly out of the tulle forest, into the eyes of Theo.

"Does it hurt?" he asked. "Does it fucking break you up inside?"

His eyes pierced me. The green in them fractured like cracked gemstones, furious emotion shining through. Naked he was so breathtaking. All sharp glistening edges—naked because of *my sister*. Three parallel scratch marks slid down his pec. He was *mine*. He was mine, and she'd marked him and he'd let her.

I found his eyes again, but they were too tender. I needed him to be cruel as betrayal's knife twisted in my side.

"Do you still want me to stop, Abigail?" His touch on my ankle was soft now. His thumb stroked the bone, back and forth, too light. Too sweet.

I couldn't breathe.

"Say no, Abigail." The way his voice lowered into a vibration made it sound like a threat, but he was threatening me to make him *stop*.

I couldn't do it, either way. I couldn't say no.

"There's no going back, Theo."

Misery. That's the brine on my tongue.

I promise by the time I'm done with you, you'll be ruined for everyone but me.

He was right in the end.

Some emotion flickered across his features at my words. It was followed by another barely-there second of that addictingly sweet touch; then his grasp hardened, and he yanked me to the edge of the bed. He lifted one ankle to his shoulder, and then leaned over me, hands at my neckline, tearing my dress down the middle.

Hours before he'd wondered if it was held up by magic; now the lace was torn between his fingers.

His touch left me too soon, but one hand returned, between my thighs.

"Oh, I get why you didn't want to stop." He laughed, rubbing my panties into me. "What did it? What part of this is getting you so fucking wet, Reject?"

I was stuck on him, the way he watched me. It was reminiscent of our first night together, when he drank in every sigh, goose bump, and bitten lip. But unlike that night, I had a feeling I was going to regret his worship.

He rubbed my silk panties against me, a concentric, intoxicating rhythm. I wanted him to rip them off. I would deal with the emotional fallout after. All I knew was I wanted Theo's rough, knowing hands on me.

"Is it knowing you're second best?" he asked, pushing aside my panties. He slid one finger into me, and I must've gasped, but it was drowned out under his groan.

His *groan*.

Deep, strangled, and *unfair*. Unfair he gives it to me after such cruel words.

His fingers left me. I was shocked, and so *empty*. A cruel fucking tease.

But then he was at my entrance, his thick cock spreading me. He held one ankle on his shoulder, my other gripped in his hand. I'd never been so obscenely open, vulnerable, and so ripped apart.

But he waited.

For me to say no? To push him away? I should. Tears were drowning my face.

Instead, I arched my back.

He slammed into me. I arched higher off the bed, but he gave me no reprieve.

"Abigail Crowne," Theo taunted with another powerful thrust. "So unloved she can't love in return."

"Abigail Crowne"—*thrust*—"has told herself so many lies the truth looks fake."

Theo pushed deeper and deeper until I could only gasp. Deeper than I ever thought I could take, harder than I thought I could manage.

"Abigail Crowne"—*thrust*—"a pathetic, rejected princess."

"Why are you doing this?" Tears streamed down my cheeks, not from physical pain, but from the brutal, emotional battering I was receiving. Physically, Theo was driving me to ecstasy.

The combination was ripping me apart. He was weaving two existing dichotomies inside me irrevocably together.

"I thought you loved me, Abigail? I thought you loved me even if I betrayed you."

The worst, most cruel part about this is I still did love him. I wanted to take it away, I wanted to break it, I wanted to forget my love for him ever existed, but I *couldn't*. It was throbbing and bruised from what was happening, but it was *there*.

His eyes were red, and I could almost convince myself that this hurt him as much as it was hurting me, but then he pulled out, flipping me onto my stomach so I couldn't see his face. He grabbed my hips, pulling me against him, so rock hard.

He yanked my hair, pulling my ear to his lips. "You don't deserve this cock, Reject."

He dropped me, and I bounced on the mattress, and he was inside me again. The new position was too much, too deep. Every thrust driving me higher.

"Look at me."

I shook my head, so he grabbed hair that had taken hours to braid, yanking it and lifting my head. "Look at me, Reject."

The black window mirrored our image inside the diamond-shaped golden lattice. I saw our relationship, a hundred different reflections of what we'd become, dark and twisted and wrong.

I still saw Theo too clearly in the window. His beautiful, sculpted features next to me, his lips even more plump from kissing me. My hair was nearly all down. Messed. Tangled from him.

He slowed his thrusts, watching my reaction just like before, and it was so much worse. Too deliberate, almost tender, as he fucked me atop my sister's ball gown. A ball gown I could now *see* had twisted inexorably with my own. His lips came to my ear, eyes still locked with mine. His words were low and steady, gentle even, as if they weren't going to rip me apart.

"Truth or promise?"

"I don't want to play this game with you." Tears reflected back at me, my makeup entirely ruined.

He slid out, then back in—*deeper*. I gasped, clawing at the sheets—her *ball gown*—I realized. Still going the same, deliberate pace, but now deeper, harder. I was on the edge, begging to jump off, but Theo held me back by the collar.

Shivers slid inside my veins and I could barely breathe, let alone speak.

"*Truth* or *promise,* Reject, and I'll let you come."

"Promise," I gasped instantly.

He froze, body and eyes rigid, but still dug into my hip with his hand. For a moment, I saw old Theo, sweet Theo. I'd only ever made him one promise, after all.

I promise, Theo. I promise I'll never let you go.

Then he rammed into me again, this time harder, faster. I was going to come. I could feel it.

"Promise you don't love me, Abigail," he commanded, voice dark.

"What?" I gasped.

How could he ask that of me?

Theo continued to slide in and out, and I was reaching that addicting moment where you'd do *anything* to reach the peak. Selling my soul seemed like a good trade, if only Theo would...just...keep...going.

"Promise," he gritted.

It wasn't his command, or even my need, that made me say it. He was nearly out of breath, fingers bruising my thighs, like he was trying to keep himself from coming, but his thumb... his thumb softly traced my hip, back and forth. It was almost like he didn't know he was doing it. How treacherous that a show of affection would topple me.

"I—"

Just before I was about to speak and damn myself for eternity, Theo spoke over me.

"Promise you'll never say 'I love you,' promise you'll never make another goddamn promise to anyone again."

When he slammed the final nail in my coffin, it didn't matter, I was already over the edge, and the words were already leaving my lips.

We came together. As I exploded back into a thousand pieces that only *Theo* had been able to put back together, I promised I wouldn't love him.

Or anyone else.

<hr>

It still hadn't settled when Theo put on his black slacks. I didn't realize what happened, how badly we were broken. I hadn't moved, but he was getting dressed. I sat up, trying and failing to clasp my ripped bodice together.

"Where are you going?"

He eyed me, pants undone. "Somewhere. Anywhere."

"But you'll be back in my wing by tonight."

A wrinkle formed above his brow. "No, Abigail. I won't."

He continued dressing.

He was leaving me in a ripped ball gown. He was leaving *me* ripped.

"Are you going back to my grandfather?"

He shook his head, and my chest caved.

Theo was *leaving*.

Again.

For good.

"You can't leave," I practically screamed. "You're mine. I mean"—I tried to stifle my emotion—"I own you. I've owned you from day one. You belong to Abigail Crowne."

He paused.

"It says so here." I lifted my wrist, showing the bracelet I still wore. I hated how my voice trembled. "You belong to me." He'd *always* belonged to me, before I knew it, before *he* knew it.

He was mine.

I was his.

He glanced absently at my wrist, where the bracelet I'd given him as a child lay.

Then, without so much as a flitter of emotion, he ripped it off. Pastel beads clattered violently to the marble floor. My breath caught and clambered in my lungs as they bounced on the floor.

I like you having something of mine. To think of me.

Whatever strength remained inside me vanished as beads slid under furniture, vanishing into shadows. I was a broken radio, static switching from numb to broken to pained. I didn't know I could feel this amount of pain. My chest was ripping open. I thought the first time Theo left was brutal.

This...

This would end me.

Theo finished dressing. In black slacks and his white undershirt, he still looked like a celebrity. He was ruffled, and he made it look good. I resented that.

He headed to the door, and I thought I would have to watch him walk away. I thought he was through with me. I was foolish. I thought the pain in that moment was the worst I would ever feel. I was naïve.

He looked back at me, like I was an afterthought. "Say thank you."

At first I couldn't do anything but stare back, my words lost in shock. He couldn't be serious.

Theo didn't so much as smirk at me. He waited, bored yet still infuriatingly hot, watching me like I was some waiter taking too long with his order. He was serious. He really wanted me to say *thank you.*

I summoned rage. Good, easy, numbing rage. "Fuck you."

294 MARY CATHERINE GEBHARD

"I will," he said, nodding, walking back to me as he spoke. "If you don't say *thank you*, I'll make you come on her dress over and over, until you associate *her* with feeling that good."

I looked up, shocked, staring into his eyes. Part of me couldn't believe it. I couldn't believe the boy who'd saved me had become this way.

Evil. Theo was evil. What did it make me that I gave in to temptation so easily? Because as much as I knew he *would* go through with that promise, I knew I would let him. I hated him, I hated myself, but I still craved him.

Bruising or tender, biting or soft, I needed him.

I was pathetic.

"Say it."

"No."

A part of me wanted to keep saying no so he would have to go through with his threats.

He tilted his head, as if reading my mind. "Sweet girl, that would break you." His voice was soft then, his touch softer.

That, more than anything he'd done, broke me.

He can't call me by such sweet names while obliterating my soul into such small pieces they can never be repaired. It fucks with my head—but that's Theo, and that's why I'm so strung out on him. Theo is the moment after agonizing pain subsides, when stark relief has you high and you've sworn you've never felt so good. It's the most addicting thing I've ever felt.

Be mean to me just so I can hear you say nice words.

I jerked my head away, but he caught me, slowly bringing my gaze back to him, digging into my jawbone, soft touch returning brutal.

I knew he was done telling me what to do, just like I

knew I had to do it. I wouldn't look him in the eye for this humiliation. His grasp on my chin still harsh, I looked down. I focused on the fine needlework of my dress now ripped from his hands. Teardrops stained the white chiffon. Soon everything blurred in my tears.

"Thank you," I whispered.

It burned through me like hot smoke, staining my insides irrevocably.

Theo laughed and dropped my chin. "You're welcome."

TWENTY-NINE

THEO

I'd barely made it out of the room before I doubled over, heaving whatever was in my stomach. It didn't help. I was still festering inside.

Promise you'll never say I love you, promise you'll never make another goddamn promise to anyone again.

Fuck, I hadn't meant to say that. The thought of Abigail loving someone else tore me up. It had no right, but it did.

Selfish.

Cruel.

Unavoidable.

Another round of heaving seized my gut, this one dry.

"That was one of my favorite vases."

I stood up, wiping my mouth with the back of my hand. Tansy Crowne leaned against the railing, behind her the domed ballroom ceiling and massive chandelier. If there was one good thing to come of this, it would be never seeing Tansy Crowne again.

She arched a brow, like she'd read my thoughts.

"You wanted me gone, I'm gone. She's not following."

"You're so sure—"

"I fucked her sister."

Her brows rose, and she blinked thrice.

I'd surprised the implacable Tansy... with a lie.

It didn't matter; it had still burned like the truth. Abigail had still been crushed under its weight. I still wouldn't be able to go back to her, couldn't save myself and say, *Love me again. I'm not who you think I am. I'm not actually that guy. You were wrong.*

Truth, lie, it was still razing and blighted betrayal.

The only difference was I might be able to sleep at night.

Maybe.

All Gemma and I did was kiss, and that was for show. I probably should have done more; it would've made the break cleaner. Would've made the temptation to go back to Abigail easier to avoid, but it was simply transactional between Gemma and me. Gemma needed something of mine, and I took that opportunity. In exchange, Gemma gave me her dress and lingerie. I don't know why she needed what she took. She wasn't going to tell me, and I didn't have it in me to care.

I glanced down the hallway. I didn't know how long I had until Abigail got off the floor. I rubbed my chest, trying not to think about her on it. Below us, the party still continued on... her engagement party.

"Your turn," I said.

There were two things I needed from Tansy Crowne. Abigail's security updated, and Edward Harlington gone from her life forever. In exchange, I had to do one terrible deed. In the long run, it was nothing.

Break up with her.

But not just break up with her. Tansy made it pretty fucking clear Abigail couldn't follow me, couldn't contact me, couldn't so much as look for me. In return, she'd break off the engagement, she'd get her guards, she'd get a life she should've had, the one I couldn't give.

The life she should've had.

"Abigail was curiously absent for her engagement party and photos." Tansy pinned me with a knowing look, and another wave of nausea hit. "It will be easy to change the story. No one will ever know there was an engagement. It was just another party."

It seemed like every ugly, jagged piece of this puzzle had fallen into place. But I did wonder what was in this for someone like Tansy Crowne.

She arched an artfully plucked brow. "Something on your mind, Theo?"

"Why?" I didn't expect Tansy to tell me, but I had to ask.

"You don't belong here, Theo. You never did. Abigail's weakness threatens all of us."

I don't know why it had taken me so long to realize Tansy Crowne was the puppet master pulling and ripping apart our strings. If I'd taken one look beyond us, it would have made so much more sense.

"It was you. You sent me away."

She tilted her head. "Of course."

That single head tilt threw me, nearly made it impossible to speak. Tansy was never trying to hide she'd done it. Abigail and I were both just too blinded by our fears.

All these years wasted, and now too late for any more.

"Would you ever have approved of me?" I wondered.

"No," she said easily.

It didn't matter anyway. It was over now.

I straightened.

"I'm sure you know if you don't come through on your end of the deal, I'll be watching," I said. "I don't have a billion dollars or endless resources, but I love her, and I have nothing to lose now."

Tansy watched me with a shrewd look, rubbing two fingers together absently. I decided I was done staring into the face of the devil and turned to go.

I knew a happily ever after with Abigail wasn't in the cards. When I took this charge, all I ever thought I could hope for was revenge. Yet hope for something more had broken through like weeds in the cement. There were moments after Tansy presented her deal when I'd thought love could overcome everything. I'd nearly caved when Abigail told me she found my mother.

Could she see how much it meant to me? Was my anger too transparent? Did she see the hurt beneath?

Abigail was the only one who ever cared.

Still, at every turn, I was reminded how fucking naïve that was.

Abigail and I were a fairy tale I was foolish to believe in. At least when I left, she would be taken care of, for real.

THIRTY

ABIGAIL

It's my birthday, I thought blandly.

It's been a week and I haven't changed out of the ball gown Theo took me in. I'm sure I smelled. Mother nearly threw a fit when I appeared at my engagement party looking like a *Pride and Prejudice and Zombies* reject.

I don't give a shit.

I haven't moved from my bed, either. No, that was a lie. Theo left his hoodie, and like a junkie addicted to the drug that's nearly killed her twice, I put it on. To cover my ripped bodice, I said.

Not because it smelled like him.

Or felt like him, soft and warm.

A week hasn't done anything. It still feels like it's happening. I relived it over and over again. I couldn't cry anymore. My tear ducts threw up their hands, out of water. I felt the moment inside me, though. Like too much alcohol or bad seafood. Felt him choose her and leave me. Felt the stupid hope I had that I could have had some kind of happily ever after, been more than Abigail Crowne, Reject Princess.

Someday I will be special. Someday I will mean something to someone. Someday I won't be so alone.

I think it's ironic the hope that was once the only thing keeping me going, was the very hope Theo Hound used to obliterate me.

Sweet girl, I would never leave you, not willingly, not unless I had to.

The words he'd spoken to me the day I'd dropped my walls once more for him zinged through me.

Fucking liar.

I wiped my eyes, wishing anger would drown out the sorrow.

My laptop pinged, and I eyed it warily. A new email. Using it for the distraction it was, I dragged it off the floor and into my lap.

A new message from the private investigator I'd hired, letting me know he'd found Theo's mom's address.

I didn't want this information. I didn't fucking want it. It assaulted me. I didn't want to know anything about Theo, let alone have this information, anchoring me to him.

I slammed the laptop shut, breathing heavy. I focused on the sound of the waves, trying to steady my breath, when I noticed my freckle. All hope of steady breath vanished.

That was the difference between Theo and me. He'd ripped that bracelet off me so easily, but I still have him inside me, just a few millimeters away from my bloodstream.

I couldn't fucking take it anymore. I jumped off my bed and got out of my stifling room.

I hate Gemma, and the last few days I've been imaging

302 MARY CATHERINE GEBHARD

various ways I can ship her to Antarctica, but she can still help me.

I opened my door and stopped short. Four tall, menacing-looking men in black suits stood inside my suite. Just like that, four Theo shaped holes blasted into my chest.

When I moved from my suite, they followed me like shadows. I looked over my shoulder, slightly unnerved. They were even armed. When I opened the door to my wing, a fucking alarm went off.

I wondered what I'd done to piss off my mom so much to gather this much oversight.

They followed me all the way to my sister's wing, not speaking when I entered her room without permission.

Theo would've said something.

And there was that pain.

Gemma had a secret she thought no one knew. I pulled an orange bottle out of a Louis Vuitton clutch she kept in her closet, opening the cap and dumping the contents into my hand. Little white pills fell into my palm. Little white pills she'd stolen from Mom, pills Mom didn't need a reason for, because she donated so much to the hospital the doctor would prescribe whatever the fuck she wanted.

I dropped them into my mouth.

Everyone at our old school had been on some kind of prescription, usually doing a combo of the Holy Trinity: Xanny, Addy, and Oxy. Gemma's drug of choice was Xanax.

It took a moment for the pills to kick in. When they did, the pain was still there, the constant ache, but it was dulled, fuzzy around the edges, not cutting into my heart so much.

Suddenly I wasn't dreading another forgotten birthday, but I was *hungry*.

I couldn't remember the last time I'd eaten... maybe two

days ago, when the mysterious food from my favorite Crowne Drive-In Diner appeared. I couldn't imagine Mom bringing that to me, let alone *going* to a drive-in diner.

When I came downstairs, there was a party.

A fucking party. On my birthday. That was just too much. Everyone was present: my family, the Harlingtons. The only one absent was my fiancé.

Pity.

My eyes zeroed in on Gemma.

Her hair glowed under the chandelier lights, her smile was radiant, and she laughed with Gray and our mom. I couldn't take it.

Even on my *birthday* it was about *her*.

I wasn't trying to be sneaky; it was just that everyone's eyes were on Gemma all the time. Even with four certified bulwarks surrounding me, they focused on her. I grabbed a pair of scissors off a table filled with presents and approached Gemma.

I grasped a chunk of Gemma's hair. The hair Theo'd probably tangled. The hair that lay on the same bed—

And cut off a chunk.

I could almost hear the party come to a crashing halt as eyes landed on me, my sister's hair in my hands. Her flowing rose gold hair, the hair synonymous with being a fucking *Crowne*, and once voted most likely to drive a boy insane in boarding school, was now dead in my fingers.

Gemma's hands flew to her head, feeling the empty space once filled with luscious tresses.

Gray laughed.

Mom looked at my ripped dress, my unwashed hair, still messy from the way Theo had tangled his hands in it, and the hoodie I wore over the bespoke dress, culminating in what I was calling broken-heart chic.

Her eyes narrowed on me, focusing on my probably glassy eyes.

My mom's smile was tight when she spoke. "Abigail, are you *unwell?*"

That was Crowne for *Are you fucking high right now?*

Gemma had been asked that a few times too many. Gray occasionally.

I looked at the rose gold strands glimmering between my fingers. I felt empty. This didn't erase what happened. Theo had still chosen her over me, like everyone else.

"What...the...*fuck?*" Gemma finally screamed, coming out of shock. Her hair fell from my grasp, fluttering to the floor.

"You take *everything* from me," I yelled at her. "My family, my love, my own *birthday.*"

I didn't care Mom was watching, or that I was confirming who Grandpa had accused me of being. I was Abigail, the fire starter, the worst of them all.

All I could think about was her *fucking hair in his hands.*

She never even looked at me funny, never even looked slightly guilty. I wasn't insane enough to expect an apology, but it was like I'd imagined it all.

So I lunged for her, my fingers tangling in her now unevenly cut hair. We were barely at each other for a few seconds before the men at my back pulled me away, and the men at her's did the same.

"You idiot!" Gemma's crudely cut blonde hair was mussed. "This was for *you.*"

She waved her arm around, at the smashed cake. At the champagne fountain, smashed to crystalline shards on the floor, leaking gold to the marble.

Then I noticed more little details. A table of presents

with my name on it. The dining table had a name card for me between my mother's and Gemma's. This was the birthday I'd always dreamed about.

The cake was so smashed the letters now read *appy irt day gai*.

"Surprise."

Hours and a few more pills later, I found my sister in her room.

"Gemma," I said.

"If you're here to cut off more of my hair, could you wait until the mask I've put on sets." She eyed me from the oval mirror set in gold in her vanity. "I'm deep conditioning."

I sobbed. I fell to her floor in a heap and sobbed, sobbed, and sobbed.

I'd meant to come up here strong, but the minute I opened her door, every goddamn thing I'd been trying to ignore flooded me, and my knees gave out.

I don't know how long I was on the ground, but Gemma whistled when I was done. "You're fucked up."

"Why did you do it?" I lifted my head, looking up at her through bleary eyes.

"How high are you right now?"

A minute passed. I summoned enough energy to get to my feet. "Why did you have to sleep with him? You can have anyone you want. Why did it have to be *him*?"

"*Who* are you talking about?"

"*Theo!*"

Guilt slashed her pretty face—I've never seen her look guilty—but all she said was, "Ew."

I flew at her before I realized what I was doing, my

hands sliding through the creamy conditioner in her hair, pressing her into her bed. She yelled, trying to shove me off. All I saw was white hot rage.

"Get off me." She elbowed my stomach. "I don't like him."

"That's worse you sociopath!" I got her on her back, arm pinned behind her, using the move Theo taught me. I pressed her arm down and she yelped.

"I had no choice!"

I didn't let her go, but I eased up the pressure on her arm.

She huffed, turning her head so she could somewhat catch my eyes.

"Do you want me to say sorry? That I felt bad? I didn't. I didn't think about your feelings, like you didn't think about mine when you had Horace's tongue in your throat and hand up your leg."

Shame swamped me, and I slowly got off her. She climbed up, sitting against her jewel-toned satin pillows, her long, elegant legs stretched so they nearly met me at the foot of her bed.

"We didn't have sex, Abigail."

I glared, wiping my nose. "Do you think I'm an idiot?"

"Kind of."

She climbed atop her pillows at the look on my face. "Did you actually *see us* fucking, Abigail?"

"I saw your dress. I saw your lingerie. I saw you *kissing*. I saw the photo and the marks you left on him. I saw the condom. Don't fucking try and say that wasn't something."

She paused, like she was struggling with something deep, but all she said was, "We promised not to talk about what happened, but I didn't have sex with him."

He'd made a *promise* with her? I didn't know my heart

could break anymore, but I felt some last clinging edge chip off, crumbling to ash.

"I don't believe you." Still, doubt sewed its way into my mind.

She threw up her hands. "You got me. I'm secretly in love with Theo Hound. Tonight I'm going to confess my love for him at a Walmart or something."

"That's not funny."

"It is, because it's so ridiculous."

"I *can't* believe you, Gemma, because what does that mean? He left. He... he *fake* fucked you, and he left. After obliterating me with a lie for *no reason*." It didn't make sense. Why would he lie? Why would he say he slept with her when he didn't?

"Sister, the day I have sex with someone like Theo Hound is the day this family is really and truly fucked." Gemma stared at me with her bright blue eyes, unblinking.

A Crowne didn't lie... at least, a good Crowne didn't. Gemma was a good Crowne. Not like me, who got so messed up and tangled in her lies she could barely see the sunlight beneath their wicked, curving branches.

I fell to her bed, the truth sinking in.

That was so much more terrible.

She went through that night from her perspective. Theo had approached her, and she'd suggested a trade. They'd kissed, gone up to that room, where she'd changed into sweats, and then she'd given him her dress.

"What did he give you? What could he possibly have given you?" Theo was nowhere near the street kid I'd found years ago, but Gemma was a Crowne. She had everything. If she didn't, she'd buy it.

What could he have traded her?

She grew quiet, twisting her oversize sleep shirt

between her fingers. The front of the white shirt read in black, blocky letters:

NO SOCIALIZING,
NO PANTS,
NO SHITS GIVEN,
GIRL'S CLUB.

"I have a debt," she whispered. "I'm trying to repay it. Theo had what I needed."

"But—"

"That's all I'm saying!" Gemma went to her drawer, pulling out a jar of pills and a bottle of tequila. "Pick your poison."

I pointed to the tequila. She raised a brow and shrugged.

"I think I preferred it when I thought it was real," I said. "It was cleaner. I don't know what to do with myself now. It still feels the same. There's still a hole inside me. I still can't trust him. But now those feelings feel *wrong*."

It was wicked, and classic Theo. I could never be clear in the head, emotions simple and with a logical beginning, middle, and end. He had to step in the middle, throwing them to a thousand different beginnings and endings.

I'd told him lies to protect him—at least, that was what I told myself.

If Gemma was telling the truth... I took another long swig of tequila, relishing the burn and bite. Theo and I played our games of truth or promise, but with every truth, more lies bled, and our promises were made with fingers crossed.

Gemma and I drank and got drunker. I chewed on my hoodie string. It tasted like wool and faintly, so faintly, *Theo*.

The part of the hoodie I'd spilled wine on was faint, but visible. I rubbed it, remembering him, his promises to me.

The drunker I got, the more mishmashed my emotions became, and the looser our tongues got.

"So, like... how does he fuck?"

"Gem—" I coughed on the tequila. "Gemma!"

Theo was safe. The reckless, exhilarating, *freeing* kind of safe that was falling strapped to a bungee cord or skydiving with a parachute. Even the night he destroyed me, Theo had been my safety net.

Sweet girl, that would break you.

I swiped away hot tears.

"Yikes, that bad?"

"No..." A jagged, cutting sigh. "That good."

I focused on the blurry tequila.

"So we're like friends now?" I asked, eyeing Gemma. This had been the most we'd talked to each other in years.

Gemma laughed. "Fuck no. But not enemies is a start. Maybe we'll throw less food at each other."

"No promises." I paused with the tequila to my lips, a small smile escaping. "Not enemies."

I handed her the tequila.

"Not enemies," she agreed.

Something inside me slammed together at her words, tightening, fixing.

Your bracelet will break if you keep building it with brittle wire.

Theo had seen into me. He'd always seen into me, and he'd known I'd used corroded wire to hold my most precious feelings. Over and over it had broken, leaving me in shambles. But now one wire had started to heal.

Gemma shoved the tequila in my face. "You look like you're going to cry. If you do that, I'm going to kick you out."

I took the alcohol, focusing on the burning in my throat and not the constant burning in my eyes.

"So, look," Gemma said suddenly. "Newt is a total dildo, and you deserve better"—I opened and closed my mouth in shock at the compliment—"but do you think you could give this all up? I know you like your dog—"

"Theo," I all but growled.

She raised her eyebrows like *okay, whatever*. "I know you like him but, we have *everything*. Do you know how rare that is? We are above laws. We exist in a world only a few will ever taste. This is as close to paradise as anyone can ever know. Horace doesn't expect me to be loyal. I don't expect it of him. Nothing is going to change."

Maybe that was the problem.

Eve had thought paradise was a prison, so she took a taste of something else.

"Not much is asked of us," Gemma said. "We just have to marry. We can fuck whoever we want. You can live in an entirely separate part of the world from Newt so long as you play nice for parties. I don't want to be like Uncle Albert. He has *nothing*. Do you want to be like that?"

Maybe... and maybe that wasn't the worst thing in the world.

"It doesn't matter," I croaked. "Theo's gone."

Gemma rolled on her side, catching a strand of my hair and twirling it between her fingers.

"What if he came back and was all like"—Gemma lowered her voice, sounding like a caricature of a tough guy —"'*Babe, I made a mistake. Take me back?*'"

"That impression is on the money, Gem."

She paused, looking up at me. "You haven't called me Gem in years."

Weird, I hadn't. The old name just slipped out.

I brushed past it.

"Theo and I are old tape. We come together, we fall apart fast."

"Orrr..." She stretched out the word, taking a swig of tequila. "You're two points of a rubber band, like... a..." She slammed her hand on her nightstand, rooting around until she found a bracelet, then she stretched it out, emphasizing her point.

"A bracelet! You come together, stretch apart, come together—but you're always connected."

I narrowed my eyes. "Since when are you this poetic?"

"I've always been this way." She yawned. "You were too up your own ass to notice."

I exhaled.

Maybe.

I closed my eyes, but Theo's wicked grin from the week before slammed into me. The feel of his hands on my body, his warm breath at my ear, and suddenly it was like he was in the room. Most importantly, I heard him again, forcing me to promise never to love him, or anyone else.

He'd made a promise with my sister that day, too, and the truth was wrapped up in that promise. Maybe it would explain why all of this happened. It could alleviate this brutal pain and take us back to before. Or, more than likely, what was left of my brittle wire would crumble.

I lifted my wrist, staring at the bare skin.

"Bracelets can snap," I whispered.

But Gemma had already fallen asleep.

I stumbled out of Gemma's room, still drunk, and spotted Gray in the shadows of the hallway. He had his hand to the wall, arm outstretched, above *Story*. It looked like he was talking to her, though her eyes were on the floor.

I shuffled over, interrupting whatever they'd been talking quietly about.

"Why is *she* with you?" I pointed at the girl. "She's *my* girl."

"She's *my* girl now."

He stepped in front of her like he had the first time I'd spotted her. Had he been keeping her all this time? All the while I'd been looking for her? Drunken anger smothered and softened all the other nasty emotions pricking my heart.

I reeled. "What? Why?"

He smiled. "I don't really think that's any of your fucking business, Abby."

I held out my hand to Story. "Do you want to come back?"

Story and I weren't ever close, but I couldn't imagine life with my brother was better than with me.

Story rolled her lips, then shook her head. "No, Ms. Crowne."

I think that was the first time I'd ever heard Story speak. She had always been quiet as a mouse when attending to me. So of course, like every other person in my goddamn life, she was using her voice to leave me.

Gray grinned and turned away, but I grabbed his bicep, pulling him back to me. He hadn't been expecting that. As much as a prick as Gray was, I rarely stood up to him. He knew just the right buttons to press to piss me off without taking it too far.

"I think it fucking is, Gray." I jabbed his chest. "You can't just take, take, and take. You can't just take pieces of me that don't belong to you."

I was tearing apart. I never stopped.

Why had Theo left me? Why? Why would he be so vicious? It didn't make sense. The little hope I had that *my* Theo might still be out there somewhere was proving so much more eviscerating. It cut and it cut and I bled.

I shoved Gray with both hands. "You can't rip parts of me out, act like you'll be there to put them together, then fucking *leave* without warning. You can't keep *doing that*. Why do I keep letting you?"

I hadn't realized I'd been crying until I couldn't see anymore. The hallway was a blurry, watery mess, like when it rained so hard the windows slammed with anger.

I passed a hand to my aching head. My lip was wet and warm—my nose must have been running.

Gray blinked, then shook his head. "Yeah, I don't think that was meant for me."

He waved a hand over his shoulder, motioning for Story to follow. She threw me a concerned glance, before looking at the floor and following Gray.

I fell to my knees.

THIRTY-ONE

THEO

Abigail hadn't left Crowne Hall in over a week. I couldn't see what was going on inside, but I got snippets of information from certain servants. She had the guard, and Ned hadn't been allowed inside Crowne Hall. Tansy was keeping up her end of the deal.

I kept hoping I could catch a glimpse of her.

"Welcome to Crowne Drive-In Diner. We hope you have a royally pleasant day. Can I take your order?" a scratchy voice said through the speaker.

I ordered a double cheeseburger with extra special sauce, fried pickles, and a drink. When the kid came out to hand me my meal, I told him I wanted him to deliver it.

"This is a *drive-in* diner," the teenage boy said. "We don't do delivery."

I pulled out a wad of cash, counting as much as it would take to bribe him. His lips parted when he took the thousand dollars. When I told him where to take it, he stopped looking at the cash, raising both brows.

"Are you sure? It might not get through—"

"Go to the servant entrance and use this code."

It was a lot of money for an uncertainty. I still wasn't sure Abigail ate the last meal I sent her, but it was better than nothing. Every report I'd received from inside said she wasn't attending meals.

I didn't stop moving after Crowne Drive-In Diner. I hadn't stopped since the ball. If I even so much as slowed down, I'd feel it all. Feel the poison still inside me from the thing I'd done. It was crippling.

The ugly fucking truth is all the while I've been trying to break Abigail, I've been the broken one. I love Abigail. I love her without walls and reason. I will always fucking love her. I'm the poster boy for unrequited love, and I have been since the first day I saw Abigail Crowne.

She abandoned me like everyone else, and the first chance I got to come back to her, I took. Because with her, the knife is in me, and I'm gutted, but without her, I'm bleeding.

There'd been a time when I had dreams, and I'd wanted to help kids like me. Now? The only reason I hadn't completely faded away was the urge to keep moving for Abigail, to fix what I'd broken.

At least I could help make Abigail's dream come true. Her dream college was one of the few who accepted fall applications late into August. Maybe that was fate. She was so fucking talented, and she deserved to follow her dreams.

I dropped off the application in the post, then met my next stop under the pier. He leaned against the wood column, on his phone, a hat shadowing his face, white designer sneakers digging into the sand.

He looked up, spotting me.

"You look like shit," Gray said, shoving his phone in his pocket.

I don't know if I've slept, really slept, since that night.

"Where are you staying?" he asked.

I arched a brow. "Miss me, Crowne?"

I'd been staying at the one motel in Crowne Point, a little thing inland, up on a hill, with a view of the ocean. I kept saying I'd leave. This place was never meant for me. But every day I thought of something new Abigail needed.

"You're the ant infestation I've been trying to rid us of for years. You're almost gone. Just a few more bug bombs and your ass is finally out of our lives."

He grinned, and, done with catching up with Gray fucking Crowne, I moved on with the point of meeting him. "Did you get the cake?"

"Yeah—"

"Presents?"

"Yeah—"

"And you went? All of you?"

"Yeah, *but*"—he snapped his fingers—"I think you're forgetting something, dog."

I pulled out the last of my cash and shoved it at Gray's chest. "That's the last of my savings." Gray scrambled to keep it from blowing away in the salty air. "You make her feel like a fucking princess. A *real* one."

Gray arched a brow without looking up, counting the cash I gave him. "You're a thousand short."

"Something came up."

"It doesn't matter," he said, reaching into his back pocket and pulling out a lighter. He put the flame to the green corner of the stack.

Nineteen thousand dollars. All the money I'd managed to save working under Crowne.

Gone in an instant.

The last of it fluttered in the wind, glancing my cheek like butterfly wings.

"I didn't even want this," Gray said. "I just wanted to see the look on your face. It's... underwhelming." He sighed like I'd put him out.

Prick.

Whatever. Whether he wanted to use it, burn it, or shove it up his ass. It had served its purpose. At least I was done with him. I turned, not wanting to stay another second longer than I had to with Gray Crowne.

"Why are you doing this?" he called to my back. "You lost. You'll never be one of us."

Leave it to Gray to assume that was why I was ever here.

Someone had to stand behind that girl. Someone needed to be her dog.

THIRTY-TWO

ABIGAIL

They were making my birthday up to me.

Up to me.

A Crowne didn't apologize, let alone make amends. It was so surreal. They'd rented out the pier so we could have a family day, and I wondered if I'd stumbled into an alternate universe, one where my family members loved me more than Theo Hound. My mother even let me wear the Crowne tiara and would join us soon.

The wooden railing was decorated beautifully with white satin ribbons. We had balloons, and they'd even washed and repainted the wood.

We fed swans off the pier. Most people thought of swans as freshwater animals, which was another reason our swans are so popular. It was one of the only places you can regularly see swans swimming in the ocean.

In the right light, it looked like magic.

So of course my sister and brother were on their phones, bored.

I had everything I'd ever wanted. My mom's affection. My sister and brother not being total a-holes. The fucking *tiara*. Yet I looked around me, as if the sunny beach air would suddenly explain to me why I still felt so empty.

When I'm finished with you, will you be lost forever, Abigail?

The words Theo said to me the night of the Swan Swell slammed into me and I dropped an entire slice of bread into the ocean.

Commotion sounded by the pier's entrance—paparazzi. They were vultures, scavenging anywhere we went. We had guards stationed to keep them out, and I noticed my mom had finally joined us, almost at its mouth.

"Maybe it's the dog," Gray said. "Back to give us more money to love you." Gray lounged against the pier railing, looking casually unaffordable in a thousand-dollar white shirt, jeans, and limited edition sneakers.

"What?" I lifted my head. "Theo gave you money? When?"

"Take a wild fucking guess. Do you think we all volunteered to play happy family for your birthday?" He lifted his arm slightly off the railing, looking disgusted at something I couldn't see. "I fucking wish there was money involved today."

I looked at my sister. "Gemma?"

"I said I would go if Gray promised to let me see the look on your face when you found out." At my face, she quickly added, "This was before you started being cool again!"

It didn't bother me my family had lied about their intentions. It would have been weirder if overnight they'd suddenly become good, caring people who loved me. Being bribed made the most sense and was still, in a twisted Crowne way, some kind of affection.

What had my heart hammering was Theo's inclusion in all this.

"Dear," my mother's trill voice called out.

"Someone tell me what the fuck is going on," I said.

"You didn't kick your dog hard enough, sis," Gray said. "He's following you around, biting all the bad guys at your heel... which maybe isn't such a bad thing."

Gray frowned at something over my shoulder.

It wasn't the ocean in my ears; it was blood. Rushing, pounding blood.

I chewed my lip until I tasted blood. "Am I the only one who hasn't seen Theo since my engagement party?"

Gemma raised her hand. "I haven't. Gotta leave 'em wanting more." Gemma smiled, batting her eyelashes at me. I rolled my eyes.

Theo had been behind the scenes, making sure I had a happy birthday. A wrinkle formed on my brow as I thought about the lie. None of it made sense.

My mother grabbed my elbow, spinning me away from my siblings. "Have you gone deaf?"

Beyond her, *Ned* stood beneath a white-and-gold balloon arch.

My gut dropped.

I'd had a week-long respite from Edward Harlington, and I almost believed he didn't exist anymore. My mother left me to grab him, set him next to me, and lift my chin, elongating my neck.

"You disappeared before we could get a proper photo," my mother said, referring to the engagement party when I'd stumbled down the steps brokenhearted.

She situated us next to each other like dolls.

"Is this why you let me wear the tiara? The family... all of it... were you even making my birthday up to me?"

"Making what up, Abigail?" She put his arm around me, on my fucking shoulders. "The cake you smashed all on your own, or the hair *you* cut from Gemma's head? Which part of that should we *make up?*"

Before this summer, that would have destroyed me. Before Theo, I would've thrown myself at her feet for approval.

Theo always poked the sorest parts of my soul. The parts of me I didn't want to acknowledge. My mother didn't love me, or, worse, *no one* can love me. He made me look at those parts and question why the wound existed and who had put it there.

It was cruel and horrible, but the thing is, if you didn't acknowledge a wound, you can't heal. It sits there and gets infected. It grows and it takes over. A wound on your soul changes who you are. If you didn't love yourself first, you can't love anyone.

I thought my grandpa loved me. It had taken one word from Theo to change it.

That isn't unconditional.

Theo was cruel and heartless, and somehow the only one who loved me unconditionally.

I shoved her off, stepping far, far away from her and Ned.

I rolled my lips, focusing on breathing through my nose and not the ache in my chest.

"Do you even care the man you want me to marry has been stalking me for over a year?" I asked, for the first time genuinely curious.

Was I going to live like this forever? With a man who

thought I was his property, with a mom who saw no problem selling me to him, and whose affection hung like the sword of Damocles.

Ned shifted, smile tight on the press approaching.

Gray and Gemma had put their phones away, watching us. Though my and Gemma's relationship was better, and Gray had been decidedly less of a dick, I still didn't trust it. Old fear scraped at my gut, worried at how they might use this information against me. At the same time, I wasn't going to let it stop me.

I was done hiding, through pretending, finished caring more about reputation than well-being.

"You know who he is. You've seen everything. The evidence—you *saw* how he treated me. Is our name really that important?"

"Where is this coming from?" Mom asked through clenched teeth.

I saw my future crystal clear and blinding in my mother's tight smile. Loveless, cold, married to a name not a man. Children who fought for scraps of affection. If I was lucky, I could hold on to the memory of Theo.

"He drugged me. He drugged me, and he probably would have raped me if Theo wasn't there."

"Always with the melodrama," my mom sighed.

Just a month ago I would have given in to this marriage, given up and into a life that was less than in so many ways.

"Nothing I do will ever be good enough for you," I whispered. "For this family." She probably couldn't hear it above the seagulls and crash of the waves, but it was more to myself than her.

Because that was when I finally understood she would never love me the way I needed. None of my family could. We were all too fucking broken. We were jagged facsimiles of a family. When we tried to love one another, we cut.

Tansy Crowne honestly didn't see the problem with marrying me to someone like *Ned* for the rest of my life.

It was what she'd had to do, after all, what we all were expected to do.

But that was the moment *I did*.

"Fuck you all." I tried to rip the tiara off, but it had been bobby pinned to the point of superglue. I yanked and yanked until my hair ripped out. "Fuck this family and fuck *you*."

If I could've thrown the tiara at Ned, I would've.

In the end I walked away, tiara still on but lopsided, my head aching.

I ran past the paparazzi clamoring for a photo. I ran and ran, under the pier and down the beach, until my heart would give out, but eventually I escaped them, hiding behind the pier's wooden columns. I watched as a few vultures sprinted by me, assuming I'd gone toward Main Street.

When the last of them had disappeared down the street, I turned to go somewhere else—anywhere else—and ran headfirst into someone's chest. He was already walking in the opposite direction down the sandy shore when I looked up. Even far away, even with his back to me, I knew him too well. His tall, slightly slouched shoulders. The sheen on his wavy chestnut hair.

"Theo?"

He paused, then kept walking.

"Theo, wait."

I was propelled after him, latching onto his bicep. He turned around, and when he did, I nearly lost my breath. His stare was harsh, his jaw hard. Those green, green eyes were so pained. With the sunlight behind him, he looked like a fallen angel.

"You were just going to keep walking?" All the strength in my voice was gone. "Like you'd never seen me before?"

The words my family had said were fresh in my mind. Theo was down in the most deserted part of the beach, and there was no reason to be here. But above us, I could see the black satin elbows of my brother's bomber jacket, my sister leaning over the edge, lips twisted in a bored pout.

Has he been watching me? Following me? Taking care of me?

He leaned forward, and I closed my eyes foolishly, breathing him in, as if he was going to kiss me.

There was too much water between us.

I couldn't trust him, but I couldn't hate him either.

A salty, breezy moment passed before I opened my eyes. He was feeling the sharp point of my tiara. So sharp it had cut many maids. His eyes were on me. Soft. Sad. So not the boy who'd broken me just a week ago.

"Are you happy?" he asked.

Theo knew better than anyone this was my dream come true. My hair was messy from trying to *rip* the fucking tiara off my head. I'd been all but forced into the shower yesterday. Ned was above us, hidden from view like the cockroach he was. Each second another piece of my heart sloughed off like papier-mâché.

I'm sleeping with the light on again.

"Yes," I lied.

The one time I wanted him to catch me in a lie, he just nodded to himself.

"Your party, it was good?" he asked. "You got the presents?"

"I didn't get a chance to open them," I admitted.

He pulled his hand from the tiara until he was almost touching my cheek. I could feel the whisper of his fingers on my skin. I just needed to step forward and he would caress me like he had a hundred times before.

Why did you lie to me?

Why did you leave me?

Why won't you come back?

"Truth or promise, Theo?" My words were barely a whisper.

His brow furrowed. I was sure he would say no, leave me dangling on the spiderweb of lies and half-truths we'd built.

"Truth," he said.

"Did you lie to me when... at the ball?"

Theo clenched his jaw so hard the muscle twerked, watching me with a such a painfully intense stare my belly ached, and then his fingers brushed my forehead. I closed my eyes again as he pushed a strand of hair behind my ear with a tenderness so opposite the tension in his body.

"Yes," he finally said.

I opened my eyes. "Why?"

"It's my turn."

"I don't care. Why?"

"It was the only way I could think to protect you."

Frustration built, water rising and stuck in a fire hydrant. What did that even mean? How did this protect me? Then I thought to the four mysterious guards who appeared overnight. The new alarm. The conversation I thought I'd dreamed up between him and my mother.

I knew my mom was involved somehow. She'd been the

one to assign the guards, to have the new alarm installed. Our love lay brutally massacred, and her fingerprints were all over the crime scene.

I just didn't know how, I didn't know why, and I didn't want to believe it, that Theo could have stomped my heart into a hamburger for something so pointless.

"Did you even think about what it would do to me? Did you care? Four guards..." I tried not to laugh, to ease the bitterness blacking out my heart. His touch was light on my neck, and it would be so easy for him to grab my neck, crush me to his lips. "You're better than any number of guards."

His fingers tightened. "It wasn't just guards, Abigail."

I stared into his eyes, trying to figure out *what* would have made Theo tell such a horrible lie, all in the name of protection. What could my mom have offered him?

In the end, I couldn't think of anything.

"I don't know what trade you made, but it wasn't worth it. In every scenario, you're worth the risk."

His grip tightened on my neck, pulling me until our lips were so close to colliding, but there was no heat in his eyes.

"I'm not worth it, Abigail," he gritted. "I could never ask you to risk your life for someone like me."

It was a while before I responded, the wind blowing.

"I know," I whispered. "You would never ask."

He searched my eyes, then dropped me.

My skin was colder than before he'd touched me. I could too clearly remember the heat of his touch, his breath warming my lips. He exhaled with so much force his shoulders moved, and I knew he was going to leave. Going to God knows where. I didn't know when I was going to see him again.

"Truth or promise," I asked. "Do you still love me?"

His eyes were hard. "I'll never stop."

My eyes were watering, his image blurring. No matter how much focus I put on keeping my chin up, my back straight, I couldn't keep the tears away.

"T-Truth or promise." My voice was shaky with unshed tears. "Would you do it again?"

Say no. Say you regret everything you did to us.

"Yes."

His answer knocked the wind from me. I couldn't stop him from leaving, too busy trying to breathe. So I watched him walk away, his footsteps disappearing in the tide.

I was desperate for anything to make him come back.

"Your mom," I yelled at his back. "Um... I have her address... I know you don't want it... but..."

He stopped. This was *so* not the way I wanted to tell him. I rubbed my forehead, anxiety spiking with each silent minute. The tide kept coming in and going out, washing the sand anew. Then he turned to face me.

He was still silent. About a foot of sand separated us. Wind whipped his wild, silky brown hair around his sharp, beautiful face.

"She's been looking for you," I said. "You're hard to find, since she wasn't the one to give you your name. Hers is Miranda Lemaire, and she lives in town. You can find her online easily. She's been here the whole time."

He looked like he wanted to say something, and my heart stood on tiptoes. Then his eyes lifted over my shoulder, and he turned from me, walking away without another word.

I looked to where he had and saw my mother. She had black sunglasses on, but her arms were folded, and she was looking in my direction. Theo left because he was protecting me, but there was only one person who could

328 MARY CATHERINE GEBHARD

provide such thick armor he'd leave my side. I stared at my mother, a realization curling in my gut.

I hadn't been back at Crowne Hall for even an hour before I went to my sister's room, kicking open her door.

"What did he give you?" I asked, not waiting for her to let me in. The question wouldn't stop plaguing me. It felt like it was the secret key that would unlock everything.

"What could Theo Hound possibly have given you to make you trade your dress and *kiss* him publicly—"

I stopped short. Grim was in my sister's room. Grim, the scary head of four guys who used to sit atop lunch tables, smoking and glaring, scaring teachers as much as they had the student body. Now he led them as the Horsemen gang, controlling any and all crime in Crowne Point.

Seeing me, Gemma startled. "Abby!"

Grim, on the other hand, barely reacted to my presence. His dark eyes glanced in my direction, then he moved to leave, brushing past me without a word.

"I..." I trailed off, noting the item in his hand.

Theo's mom's *diary*.

I snatched it without thinking. Keyword: without thought.

Grim was scary in high school; he was scarier now.

He was tall, tattoos decorated tan skin spiraling up his neck. Wild, inky black hair fell over his eyes. He reminded me a little of the grim reaper, which was fitting.

But this was the last piece of Theo's mom. An item Theo rarely let me see, let alone touch, was in a stranger's hands.

"Abigail, stop!" Gemma ripped it out of my hands, shoving it into Grim's. "Theo *gave* this to me."

Grim turned it over in his hand, then gave me another one of those barely interested looks from down his nose.

I had to watch helplessly as he disappeared with Theo's *mom's* diary.

"See you soon, rich girl." Grim's smooth, amused voice trickled back. It lingered like smoke.

Gemma stared after him, lips parted, as if caught in a spell.

"What the fuck? Was that who I think it was?"

She looked away. "I don't know."

"Why does he have Theo's mom's diary? Why did *you?*"

"I told you, it's what he gave me, and I was trying to pay off my massive, Abigail's muffin-top-sized debt."

Her insult had my Gemma Defenses rising so quick, I nearly didn't catch the most important part of what she'd said.

Why would Theo trade the one thing left of his mother so he could *lie* to me and ruin us?

"Did he really?"

Neither Gemma nor I had moved since Grim left, feet planted in her plush rug near the door. I stared in her blue eyes, willing her to be honest with me, trying to trust her despite the rusty beams propping up our sisterhood.

She slowly nodded.

Fuck.

I officially welcomed myself to her room for the second time in as many years, going to her bed.

"Why did the Horsemen want it?"

She shrugged. "They don't tell you that."

Gemma had her hair cut cleaned up, and now it sat just above her shoulders. It was all at once chic and grunge, totally in style. I tried not to be jealous, because we were trying to be better about that.

I fell to my back, head landing flat on her comfy sheets. "The more truth I learn, the more I don't understand. The lie was easier. It made sense."

Gemma had a pretty ceiling with gilded molding and a crystal chandelier. The crystal drops refracted soft, yellow light. I wanted to know everything that led Grim to be in our house, but I knew Gemma wouldn't tell me anything.

Of all the people to have it, he was the *worst*. The one person that couldn't be bribed. The one person neither beholden to law nor above it, but below it, untouchable in its seedy underbelly.

"You're not really going to end up dead? Right?"

"No." She laughed. "That would be too easy. I'll be fine..."

The way she trailed off had me staring at her.

She cleared her throat. "I'm Gemma *Crowne*. There is no one scarier than me."

"I've kicked your ass a couple times."

"You wish."

My phone buzzed with a notification, a new email.

Dear Abigail, we are pleased to inform you you've been accepted...

An acceptance letter to the college of my dreams, for this fall semester. Except, I'd never applied to college. I didn't know what to do with this information, or how to process it.

When my mother had thrown all the pamphlets in the trash, a part of me accepted my dream had gone with it.

There was only one person who knew enough to apply for me, and would do something like this for me. My heart cracked with the knowledge.

I left Gemma, my head swirling too much to continue talking. I kept thinking *why?* I was sandwiched between Theo's cruel deeds and sweet actions, jagged on one side and pillowy soft on the other.

I went to my room and dragged my box out from its spot. I had one secret left, one neither Mother nor Theo knew about. Inside were pastel beads, beads I should've left abandoned like he'd abandoned me. Instead, in my ruined dress, I climbed on the floor, grasping into the shadows, until I'd recovered every last one... well, except for one. I couldn't find the *F* for forever.

And it still ate at me.

I carried my box to the balcony, swinging my legs over the edge, looking at the pastel pieces. They were all broken apart, but they were still *there*. That was how I felt. Broken apart, but impossibly in love with him.

AC + TH

I traced the letters. I was pretty sure I knew what happened. Theo did what he always did—he protected me. He protected me in the only way he knew how, like the time he tried to get Gemma to tell him he wasn't good enough for me.

Theo sacrificed himself.

When would he trust that he was more than good enough for me? That he didn't need to keep leaving me? *I* was the one who didn't deserve someone like Theo.

I still didn't know *how* he'd protected me, and what made him leave me... again. I pushed the beads around, and they rolled to the unevenly weighted corners.

There was something that's been bugging me, some-

332 MARY CATHERINE GEBHARD

thing Theo said that has been sticking like a thorn in my side. He said *I* abandoned him. I would never do that...

But I knew somebody who would, and seeing her at the beach pushed the thorn deeper. I still wanted to believe my mom loved me, and that love meant she wanted me to be happy.

Another bead rolled, and I caught it in the middle, holding the square pastel piece between my fingers.

Of all the things that hadn't made sense—Theo sleeping with Gemma, Theo stabbing a knife in my open wound, Theo leaving, Theo lying about it all—my mom being the cause fit perfectly.

Mom was sitting in her favorite room, in a chaise against the now-dark window.

"Why did Theo leave?" I asked. "All those years ago, why did he go work for Papa?"

I'd never asked her. I'd never thought to ask her. I saw him with Gemma, and I assumed he didn't want to be around me anymore.

"I was protecting you," she said simply, without looking up from her book.

I was getting real fucking sick of people *protecting* me.

I barely whispered my question. "Is that why he left again? Did you make some kind of deal?"

She looked up, eyes slowly finding mine. "You were never going to marry Theo, Abigail."

I had to swallow every emotion. Rage, betrayal, anger at myself for being so foolish.

"You were protecting *you*." The truth was charcoal on my tongue. "You let me believe Gemma was better than me.

You let me believe Theo *loved her*. No... you made it impossible for me to believe anything else."

The pain came out of me jagged and rough, and I stumbled, grasped the back of one of the two wingback chairs between us to keep from falling over.

"All this time it's been about you, your insecurity, your need. I wanted your approval so *badly* it kept me up at night. It destroyed my chance at love, but you never wanted me to win. You just wanted to keep watching me lose."

I gripped the wingback until the fibers groaned against my nails.

"Why?" I probed. "Because I was happy? Because I still had my Theo?"

Mom looked away. In all my life I'd *never* witnessed my mother avert her eyes or show any kind of weakness. Her jaw was tight, and she swallowed roughly. For a brief, blinding second, I thought I would see some of my mother's humanity.

Real humanity.

But as quickly as it came, it vanished.

"That's quite the story you wove," she said coolly.

Uneasy is the girl who wears the name Crowne.

This fight has never been with Ned. If it were just about that, it would've been over already.

We were all chess pieces fighting to be queen.

Ned was a pawn.

It's a good thing I've been warring with the best queen since the day she gave birth to me.

"I'm not you. I'm not going to let the love of my life go because I was too afraid."

She looked up, eyes slowly finding mine. "You don't get to stay a princess and marry a pauper, Abigail."

"Maybe I don't want to be a princess," I said.

"You will always be a Crowne, Abigail," my mother said. "Unfortunately."

To be a Crowne was more than a name, it's blood, it's the insidious connections laid root centuries before you were ever born. I could change my last name to Squarepants and still be a Crowne.

"You underestimate me. You always underestimate me. The next time we meet, I will be *just* Abigail."

Her brows furrowed, but I walked out, not giving her a chance to respond.

I was Abigail Crowne, fire starter, attention seeker, scandal maker. The Reject Princess. Unloved, uncared for, unwanted. There was only one way to dethrone a princess. As my mom said, you don't get to stay a princess and marry a pauper, and a Crowne without a castle is just a hunk of metal.

THIRTY-THREE

THEO

The house was inland of Crowne Point, up on a hill so you could still see a brief glimmer of the ocean, like a sapphire line coating the horizon. It was a sprawling mansion, one of the newer ones built in the last few years. When I was a teenager first living with Abigail, this land used to be grass.

We used to come up here and smoke weed, watching the sunset.

I was certain I had the wrong name and number, but I'd double and triple checked. This was the home of Miranda Lemaire, my mother.

I knocked on the door and waited. It wasn't long before the door opened. I don't know who I'd expected to open it, but I'd hoped it wouldn't be my mother. A useless hope borne from the pounding in my blood, a reminder I wasn't ready.

Maybe I never would be.

Just a moment later, the door opened. She was pretty,

with pale green eyes and long, brown hair. She looked familiar, but I couldn't place her. I wrote it off as nerves.

Her lips parted when she saw me.

A stretched, stiff silence passed.

Say hi, idiot.

"You might not know me," I started.

She stared at me like I was a ghost. "Theo?"

"Uh, yeah—"

She dragged me into a hug, cutting me off. I could count on one hand the number of people who'd hugged me in my life—one, Abigail. I didn't know how to respond, so I just stayed put, stiffly accepting this woman hugging me.

My mother.

After a minute she pulled back, shaking her head. "Sorry. I'm so sorry. I never thought I would see you again. Will you come in?"

Another moment of silence.

Come *in*? I didn't have a game plan for this. You prepared for nightmares. You prepared for the worst possible outcome. What do you do when your dreams come true?

"Uh, yeah."

She brought me into a sitting room bathed in warm light, and I awkwardly took a seat, perched on the edge. I felt massive on her furniture.

She was nervous. Her hands in her lap, then beside her thighs, then back in her lap. She proposed tea, and I wondered if it was so she could have something to do with her hands. I said yes, just so I could say something. She stood, walking out of the room into what looked like a kitchen.

On the mantel were plenty of pictures—no kids, it appeared—and I hated myself for being grateful. Most were of my mom and another pretty woman with silky dark-chocolate skin and braids that looked like a crown, one on their wedding day, it appeared. I knew the woman. Everyone knew the woman. She was Penelope "Penny" Lemaire, the mayor of Crowne Point.

I realized then I knew where I'd seen my mother before, at a party. The mayor wasn't always in attendance—for example, a local politician would never receive a July Fourth invite, but no doubt she'd been at a few. My gut bottomed out, realizing I'd once been feet away from my own mother.

I should've pieced it together earlier. Lemaire wasn't exactly a common surname, but I just never imagined my own mother would be part of the rich and powerful.

And I would be a dirty secret.

Again.

I worked my thumb, waiting for her to politely kick me out, bribe me to keep my mouth shut.

She came out with a glazed wooden tray holding steaming porcelain cups.

"There's so much I want to say to you," she said. "I can't shake the feeling we've met before. Probably just the guilt." She gave me a weak smile.

"I used to live with the Crownes," I said.

Her eyebrows raised, and I saw she was making the same realization as I was.

"I see it now. You and the youngest..." The tray she was holding shook. She set the tea down next to a stack of magazines, and I saw what was beside them: a bound, red-leather book with a burned tree design. The last time I'd seen it I was handing it to Gemma, for whatever reason I didn't want to think about.

Now my mom's diary—*her* diary—was beating between us.

She must have noticed me eyeing it, because she said, "You probably don't remember, but I gave this to you."

"I've kept it with me for twenty-three years." Silence engulfed us. When I dreamed of meeting my mom, it was beautiful and rosy, with no place for anger and rejection.

In reality, all I could feel were my scars breaking open.

"Why the fuck do you have it?" I couldn't look her in the eyes.

"I...I was looking for you. I only recently learned you never went to a family, Theo," she explained. "I've been looking and looking for you, but everyone who was there when I left you at the station was either dead or a dead end. I got desperate. This was my last hope."

She caressed the leather front. "I got the diary... I didn't get you. They wouldn't even tell me how they got it, or *where* they got it."

I ground my jaw, fighting the urge to stand up and leave, but at least I found my mother's eyes. Pale like mine.

"But you found me anyway. You followed my map."

Abigail would say it was fate. In her romantic, starry-eyed view of life, she would look at all these coincidences and say it was fate. I got rid of my mom's diary. I'd chucked it, assuming I'd cut it and that part out of my life.

It led me back to her.

"Why did you leave me?" My pain came rushing out in a jagged yell. "You abandoned me. You just let me go. Now you're saying you wanted to be found?"

Her brows caved. "I thought I was giving you a better life."

I looked around at her mansion, her beautiful things and apparently perfect marriage to one of the most powerful people in Crowne Point.

I scoffed.

"More like you were burying a dirty fucking secret."

"I didn't used to live like this. I was fifteen and poor, with strict conservative parents who promised you would go to a better family if I just let you go. I believed them. Anyone was better than me. I can't erase what I did. I can't take back those years—"

"Would you do it again?"

Say no. Say you regret everything you did to me.

"Yes."

I stood up.

"Have you ever done something awful for the right reasons?" she asked my back.

"No," I lied.

"Well... good. If you had grown up in the house I did, with the parents I had, you would've."

I spun around. "You should've stayed. You should've kept me."

"I wouldn't have loved you, not how you should've been loved. I wasn't able to love you. Just being there isn't enough."

I ground my teeth, wanting to argue, not knowing how. I'd watched Abigail with a mother who stayed and who destroyed her with it. Which one of us had it better? It was an impossible question to answer.

I wanted my mother to regret everything.

To say she was sorry, that if she could've gone back in time and made things perfect for us.

"Where are you living now?" She sounded choked.

"The motel."

She frowned at that. "Are you happy there? Do you..." She trailed off, more lines growing between her brows. "We have a lot of empty rooms in this house. I mean—this is presumptuous. You don't even know me. You probably hate me. I should be better at this..."

She couldn't be about to ask me what I think she was.

She didn't know me. I didn't know her. This was the first time we'd met since she *gave me up*.

I still resented her, anger still burned my throat.

She exhaled. "If you're going to leave, at least take the diary back. It belongs to you." She bent down, lifting it off the coffee table, and then I saw the newspaper. On the front page, an announcement for a wedding: Abigail Crowne and Edward Harlington. My mom's voice blurred into the background.

Ned had his arm around a stiff-looking Abigail. That was just two days ago, on the fucking pier. How had I not seen him?

"Theo, I know we can't start over, but can we try and start again?"

I headed to the door without thought.

"Theo?"

I looked back, realizing Miranda had been talking.

A wrinkle formed on her tan forehead. "Is something wrong?"

I was more torn than I'd ever been. I wanted to sit back down and talk to my mom. What if this was my only chance to ask her the questions burning cigarette holes in my soul?

This was all I'd ever wanted in life. I was moments away from no longer being the lonely boy sitting in the sand.

"I..." I raked a hand through my hair. "I have to go."

Sadness washed her features, but she nodded. She followed me out the door and gave me her phone number at the doorstep. "Call me, please, Theo. If you need anything, anything at all."

I took it, a foreign feeling in my gut. Hope? Then I turned my sights toward the sea, where Crowne Hall's jutting and pointed black pepperbox turrets were visible against the sparkling sea.

They wouldn't let me inside Crowne Hall willingly, but fuck willing. I used my servant code to get inside the gate, and my fists to get inside the main hall once I was spotted. I left a trail of catharsis, of groaning bodies and blood in my wake.

I might've forgotten why I'd come in the fury, if not for one single burning thought: *Abigail*.

I could take two on one, even three on one, but once four fully trained guards surrounded me, fists landing on my jaw, my gut, flying all at once, it was touch-and-go. I wouldn't give up.

I wouldn't.

"Stop."

All at once they let me go. Tansy stood in the middle of the hallway.

"You have made quite a mess," she murmured, looking at the blood staining her priceless black-and-gold rugs, the groaning bodyguards. I spat blood.

"You...broke...our...deal," I said my words through heavy breaths, my shoulders dragging up and down.

She *tsked*, shaking her head. "I've upheld my end. Edward was off the property. Abigail had guards. We broke the engagement for the summer... we never discussed the fall."

Evil. Tansy Crowne was straight-up evil.

"You, however, you've been everywhere, haven't you? Checking with the staff to see how she's eating and sleeping. Sending her food. Buying her presents. Bribing my son as if I wouldn't realize who was pulling the strings. You were supposed to leave, and you never left."

"We never discussed *how* I would leave," I said, throwing it back at her.

I swear her face twitched with a smile.

"Where is she?"

She looked at her clock. "Fulfilling empty threats."

I ground my knuckles into my palm, resisting the urge to tear the entire goddamn mansion apart. I was done playing by their rules. It was a mistake to ever think I could. I should've played to my strengths. People like them stayed up in their ivory towers so blood never stained the soles of their designer shoes. It was time to get brutal, vicious, and *dirty*.

"As long as she's a Crowne, you can't be together, Theo," she sighed. "Trying will just bring destruction. For you."

"Maybe." I wiped sweat off my lip with the back of my hand, staining my lip red with blood, eyes locked with Tansy's. "But I hope you know you've just signed his death warrant."

THIRTY-FOUR

ABIGAIL

I found my mother in the room that started it all. It was hard to believe only a few months ago I'd stumbled in here, still drunk from the night before, about to have my life upended again. I was bleeding from wounds I wouldn't acknowledge. Now I was healing, I sorta-kinda got along with my sister, and I'd loved.

I'd really, truly loved.

Blood was on the carpet—fresh blood—and I stopped in my tracks, forgetting the reason I'd come. Servants scrubbed it out of the pearly fibers, soap mixing with the blood into strawberry foam.

"What happened?" I asked.

"A dog got loose in the house," my mom muttered. "You just missed him."

Theo?

My heart hammered. Why had Theo come, and why had he left a trail of blood?

I shook my head.

I had to stick to my plan.

"I've eloped," I said.

I saw the shock my mom tried to hide. Her jaw clenched, and she nearly knocked over a bucket of soapy water. The maid was there, ready to clean it up.

"I've got it," my mother hissed.

Her eyes landed on mine.

"That joke needs some work, Abigail."

I threw down magazine after magazine after magazine, just like my mother had done months before. On every cover was a picture of me and a blacked-out picture of a man. Variations of the same title slashed across the glossy fronts, ABIGAIL CROWNE ELOPES WITH MYSTERY BODYGUARD.

A small rectangular picture of Ned was in the corner. The worst photo I could find. They'd spent the time trying to guess whom I'd married over *Edward Harlington*.

Neither my mother nor Ned were those you can win by force. I couldn't call the police. I couldn't call my lawyers. In this world, you won with psychological warfare. You couldn't get caught up in right and wrong. As my grandma once told me, *You can be in the right and lose.*

This time *I* came to the paparazzi with a scandal. The people who'd burned down my life over and over again, I'd handed the matches.

I held out my left hand, where a simple rose gold ring wrapped around my finger and small, rough-cut pieces of translucent seashells refracted light. I thought it some kind of poetry to use my own jewelry.

I was saving myself, after all.

It didn't matter there was no record of any marriage. I gave the press a good story and enough information for it to seem legit. *Oh, what a scandal.* I eloped *right after* the press announcement of my engagement. Everyone ate it up. I'd been on such good behavior, after all, but now I was back to starting fires.

"They came out this morning," I said. "I fell in love with my bodyguard. All those late nights and close quarters. Guess they figured it out."

It wasn't entirely a lie. I had fallen in love. For the first time, I recognized the power in truth. It not only destroyed my mother but cut me in the process.

"Do you have any idea what you've done?" she all but hissed.

"I imagine the acquisition will fall through. Marrying Ned will as well. You'll take away my trust fund, my equity, and leave me with nothing, then kick me out. Oh, and you'll have to disown me. Publicly."

Her eyes slimmed. "You *want* a punishment?"

"A reward."

I swear I saw a look of admiration in her face, but it faded quickly.

"I was never a princess. I was always a reject."

A moment passed, Mom studying me like I was some new creature, not her daughter.

"Was it worth it?" she asked.

I would lose my family, my mother, my grandfather, and my siblings. I'd be left with no money—*nothing.* Was it?

Yes.

I kept waiting for the time I wouldn't be afraid, as if that was the moment my love for Theo would become real, but love isn't real without fear. Love *is* fear. Fearing it can be taken away, but trusting him not to. Jumping into a black abyss without a bungee cord.

"You might want to find that dog of yours before he runs

loose," she said obliquely. "Take what you want out of your room. I don't know how you're going to carry it, or where you're going. I don't care. You're gone by tonight."

Oddly enough, she wasn't angry, and her eyes had softened.

I nodded, smiling now, and turned to leave, fully expecting to be cut out like the stories had led me to believe.

I was at the door when my mother's voice stopped me.

"Abigail," she said. I spun around, bracing for the next round of Tansy's bullets. "That ring is quite lovely."

It was the first time my mother had ever said anything about my handmade jewelry.

"See you at Christmas… daughter."

Then she smiled. My mother *smiled*.

The gates to Crowne Hall were swarming with press, and Ned was just inside them, walking up the cobblestone steps. When he saw me, he ran.

"Why would you do this?"

"It's all a mistake," I said. "We can still be together, Ned. Run away with me."

He ran a hand through his hair, obviously torn. I stepped closer to him, eyes big. Lush, green hedges fenced us, the flash of the paparazzi just a few feet beyond.

"We can live off the grid, foraging for our food. I saved all your roses"—*lie*—"we can eat them and live off our love."

He took a step back, having the gall to be *frightened*. I smiled wide, doing my best to look out of control.

"I thought you loved me? I'll give you what you deserve, Ned." I reached for him and he backed away until he was pressed against a perfectly trimmed hedge.

"You have no money," he said. "You have no name. You have nothing." Shock usurped his breath.

While he looked at me like I was an alien, I bit back my smile.

I never thought hearing those words would feel so damn freeing. I thought all my life I wanted to be the best of them, but now it was like I'd just grown wings.

I tilted my head. "So you don't love me?"

"I never want to see your face again. I don't even know who you are anymore."

I acted sad, watching Ned run out of my life, into the paparazzi.

There was still one person who would know who I was, but he'd made it clear he didn't want me anymore. After my mom's ominous statement and the blood on the carpet, I was even more confused about his intentions. Still, I was determined to find him. I'd put it all on the line, one more time.

THEO

I found Ned running out of Crowne Hall. This time I wasn't letting him get away. I wasn't going to put my faith in anyone else. This time when I saved the princess, it's going to stick.

Even if I have to give up everything in return.

THIRTY-FIVE

ABIGAIL

I spent all day looking for Theo, magazines in my hand, practicing in my head what I would say. That was the thing with Theo, he always showed up. I had no idea where he was or how to find him.

Discouraged and dejected, I went to the pier where we'd first met.

That was when I found him.

I felt like an idiot for not checking there first. When I saw him, the magazines fell out of my hand, and everything I prepared vanished.

Ned was a bloody heap at his feet, the sand beneath them dark burgundy, like the wine stain on my sheets the first night we'd made love. The moonlight created a shocking outline. His shirt whipped in the dark night wind, exposing the cut muscles of his lower back. He was a god dispensing justice.

"Don't do it," I yelled, still too far away.

Theo froze, his fist in the air.

I took a tentative step forward. "You'll go to jail."

Ned was barely conscious.

Theo glanced at me, then at my finger. My *ring* finger. He looked like he was going to rip apart Ned all over again. I should've explained everything then, but months—no *years*—of half-truths spurred me on.

"Does the idea of me marrying someone else bother you?"

"Yes," he gritted.

"Why?"

"You promised," was all Theo said.

"I promised not to love. I didn't say I wouldn't marry."

Theo placed his black sneaker to Ned's cheek and ground, watching me with restrained interest. In his eyes a war blazed.

"What are you going to do?" I asked, hoping to win the war. "Follow me around the rest of my life?"

"Maybe." He looked away, back to the bug groaning beneath his sneaker. My heart dropped.

"So you'll be at my heels while I'm married to an asshole, making sure he treats me right?"

He ground the rubbery sole into Ned's cheek. "If I have to."

I glanced at the harsh action, then back at Theo. "Why don't *you* stand by my side?"

Theo froze.

I took that small victory, edging closer to him. The wind picked up; above us the sky was dark, no stars visible beneath a blanket of black clouds. The ocean crashed and sprayed.

"You treat me right," I said softly. "You know what I want. Why can't it be you?"

I was pleading with him, and he turned his head slightly, enough for me to see the surprise wash over his features.

"I know it was you," I continued. "I know you were the one who applied to college for me. When I got the acceptance letter, I knew only you would do something like that."

"You got in?" A small smile broke through the storm on his features. "That's fucking amazing, Abs."

"I don't want to go alone. I don't want to be the only one following my dreams. Don't throw everything away. Come with me. Be the boy who wanted to change things."

And just like that, whatever glimmer I'd seen vanished into stone, his jaw iron, his eyes black. He moved his foot to Edward's throat and pushed.

I closed the distance and brought his hands into mine. They were bloody and broken open. "You don't have to worry about me anymore, Theo. Ned isn't going to bother me. Neither will my mom."

"I will *always* worry about you." His words were gravelly, and his chest warbled with the word *always*, like it hurt coming out.

My fingers lingered, a frown forming. "What are you planning to do to him?"

"Whatever it takes." The way his eyes darkened and cracked, I knew he meant it.

Whatever it took, no matter the cost for Theo.

Hadn't that *always* been the case, though?

My thumb grazed his split lip. "It's over. I did something today. He doesn't want me anymore."

His brow furrowed, unconvinced. "Even if that were true, it doesn't make what he did to you okay. You expect me to forget? To let him go?"

I didn't take my eyes off Theo, but whatever he did

caused Ned to groan in pain louder than he had before. Theo touched my cheek, so, so tenderly. I closed my eyes, leaning into his calloused, wet-with-blood touch.

"If I had known what would happen, I would have ended the problem that night. I shouldn't have left you alone, sweet girl. I'm sorry."

He dropped his hand from my cheek. The loss of contact was like a Band-Aid tearing.

"He's not worth it," I pleaded. "He's not worth you losing everything."

He looked at me like I was crazy. "*You're* worth it, Abigail. I would throw my life away for you over and over again."

As if that was the last thing worth saying, he turned back to Ned, determination on his face.

"But would you keep it?" I asked. It came out as a squeak, and I cleared my throat. His body language had changed, tight and coiled.

"Would you keep your life?" I asked, voice louder. "Would you love yourself the way I do? Can you promise that?" I swallowed, taking a breath. "I'll try... If you do."

He threw me a look over his shoulder, eyes furious. He was a noir, black and white, moonlight and shadow, a nightmare and a dream. I wondered when his muscles had gotten so sharp, his veins so defined, or if he appeared so because in this moment he was deadly.

His eyes softened.

Then they calcified to rock.

"This is it for us, Abigail. This has always been us." He gestured at Ned's prone body on the soft sand. "You're the princess. I'm the dog. Just let me do my fucking job."

He turned away, and I knew he was officially *done* humoring me.

Panic crawled up my lungs.

Ned didn't get to take this from me. Not Theo. Not after everything I'd sacrificed.

So I did the only thing I could think of—I lunged at Theo, grasping his arm, pinning him with the move he'd taught me.

THIRTY-SIX

THEO

"What are you doing?"

"What does it look like?" She pressed my right arm to my back. "Pinning you to the ground."

I exhaled, took a breath, and stood up, shaking Abigail off. She was easier to get off my back than an ant—too easy. Abigail flew backward and I grasped her wrist, catching her before she fell.

Her eyelashes fluttered, eyes wide.

So pretty, too fucking beautiful. I was distracted, distracted by her big, surprised eyes. By the muted red of her lips in the dark night.

Fuck, I'd missed her.

It wasn't lost on me she'd used a move *I* taught her, and that made me want to crush my lips to hers, pin her myself and slam my dick in her until she submitted. I was distracted by the *Abigail* of it all.

Too distracted, because in the blink of a second I'd lost myself, Ned stood up and ran away.

She grasped my wrist with two hands. "Let him go, Theo."

Ned ran awkwardly down the beach, slipping on small dunes of sand. I ground my jaw, split between wanting to catch him and keep touching her.

"I've let him go too many times," I said.

Her eyes were shining. "You've let *me* go too many times."

The wind blew, whipping her sable-brown curls around her cheeks the same way it had the night she'd picked me off this beach. And with that distraction, I watched Ned Harlington run the fuck away.

"He'll hurt you," I said.

"He doesn't want me anymore."

"How can you be so fucking sure, Abigail?"

"I'm... I'm not," she admitted. "But I'm pretty sure." The engagement ring on her finger sparkled in the moonlight. It looked more like Abigail than it did Ned.

I looked down the beach. I could still get him.

She grasped my face, palms cupping my cheek, drawing my attention back to her.

"I love you, Theo. Even if you don't want me, even if you can't give me your love, even if you never will. I love you."

"I can't give you what you need." My voice was hoarse, raspy. I hadn't intended that, but the pain in my chest scraped at my throat.

She was a fucking princess. Her blood was blue, but fuck all of that—she was *Abigail*. Abigail who loved blind, Abigail who gave her whole heart to mend yours. She deserved to be kept and cared for by someone worth something.

"You're the only one who can give me what I need. It's only ever been you. You're it for me. I feel it in my bones. You're in my blood. You're in me. Why can't you see it?"

I ground my jaw until it felt my teeth would become dust.

Abigail's eyes narrowed. "Ned was going to give me the world. Should I go back to him?"

She took a step back, but I grasped her wrist, stopping her from leaving, keeping her palms pressed to my face.

"I'm scared. I'm scared you'll leave me, but I'm jumping anyway, hoping you'll catch me this time. *Catch me.*"

A split second followed her declaration, marked by the waves crashing into the sand, and then our lips collided— crashed, slammed. It was violent like the surf, the thunder roaring above us, the lightning flashing our world white.

Then she ripped her lips off mine. I went right back in, but she turned away, breath louder than the wind.

Our foreheads were still pressed together, her eyes on the sand.

"Loving me at a distance is selfish and cowardly," she whispered. "I won't let us do it anymore."

Her eyes found mine. "You either love me in public, proud, where everyone can see, or not at all. I don't want your burgers, I don't want your presents, I don't want secret acts of love, and I don't want your protection. I want *you.*"

"Selfish? Cowardly?" I growled.

True, the voice in my heart whispered back.

"I'll wait for you," she said, finding my eyes. "Come find me. Come keep me. Please."

She took a step back, breaking our connection. Then

with one more searing moment of eye contact, she left, just as the rain started to slam into the ocean.

I woke with a hangover—an Abigail Crowne hangover. I should be used to them by now—I'd received enough of them in my life. It's a throbbing ache that starts in your chest.

She'd called me on all my shit and offered me my greatest dream.

Why couldn't I just fucking take it?

I groaned into my pillow just as there was a knock on the door—the newspaper. Whether I wanted it or not, the motel delivered the *Crowne Point Tribune* every goddamn morning.

I answered the door in my boxer briefs and nothing else. My hair was a mess and fell over my eyes, and the sun felt too hot. At my feet, in black and white print, Abigail's face stared back under the headline ABIGAIL CROWNE ELOPES.

My heart bottomed out. Had she fucking eloped with *Ned*? I tore the paper off the ground as an older woman walked by, staring at how little I wore.

"Take a fucking picture," I said, slamming the door.

I gripped the paper. It wasn't an announcement about her and Ned. They said she'd *eloped* with her bodyguard. Something about her falling in love with a bodyguard and calling off the engagement.

I threw on jeans and T-shirt, heading to Main Street to see if any other publications had covered it. This had to be just another Abigail scandal. She wouldn't really go through with something so nuclear.

When I got to Main Street, Abigail was front-page news on multiple national and international magazines. Not only that, morning news was covering her. They all said the same thing.

"My little reject..." I thumbed through the magazines. This was what she'd meant when she said she'd gotten out from under Ned.

The Crownes didn't have many *enforced* rules, but there was one: you marry who you're told to marry. If they let you marry for love, then how would you stay in power? How would you stay a Crowne?

I looked to the beach, to the black palatial house visible from anyplace in Crowne Point.

I needed to find her.

When I went to Crowne Hall, I decided to take a less bloody route. Many times I'd scaled Abigail's wall so I could catch her when she snuck out. There was an easy-to-climb lattice on the shingled wall, and garden boxes to get your footing. Her window was high up and always open.

The alarm went off when I opened the window, so at least Tansy wasn't lying about that. She had gone through with that part of the deal.

Her room, though? Fucking empty.

I went to find Tansy. They couldn't have really fucking kicked her out, right? Tansy was where she always was—in the damn sunroom.

"Where is she?" I asked.

"Good question," she hummed, not even surprised by my presence. She flipped a magazine, not looking up.

"She's your daughter."

"As far as I, and the rest of the family, are concerned, Abigail isn't a Crowne. She took her things and left yesterday."

It took a minute for what Tansy was saying to sink in. Yesterday, when Abigail had found me, she'd been kicked out? She gave up everything?

I was such an asshole.

"You kicked her out?" I asked, to be sure.

"She chose this. Abigail stood her ground for the first time in her life, over you." Tansy lifted her head, pinning me. "Are you worth it, Theo?"

That was an easy question to answer. "No." I nearly laughed. Hell fucking no. That wasn't the answer I was focusing on anymore.

Tansy looked down at her magazine again, earmarking pages with five-layer cakes.

"But Abigail thinks so," I continued. "So I'll spend the rest of my fucking life trying to be whatever she sees in me."

Tansy slightly raised her brow, flipping another page, earmarking another dessert. She didn't acknowledge my presence further, and, either way, I was done talking to the Crownes.

Abigail left her family, left her entire world behind for me. She was somewhere—*alone*, with nothing.

I'd barely left the sunroom when I heard Gray's apathetic voice drift over my shoulder. "This is the problem with feeding a dog. They keep coming back. They think they belong here."

When I turned, he was speaking to the girl, Story, apparently now a fixture at his side.

Gemma was a few feet away, by the huge double doors, leaning against the stone walls, a cup of tea in her hands, watching my and Gray's exchange with interest.

"I thought you were smart, Gray," I said. "Don't you know yet? You can kick me out, you can send me away, but I'll come back. I'll always come back. I'll always be here. As long as Abigail will have me—and even when she doesn't want me—I'll fucking *be here*."

Gray sighed. "What a fucking miracle she doesn't live here anymore, then."

Without another word, I kept walking.

"You ruined her life," Gemma said as I was about to leave.

I stopped, and Gemma kicked off the wall. "She was a Crowne and now she's nothing."

"I'd fucking do it again too," I said. "My only regret is not doing it sooner."

She frowned, and just as I was about to push open the double doors and leave this place for good, Gray spoke.

"You should've told us about Newton," Gray said. "My mom might not care, but only I get to fuck with my sister."

"And only I get to rip out her hair," Gemma added.

I paused. I nearly had the doors open. I could see the cobblestone path that wound around the crystal fountain and down to the wrought iron fence.

I turned around. Gray and Gemma stood side by side.

I didn't know what the fuck this was. Were they seriously acting like they cared about Abigail?

"What are you planning on doing with him?" Gray asked. "Some blue-collar appeal to the police. It won't work. He'll have them paid off before you finish your sentence."

I pushed my cheek out with my tongue. "You want to help or something?"

"Or something," Gray said.

"That weasel Newton is out. *He's* the one getting excommunicated," Gemma said. "Out of our lives. Out of our world. We'll handle that part on our end." Gemma glanced at Gray. "But when you blow up your life for Abby —as I'm sure you're planning on doing—be sure to get Newt caught in the crossfire. Say Gray and Gemma Crowne were there. We'll back you up."

"Just this once," Gray added.

Gemma rolled her eyes. "Duh."

"Or," I said, taking a step to them. "You'll use it as an opportunity to fuck her over."

"That would be hilarious," Gray conceded. "But there is no fucking universe where I would side with *Newt* over a Crowne, not even for a joke."

Gray stared back at me, bored.

If there was one thing I could trust, it was Gray's unyielding arrogance about being a *Crowne*. This could work. This could save Abigail.

I grinned. "See you around then, *brother-in-law*."

Gray glowered at my words as I pushed open the door into the bright summer sun.

Outside I caught a rare glimpse of Beryl Crowne getting out of his town car. He froze when he saw me, halfway in the car.

"Was it worth it, Theo?" he asked, straightening, righting his lapels. "Was it worth losing all of this?" He gestured around him, at the sprawling palatial home. "You could've climbed high."

For five years I'd stared at the back of Beryl Crowne. In some twisted way, I think he cared for me. In this world, that was the best you can hope for. A mother who played games with her daughter's love, a father figure who chose when you looked him in the eye.

"It was never about this. It was always about her."

I kept walking, down the cobblestone path so long most

drove up it, past hedges and glittering fountains, and out of the wrought iron gate that Abigail Crowne had opened for me.

I had one stop to make before I found her.

It was time to let the world know she belonged to me, that we belonged to each other.

Abigail had put a photo of some random shadow on the cover, so if I wanted, I could go and find her, live in the background like I had been—but Abigail was mine. She was mine the day she gave me that bracelet.

The *Crowne Point Tribune* offices were on Main Street, one of the original old-style buildings marking the street. It had been touched up, the Carolina-blue shingles and white trim bright in the sun. Very nautical, and very Crowne Point.

There was no going back. I could put it all on the line, and she could leave me. I could lose her. At a distance, I'd always have Abigail in some way, but she'd never be mine.

Today I would catch her. I would keep her. I would never let her go.

I just hope it isn't too late.

I pushed open the door into a too air-conditioned room. The receptionist looked up at me with bored interest.

"I'm Theo Hound, Abigail Crowne's husband."

THIRTY-SEVEN

THEO

Abigail was sitting on the beach, just like I had all those years ago when she'd found me. The sunset glowed orange on her skin, her feet buried inside the sand. Black leather sneakers were beside her. She set her chin on her knees, the sun bright on her cropped white shirt.

She was a literal dream come true.

All at once she stood, stumbling in the sand. I was there just in time to catch her. One arm anchored her waist as the ocean glittered citrine in a fading sun. We looked like a still from an old Hollywood movie.

"Theo," she breathed.

I groaned. "I don't think I'll ever get tired of hearing you say my name."

Her grip tightened on my shirt. "What are you doing?"

I grinned. "Catching you."

We had three uninterrupted seconds as she registered

my words and the meaning behind them. Then the necessary evil I'd brought to show my love ruined the moment.

"Abigail," the horde of paparazzi just a few feet away yelled, cameras flashing.

Abigail scrambled off me. "What the hell?"

I trailed my knuckle along her jaw. "You lied to me, sweet girl." I inclined my head at the ring. She covered it, looking away.

"No, I didn't. I should've, because you lied to me... but I simply didn't correct an assumption."

"So, a Crowne lie."

She shrugged. "Old habits."

Another moment passed. "Is that why they're here? Do they think it's you? Theo, I'm so sorry. I didn't mean to drag you into the spotlight."

I stuck my tongue into my cheek to keep from smiling. "My little reject always getting in over her head. What did you say? Something about in public and proud. And about not wanting my burgers... you're going to regret that."

I unrolled the magazine I'd brought with me, handing it to her. She held the glossy pages, a line forming between her brows as she read the headline.

ABIGAIL CROWNE'S SECRET HUSBAND REVEALED.

I grasped her chin, pulling her eyes back to mine. "Didn't you know if you made that kind of statement, I was going to cement it? Bind it and wrap it in steel."

"No," she whispered. "I didn't."

I grazed my thumb back and forth across her chin. I wished I could take all the hurt in her eyes away, heal the bruises on her heart. Maybe if I filled her chest with enough bliss, she wouldn't feel them.

"I was always afraid to love you, Abigail. At first I

thought if I kept my distance just enough, then maybe it wouldn't hurt when you left me. Then it became, if I keep *us* distant, we can't get close enough to break apart. You're the one person I want to risk everything for. You wanted a grand gesture, this is it, Abigail. That magazine goes out tomorrow, but this is live. The whole world is watching. They know you're mine. You belong to me. Forever."

Something mischievous flickered in her clay eyes. "What if I said no?"

"It's too late for that. This is for the *world*, Abigail. So people like Ned know what it means if they try and take you. So they know who's going to rip their throat out. But us?" I leaned closer, so the words throbbed along her neck. "There's no going back. We've belonged together for years. I'm keeping you. You don't *get* to let me go, Abigail."

When I pulled back, there were tears in her eyes.

I thumbed them away.

"I'm scared," she said. "Every time I get close to my happily ever after it always crashes to pieces at my feet."

I gripped her jaw tight between my fingers, willing her to feel my determination.

"Sweet girl," I said. "I will always be there to pick up those pieces." She chewed her lip, still uncertain. "I was saving this for... Fuck it."

I reached into my back pocket.

"What are you doing?"

"Proposing. Properly."

Inside was a bracelet, not a ring. It wasn't anything someone like Ned could give her. It wasn't worth more than a house. It wouldn't sparkle in the sun.

But it meant something, and it was years in the making.

I grasped her wrist.

"I'm going to keep you, Abigail." I clasped the bracelet

on her wrist and rubbed the material, loving the way it looked on her.

Then I looked up, catching her eyes. "Will you let me?"

She touched the bracelet. "What is all this?"

"Sea glass from the night you kept me. Origami from the first romance I read—the moment I knew I couldn't lose you. The wine cork from the night we made love. One bead from the bracelet you gave me, the night I broke it and your heart..." There were key pieces from all the moments in our life, totaling fifteen charms. I hadn't saved them for this purpose. I'd kept them because I'd wanted something to remember the moments by. When I'd been looking for something to propose to her with... it felt right.

Abigail always cared more about found treasures than any expensive piece of jewelry. I'd been finding and keeping our treasures secretly for as long as I could remember.

She touched the *F*, the bead I'd managed to save the night I nearly wrecked us irrevocably. Silence stretched on and on as she stared at the baubles on her wrist.

I needed something to break the silence.

"Bet you wish I'd given you a burger—"

Abigail jumped at me, and I stumbled back, barely keeping us from falling over. Her legs wrapped around my waist, and I anchored her with my arm.

The cameras flashed behind us.

"You... you saved the bead?" she asked, eyes wide, but before I could answer, she asked another question. "You kept all of this?

"I keep all of you, Abigail. Every laugh you make and

every tear you drop. Every bruise I put on your heart. I keep it all. You're inside me too. You wove yourself inside me before you even knew who I was."

She crashed her lips to mine, furious, hot, fast. I could barely keep up with them, on my lips, on my neck, on my jaw, back to my lips again.

"Is that a yes?" I asked through her feverous lips.

She chewed her lip, and I fought the urge to bite it myself.

"It's too late for that, Theo." She lifted her eyes, using my own words. "We've belonged together for years. This..." She lifted the bracelet. "This is just for the world."

I crashed my mouth against her, kissing her as the world watched, making up for all the times I'd loved in secret. It was furious and gentle, and it wasn't enough. I wanted to swallow all of her. Her lips, her tongue, her soul.

I broke on a groan. "I need to get inside you right fucking now."

THIRTY-EIGHT

ABIGAIL

"I've always wanted to fuck you on this beach," Theo said, voice low at my ear. "There were times I wanted to drag you back here and make you pay for finding me, and there were times I wanted to worship you in the sand for saving me."

My lips parted. "What do you want to do now?"

He grinned. "Both."

Theo bit my ear, dragging at the lobe, swirling his tongue along the shell. He was so strong and he held me up as if I weighed nothing—I *knew* that wasn't true. His focus was on my neck, then my ear, my collarbone.

I got lost, my head falling back.

Then I saw them.

"The paparazzi are still here," I said on a sigh.

From their perspective, I was hugging him. He ignored me, popping the button on my jeans with his free hand. He slid his hand under my panties, fingers cool from the beach air, my skin hot. The fact that people—*cameras*—were feet away only made me hotter.

His jagged groan ricocheted like shrapnel through my body. I gripped his shoulders for support. "If I wanted to fuck you right now, you would do it."

God help me, I would.

"I won't give that to you, Reject. I don't want anyone to see you but me."

He slid out of me, and I missed him like my own blood. He let me go, and I clung to him, sliding down his body. He grinned down at me, cocky, pushing hair out of my face with the hand that had just spread me.

Then he turned to the paparazzi, smile evaporating. "Fuck off."

"That doesn't work with them," I said. If anything, it fueled them.

Sure enough, they stayed put.

Theo rolled his shoulders and closed the distance between us and the paparazzi. He focused on the guy with the video camera, grabbing the lens, smashing the thing to the sand. I was reminded of when he'd first come back to me, the very first times he'd stuck up for me. They yelled something about a lawsuit, cameras flashing with more vehemence. Theo laughed.

"Unless you want your exclusive to disappear like sand, get the fuck out." He growled the last bit.

When they didn't immediately move, he reached for another camera, and that had them scattering. He looked so intimidating, so *Theo*.

They took a slew of photos as they left, and I wondered what they were going to print now. Something about how Abigail Crowne had found someone just like her, maybe.

Married a man with no regard for civility, aggressive and rude.

What a pair they were.

That worry vanished as Theo came back to me.

He picked me up, grabbing my thigh and lifting me up, wrapping my legs back around his waist. He buried his face in my neck, biting and sucking.

"First I'm going to fuck you against the pier, then I'm going to fuck you in the sand. If you're good, maybe I'll let you suck my cock."

"Splinters," I managed to breathe against his intoxicating lips.

He laughed. "Sweet girl, you should be worried about more than splinters."

He moved us underneath the pier, but when he backed me against the column, he took off his zip-up hoodie, draping it over my shoulders. I had a very good cushion against *splinters*.

My Theo barked, and he bit *hard*, but when it came to me, he was always so protective.

My fingers glanced down his chest, to his jeans, unzipping him. I pulled him hot and hard out of his boxer briefs, into my hand. He hissed, tightening the hoodie around my shoulders.

"I don't have a condom, Abigail," Theo said, voice rough.

"I don't have any birth control."

Our eyes locked. This was my out.

I wrapped my legs tighter around him, pushing him closer to me, just barely spreading myself.

"Fuck," he groaned into my neck. "I've missed this pussy." His teeth found my neck, biting. "I'm going to mark you." He dragged his teeth along my collarbone. "I'm going to drip down your pussy."

He slid a hand up my shirt, palming my breast —*bruising*.

I arched on the rough, wooden pole as he pushed deeper but not deep enough. Not nearly.

"Where you saved me all those years ago, now you're going to give me *everything*. No more barriers, no layers between us, nothing hiding that I'm yours and you're mine."

Theo lifted his head enough to find my eyes. The ocean breeze blew soft chocolate strands around his face, softening the hard lines.

"You might be the artist, but you're my masterpiece," he said. "All my life I've been painting you on a canvas, and now I'm going to unravel you thread by thread."

He captured my lips at the same moment he speared me on his cock.

The world disappeared into Theo.

The water nipped at our toes, my head on Theo's bare chest. I dripped down my thighs, dripped *him*.

"I need to clean up," I murmured into his hot skin.

In response, Theo cupped me. He stared up at the wood pier, the stars peeking through, lazily spreading his come all over my lips. One finger, then two, slid back inside, pressing it back inside me. The movement was enough to get me hot and prickly.

"I like feeling me on you," he said casually, still staring up at the slatted sky.

I couldn't breathe.

His free hand came to my chin, gently tipping it up,

until my eyes met his. His head was tilted slightly, eyes narrow, drinking me in as he pressed in and out, in and out, a delirious rhythm. He watched me like he had the first night, only now I was wet with him. Marked—covered—in Theo.

I was still sore from Theo, but his fingers transmuted the pain into a delicious need. Soon I was working myself against his fingers. Theo using his come as lube was boiling my blood.

"I like feeling you in me," I admitted, breathless.

His grip on my chin tightened, eyes blazing. He flipped me on my side, hot skin flush against mine. His thick, muscled arms wrapped around me, holding me close, his lips on the back of my neck, my ear, my shoulder.

I felt him at my entrance and I pushed back.

"Please," I managed to whimper.

"Sweet girl." He groaned my special term of endearment, sliding inside me.

THIRTY-NINE

ABIGAIL

Theo wiped a bit of sauce from my lips, licking it from his thumb.

"What?" I asked. He watched me, looking too damn smug. After Theo made true on his promises, we'd dressed and were now getting burgers.

Theo insisted I needed to be fed.

"Just picturing your lips dripping with something else." I looked away from his green eyes, which seemed to glow in the night. "Is Abigail Crowne blushing?" he asked, sounding like a startled Southern belle.

I glared, taking a bite of my burger.

I *was* hungry after the pier. Theo was... insatiable.

Theo hadn't stopped touching me. When walked here, his arm was around me. Now he kept one hand on my shoulder, his other between my thighs. It was intoxicating, distracting, marvelous. I still wore his hoodie, and it was soft and smelled like him. I kept lifting the fabric to my nose, inhaling the musky, spicy scent.

"Not Crowne," I said, dropping the sleeve after Theo gave me a knowing look. "Not anymore. Hound... maybe..." I chewed my lip, nervous at suggesting I take his last name.

When I looked up, a need blazed in his eyes that nearly floored me. Then a slow, intoxicating smile curved his pink lips and broke his cheeks, white teeth and all.

Oh. Wow.

"What did you tell the press?" I asked, blinking out of my stupor.

"Our story. How you saved me, how I fell in love with you despite our worlds."

"Even Ned?" I wondered.

"The right thing to do would be to tell you it's your story, and so I didn't say a word of it."

I looked up, peering into his eyes. "So you didn't tell it?"

His jaw was hard, and his grip on my thigh tightened. "I'm not a hero."

"You've always been my hero."

He worked his jaw. "Maybe I knew if I told that story with your name attached, you'd be dragged through the mud, so maybe I told a different truth."

A wrinkle formed on my brow. "A different truth?"

Theo told me how he'd painted a picture of Ned as a backstabbing coward who only wanted to marry me to get close to my money.

"Gray and Gemma helped," he admitted. "They backed me up and said they would excommunicate him from your world."

That would *obliterate* him.

He might not go to jail, but he could never show his face in Crowne Point again, or in our world. His reputation would be ruined. For some reason, we lived in a society where it was okay for men to terrorize women, but they could never be foolish, and they could *never* be weak.

"They helped?" I couldn't stop the awe in my voice. Theo nodded, and I grinned and buried my face in his chest. "You're my hero."

He hadn't told my story, but Ned was ruined anyway.

"He loved Abigail Crowne," I mused. "He didn't know what to do with just Abigail. Now he has to live as *just Ned*."

"I knew he was an idiot," Theo said, eating a fry. It was unfair how hot he looked just eating a stringy potato. All thoughts flew out the window, stuck on his pillowy lips. As if he knew what I was thinking, he grinned crookedly, arching a brow.

"Where are you living?" he asked suddenly, eyes hard.

I paused.

Oh my God—where *was* I going to live?

"I was sleeping at the motel. I don't really know where I'm going to live." I charged the room on my credit card, but my mom was going to cut that off soon.

I set down my burger.

"Abs," Theo said. "What are you thinking?"

I could barely hear him.

What was I going to do?

I have nowhere to go.

Was this what a panic attack feels like? I couldn't breathe. Don't get me wrong, I would do it again in a heart-beat. I'd always choose Theo, *always*. I just... I'm scared. My life had always been comfortable and easy. I've never had to worry about material things.

I was homeless.

I had no money.

"How comfortable was the beach?" I asked Theo. "It probably got cold in the winter. Oh my God, you didn't have internet. Or *maids*. Or running water."

"Of course Abigail Crowne is more worried about maids than running water," he said.

My wide eyes found him, unable to laugh at his obvious joke. Sometimes it snowed in the winter, covering the sandy beach in a blanket of beautiful white powder. I always thought it was magical.

But not if I was *sleeping* in it.

"Was it warmer under the pier?" I asked.

His fingers were at my chin, drawing me to him. "Hey. We'll figure it out. I'm not letting you sleep on the beach."

"But—"

"I can't promise you servants, Abigail, but I promise you will always be comfortable and always be protected."

My heart rate slowed as I stared into his green eyes. I believed him.

"Maybe..." Theo dropped my chin, warring with something in his mind. He shook his head, and it was my turn to press him.

"What are you thinking?"

"It's stupid," Theo said. "I shouldn't have even thought it."

"But you did. What was it?"

"I wondered if maybe we can stay with my mom. She gave me her number and for a moment I thought she was going to ask me to stay with her."

"Your mom?" I gasped. "You saw your mother?"

"Abigail Crowne?" someone said, at the worst fucking moment. To our left, a crowd of teenagers was looking over. I looked at my unfinished burger, at Theo's barely touched fries.

"It's Abigail Crowne and her new husband!" another said.

Theo grabbed my hand, pulling me off the rubbery chain-link table. Holding hands, we ran out of the diner. For once, the thought of marriage hadn't filled me with dread.

Married to *Theo*.

What a dream.

- - -

After escaping the gathering crowd at Crowne Drive-In Diner, we walked hand in hand along bluffs, below us a sandy shore.

"So you met your mom?" I asked.

"Briefly. I got distracted by your marriage announcement." Theo shot me a crooked grin.

I buried my face in my free hand. "Oh my God. I'm so sorry."

He pulled me to his warm, solid chest, back to the ocean. "Never apologize for what led me back to you."

The wind and waves whipped a small flurry, and I buried my head deeper into his hard pecs. Was it possible I was really safe? *Finally* with Theo, after everything? I never wanted to move from this warm embrace, but then he spoke.

"You were right," Theo said and I lifted my eyes to his. "About the diary. All this time, my mother was trying to find me, hoping I would find her. It was a map."

My heart cracked like an egg for Theo. In all the years I'd known him, this was the dream I'd hope would come true. As if he could see the words in my head, Theo pulled me to him and grasped my chin.

"I should've listened to you, my princess and my reject, my lying, fire-starting, romantic..." He pushed a strand of hair behind my ear with one finger, eyes throbbing with tenderness. "My perfect contradiction."

Theo was the only person in the world who knew exactly what to say to make me bloom. Which made sense, I guess, because he also knew exactly what to say to destroy me.

I stood on my tiptoes, angling to kiss him. I could taste the buzz of him on my lips, our static electricity already dancing when suddenly I remembered.

"Grim has your mom's diary now!" I said. "My sister gave it to him."

Theo's brow wrinkled, but not with concern, like I'd expected. "My mom had it when I found her. He must have given it to her. She said she was given it looking for me."

"What? Why would he do that?"

"You know the Horsemen will do any job, for the right price."

I briefly thought to my sister, to her debt. Had she needed a job from the Horsemen?

"My mom's wife is the mayor of Crowne Point," Theo continued, pulling me back. "There isn't much she can't afford."

That was why she looked familiar. She was one of the many faces I'd been forced to mingle with. They all blurred into one blob after awhile.

"What about you, sweet girl? Can you really give up your entire family?" He arched his head forward, eyes digging, unwilling to let me gloss over this.

"Yes... but my mom didn't seem angry with me. She said see you at Christmas. I don't know, she might not totally have excommunicated me."

I could tell he was worried, unsure if that was good or bad, unsure what that meant for us.

"Whatever happens," I said. "You'll be with me, by my side. I made that clear."

Theo dragged me the last few inches to his lips.

Kissing Theo was addicting. I loved everything about it. Standing on my tiptoes as his arm anchored my lower back, tugging me higher and pressing me flat against him, so I felt *him*. His flat abs, his hard cock.

I got lost in his soft lips and the firm pressure he applied, his skillful, teasing tongue.

The free hand he wove to the base of my neck, pressing me harder against his lips.

A smattering of raindrops fell, and I opened my eyes, breaking me out of his trance. My arms were wrapped around his neck, and I saw the bracelet he'd given me for the thousandth time that night. I realized something then, something so important I'd yet to give Theo.

"I need to go back to the motel," I said against his lips, breathless.

"Now?" he asked, lips at my neck, then jaw, kisses leaving a trail of fire and need.

"Now," I breathed.

He groaned, biting my lip, but let me go.

When we got back to the motel, he eyed my room number with mild amusement.

"What?" I asked.

His lip curved. "I'm 302."

I looked at the white painted wood number on my door: 301.

"We're next to each other?"

Of course we were next to each other.

All Theo did was grin.

I opened my pale-blue door, and Theo followed me. I placed a hand on his chest.

"Stay here."

He grinned wolfishly, taking another step, pushing me back into my room. I stumbled over my own feet.

"I want it to be a surprise," I all but begged.

His eyes gleamed, but he raised his hand, stepping back onto the whitewashed porch that wrapped around the motel.

I fished around my room, looking for my box. Despite being a motel, the room was beautiful, with a weathered seaside decor, queen bed, and valet if you needed. In any other town, it would be a four-star hotel, but this was Crowne Point.

Theo was leaning against a railing overlooking the ocean, arms folded. When he saw me come out, he stood off it.

"My mom told me to take what I wanted from my room..." I said, suddenly nervous. "This is the only thing worth saving."

His green eyes flickered from my eyes to what I held in my hands.

Too silent.

The waves too loud.

"I fixed it..." I trailed off, fiddling with the bracelet. I still felt hopelessly vulnerable. I'd fixed it without any certainty he would come through and catch me. Holding it in my hands reminded me of when my heart beat raw.

Theo wrapped his arm around my waist, thrusting me to him.

His lips were on mine, sucking my breath from my body, thrusting his tongue into my mouth. Any inch I gave him he took and demanded more. More breath. More tongue. More lips. More.

He finished with a quick bite of my lower lip.

I could barely breathe.

"Do I get to wear it?" He arched a brow. I could only nod at his beautiful face, sliding the bracelet on his wrist.

Seeing those restrung pastel pieces back on his wrist, only missing the one *F* now on my bracelet, something clicked into place. The final broken part of us fit back together.

He kissed me again, pushing me back into my room. The door slammed shut behind us on a seaside summer night. I wrapped my arms around Theo as he carried me to bed.

My best friend. My tormentor. My bodyguard. Now my fiancé.

My everything.

EPILOGUE

ABIGAIL
Two months later

I tried to focus on the girl talking to me as we walked to our next class. I had just finished my first of the semester, attending the college Theo had applied to for me. *College.* I was mid-conversation with her when all of a sudden I was yanked by the wrist into the girls' bathroom.

I stared at the door a moment, lips parted, before turning into the eyes of Theo. He leaned against the sink, one leg propped, green eyes bored.

"I was talking to someone," I said at last.

"Tough shit, Reject." He snatched my wrist, spinning me around so I was pressed between him and the sink.

I looked around at the pink tiles. "Did you go in the wrong bathroom, dog?"

He kneed open my legs. "No one's going to think twice about your bodyguard accompanying you."

"You're not my bodyguard anymore."

"Hmm... tyrant? Tormentor?"

"Nope," I said.

"No?" He leaned over, biting my neck. "Best friend?"

"Closer..." A smile twerked my lips.

Theo engulfed me. His muscular arms on either side of me, his green-eyed stare digging into me, his big hands on the sink, finishing the cage. My space, my air, everything.

"Husband, then?"

Warmth filled my gut almost as much at the word, as the way his lips soothed his bite. *Husband.* Theo Hound was my husband.

"Shouldn't you be in class?" I all but breathed.

I wasn't the only one pursuing their dream. Theo was finally getting his degree in social work so he could help children like himself.

"I have a surprise for you," Theo said, voice gravelly. He pulled back, eyes dark in the way I loved. The way that said he was about to fuck me in a bathroom, and I was going to let him.

But then he stepped away.

He grinned at my face, tracing his knuckles along my jaw. "If we don't go now, you'll miss your next class."

I seriously contemplated it, but in the end, I let him lead me out of the bathroom.

After a short taxi ride, we arrived at a tall, jutting skyscraper in the middle of Manhattan. After the doorman opened one of the gilded double doors, I followed Theo, confused and a little wary, into a polished foyer.

"Are we meeting someone?" I asked.

He looked at me with a small smile. "I'm not ruining the surprise."

We rode the elevator to the top floor. The doors opened on an empty, vaulted ceiling apartment sweeping what appeared to be the entire floor. It had views stretching all the way to Central Park.

After the doors nearly closed on me, Theo dragged me to the center.

"I would've asked if we were burgling, but..." I gestured at the lack of furniture, the barren hardwood. "What is this place?"

Theo watched me softly. "Every hero needs a lair."

"This isn't a *lair*, it's—wait, this is *your* place?"

He came to me. "*Our*. It'll be nice not living with my mom."

My palm pressed to his cheek. "I don't mind."

"I'd like to fuck you anytime, anywhere," he practically growled. "I don't need to feel like a teenager, waiting to fuck you in my bedroom when my mom is gone."

I smiled, remembering the past two months.

"I like fucking you in secret."

Then his lips were on my neck. Theo never stopped touching me now, like he's making up for years he could've been. Sometimes it was an innocent touch, a hand on the back of my neck, a kiss on my forehead. Sometimes it was ravenous, wild, teeth and tongue and bruising hands.

And... yeah... it's a little uncomfortable when you're living with his mom.

"Not to mention..." He gripped my hand, dragging me out of the main room to the only decorated room.

I nearly lost my breath.

A nursery.

Theo embraced me from behind, surrounding me with his warmth, his palms landing gently on my belly, nearly encapsulating the entire thing. He buried his nose into my neck, lips warm on the flesh when he spoke.

Theo kissed up and down my neck. "It's gender neutral."

Gray-and-yellow chevron walls, a softly colored crib with a mobile hanging above, even a fully stocked library next to a rocking chair. Swans dangled from the mobile, *laces* tied the crib together in pretty bows, and a Crowne Point blanket hung over the rocking chair.

They were little bits and pieces of us, of our relationship, incorporated into our future. I blinked away tears.

"If you don't like it—"

"I love it."

Theo, who always acted so uncaring, but always cared the most.

We were so young, and probably not ready in any sense of the word, but nothing had ever made more sense, had never been more *right*, until that little stick said *pregnant*. All my insecurities, my need for love, vanished. I said I would give all the love I'd always needed, the attention I'd always craved. I would make sure he or she would grow up never knowing that void.

Theo was the same. That fear of abandonment, that ache of being left, they would never know it. Every hurt lashed on us had been leading us to this moment.

It was perfect and right and whole.

"We're close to your school, and just two hours from Crowne Point, so you can still visit your family on the holidays and get Crowne Drive-In Diner on the weekend, and when you finish, you can open up that shop you've always dreamed about, because you *will* open up your shop—" He ended abruptly, as if realizing he was rambling.

"How can you—err, *we*—afford this?"

Theo was quiet, and I pulled out of his embrace, coming to a conclusion. His mom lived in a swanky house, nothing compared to what I'd grown up in—but then, I was the one percent of the one percent.

"Wait..." I bit the inside of my cheek to stop from smiling, but it was pointless, because a mischievous smile lit up my face. "Theo Hound... are you a trust fund kid now?"

He barked a laugh. "Hardly."

"Theo Hound, who always made fun of us. Theo Hound, who always looked down on us. Theo Hound is now *one of us*—"

He gripped my cheeks, pulling me in for a harsh kiss, cutting off my words.

When he pulled back, I was dizzy.

"Now I'm the poor one," I whispered.

He caressed my cheek. "I'll be sure to treat you as well as you treated me."

My eyes grew even wider, and he grinned. He pulled me into an embrace, into his chest. I turned my head on his soft shirt, taking in our new apartment.

"This feels like a happily ever after," I said suspiciously against his chest.

"No way," Theo said, and I lifted my eyes to his. "This *is* a happily ever after, Abigail."

I let that sink in as he wrapped his arms around my waist, pulling me tighter against him. Theo's heartbeat thrummed steadily against my ear.

"Truth or promise?" I asked against it.

He grinned against my forehead. "Promise."

"Promise you won't break my heart?" I asked.

"Promise."

BOOKS BY MARY CATHERINE GEBHARD

The Hate Story Duet

Beast: A Hate Story, The Beginning

Beauty: A Hate Story, The End

Owned Series

You Own Me (Owned #1)

Let Me Go (Owned #2)

Tied (Owned #2.5)

Come To Me (Owned #3)

Patchwork House

Skater Boy (Patchwork House #1)

Patchwork House #2

Patchwork House #3

Patchwork House #4

www.PatchworkHouseSeries.com

Standalones

Elastic Heart

Heartless Hero

ACKNOWLEDGMENTS

With each publication, the list of those I'm grateful to expands and grows. My team—my tribe—is as essential to this process as writing the book.

Those I'm forever thankful to for helping me bring *Heartless Hero* out into the world includes, but isn't limited to:

My betas, who read my raw writing and gave me great feedback. Sonal, Kris, Kat, Nikki, Sarah G. S., Caoimhe, and Sarah G!

The Diehardy Girls, who promo their asses off and are just, in general, an amazing group of people.

My reader group, GetHard. You continue to be a safe and welcoming place on the internet.

My PA, Melissa! A brilliant twist-of-fate brought you into my life and I couldn't be happier. You work so hard and your passion is so bright. You're just the bee's knees.

My editors, James Gallagher of Evident Ink, Ellie with My Brother's Editor, Amy Halter, and Becca with Edits in Blue. You all polish my story so it can become what I dreamed it would.

My cover designer, Hang Le, who blew me away *again* with such an amazing cover.

Sarah with Teasers by the Modern Belle, who continues to make stunning graphics that capture the essence of the story.

My promo team, Candi Kane, Give Me Books, and Essentially Chas, who work hard to make my release a success.

The bloggers and bookstagrammers who sign-up, promote, and devote their free time. Your passion always blows me away. I'm so grateful to everyone who signed up to promote me.

The authors in this community, who build up instead of tear-down.

My husband, family, and my friends.

Last but not least, *you*, the reader, the reason I publish!

And to everyone and in-between...I love you!

Now this is a little different but, I want you to write your name in, whether it's in ink in your paperback or a highlight on an ebook...

_____

Because thank YOU for helping me on this journey and continuing to support me.

Made in the USA
Columbia, SC
05 March 2020